The only sound was the snow crunching under their feet.

Nora leaned into Rush as they walked to the cabin.

Crack!

The gunshot sprayed the snow a foot from them.

Someone had been lying in wait, Rush realized. To get her. To get them.

"Run!" When Nora obeyed his command, he ushered her behind a tree.

Another shot fired, this one splintering the bark, and he fired back. Grabbing Nora's hand, he hauled her into the woods with him.

When they'd made it deep inside, the firing stopped.

"Now what do we do?" Nora asked, her panting breath coming out in plumes in the cold night.

Either the shooter had given up...or he was tracking them quietly. Stalking them.

"We double back to the chalet and call for backup," he told her.

But his deputy sheriff's mind reeled with the potential danger. With a list of potential suspects. Someone had planned this attack carefully. Could be anyone. Nora's mother had had a slew of deadly secrets...

And now one of them

YULETIDE MOUNTAIN PURSUIT

JESSICA R. PATCH
&
LIZ SHOAF

Previously published as *Cold Case Christmas*
and *Holiday Mountain Conspiracy*

LOVE INSPIRED
INSPIRATIONAL ROMANCE

LOVE INSPIRED®

INSPIRATIONAL ROMANCE

ISBN-13: 978-1-335-23095-9

Yuletide Mountain Pursuit

Copyright © 2020 by Harlequin Books S.A.

Cold Case Christmas
First published in 2018. This edition published in 2020.
Copyright © 2018 by Jessica R. Patch

Holiday Mountain Conspiracy
First published in 2019. This edition published in 2020.
Copyright © 2019 by Liz Phelps

This edition published by arrangement with Harlequin Books S.A.

For questions and comments about the quality of this book,
please contact us at CustomerService@Harlequin.com.

Love Inspired
22 Adelaide St. West, 40th Floor
Toronto, Ontario M5H 4E3, Canada
www.Harlequin.com

Printed in U.S.A.

CONTENTS

Jessica R. Patch lives in the Mid-South, where she pens inspirational contemporary romance and romantic suspense novels. When she's not hunched over her laptop or going on adventurous trips with willing friends in the name of research, you can find her watching way too much Netflix with her family and collecting recipes for amazing dishes she'll probably never cook. To learn more about Jessica, please visit her at jessicarpatch.com.

Books by Jessica R. Patch

Love Inspired Suspense

Fatal Reunion
Protective Duty
Concealed Identity
Final Verdict
Cold Case Christmas
Killer Exposure
Recovered Secrets

The Security Specialists

Deep Waters
Secret Service Setup
Dangerous Obsession

Visit the Author Profile page
at Harlequin.com for more titles.

COLD CASE CHRISTMAS

Jessica R. Patch

The name of the Lord is a strong tower:
the righteous runneth into it, and is safe.
—*Proverbs* 18:10

To the lonely and fearful hearts. God sees.
He knows. He loves you and is always for you.
Stand firm in your faith and trust He's working
on your behalf. Perfect love casts out all fear.

As always, thank you to…

my brainstorming partner and rough-draft reader,
Susan Tuttle; my wonderful agent, Rachel Kent;
and my brilliant editor, Shana Asaro.
It takes a village to birth a book.
Thank you for being my village!

Special thanks to: Michael Fagin
at West Coast Weather for helping me with the
forensic meteorology portion of the story. Any
mistakes or stretches I made for fictional purposes
are all on me! You were wonderful to talk to and
provided a plethora of information. I appreciate
your time in answering all of my questions
thoroughly and professionally.

ONE

A country a version of "Holly Jolly Christmas" played inside Chief Deputy Sheriff Rush Buchanan's Bronco. His coffee steamed from the insulated thermos and sleet pelted his windshield. Blue lights flashed and cast eerie shadows over Shepherd Rock Lake. Wind jostled his vehicle as he slid his hands into his lambskin gloves. Nothing about this moment was "holly" or "jolly."

He opened the door and braved the nasty weather. East Tennessee had its perks, though. Splendor Pines was the gateway to the gorgeous Smoky Mountains, capped in white at the moment. But now, in the darkness, with the mountains shadowing the horizon, everything appeared sinister, especially with the headlights shining on the rusted and mud-caked car they'd dragged from the lake.

The crunching of tires on gravel turned Rush's attention from the car and the pit in his gut. Sheriff Troy Parsons parked beside him and climbed out. He frowned and flipped his collar over his ears. "Well?" he asked in his gruff voice.

"It's a Jaguar. Deputy Tate ran the plates. It's hers."

Troy grunted. Rush didn't need to expound. Marilyn

Livingstone had driven a Jaguar and she'd been missing since Christmas Eve seventeen years ago.

"Remains inside?"

"Skeletal. I think DNA is going to confirm it."

"Any other remains?"

"No."

Troy cocked his head, studied the vehicle dripping with water and debris. "Theories?"

Rush had plenty. But speculating aloud wasn't smart. Especially with the small crowd that had gathered. He moved closer to Troy, his mentor and father figure after Dad became a shell of the man he once was. "I know rumors say she ran off with a man that Christmas Eve." One of many she'd been whispered to have had affairs with. Not all were lies. Rush had witnessed it with his own eyes on the very night Marilyn vanished. Only Troy knew his secret.

Troy hunched in the cold and rolled his toothpick around lips that were hidden by a dark mustache and beard. "You want to call the Livingstones? Or would you rather not deal with talking to the eldest daughter?"

"You can say her name." Nora. The woman Rush thought he was going to marry. Then Marilyn went missing and metaphorically, so did Nora. She retreated into herself and broke things off just before she left for college. Rush sighed, took his flashlight and trudged through the snow to the car. A crime scene tech was photographing and collecting materials. "Find any-thing?"

"A round, silver cuff link and partial remains of a man's masquerade mask."

Could they have belonged to the man Rush had seen

Marilyn with that night? He turned to Troy. "How do you want to proceed?"

"I don't know why she'd be out this far from home with the biggest event of the year going on, but it turned into a tragic accident. Pretty cut-and-dried, don't you think?"

Seemed so. "Suppose we'll know more once Gary can examine the bones. Course he won't be able to determine cause of death if it's drowning," Rush said.

"What else would it be? Other than maybe the impact of crashing into the lake knocked her out. I'll be honest, I hope that's the case and she wasn't conscious when the waters took her. But let's leave it to Gary. He ought to be rolling in soon."

Rush agreed.

"We need to call Joshua," Troy said. "He'll want to know we've discovered his wife." Joshua Livingstone owned the biggest resort and lodge in Splendor Pines. A powerful man, but one of the kindest Rush had ever known. He'd handled the many rumors about his wife with poised grace. Which—if Rush hadn't witnessed Marilyn kissing a man in a Phantom of the Opera mask that night of the annual Christmas Eve Masquerade Ball—he wouldn't have believed. What kind of man wouldn't have a meltdown over his wife cheating on him? Numerous times—if all the tales were true.

Rush adjusted his wool collar; icy beads had steadily slicked down his neck, but he didn't mind. His whole body was flushed. "I guess Nora will come home." Granted she came every Christmas Day, but only for the day. Rush had to share some of the blame for that.

"You ready?" Troy asked.

Was anyone ready to see the person they thought

they'd have the rest of their lives with? "I've moved on, Troy."

"And your last date was?"

"Six months ago with Brandy Walker." She was sweet. Lived in the neighboring town. They met at a church singles social. But he hadn't felt a spark. Would he ever? Would he always be a lonely bachelor living in a house too big for one man on the side of the mountain?

Troy grunted. "I know Nora was a pretty little thing. Still is. But at some point, you're going to have to stop comparing other women to her. Who's to say you'd even have a thing in common with her anymore?"

The downside to father figures. They felt the license to say whatever and whenever. And however. "I'm over Nora Livingstone. Not finding the right woman has nothing to do with her and everything with God's timing." Which was slower than Grandma Buchanan's homemade sorghum. "Sometimes I wish you weren't my mentor," he deadpanned.

"Sometimes I do too." Troy smirked. "I'll call Joshua and give him the news. Merry early Christmas."

"And a happy New Year to no one," Rush muttered.

Troy shook his head and climbed back inside his vehicle to make the call, leaving Rush to the wreckage. The body. *Why would you leave Nora and Hailey, Marilyn?* She may not have been faithful to her husband, but she'd doted on her girls.

New gawkers arrived with local media.

"Is that Marilyn's car?" a few asked.

"Poor Joshua."

"He's probably relieved to be rid of that..."

Insults, opinions and gossipy speculation rode on the wind, slapping Rush's face with frozen fingers. Gossip murdered the spirit. He'd witnessed it happen to his own father. Over ten years now and he'd never returned to pastoring or part-time law enforcement no matter how hard Rush and the rest of his family prayed. Dad had chosen to hide from everything and everyone.

Rush turned on the crowd. "Someone is dead. This person had family and friends, so show a little respect, please, or I'll have every last one of you dragged from here. Am I clear?"

The onlookers quieted. For now.

Before long a black Escalade pulled up next to Rush's Bronco. Joshua Livingstone—larger than life in his long, black fancy coat—stepped out. Jet-black hair and intense eyes, the same color, focused on Rush. "Troy called." His voice was baritone but soft. Rush recognized the sorrow, the need for answers. Hailey, Nora's younger sister, sat in the passenger side, tears rolling down her cheeks—she looked so much like her sister, only her hair was a darker blond and she had Joshua's eyes. She'd been through a lot lately with her separation from her husband. She and their son lived at the main house with Joshua. Rush hated to be the bearer of bad news, but now they might be able to find peace.

"All we know is the car is registered to you, and I'm sure you can tell it's Marilyn's. The…remains need a DNA test but I'm pretty sure they'll come back as your wife's. I'm so sorry for your loss, Joshua."

Troy returned and shook hands with Joshua.

Joshua stared at the car. "Any idea what happened?"

Rush sighed and glanced at the car that had once been shiny and sleek. "You know what the weather is like up here this time of year. Seems a tragic accident."

Joshua nodded. "When can we have her for a proper burial?"

"We need to officially confirm it's her. After that, I see no reason why you can't have her back."

They stood silently staring for several long minutes until another set of headlights flashed behind Joshua's Escalade. Rush squinted, blinded by the lights. The driver didn't bother to kill them before the door to the car opened and a woman's figure stepped out, slipped under the crime scene tape and stomped toward him.

"Hey," he shouted. "You can't be out here."

"The cumulus clouds I can't!" she hollered back.

Rush wouldn't freeze from the nearly single-digit temps. But his heart froze at the sound of Nora's voice. Sassy. Southern—though a little less country in it than he remembered, but then she'd moved to Knoxville and taken a prestigious job as Chief Meteorologist. He watched her every night at six online. Didn't much care about the weather unless it affected his townspeople. He watched to see her sunshiny smile with a chance of twinkle in her blue-green eyes.

Right now, she was all storm clouds and thunder. But even so she was a sight to behold, dressed in a soft but thick coat, gray beanie and knee-high leather boots. He couldn't seem to find his voice.

Nora marched up to him, as if the weather didn't bother her in the least. She nearly reached his chin flat-footed. The smell of cherry blossoms and vanilla filled his nose, and the familiar scent brought a wave of memories. He'd been crazy about her since third grade. But he'd gained the courage in eighth grade and asked her to a dance. They'd dated all through high school.

"Don't just stare at me, Rush. Answer me."

What had she said? "Repeat the question, please."

"Is it my mom?" She looked to her father, but he stood stoically.

Rush shook out of the memories. "DNA will confirm it, but I think it's safe to say it's your mama." Did he hug her? He wasn't sure what to do. "I'm sorry, Nora Beth," he murmured.

Nora's chin quivered and for a millisecond Rush thought she was going to fall into him. And that'd be okay. But she turned at the last second and ran into her father's arms. Looked to him for solace.

Joshua kissed Nora's cheek. "It's going to be okay, honey." She shuddered against her father's chest, then gained resolve and faced Rush.

"Do you know what happened?" she asked lightly.

"We don't, but it's dark and we haven't had a chance to thoroughly examine everything."

"You will, won't you, Rush?" She sniffed and wiped a tear.

Rush closed the gap between them and grasped her gloved hand with his. She never wanted to believe Marilyn had abandoned her family. But, here in the lake leading out of town, it appeared that was exactly what she'd done. Rush didn't know how to spare her that pain. He'd tried to spare her then by never revealing what he saw that night with Marilyn and the Phantom. But now? The evidence was right in front of her eyes.

Troy gripped her shoulder in a fatherly manner. "The roads were bad that night. Probably hit a patch of black ice. The only thing left is to confirm it is your mama and put her and this to rest, hon."

Nora gaped and freed her hand from Rush's. "Unacceptable."

"Nora," Joshua said calmly.

She shrugged him off. "Doesn't anyone want to know why she was out here? On Christmas Eve night?"

"Of course we do, but that's not relevant or even possible to know now," Troy offered.

Nora pointed with her black glove toward the car. "I know what you're thinking. The whole town has thought it for years." Her voice rose with each word. The crowd attentively listened, reporters salivated. "She wasn't leaving us. She was out here that night for a reason, and I'm going to find out if I have to turn over every rock, crawl into every hole and re-create every weather pattern for a week leading up to the event. My mother didn't leave me!" Her watery eyes met Rush's. "She didn't."

Rush itched to comfort her, but she'd push him away. The last time she left his arms, she'd called him a cheater, a liar and a jerk. He'd own up to two out of three. He didn't embrace her but he did pull her aside. "What if you don't like where that night takes you, Nora?" he asked softly. "Let it go. Be content with the fact that she loved you."

If Nora dug, it could turn up a lot of dirt.

"I will not be content until I know what she was doing out here. And just because you assume it's an accident doesn't mean it was." Nora shivered. "What if someone hurt her?"

He couldn't rule out foul play yet, but it was unlikely—even with the evidence retrieved from Marilyn's car. Nora wanted any answer other than the one that claimed her mother was leaving town without so much as a goodbye. And they'd never know the reason. It had been nearly two decades. "I told you I'd look into it, Nora."

"You promise?"

"Nora, I've never broken a promise to you. I won't break one now." He hadn't broken the promise to be together forever. She had. He'd tried everything to coax her back into the land of the living—back to him. In the end, she'd left him picking up the shattered pieces of his heart.

Her lips soured. "No, I suppose you haven't broken a promise to *me*. But you have broken them."

She hit him square in the frozen heart, thawing it to a burning muscle that pulsed with regret. He hadn't broken a promise, but he had broken a commitment to the girl he was dating when Nora came home after graduating college for a job opportunity with a radio station. He hadn't expected that, or for her to call him and see if they could grab dinner, catch up, since she'd pulled away from him after her mom went missing.

It was as if nothing had ever come between them, and she'd been planning on moving back if things went well with her interview.

Things escalated, snowballed. He honestly meant to tell Nora about Ainsley, and that he'd already intended to break things off with her anyway—it was the truth. But before he had the chance, Ainsley caught him and Nora in a heated kiss on Lookout Tower.

Angry words had been hurled. Words like *You're just like your mother. A home-wrecker*. Statements like *Wait until the town hears that perfect Nora Livingstone is her mother made over*. Nora wouldn't let Rush explain, and really what could he say? He had cheated on Ainsley with Nora. He was wrong. He admitted it.

He'd made amends with Ainsley since, and she was now married to Dan, Troy's son and Rush's good friend. Water under the bridge, but Nora had tucked tail and run to Knoxville, never looked back. Never answered a call from Rush.

He glanced at Troy and ignored his disdain over Rush's declaration to look into things. It might be a waste of time and manpower, but he'd oblige Nora this one thing.

He owed her.

Nora's heart might explode. There were so many emotions going on right now. She'd come home twelve days before Christmas—not by choice—only to arrive at the lodge and be told that Dad and Hailey were out at Shepherd Rock Lake with the police. That alone sent knives to her gut. But now here she was face-to-face with Rush. Time had filled out the young man's body into a grown man's, muscled by hard outdoor work more than gym visits; she'd heard he'd built a log cabin up farther on the mountain.

His hat covered his toasted blond hair, but eyes the color of Hershey bars drilled into hers. Rush wasn't a promise breaker. He used to be the most noble and honest person she'd ever known. And he could make her laugh on a dime. But then he had hurt her and at the moment she wasn't sure he'd give the investigation all he had. Troy Parsons wanted to end it right now.

But Mom was here for a reason and Nora couldn't let it rest. However, arguing about it when she was standing in the middle of a monster Christmas storm coming through wasn't wise. She'd predicted back in September low pressures off the Gulf Coast and arctic outbreaks across the Southeast. Snowflakes had begun in early October. This was likely to be the worst snow and ice storm in twenty-five years, but she couldn't afford to fly south for the winter. She was upside down in debt and she'd been pushed out of her Chief Meteorologist job at channel six in Knoxville.

To say she was touchy was an understatement.

Dad approached her. "I'm taking Hailey home, honey. Don't stay here any longer than you feel you have to. I'll have the guest chalet stocked for you." He kissed her forehead.

She nodded at Dad and watched him climb in his vehicle. Hailey hadn't once stepped out. Not even to acknowledge Nora was home. She didn't handle hard situations well. Neither did Nora, but someone had to be Mom's voice. Someone had to find out the truth.

Nora walked closer to Mom's car. All these years, she'd been submerged. Christmas Eve used to be Nora's favorite night. The resort and lodge was always booked with families and couples from all over the world, antic-ipating the renowned Christmas Eve Masquerade Ball. A glorious night decorated in red, green and gold. A nativity ice sculpture. Fountains of gold sparkling cider. Christmas music. Friends. Family. Fun.

Nora's heart ached. Her father still put on the event as if her mother hadn't gone missing that night. He had barely said a word about it. Didn't push or force the in-vestigation. Maybe he had believed the vicious mur-murs about Mom.

Well, not Nora.

"Nora." Rush's voice came softer than moss. "Don't go any closer. Some things can't be unseen."

And some things couldn't be undone. "Do you remember it raining and being slick that night?"

"I don't know," he said sadly. She glanced at him, his nose red and eyes deep with compassion and pity. If only he knew how pitiful Nora was. Not two pennies to rub together. But he'd never know. No one would. It was all too humiliating.

"I don't." Nora had always been fascinated with weather, which was why she remembered there had been snow earlier but the temps had been mild for December. "I need to trace her steps that night and find out what time she left the party and ended up here. Someone saw or heard something. They had to have." If she could piece together the weather from that fateful Christmas Eve, she might be able to determine if the car going into the lake was related to weather conditions or not. Her part-time work as a forensic meteorologist had her doing this often, helping insurance companies with claims.

Rush licked his lips and pawed his scruffy face. "Let me do it. Spend your time with family. Isn't that why you're home so early?" He cocked his head, and plumes of air trailed from his mouth.

She was here because she had nowhere else to go. When the news played and she wasn't on-screen they'd know. "I left channel six."

Rush's eyebrows rose. "Really? Why?"

The cold seeped into her bones and her teeth chattered. "I'm ready for warmer weather. Going to take a job in Florida." She hoped anyway. She ought to know in the next week or two. And right now she did want warmer weather. She was a human Popsicle.

Rush frowned. "You love mountain air. Skiing. Snowball fights."

"I do know how to pack a snowball," she quipped. "But people change. I'm ready for palm trees and water-skiing." She adjusted her knit cap and rubbed her hands, her gloves not keeping her as warm as she'd like, and stared at Mom's car. "Anything inside besides…her?"

He scratched the back of his neck. "We found a cuff link in the car, partial male masquerade mask. Haven't checked the trunk yet, but we'll gather the evidence, see what we see."

A cuff link. A mask. "A man was in the car that night?"

"Seems like." His eyes were shifty.

"What are you keeping from me?"

"Nothing pertinent to the case."

"Promise?"

"Nora, trust me."

She laughed humorlessly. "Last time I trusted you, Rush, you broke two women's hearts and made me look cheap. I'm sure the whole town thinks it." Ainsley surely spread it all over the world.

"No one thinks that, Nora, and you'd have known that if you hadn't gotten out of Dodge at world-record speed. But that's what you do." He shoved a hand on his hip and heaved a breath.

Nora's temperature rose a few degrees. "And cheating on women. That's what you do?"

Rush's jaw ticked. "We were kids. And I was going to tell you."

"We were twenty-one. And you didn't. You gave the town a new tale to spin." But fighting about it was pointless, and Nora was cold and exhausted. "Can you find prints on the cuff link?"

Rush inhaled and rubbed his chin, then exhaled. His shoulders relaxed. "Doubtful. But I'll try. I'll try everything." He held her gaze and she fidgeted. Angry at him or not, she wasn't blind. The man was attractive. Always had been.

"How did you find the car?" It had been seventeen years. Why now?

"You remember Brandon Deerborn?"

Few years ahead of them. "Yeah."

"His son was doing a project using Google maps and our town. Found the lake and noticed something in it. Like a shimmer, he said. He went out there, climbed a pine to check it out—fell out of the tree by the way and broke his arm…also he's grounded for leaving without asking—and Brandon called me. Put the divers in and we hauled it out. Water was too murky to notice it at ground level."

"Google maps. Invasive yet…" She shrugged. "He might be grounded but he'll be a town hero." Or maybe not. If what people said about Mom was true, there'd be a few who wouldn't be too thrilled the Deerborn kid had found her.

Rush didn't say anything and kept his eyes on the sky. "Storm's coming in. But I guess you know this already." He smirked.

She grinned, then sobered. "I'm serious about investigating. I want answers before I leave here, and I won't bring up our past again. Better if we leave things on the personal side alone. Focus on the case."

"We don't have a case. Yet." The freezing rain slacked up.

"Never hurts to ask questions."

"Yes, it does. Sometimes." Rush shoved his gloved hands in his pockets. "Go home. Be with your family. I'll call you tomorrow."

He was right. Nothing she could do tonight. She walked back to her car, opened the door when Rush called out. "Nora Beth, be careful. The roads are slick. Watch for deer."

Her middle name was Jane, but Rush had never once used it. A little nod to *Little House on the Prairie*. In high school, she'd forced him to watch reruns, but there hadn't been much Rush wouldn't have done for her. Manly called Laura *Beth*. Only him. Rush had started that at fifteen. It warmed the chill seeping into Nora's bones. "Will do."

She climbed inside and blasted the heat. She'd regretted pushing Rush away after Mom vanished. She'd been hurt. Wanted a fresh start, to pretend she lived in a town where gossip about Mom hadn't abounded. Where she didn't feel shame. But coming home after college— she'd missed Rush so much it ached—she thought he might be willing to give it another chance, and if so she'd stay. And he'd done the one thing she'd worked hard to avoid—made her the subject of ugly rumors.

She drove carefully through the winding roads and spotted Mom's favorite café. Charlee, the owner, might know a thing or two. Inside, Charlee met her with a wave. "Well, look who the cat dragged in." Her face paled. "Sorry. Bad use of words. I heard about your mama. I'm so sorry." She poured a steaming cup of coffee and slid it to Nora as she sat on the bar stool.

"Thanks. Did you know anything about that night?

Why my mom might be heading out of town or be near the lake?"

"I wish I did, hon. I loved Marilyn, but she only let one get so close before she distanced herself."

Nora sipped the brew and talked with Charlee until the weather picked up. "I better get on back. If anything comes to mind, call me."

Charlee nodded. "Be safe, Nora."

Nora inched along the roads until, almost thirty minutes later, her father's vast lodge peeped out from the evergreens. A wintry, dark sky overhead seemed to close in on the structure that housed two hundred and fifty-two guests. Nestled in the mountains behind were fifty chalets. Every room, every wooden cottage would be occupied, except the guest chalet where she liked to stay.

White lights clinked in the trees as gusts of wind barreled through the pines. The smell of evergreen, wood smoke and cinnamon wafted into her car—the smell of home. She stepped out of the car, pinched the bridge of her nose, inhaled deeply and trudged up the walk; someone had plowed the drive for her. Fresh snow hadn't quite blanketed it again. Something stole her nose's attention. She sniffed. Was that paint? She followed the scent to the side of the chalet and gasped.

In the moonlight, she made out one of her two most hated words to call women along with a note painted underneath telling her to die like her mother. Shock sucked the breath from her, and then she caught sight of a shadow moving toward her. She had only seconds to block the blow and failed.

A meaty fist covered in camouflage gloves connected with her face, knocking her into two feet of snow. White spots popped in front of her eyes and her head spun.

"Take the warning and take a hike," the masked man growled. "Or you'll regret it."

His feet crunched along the snow.

Buzzing whizzed in her ears and then silence.

When her eyes fluttered open, a man had her. Panic shot through her system and she flailed, scratched and punched.

"Hey, hey! Nora. It's me. It's Rush. You're safe. You're safe."

Rush. Rush punched her? No. Her head was fuzzy and aching. Rush had her in his arms. It felt familiar, but also strangely new and wonderfully safe and warm. Her stomach dipped and as if he could feel her thoughts, he nestled her closer against him.

"I got hit," she croaked.

His grip tightened. "And I'll be sure to return the favor when I find the guy." His tone was raw steel. She laid her head against his chest, heard the staccato beat of his heart. "Did you see him?"

"No. Just the writing on the wall, and then he stuck it to me and knocked me out." Her limbs were numb and stiff. Her teeth chattered. Rush carried her up the porch steps.

"Do you need a doctor?"

"No. It's no worse than when I got bucked off that horse that time."

"You had a mild concussion then, Nora Beth." Rush chuckled and swung open the front door and stepped inside, then flipped on a lamp on the side table.

"Right. Not the best comparison. Well, I'm fine.

Honest. Just sore." She peered into his rich eyes and nearly got lost. Certainly got choked up.

He laid her on the soft leather sofa and tucked a strand of hair behind her ear. "I'll get your bags. You need to get into dry, warm clothes and I'll start a fire for extra heat." He stepped outside before she could speak, brought in her luggage and carried it to her bedroom, then returned. "Make some coffee. Yeah?"

She nodded.

"Sure you don't need a doctor?" He touched her face. "Lying in the snow probably helped the swelling, but…"

She shivered and he pointed to the bedroom. "We'll talk in a minute. Or I can take you to the hospital."

Shaking her head, she shuffled to the bed and he closed the door. If Rush hadn't come to her rescue… She didn't want to think about what might have happened.

Clearly, she'd angered someone. But who? She'd seen dozens of locals on the scene; they'd heard her rant. By now, Nora sticking around to find out what happened that night was bound to be spreading all over Splendor Pines like lice in a day care. Between talking to Rush, leaving the scene, stopping to talk to Charlee—someone had rallied fast. Not fast enough or Nora wouldn't have walked up on them.

After throwing on sweats, wool socks and an oversize Vols sweatshirt, she looked in the mirror. No swelling but her right cheek had a purplish tint. Wood smoke and coffee brewing drew her into the living room decorated in cozy earth tones. The fire reached out and hugged her cold skin. She inched closer to the large brick hearth and sat.

"How you feelin'?" Rush made himself at home in the open kitchen. He took two white mugs from the cabinet and poured the coffee, then opened the fridge and frowned. He rifled in the other cabinets until he found powdered creamer and sugar. He carried everything to the living room and placed them on the coffee table.

"Oh, ya know…like I got punched and knocked into the snow." She touched her cheek.

"What exactly happened?"

She gave him the rundown. "Told me to back off or I'd end up like my mom. Almost did if you hadn't shown up. Why are you here?"

His neck flushed as he handed her a cup of coffee. "Honestly? I don't know. I guess to check in on you."

Whatever the reason, she was thankful. She added cream and sugar to her cup.

"You recognize the voice by any chance?" Rush hurriedly asked, as if hoping to skim over the topic of his popping in.

"No. I was kind of busy being terrified. Sorry."

Rush sat beside her, laid a gentle hand on her knee. "I'm sorry too."

Half of her wanted to jerk his hand away, but the frightened half needed the tender contact, the reassurance and compassion. He removed his hand and she sipped her coffee, relishing the warmth of the fire and the brew.

The fire crackled.

He studied the purple mark on her face and balled a fist. "Nora, I don't think it's a good idea for you to go poking around after what happened. This is my job. Better to let me handle it."

Nora huffed. "Someone doesn't want me looking into my mother's death. Which means it might not have been an accident. More than ever, I have to."

Rush drank his coffee and kept quiet, his jaw slowly working.

"What's the matter? I know that face."

Rush pinched the bridge of his nose. "Everything is the matter, Nora Beth. From the minute we pulled the car from the water to right this second. No, it might not have been an accident, but chances are it was, and this attack on you might be from someone who is afraid you'll discover…you know…an affair. If even a quarter of the rumors are true, then there are a lot of people who won't want the past hauled into the present. Next time it might not be a punch to the face." He skimmed the bruise with his fingertips, bringing a wave of emotion she'd tried to bury years ago.

She turned away enough to force him to keep his hands to himself. She didn't need the attraction or the old feelings. But he did have a point. "Then those men shouldn't have had those affairs. What happened to nobility, fidelity and honesty? If their dirty secrets get exposed, then so be it. They shouldn't have done it." Mom shouldn't have either. Why would she?

Rush's nostrils flared, but he didn't respond.

"What happens when *you* investigate? Secrets will be exposed. One way or the other."

He drained his coffee and set the cup on the hearth. "I'm not worried about my safety. I am worried about yours. Besides, I'm going to be more discreet than you."

"You're going to have to talk to more than men you suspect could be guilty. You'll have to talk to neighbors, friends and, sadly, wives. It is what it is. I don't want to hurt people. But I do want the truth about that night. Someone has answers to my thousands of questions."

One being why Dad never stayed on top of the investigation. Why didn't he hire a private eye? Was he glad to be rid of Mom? Was he tired of having an unfaithful wife? Nora couldn't ignore these rumors like she had as a teenager. They were staring her down and now that she'd been attacked and told to back off, denying that even one of them were true would be naive. *Mom, why? Did you not love Dad?* He was amazing and wonderful. He gave them everything.

Or maybe Nora was only seeing what she wanted to see.

A faithful mom.

A devoted husband.

Maybe neither were who they seemed.

"What if you never find out why your mom was heading out of town?"

"How do you know she was?"

Rush stood and turned away from her. "Because we found two cases in the trunk. One had clothing in it." He faced her. "She was going somewhere, Nora."

Nora's hands trembled, and she steadied her cup between her knees.

"I know that's not what you want to hear. And you have to understand that no matter what turns up, you won't get every single answer to your questions. And that's not even the most frightening part of this."

"No?" She peered into his eyes, firelight casting shadows on his face. "What is?"

"You won't back down, and I don't believe whoever did this to you is going to back down either. Which means you're not safe as long as you're snooping."

Nora swallowed the fear clawing in her throat. "I can't sit back and do nothing."

He collapsed beside her again and groaned. "I had a

feeling you'd say that. I think you should stay up at the main house. You'll be safer there."

Her first instinct was to say no, but Rush was right. However… "Hailey is staying with my dad. Which means Dalton is also. He's only six. If someone comes after me again, he could be in harm's way. Hailey too. While I agree that I should stay at the main house, it scares me not to stay here." Scared her to stay here too.

"I heard she was living back home for a while."

Nora shrugged. "I don't suppose any marriage is perfect. Except maybe your mom and dad's."

Rush grunted. What did that mean? Bringing up Rush's parents gave her an idea. "Hey, your dad was a part-time deputy back then. I remember him coming to talk to my dad. Maybe he knows something about that night or he overheard a conversation that would help. We should talk to him."

Rush's jaw flinched. "Yeah… I'll talk to him."

Nora wasn't so sure she believed him. Something was up with his parents, but now wasn't the time to pry. She had to stay somewhere safe. The main house wasn't it. "I can't stay at the main house. Just in case. Besides, Dad has security that patrols all night. Guests love added security measures."

Wind howled and sleet started up again, pelting the windows. "I don't like it, but I understand. Take my number. Call me if you need anything. Anytime of night."

Rush rattled off his number.

Nora laughed. "Seriously? The last four digits of your number is four, five, six, seven?"

"Hard to memorize, huh?" he teased.

"It's probably the only number in my phone I can."

She saved his contact information and closed her eyes. "Rush, you do think it's only a threat, right? No one will actually try to kill me?"

Rush stopped at the front door, raised his coat's wool collar. "Nora, you're about to unleash an avalanche. What do you think?" He bent over and lifted his pant leg, retrieving a handgun from an ankle holster. "This is my personal piece. Lock the doors and keep it on your nightstand."

Nora accepted the gun and prayed she wouldn't have to use it. "Rush?"

He turned before leaving. "Yeah?"

"You said two cases. What was in the other one?"

"It was your mom's camera case." His mouth formed a grim line. "With two hundred and fifty thousand dollars inside."

TWO

"How'd you sleep, honey?" Dad looked up from his desk with tired eyes.

"I'm guessing about like you. Harrison stopped in at first light." Dad's Chief of Security had scared her half to death. He ought to be thankful he's alive. She almost shot him.

"I should have called and told you he'd be by to paint over the graffiti. I wanted it done before too many people saw it. I'm sorry that happened." He scooted out from his mahogany leather chair and crossed the room. Dressy jeans. Dress shirt that brought out the lighter flecks of brown in his eyes. She'd always wished she'd been blessed with her father's eyes. He opened his arms to her, as he always did.

She walked into them and let his comfort shield her and make her feel safe. A different safety than how she felt in Rush's arms last night. She didn't want to think too much on that. There was nothing left between her and Rush romantically.

"I had him put more security around the chalet for you." He touched the tender area on her cheek. "Rush taking care of this?"

"He is." She pulled away, cleared her throat. "Dad, I've never asked because I never wanted to know. Or I didn't believe. But after last night there has to be some truth to the gossip." She peered into his eyes, waiting for the bomb to drop.

Dad didn't speak for what seemed like an eternity. He touched her shoulder; his eyes held a mix of resolve and sadness. "Nora, why don't you remember your mother in all the good ways like Friday manicures and pancakes on Sunday. Or even that silly song she sang to help you sleep that only made you giggle and stay up longer. I think she did that deliberately to have more time with you. Don't try to pull up anything ugly. You'll find no peace there."

Nora held back the burning tears. Those were the memories fueling her search for truth. Mom had loved her, but did she ever love Dad? "You're not denying it. Is that why you didn't go on a mad hunt to find her after she disappeared? Were you relieved she was gone?"

Dad's jaw ticked and he inhaled sharply. "I loved your mother, Nora. The only relief I have is that now I have some closure. Let Rush look into who assaulted you and vandalized my property, but as far as the past, you stay out of it."

Nora had zero closure. *Stay out of it?*

Dad wasn't going to give her any answers; no point in bringing up the fact Mom had a huge sum of money in the camera case. If he did know about it, he wouldn't tell her. Nora had searching to do. Searching no one else seemed to want to do. Rush believed the past was an accident. He wouldn't put the proper time into it. Someone needed to fight for the truth.

"Now, why are you really here?" he asked. "I'm thrilled to have you. I hate that you came home to this."

"Can't a girl come home longer than Christmas Day?" She didn't have the courage to admit the truth. Besides, he was keeping secrets of his own.

He raised a dark eyebrow but didn't push. "You can always come home, honey."

"I know." Outside the sky was painted gray. Trendy on walls. Gloomy in her heart. "We'll have snow again soon. More rain and ice too."

"Knock, knock." Rush rapped on the side of the door frame. In uniform. He'd shaved and his fresh, soft cheeks held the dimples she'd always loved. "I see you got the spray paint covered up. You wanna report it officially?"

Joshua nodded. "Absolutely. I'll go down to the station this afternoon. I put Harrison and the night security on more rounds, especially at the chalet."

"Good." Rush cleared his throat and glanced at Nora. "How's the noggin?"

"Thinking about the next step." In between the thumping. "Which is breakfast," she added.

He chuckled. "I'll walk you down to the dining area, if that's okay."

"See you tonight," she said to her dad.

"Honey, remember our conversation."

She would. But it wasn't going to change her mind. As they walked down the hall to the elevator, she spoke. "Dad thinks I should back off. But why wouldn't he want to know what happened that night?"

Rush hit the elevator button. "He might want to spare himself further pain. Or he could know more than he's letting on to spare *your* feelings. Sometimes people keep secrets to protect loved ones." They stepped in and he pushed the first floor to go up from the basement offices.

"Secrets don't protect people. They hurt people." She slid him a sideways glance. He'd kept the fact he was dating Ainsley from her, and it hadn't spared her feelings. It had hurt more than anything. Her secrets of why she was back now would hurt and disappoint Dad.

They stepped off the elevator and took in the beautiful snowcapped view from the wall of windows that lined the hall and the dining area.

"I'm going to try to follow that money trail, Rush. It came from somewhere. If I can track it, I can get answers."

Rush pulled a chair out for her and sat across from her. She didn't miss his grimace. "I reviewed the initial police report from when she went missing, and the follow-up notes from Sheriff Parsons. Nothing about money. Nothing at all that would be a lead."

"What did your dad say?"

Rush unrolled his silverware, a grim expression. "I haven't had time to talk to him."

"You haven't had time?" She stared at him dumbfounded.

Rush balled his fist on the table. "Anything he would know would have been put in the report, Nora. And I was a little busy last night taking care of you."

Nora counted to ten. Rush had rescued and protected her. "Okay. But I still want you to talk to him. Or I can—"

"I'll do it. I'll do it."

The server came and Rush ordered coffee and toast. Nora ordered pecan pancakes with vanilla syrup and a side of bacon. She ate when she was wound up. She shivered and scanned the room. No one looked suspicious, but she couldn't shake the feeling of being watched.

When the server left the table, Rush continued. "Right now, I need you to be objective. Think back. Do you remember your parents ever fighting? Especially within a day or two of the ball?"

Nora shook her head and sipped her Irish breakfast tea with honey. "My parents never fought. I mean, if they did, then they kept it from me and Hailey. Plenty of space around here to raise voices and no one but the mountains to hear." She leaned forward. "Why? Do you think my dad had anything to do with this? I mean, I know he hasn't searched hard, but to murder my mom?"

"Whoa!" Rush put his hands up. "Don't jump to conclusions and certainly not out loud where diners can hear. I never said that." He scowled across the table.

"Well, you certainly implied it."

He shifted in his seat. "I didn't mean to. I'm saying if you could remember them arguing, you might remember some of the dialogue, which might be helpful."

She couldn't drum up one heated conversation. "Maybe he didn't know she was having affairs."

Rush gave her the get-real face. "Rumors flew through town. There's no way he hadn't heard them. Possibly approached her. A man was in that car at some point that night or around the event. Could be he caught her with him that night."

And did what? "For not meaning to imply, you're doing it again."

Rush's neck reddened. "We need to find the man who

owns the cuff link and mask. He might have answers. We can get photos from the party."

"Silver cuff links aren't rare. And what if the wearer isn't in the pictures?"

Rush tented his hands on the table. "I'd like them anyway."

Nora nodded as the food arrived. They waited for the server to leave before going back into their discussion. "They'd be in a storage room near the offices. I can get them for you later today."

They made small talk, dancing around the past.

"How's Hailey?" Rush asked.

"I think she's keeping a brave front for Dalton since he's already going through a lot." She added more syrup to her pancakes. "How's your family?"

Rush's jaw ticked. "Fine. Everyone's coming in for the Christmas celebration."

"Greer and Hollister?"

Rush's eyes held surprise. "You remember them?"

"How could I forget?" She remembered all those summers with Rush, including the ones with his cousins.

His phone rang and he answered; a few minutes later he hung up. "I have to go. With this weather, all hands are on deck with traffic accidents and we have one on Route 5. Turned into a brawl. Let me pay for my breakfast."

"Toast is twenty-two fifty." She held in a giggle.

Rush paused, then grinned. She'd had a weak spot for that killer smile. Guess she hadn't done enough strength training lately. It was making its mark.

"Don't worry about it. Daddy would be fit to be tied if he knew you were paying for meals here." She bit into her bacon. "I'll bring the photos by the station in a couple of hours."

"Be careful. Clearly the roads are treacherous, not to mention other dangers."

"Will do." She saluted him with the bacon but lost her appetite. Someone wasn't going to be pleased when they found out she wasn't giving up the quest for truth. She rubbed her cheek and shivered, then made her way down to the offices and storage rooms where they kept the predigitalized masquerade photos for marketing purposes. She flipped the light switch. The fluorescent lights flickered and hummed, only two lighting the dim room.

Using her cell phone flashlight, she crept into the room, highlighting the dates on cardboard boxes. Like something out of a TV show evidence facility. Dust sent her into a wave of sneezes. Halfway down the fourth aisle, she found the box. "Bingo."

A noise came from behind. Mouse? *Please be a mouse.*

Hairs rose on her arms and neck. She turned as a masked man snatched the box of photos and shoved her to the ground.

No! Nora jumped up, adrenaline pumping. With all her might, she pushed until the metal row in front of her toppled and crashed onto the masked man, boxes spilling open as papers and photos littered the concrete floor.

Nora hurdled over the boxes and debris, hands shaking, and grabbed the box he'd dropped, then ran like the wind. With one hand, she dialed 911. The dispatcher answered. Menacing words and papers shuffled in the distance. *Oh, no.* "Tell Rush Buchanan to get to Pine

Refuge Resort and Lodge." The attacker was on her tail. "Basement. Storage room. Now! Right now! This is Nora…" The phone slipped from her shaking hands as she took a hard right. Could she make the elevator? No. Where? Where could she go?

Custodial closet. Down the next hall.

She gripped the box. The attacker gained on her. She ran hard enough her chin shook.

Five feet.

Four.

Two…

She flew into the room, closed the door and locked it. The attacker banged and pulled on the knob. Could he find a way in? Could she find a way out? A small rectangular window above was covered in snow. The box wouldn't fit through it. She could escape and leave the photos, but if he got inside he'd have them, and obviously something in them incriminated someone or he wouldn't want the box so badly.

Her phone was gone.

No way to communicate. She curled into a ball until the banging and twisting on the doorknob silenced. Was he gone? Was he waiting on her to open the door?

What could be in these photos? And how did the attacker know she'd be in the storage room?

Chills slithered across her spine.

She had been watched.

"Nora! Nora Beth!" Rush stormed down the hall. Millie at Dispatch had called him, and what should have been a ten-minute drive had taken him over twenty thanks to the road conditions that were worsening each hour. Rush's heart pounded in his chest as he hunted for Nora. *God, please keep her protected.* He'd made his way to the storage room and taken in the disaster.

"Nora!"

He headed right, down another hall.

"Nora!"

"Rush. Rush!" The custodial closet door opened and Nora flew into his arms, gripping with all her might. "A man tried to steal the photos." Her shoulders relaxed and she explained what happened.

Rush brushed a strand of blond hair from her face and tucked it safely behind her ear. His gaze locked on hers and he couldn't quite make out what swam in her watery blue-greens—relief but something else.

"I was so scared I didn't know what to do."

"You did the right thing calling, then locking yourself in here." More than ever they needed those photos. Rush needed to find all the Phantom of the Opera masked men. One of them had answers or could be the one trying to hurt Nora. "Let's find your phone, get these and you somewhere safe." He grabbed the box.

Troy wouldn't want him exhausting his energy on this. As far as he was concerned, it was a closed case. He'd agreed with Rush that someone wasn't happy about Nora turning over rocks and they should be looking into that. But after two attacks and being followed, Rush wasn't so sure it was all about a possible scandal. People had killed for less, though.

The only place he knew the photos would be safe was under his care, at his house. He wasn't sure he wanted Nora there permeating it with her sweet cherry blossom scent and intensifying his loneliness when she left.

Rush led Nora to his vehicle and opened the door for her, then put the photos in the backseat. He hurried inside, cranked the heat and sighed. "You okay with going to my place?"

"Sure." Her cheeks turned pink and she gazed out the window. "I heard you built a house on the mountain."

"About four years ago. Still needs some work, but I'm only one man."

"Who's saved me twice. Thank you." She rubbed her palms together.

Rush pointed all the vents toward her. "You'd think tourists would stop pouring in. This keeps up and flights won't only be delayed, they'll be canceled."

"People pay good money to be here on the holidays. They don't care about the weather. Sometimes I feel like I'm talking to nothing *but* the camera."

Rush switched his wipers on to knock away the ice pelting the windshield. The rest of the ride was fairly quiet. He turned onto a long drive that cut up through a thick forest of evergreens. His two-story A-frame log cabin with a deck wrapped around the entire second story came into view. He loved having coffee out there and seeing the mountains for miles. It was peaceful and quiet.

And empty.

"Wow, Rush. I love how it's covered in windows. So much natural light, and what a view from up here." Nora gaped and took it all in. He felt that way every day.

He parked out front, grabbed the box and they went inside. Nora studied the cedar beams and walls. The kitchen was open to the living room. Leather furniture. Rugs for warmth on the knotty pine flooring.

"I love what you've done with it." She frowned. "Where's your Christmas tree?"

"I didn't put one up this year." One tree decorated for one man? Seemed silly.

She gasped. "Rush!"

"Did you put a tree up at your place in Knoxville?"

She collapsed on the couch. "No, but I haven't put a tree up since Mom disappeared…died." Tears leaked from her eyes, and she wiped them away with her sweater sleeves that hung over her fingertips. "You have no reason not to."

"Neither do you," he said delicately. "She wouldn't have wanted you to stop loving and celebrating your favorite holiday. Besides you're celebrating Christ's birth."

"Which doesn't call for a tree."

"You put up a nativity?"

"No. Make me some coffee and let's go through photos." She grinned and headed for the box on the kitchen counter.

"You're bossy."

"You ought to know." She slid the lid off the box. "Hey, Rush?"

"Hmm…?" He opened a bin and took a K-Cup for the Keurig.

"Nothing." Fear pulsed in her eyes. Whatever she was about to open up and say, she'd bit back.

"You can talk to me, you know. Like you used to." Before her world crumbled and she closed herself off.

"It's nothing."

Frustration knotted his neck and shoulder muscles. He gave her a cup of coffee how she liked it, with cream and sugar, and started combing through photos. He searched for men in Phantom of the Opera masks. "Do you know where there might be other photos? Not every single person is going to turn up in this box." Hundreds of people attended each Christmas. Several hundred of them local, and nearly three hundred tourists. This was a needle in a haystack job.

"Tourist center might have some put away. Locals probably have personal scrapbooks. What are we even looking for?" Nora asked, and thumbed through the photos.

"The mask in the car was a partial of the Phantom of the Opera. Look for men wearing that." He left out the other reason it was important. How did one tell an ex-girlfriend he'd seen her mom kissing the Phantom? She'd been through so much already. "And someone with silver cuff links."

"My dad wore cuff links but not like those." She held up a photo. "Look, it's you and Dan in those ridiculous masks with whisker-like things growing out of the sides." She laughed, but he heard the bittersweet tone.

"Good times." Rush couldn't manage much more. That was the night his dream shattered. He found two photos of two different men in Phantom masks. One seemed like it might be Ward McKay. He owned McKay Construction and was divorced. Could Marilyn be the rift that caused it? "Did you ever hear talk about Ward McKay and your mom?"

Nora paused perusing. "I steered clear of talk if I could."

"His wife moved away with their son. He might have been pretty mad over that even though it would have been his fault. Anger brings irrational behavior and thoughts sometimes." He couldn't believe he said that. He had no facts to support that theory. "I'm speculating and really I shouldn't be."

"No," Nora said. "That makes sense."

If Ward was the Phantom kissing Marilyn three months after he had separated from his wife, he might have wanted a more permanent relationship with Marilyn. If she rejected that, after he lost his family for her, that could have sent him over the edge. She might have been escaping him. Or something more sinister.

But they didn't have proof that Marilyn's car in the lake was intentional. And he was only speculating again. "If the car wreck was an accident, then all we're doing is meddling in people's lives to give you some comfort." A lot of damage could be done. "Is that fair?"

Nora jutted her chin toward him and glared. "What if it was your mother?"

He didn't know. Before his dad falsely accused a man of soliciting a prostitute, which ended up causing the man to commit suicide, he'd have said yes. But now? Now he wasn't so sure he'd go around prying.

"We have to question Ward, Rush. Evidence or not. What's he got to lose now?" Nora asked.

"If your mom's death wasn't an accident, then a lot."

THREE

The winter storm had slacked off, leaving a foot of fresh powdered snow and temperatures in the low twenties. But it wasn't keeping tourists and locals away from Main Street. Carolers dressed in Victorian clothing wassailed along singing inside the shops that were lit with candles and twinkling lights. Nora loved the candle store best with its cranberry, pine and cinnamon scents that wafted through the air. She'd be buying one of the candles when they got there. Small stations were set up for tourists to relax and revel with mulled cider or cocoa. With red noses and wrapped head to toe like mummies in winter garb and bags loading them down, people were having a ball.

Road crews had done a good job of clearing the roads and sidewalks. Nora and Hailey walked with Dalton, his lips coated in chocolate and whipped cream. Nora had missed so much of his growing up by only visiting once a year. She'd forgotten how much she loved these pre-Christmas festivities. They'd bumped into several people Nora had grown up with, and there had been no narrowed eyes or questions about Mom, but Nora couldn't help but feel gawked at. Rush had been called away due to shoplifters, and being here in public, Nora didn't think anyone would try something. She hoped anyway. She had her sister and Dalton with her.

"Nora, do you think you should push this?" Making a motion with her chin toward Dalton, Hailey let Nora know to talk in code so young ears didn't hear.

"Don't you want answers?"

"Yes, but not enough to bring on the extra trouble, if you know what I mean. Maybe we should move on. I don't care to know about every single indiscretion, and quite frankly, I believe there were many."

"But why? What was so bad in the marriage that would cause that?"

Hailey sighed and watched as Dalton jetted ahead, gawking in the taffy store. "People grow apart, Nora. They live in the same house, share the bills and running errands and after-school activities, but the spark dies."

"I'm sorry about you and Nate."

Hailey squeezed her hand but said nothing.

Nora had seen marriages that lasted. Burned bright all through the years. Rush's parents for one. And her grandparents on Dad's side. Mom had no family. No pictures. They'd burned in a house fire when Mom was young.

Hair rose on her neck and she scanned the area.

"So how are things with you and Rush?" Hailey asked.

Nora shook off the feeling of being watched again. "Fine. Good." He was helping her look into a case. That's it. Although sitting in his home, drinking coffee and reminiscing over old photos had shifted the place where she kept her feelings for him confined. "To be honest, I wish he'd be more aggressive on this investigation. He acts like he can't question anyone until he has proof, but he can't get proof without asking questions. It's like people who need their first job but can't get one without experience. How do you gain experience if you can't get a job?"

Hailey snorted. "You're babbling."

"I suppose I am." Rush frustrated her with his tippytoeing around. She was beginning to think he was pacifying her with his promises to look into the past. He hadn't done much of anything.

They stopped inside the candle shop and Nora bought an orange-cranberry candle. Outside, Nora spotted Candace Fick. "Hey, didn't she and Mom have lunches every Thursday afternoon?"

"Yeah, but that doesn't mean she knows any more than we do."

Carolers crooned, "Have Yourself a Merry Little Christmas."

"You never know. I'm gonna hop over and see if we can have a lunch of our own. I'll be right back."

Blue lights flashed in the distance. Looked like Rush's Bronco inching its way up the road. Butterflies swam in her stomach. Oh, no. No. No. She was not going to let herself swoon over him. For many reasons. One, she wasn't even staying in Splendor Pines. She was moving to Florida—hopefully.

Two, he'd cheated on Ainsley, and if he'd cheat on her what was to say he wouldn't cheat on Nora someday? There was no guarantee. And worst-case scenario, what if the rumors about her mother were true? What if Nora had her genes? Because if she were being honest she'd have to admit that even if she had known Rush was dating Ainsley, it wouldn't have stopped her from spending time with him, holding his hand, embracing him, cuddling on the couch or even kissing him.

She was pulled from the souring thought. Literally.

A meaty hand yanked her by the collar behind the shops, thrusting her up against the brick, her face scraping against the rough exterior. "I told you to back off!" he hissed, and cut off her scream with his thick gloved hand. She flailed and elbowed him in the chest, but his heavy coat must have taken most of the blow. It barely slowed him down. Adrenaline coursed through her veins; blood swooshed in her temples.

He yanked a strand of lights from the trim of the building and wound them around her throat, tightening them. She couldn't breathe! She grabbed at them, the twinkling rainbow hot around her neck and flashing in her eyes. In the distance, carolers sang, "O Christmas Tree." A serenade to her—Nora the human Christmas tree.

Help! Someone!

The cord dug into her neck, stinging. Her eyes watered and her throat swelled. Blood heated in her cheeks.

Using her foot, she back kicked him. She missed his groin and knocked his upper thigh. He cursed and thrust her to the ground, never releasing his grip on her throat with the lights.

Spots formed in front of her eyes.

The snow burned cold on her cheek.

He practically sat on her back as if he was roping a calf. She felt along the snow and found her bag with the candle.

"Nora?"

Rush!

The attacker released his grip enough for her to gulp a breath of air and wiggle around to use the candle as a weapon. She held the handles of the plastic bag and swung it like a bat against the side of his face; he groaned and jumped off her.

Rush moved in on him, but he scrambled and found his footing, racing ahead into the crowd. Rush radioed their location as he gave chase. She coughed and unwound the Christmas lights from her neck, breathing in the cold, fresh winter air.

Jogging, Rush came back to her and knelt. "Are you okay?"

No. But she had to show a sign of strength. "Just need to catch my breath."

He tipped her chin, searched her eyes. "Nora, be honest." Concern pulsed in his. "Talk to me."

"I'm fine." She hid her shaking hands. "How'd you find me?"

Rush blew a heavy sigh. "Hailey said you went to talk to Candace Fick, but Candace said she never saw you. I got a gut feeling. Went looking for you from point A to B."

Nora rubbed the tender area on her neck. "Anyone tell you that you ought to be in law enforcement? Private Eye? Detective? Human Metal Detector?"

"I'm glad you can find the funny in this."

Nothing about this was funny, but she didn't want to admit she might have bitten off more than she could chew. Because she couldn't back down regardless.

"That's me. The funny girl."

Rush pulled Nora to her feet. He brushed a gloved thumb across her cheek. "Nora, this is getting out of hand and I'm worried."

Join the club. "I'll be okay. I've got you around." She tried to play it off lightheartedly but it fell flat.

"I'm not always around, though. If I hadn't been just down the street…"

She'd be dead right now. With no answers. She didn't want to think about it. "Candace might know where Mom was going that night or who had been with her. They were friends."

"Why hasn't she come forward, then?" Rush asked.

"I don't know." Nora picked up the bag with the candle inside, brushed snow from it.

Rush pointed to the sleigh rides. "Why don't we take a break and hitch a ride back to the lodge."

"Isn't your Bronco still here?"

"Don't want to go 'dashing through the snow in a one-horse open sleigh' with me?" Rush winked and slung his arm around Nora's shoulders.

"As long as we don't have to laugh all the way. My ribs won't take it." She ignored her heart's warning to abandon his protective arms and charm and she leaned into him. Rumors were sure to abound.

Snuggled under a quilt with Nora on the sleigh ride had brought back so many memories. Rush had been smitten with her since he made fun of her pink sparkly tennis shoes in third grade and she shoved him down the hill on the playground. She'd been full of spunk and spice and still was. Normally, he'd appreciate that but it was fueling her need to keep pushing into the past. She didn't trust him to do his job, and coupled with refusing to let her feelings out, it was utterly disappointing. Didn't she see they were in this together?

Nora's father stood on the steps of the chalet as the sleigh ride came to its end. Rush had texted him ten minutes earlier and filled him in on the newest attack.

He met Nora as she stepped out and drew her into his arms. "Nora, how many times am I going to have to beg you to stop this? It's going to get you killed."

She didn't respond but pulled from his embrace.

Joshua's nostrils flared, but underneath the anger was fear. Fear for his daughter. "I've given the family staying next to you an upgraded chalet. Rush, you take that one until you don't need it anymore. I understand appearances." He peered into Nora's eyes. "But if you won't come back to the main house and let me take care of you, then I'll feel better knowing Rush is six feet away. But again, I wish you'd come up to the house and let Rush look into the attacks. If you stop digging, they might stop."

Rush thought the same thing, but the killer may believe Nora found the incriminating photo. If so, he would be coming to silence her for it. Rush too.

Nora looked at her dad and then at Rush. "If the results come back that there is no foul play involved, I'll consider it. But something bad happened that night. I know it."

Rush believed it too. He didn't think Nora would consider letting it go. He shook Joshua's hand. "I appreciate the chalet. I'll get my things later."

They stood quietly, a bit awkward, then Joshua tightened his scarf. "I've got some work to do." He left them on Nora's porch.

"What now?" Nora asked.

"We compile a list of names we heard rumors about and quietly investigate to see if they were true. Then we add their wives to that list. You know the phrase about women scorned."

"They buy Ben & Jerry's?" A slender eyebrow twitched north, giving Nora a sly, flirty look.

Heat swarmed Rush's gut. "Something like that."

Nora unlocked the chalet and they stepped into the warmth. She hung her coat on the hook by the front door and dropped her purse, hat and gloves on the kitchen counter, then lit the candle she'd wielded as a weapon earlier. Didn't take long for the chalet to become enveloped in orange and cranberry with a hint of cinnamon.

"We should make a list of the people who were there when the car was taken from the lake too," she said. "I always stay at the guest chalet. Someone knew it, knew I was home and that I was coming after them. Had to be someone who was there."

"Not necessarily. Anyone could have picked up the phone to gossip and shared it with the wrong—or right—person. I'll work on the men with rumored affairs and their wives." He'd spare her that dreaded deed. "After I build a fire."

"I'll make coffee."

They went to work on their tasks, then sat on opposite ends of the sofa, notebooks in hand, stopping every once in a while to pour more coffee. Nora pulled a box of ginger snaps from the cupboard that had been stocked. Rush was thankful for them; he hadn't eaten dinner.

"I only have about ten people on my list, and I know more were at the lake that night." Nora tapped her lead pencil on the notebook and scowled. He'd always loved her perturbed look. It made her nose perkier and her full lips poutier.

He tried to ignore his attraction and focus on the work. "Read off the names and let's see if any of them match mine, then we'll circle them and put them at the top of our suspect list."

Nora smirked. "You got it, Matlock."

Rush chuckled and Nora read her list. He circled the names she called out that he had on his list of rumored affairs: Ward McKay, Len Franklin and Harvey Langston. He still had three more names on his list. Martin Hassleback, Kent Sammons and Rodney Jones.

"Let's start with the first three we matched and then move on with the other three. Ward, Harvey, Len and Martin are divorced so they rank even higher as the chances of the rumors being true are greater," Rush said.

Nora rolled her pencil along her bottom lip. He cleared his throat. "I'm only speculating. Don't take it as the gospel truth."

"Why do you keep prefacing your speculations or putting that addendum on there? Cops speculate, Rush. It's not like you're accusing anyone of anything…yet." Nora laid her notepad and pencil on the coffee table, stretched and yawned.

"I don't want to falsely accuse anyone of something. It could wreck them." And himself.

"Flne, but we have to process our ideas. I'm not going to go out there and tell the world these things."

No, just the men whose names are on the list. And if they didn't have an affair, it might circulate once again and marriages could fall apart and worse. Rush's cell phone rang. Gary Plenk. "It's the coroner."

"Put him on speaker," Nora said.

"Hey, Gary, what's up? You're on speaker with myself and Nora Livingstone."

There was a pause on the line. Gary had bad news. Rush glanced at Nora and she nodded. "It's okay, Gary, you can say what you need to say."

"I'm so sorry, Nora. The DNA was conclusive."

"I was prepared for that. Thank you," Nora said but her voice choked up and she stared at the floor.

"Uh… Rush, could we talk a minute?" Gary asked.

Nora held up her hand and shook her head. Words wouldn't come. Right now, he wanted to tell Gary to call back later, take Nora into his arms and comfort her, but he doubted she'd let him. She may have been prepared for this call, but the reality was Marilyn was gone. Forever. It was official.

Rush paused, but the look in Nora's eye told the tale. She wanted to hear it all—needed to. "Go ahead, Gary."

Gary cleared his throat. "I'm ruling this an accidental death, but when you look at the report and photos, you'll see some striations on the…on the skull."

"Cause?" Rush asked, his stomach roiling over what Nora might be imagining. He should have taken Gary off speakerphone.

"Unfortunately, they're inconclusive."

"Meaning there could have been foul play involved?" Nora asked, but her voice cracked. "Have you double-checked?"

"I'm sorry, Nora," Gary said. "I have. They could have come from the impact of the car hitting the water, causing her to hit her head on the steering wheel or another part of the vehicle, but I can't be one hundred percent sure."

"Then it's possible that something else caused those marks."

"I don't believe so, no," Gary said, this time a bit firmer. "I think what we have here is a terrible tragedy, and I am sorry for your loss and the loss of your family."

"Thanks, Gary. I appreciate it." Rush hung up before Nora pressed on.

She stood, then sat. Tears spilled over her cheeks as

the harsh reality sank in. Rush tried to hold her, but she pushed him away as expected. Instead of getting upset over the fact that she didn't want him or his comfort, he quietly sat while she dealt with the death inwardly, and then she hurried to the bathroom, closing herself off even further from him. When she returned, he stood. "I'm so sorry, Nora Beth. Is there anything I can do?"

"No. She really is gone. Dad will want to have a proper burial. I need to work on the arrangements." She sniffed, wiped her nose on her sleeve and composed herself outwardly. "But I can't dismiss the fact that the striations are inconclusive. That means it's not definite and you know it."

There was no arguing that Gary had been the coroner for over a decade and a doctor for twenty years prior. Nora had latched onto the idea that Marilyn had been hurt that night. Rush massaged the back of his neck, working the tightness out. She had a point, even though it was slight.

"And even if she wasn't murdered, there's money involved. What if she was blackmailed for something—or forbid it all, blackmailing someone— Money laundering, payoffs…the list is endless. Rush, you're a total cop. Tell me you think it's all coincidence and it should be laid to rest and I'll believe you."

He couldn't give her that, as much as he hated to start tearing up innocent families with accusations. "I can't say that. And you know it. I also know you, and you have no plans of laying anything to rest anytime soon. You were pacifying your dad earlier."

"So?"

"So I think it's a good thing he put me next door."

FOUR

Sunday morning had come earlier than Nora would have liked. She'd been sleeping in on Sundays for a while now, but she'd agreed to go to church with her family and she had. First Community Fellowship and its congregation hadn't changed much. Rush had been two rows back with his family—minus Pastor Buchanan—which had been a surprise. Looked like his dad had retired. Nora hadn't kept up with the town news and Dad and Hailey never spoke of Rush. She was thankful for that.

They'd eaten Sunday dinner and now she was bundled up and at the town square for the annual snowman building competition. She'd promised Dalton she'd build one with him. She could count on both hands the years she'd entered this contest with Rush.

Dalton found a good spot next to a bench. "I want to build here."

"Perfect."

"I had a feeling you'd be here today," Rush said with a measure of pep in his voice. "You ran out with your dad pretty fast after the service."

The sermon on the Prodigal Son had unsettled her heart. Truth did that sometimes. She wasn't ready to deal with the messes she'd made trying to be someone she wasn't. "Had to get ready for this." Was he here to babysit her? Or... "You building a snowman?"

"No. My sister's kids are." He pointed across the square to his younger sister and her two littles.

"Do you *wanna* build a snowman?" she asked.

"Do you?" His eyebrow slyly arched.

Their gazes held. Memories flooded her mind and trickled all the way down to her tummy. Was he thinking of all their fun in the past? The snowball fights. Hot cocoa and kisses.

"I am." She motioned to the spot she stood on. "With Dalton. We could use some help."

"And how will that look when we whip all the competition, including my niece and nephew? They'll cry for weeks." He chuckled.

"They'll thank you for not helping them. You're terrible at it. Remember the year we built Frosty? You didn't have carrots."

"Hey, the celery worked. Frosty with sinus congestion."

Nora snorted and laughed. "It was gross."

"What? I put a white hanky in his twig hand." Rush's boyish mischief could always melt her like snow on a sunshiny day. "And now I have the urge to build a snowman."

"Then help us and your niece and nephew, but mostly us." She winked.

"Deal."

They began to pack the snow and roll the balls. Rush showed Dalton how to pack it tight and keep it from crumbling as they talked about superheroes and Dalton's enormous Christmas wish list.

"What do you want for Christmas?" Nora asked Rush.

"Easy. Season tickets to the Vols games next year and worldwide peace. Or I'd settle for you being safe... and at peace."

Nora packed snow on the base of the snowman. "I will be." She caught his eye and held it. Then smacked him with a snowball, launching an all-out war.

"Hey, we're gonna lose if you use up all the snow on each other!" Dalton hollered and broke up the fight. They resumed building.

Nora's toes were cold and some snow had trickled down her collar. She was smoothing out the snowman's midsection when she spotted Len Franklin. He was on the list of people rumored to have been involved with Mom. Rush didn't seem too keen on doing anything but making lists. Nora wanted answers. Fast. Now. "Hey, give me a second," Nora said and darted across the town square, weaving through snowmen, families, friends, couples and benches until she found Len with a middle-aged woman building a snowman.

"Mr. Franklin, I'm Nora Livingstone. Can I talk to you a second?"

Len raised his sunglasses and peered at Nora, his mouth covered with a scarf. "I know who you are, but I don't know why you'd want to talk to me."

She glanced at the woman, who was watching with curiosity. Nora didn't recognize her. Had Len remarried? "It's about my mother, Marilyn, and the rumors surrounding her affair with you."

The woman gasped. "Excuse me," she said in a shrill voice.

A few participants stopped building and gawked.

"And who are you?" Nora asked.

"I'm his wife. And I think I'd know if he'd had an affair. Furthermore, this isn't the time or place to discuss such things."

Nora ignored the woman and felt a hand on her shoulder.

"You're right. This isn't the time or place." Rush had caught her before she had the chance to get answers.

"Was your divorce a result of having an affair with my mother?" Nora asked quieter. "I'm not budging until you tell me the truth."

Len Franklin glanced around and leaned in. "Your mother was a tramp and that's putting it mildly. My divorce had nothing to do with her. And I had nothing to do with her either. I knew better."

The degrading talk stung and Nora's cheeks heated as people whispered, chuckled and gasped.

"Rush, is this how you investigate these days? Sic a weather girl on innocent folks? Don't see you gettin' elected that way." He harrumphed and consoled his second wife.

Rush nearly dragged Nora through the snow and behind one of the store shops. "Have you lost your mind? You can't go off half-cocked like that. Len's wife is from Texas. She never heard the gossip but she'll want answers now, and she may always wonder if there's some truth to that rumor. Do you not understand the definition of discreet? You could have done some real damage, Nora!"

"You mad because I was pushing forward or you might lose a vote for sheriff?"

Rush's jaw dropped, then he narrowed his eyes. "I'm going to pretend you didn't ask me that. Your dad is with Dalton. I'm taking you home before you accuse the entire town of affairs and foul play."

She fell into step with him. Rush was right, though she didn't want to admit it. "I just wanted to get moving on this. We can make lists all day, but until we start asking some questions we've got nothing. And since you haven't said anything, I'm guessing you haven't talked to your dad since last we discussed it."

Rush ignored her and opened the door of his Bronco. "Get in."

She huffed and slid inside.

They didn't speak until they reached her chalet.

Rush cut the engine. "One of us has a badge and one of us doesn't. So, it's my way or I'll make sure you have zero involvement in this at all. I can make that happen, Nora." His tone held no tenderness. He had every right to seethe.

She picked at the edge of her scarf and swallowed a measure of pride. "I'm sorry for what I said. I didn't mean that."

"Fine." Didn't seem the apology was accepted.

They exited the vehicle and Nora stepped inside her chalet. An eerie feeling sent a new wave of chills over her.

"What is it?" Rush asked.

"I don't know." She walked into her bedroom.

The closet door was open. Nora was sure she'd closed it. She tiptoed to the nightstand, heart pounding. What if someone was in the closet now? Without looking, she felt for the gun Rush gave her Friday night. Breath shallow, she frantically searched to no avail.

Glancing down, she saw why.

It was missing.

* * *

Rush stood over Nora's nightstand and scanned the bedroom. While it hadn't been tossed, some things did seem to have been moved. The gun missing was the tell-tale sign, but the place was clear. "What do you think he wanted?" Rush asked.

Nora gnawed on her thumbnail. "I don't know. Can't be the gun. No one would know I had it. I think that was an opportunity he couldn't turn down."

"The only thing I can think of is the photos. He knows something valuable is in that box and he knows you know." Good thing they were at Rush's. "How did he get in?" Rush had searched the chalet and didn't find a forced point of entry.

"The window in the kitchen was unlocked. I didn't realize it until after I got wigged out that someone had been in here. I checked. I should have checked Friday night when I arrived."

No, Rush should have. He'd stayed up late watching the house, making sure she was safe. He'd even spotted the security detail make their thirty-minute cruise by the chalet. With security and Rush being so close, the intruder would have had to have been up in the trees. Watching with binoculars. "I don't like the idea of you being alone in this cabin. Six feet away in another cabin isn't going to be good enough. So before you get all freaked out, I'll stay in the chalet next door. Until midnight. From midnight until seven a.m. I'm bunking on your couch. My car will be next door. No one will think anything untoward is going on, and who's out here to think anything anyway?"

Nora's lips pursed. She didn't love the idea. Rumors were a sore spot, especially if they cast her in a dim light. Nora ran like the wind when trouble came. It was the driving wedge between them. Whether she ran physically or emotionally it was still the same—shutting out Rush. And to say he wasn't doing his job because he wanted votes? That cut deep.

"Okay, Rush. I'll agree to it." She touched his shoulder. "And I really am sorry. I know you'd never ignore your duty. I'm…"

"What?" If she would only open up. What? What would that do besides zero in on his heart and crush it again when she left for Florida?

"Frustrated. That's all."

No, it wasn't. But he didn't push. He didn't want to have to press and push. He'd watched Mama do that with Dad for so long. It did no good. They'd lost Dad to the pain and Rush had lost Nora. He needed to get a handle on that and move on. If he was meant to be a bachelor, he'd deal with it. He only wished the loneliness would go away. But better to be alone than in a marriage that felt one-sided. *God, Mama needs You to marvelously work on her behalf, and so do I.*

"I understand."

"Can I ask you something off topic? It's personal." Nora sucked her lower lip between her teeth. She didn't have to open up but she wanted him to get personal. He almost laughed, but it was far from funny. She didn't even wait for his response. "Where was your dad today? Why isn't he pastoring anymore? How long have you and your family been at First Community Fellowship?"

"That's three questions." And this topic was tender for him. Too tender to get into with a woman who wouldn't reciprocate his feelings. "We've been at FCF for about ten years. Since Dad isn't preaching anymore. He was at home today."

Nora opened her mouth but clamped it closed. "Gonna snow soon. Sleet later tonight."

That wasn't at all what she wanted to say, but relief slid through Rush. He didn't want to discuss Dad. "I know, and the tourists keep pouring in. They may not be able to get out. Tours in the Smokies have been shut down. Too dangerous out there."

Hopefully, it wouldn't slow down business. Tourism was Splendor Pines' cash cow. Especially during the Christmas season.

"Speaking of dangerous. Do you believe Len Franklin?"

"I don't know." What he did know was he hadn't found any photos that matched a Phantom of the Opera mask with the cuff link. But he had pulled a couple more photos of men in the masks. "I plan to talk to your dad when he gets home. About that money."

He hadn't had the time Saturday, and while he hated doing any kind of business on Sunday, it came with the territory.

"I'll come with you."

"I know you will. I don't want to leave you here alone, but once we get to the house, I want to talk to him by myself. If he is withholding information, it might only be from you. Give me the chance to see if he'll fess up to something to me."

"I owe you that after what I said." The next hour they spent drinking coffee and keeping relatively quiet. "Dad's probably home," she said, staring out the window.

"All right."

Nora grabbed her scarf and coat.

They locked up the chalet and drove to the house. Joshua's car was in the drive. Inside, Joshua sat on the couch watching Dalton put a puzzle together while Hailey was curled up asleep on the love seat. They made small talk, then Rush stood. "Joshua, could we talk privately?"

Joshua set his coffee on the side table and nodded. "My office."

Nora busied herself with Dalton's puzzle. At least she was following through with what she said.

Joshua closed the door to his office and perched on the edge of the desk.

Rush had no easy way of doing this. "We found Marilyn's camera case. Her camera wasn't in it. But two hundred and fifty thousand dollars was." He waited a beat, gauged Joshua's reaction to the news.

Joshua stared past Rush's shoulder, then slowly spoke. "I gave her that for an anniversary gift. Waterproof. She dropped the camera case before that into the lake. She'd cried for days over lost film." Joshua's eyebrows slightly rose and he licked his lips. "You want to know if I was aware that she had that kind of money on her person?"

"Were you?"

"No."

"But you don't seem surprised," Rush said.

Joshua's jaw twitched. "I knew she had a great deal of money. I made weekly deposits into her personal account."

"Why not have a joint account like most married couples?"

Joshua folded his arms over his chest. "We weren't most married couples. Have you ever heard of foster children hoarding food even after they've been adopted into a safe family? Even though they love the new parents and trust them, there's always this fear that they won't get another meal. At some point, they might stop doing it, but until then, they need that feeling of safety. Security."

Rush read between the lines. "You're saying her account was for her to feel secure?" Why would Marilyn feel that way? Had she been a foster kid? "You want to expound further?"

"No. Because it's not pertinent to your investigation. That account was kept open for when or if she returned. You're welcome to the bank records." Joshua opened a filing cabinet and pulled out a manila folder. "She has four thousand dollars in it. It would appear she had been withdrawing money and storing it up, since you found the cash. I can't tell you why." He handed over the information.

"Can't or won't?" Rush asked.

"Marilyn had left before. She didn't stay gone long. I don't know where she went. I think had she not been in an accident, she'd have come back. She loved the girls…and she loved me," he murmured. "I don't care what other people say. I knew her heart."

"Did you argue often?" What man would not confront his wife about rumored affairs—and so many?

"Couples disagree, Rush. Yes, we had arguments. Some were more heated than others."

If Joshua had anything to do with Marilyn's death, Rush would be shocked. He wouldn't rule him out, though. Not yet. Nora believed he was hiding something. Rush wasn't sure it was something sinister, but too many people were keeping things hidden.

FIVE

Rush slid on his hiking boots and tied the laces. At nine o'clock this morning, he'd attended the burial of Marilyn Livingstone, though he'd felt much like an outsider. Only family and a handful of friends had attended. After a small brunch at the main house with immediate family, he'd dropped Nora off at the chalet and went next door to change, and to give her some alone time. She hadn't said much, but she'd shed a few tears.

Between this case, the weather and Nora in general, his mind was muddied. Nora wouldn't let up until she had the answers she wanted. She'd proved that by bombarding Len Franklin, who had called Troy, and Rush had listened to a lecture about keeping her nose out of the investigation. Rush agreed, but clearly, she wouldn't. It would be easier to try to give her some rope and hope she wouldn't hang herself with it. If they worked together, Rush could at least contain her actions, and if things took a turn for the worse he'd be there to protect her.

Rush had filled Nora in on the bank account but he had kept the part about Marilyn's need for security to himself. He'd hoped she'd take this day to be with her family, but he couldn't trust her not to give him the slip and go off on her own. He grabbed his wool coat and faced the treacherous weather. Gray skies. Pregnant with snow. Shivering, he hurried next door to her chalet and knocked.

A few moments later, the door opened and Nora stood in sock feet with a cup of coffee. He wanted to ease into her space, wrap his arms around her and let the warmth seep into him, but those days were over. "Hey," he said instead.

Rush stepped inside and shut the door on the wintry mix coming down. His pillow was resting on the folded-up blanket he'd placed on the end of the sofa earlier this morning before he left.

The cabin smelled of fresh coffee.

Raking her hands through her hair, Nora slurped her java—didn't look to be her first—as the gales blasted against the chalet rattling the windows and whistling down the chimney flue. The fire inside popped and flickered. Snow blew from the bare branches and ice crusted the windowpanes and porch railing.

"I've been studying weather satellites online, tracking the storm heading our way. A foot of snow in the past three days and an inch of ice."

"Is that all you've been doing?" he asked and poked his nose over her shoulder. *The Old Farmer's Almanac* was open in another tab. "Don't you want a day to mourn?"

"This is my way," she said quietly and set her mug on the wooden table. "I've been looking into the weather from seventeen years ago. But there's not much to go on. No data for snow depth. Zero inches recorded for rainfall. Mean wind speed had only been four miles per hour. Maximum was seventeen. Not bad enough to knock someone off the road and especially not if the roads weren't slick with water or ice."

Rush gave his head a small shake. She might as well be speaking a foreign language. Nora had been infatuated with the weather since as long as he'd known her. Once they'd sneaked out of school their sophomore year to chase a tornado. They'd nearly died. Definitely got grounded. But there wasn't much Rush wouldn't have done for or with Nora.

"Why isn't there much to go on?"

"All weather information is collected by the National Climatic Data Center, but only what's reported. Not every station reports every day—or at all."

Nora continued to study weather satellite images and maps, jotting down notes while Rush made a cup of coffee.

She popped up from the screen. "Do you want some coffee?"

He held up his mug and winked.

A fresh flood of pink filled her cheeks. "I can get lost in research sometimes."

"You don't say."

She closed down her laptop, then poured another cup from the pot. Steam billowed into her face. "I know you're not simply here for coffee."

"I'm not." He set his cup on the table. "I'm going to talk to Ward McKay. He's renovating the hotel over on Route 5."

"I want to go."

He folded his arms over his chest. "I knew you'd say that. Which is why I'm going unofficially."

Nora frowned, then slid her glance over him and

blushed. He swallowed hard. Nora may have been aiming for stoicism, but he'd recognized approval in her once-over—attraction. "What?" he asked, forcing her to either lie or tell him she was checking him out.

"I noticed you're dressed casually. No uniform." Half-truth.

He spread his arms out. "I don't work all the time."

"Have a life, do ya?"

No. Not really. "Do you?"

"It's on hold at the moment until I hear from Florida."

"What if you don't hear from them? Then what are you going to do?" Would it ever appeal to her to stay?

"I have a few irons in the fire."

"Any around these parts?" he asked as nonchalantly as possible.

"No. I'm ready to branch out of Tennessee. See new things." Since when? "Let me change and we can be on our way." Nora hurried to her bedroom and fifteen minutes later entered the living room dressed in jeans that were tucked into knee-high black boots that matched her sweater with a droopy-looking collar. "What's wrong? You're staring at me."

"Nothing." It was hard to focus when the prettiest woman he'd ever seen was standing two feet away smelling like an orchard. "But before we go, just because I'm going unofficially doesn't mean you have free rein. I'm asking the questions and I'm going to be discreet."

She saluted him and slid her knit cap on her head. "Aye aye, *mon capitaine*." Brushing past him, she stepped onto the porch and took a step, slipping.

Rush scrambled and caught her around the waist before her backside met the wooden stair. She turned in his arms, her breath pluming between them, cheeks rosy. She blinked a few times, not hurrying from his arms. And he hadn't let go either.

A beat passed.

Two.

"You okay?" he asked, hoping his tone hadn't revealed his feelings. Having her in his arms, so close. So soft. It had unleashed a storm inside him.

"Yeah," she said with a faint voice. "Good thing you're here."

He brushed away a hair that had stuck to her lip gloss. "Guess so." Righting her, he led her to his truck parked at his chalet and opened the door for her. Once she was inside, he jumped in the driver's seat and cranked the engine. Christmas oldies blared from the radio and he adjusted the volume.

"You really do love jamming to Christmas music," she said.

"Can't a guy like Christmas?"

"Not if the guy won't even put up a Christmas tree." Rush had always loved Christmas as much as Nora. And here they both were without the festive spirit in the form of a blue spruce or Douglas fir.

"Touché." They made small talk until they reached the Evergreen Hotel.

"You didn't mention it was the Parkwells' hotel." Parkwells. Ainsley's family. He hadn't actually thought about it until now.

Tension in the air swirled over the name.

"Nora, that was a long time ago." Rush swiveled in his seat to face her. "I can only apologize so many times for not revealing I was dating Ainsley. But when we're together—I mean when we used to be together—it's like the rest of the world didn't exist. It was just you and me. I got caught up in that."

Nora looked away, then faced him. "I believe you, Rush. But I can't forget what happened, and I'm going to feel awkward around Ainsley. I can't help it."

Rush understood. "If it makes you feel any better, she won't be here. She only worked for her dad while she was in school. She's a guidance counselor for the middle and high school. Kids won't be out for a few more days."

"Okay."

"And thank you. For believing me."

She nodded.

"Now let's go see Ward McKay and hope he'll give us some information."

They hurried to the main doors and entered, shutting out the biting cold. Some of the walls were charred. Destroyed.

"What happened?" Nora asked.

"Fire last month. Bad wiring. It'll be summer before they can reopen."

The sound of hammers, drills and shuffling about drew their attention past the elevators and down one of the first-floor halls. "Parkwell can't seem to catch a break," Rush muttered as they stepped over heavy plastic, where painting crews had been working.

"What do you mean?" Nora asked.

He should have kept his mutter quiet. Ainsley had confided in him while they were dating that her father seemed to fall into bad investments and had been pretty stressed out. It was straining her parents' marriage. But then he'd bought this small hotel and things seemed to look up. Now a fire.

"Just, he hasn't been the star of the show when it comes to business deals." He nonchalantly shrugged and kept moving. Construction crew members passed by and he stopped one. "Hey, you seen Ward?"

"Second floor," one mumbled, and hauled some lumber on his shoulder into another room. "Use the stairs. Elevators aren't working right now."

"Thanks." At the end of the hall, the stairwell door was already open and they climbed the flight of stairs that led to the second floor. More noisy construction was going on up here along with some classic rock music.

Rush and Nora wandered the hall until Rush spotted Ward. Guy had been a legend on the football field—played some college ball for the Vols. But like most people, he made his way back home. Unlike Nora, who wanted nothing more than to stay gone. Being here seemed almost painful for her and not only because of the memories of her mother. Something more was going on but she refused to confide in Rush. And he couldn't push. He was keeping the kiss between the mystery man and Marilyn to himself.

Nora didn't trust him with her feelings. Rush couldn't trust her with this. She'd already proved she wasn't going to be discreet. If she found out about what Rush had seen, she'd go vigilante and ignore others' feelings. Might even falsely accuse someone. And that's another reason he'd let her come along. To test her with Ward. If she could be discreet and not hotheaded this time, he'd reveal the truth. Overly cautious was better than hurting and wrecking innocent lives.

"Hey, Ward," Rush said.

"Were you having an affair with my mom and if so, did you have anything to do with her death?" Nora asked.

So much for trust and discretion.

Heat filled Nora's cheeks as Rush's sight bored into the side of her head. Okay, she'd been blunt, but she was losing time. Florida could call any minute and she'd be leaving. And if she did, no one would put in the time or effort like herself.

Ward McKay slowly removed his construction hat and eyed her with a mix of regret and heat. "Hello to you too, Nora."

Rush needled her lower back and stepped in front of her. "Sorry, Ward."

Sorry? This man could be a murderer. She could have used more tact, sure, but apologizing? Not in a million years.

Ward ran his hand through his thick salt-and-pepper hair. "I figured you'd eventually come calling about Marilyn. Didn't realize you deputized her daughter."

Rush shot Nora a glare. "I didn't. We're here unofficially."

Eyeing Nora, Ward grunted. "Doesn't feel unofficial."

Nora couldn't keep silent. "Official. Unofficial. Either way, you might have some answers. Did you have an affair with my mother?"

Ward studied his feet, then looked at Nora. He tossed out his hands. "What do you want me to say? I'm sorry? Because I am, but I wasn't then."

His words punched her straight in the stomach. She

nearly bowled over from the blow. For the first time ever, she heard the truth from someone who had no reason to lie.

Rush lightly touched her upper back.

"Did my father know?" she choked out. There was no denying it anymore.

Ward licked his lower lip and jammed his hands into his pockets. "I never told him. Doubtful Mari did."

"Marilyn. Her name was Marilyn." How dare he use a pet name for her mother in front of her! Where was the respect?

He turned to Rush. "I suspect that Joshua has an idea. He's never approached me, though."

"How long was the affair?" Rush asked.

"A year."

A whole year? Nora couldn't breathe. This was a bad idea. Maybe she should have listened to Rush. She wasn't as prepared to hear these things as she thought.

"Did you see her the night she died?" Rush asked.

"I did. But we were over by then. She called things off." His tone held sorrow and even regret. The man had genuinely been in love with her mother! He pulled his phone from his pocket, checked it and texted. "Sorry. Work stuff."

"Did the affair contribute to your divorce and family leaving town?" Rush slightly cringed as if asking the question hurt.

"Most definitely." He paused. "Nora, I really would rather not discuss this in front of you."

"If you're embarrassed, that's on you, Ward." She wouldn't give him an ounce of easy.

"I'm not. I don't want *you* to have to hear this."

"You weren't thinking about me then! Why think

about me now?" Venom dripped from her words, all the hurt and anger. She couldn't stop it if she wanted to. "You hurt so many people! How could you?" Unwanted tears sprang in her eyes.

Rush faced Nora, his back to Ward, and he gently put his hands on her shoulders, leaning close and lowering his voice. "Why don't you go wash your face. Take a few moments. I'll finish this up and tell you everything you want or need to know."

As much as she hated it, she needed to pull it together. "Fine," she said reluctantly.

"Bathroom on the second floor isn't working. Use the one on the first. Down the hall from the pool. Under construction but in working order," Ward offered. "I'm sorry, Nora."

"Save it, Ward." She stomped from the hotel room and down the hall to the stairwell. On the first floor, she turned right, the cold draft seeping through her thick gray peacoat. Securing her scarf tighter around her neck, she passed plastic-covered walls and doors. The hard truth had left her exposed and vulnerable. She couldn't stop imagining Ward and her mother as a couple. Her father all alone. Those images turned her stomach.

Rush had warned her.

She hadn't listened.

Hammering and drilling echoed through the lonely, dark hall. Metal burning turned up her nose.

Bathroom. Covered in the same heavy Visqueen.

She shoved it aside, the rattling noise sending her insides kangarooing. Bending, she checked for feet under the stalls. She went to the mirror, ran water and waited on it to warm.

She closed her eyes, splashed water on her face.

Suddenly she was yanked away from the faucet, a strong grip on her coat collar. Through the mirror, a burly man's partially covered face stared back. He wore a construction hat and a painter's mask.

Nowhere to run.

Swinging her purse, she caught him on the shoulder but it didn't stop him. He slammed her back against the wall by the bathroom door.

Heart pounding, she dug her nails into his hands that were clutching her throat.

"You don't listen! You must have a death wish."

Snatching the hanging Visqueen from the door, he ripped it as she kicked and swung, but his grip around her throat was a force, and his hands were like vises. Nora let out a strangled cry as he draped the plastic like a tight blanket across her face.

Can't breathe!

Panic set in. Blood pounded in her temples.

Pop!

Pop!

Had he shot her?

She couldn't see. Every time she inhaled, plastic entered her mouth, the taste dirty and bitter.

God, help me! He'd yanked the thick material across her face and nail-gunned it to the wall, trapping her to suffocate! The last thing she heard was him laughing.

Nora couldn't tear through it. Too thick.

Couldn't get oxygen.

Couldn't calm down. Hysteria was taking over. With each scream, she inhaled the plastic.

No air. Spots formed. Sweat slicked her temples and back as she clawed at the plastic.

She was passing out.

"Nora! You down here?" Rush called out. "Hey, I don't want to come in, but I will if you don't say something."

Barely any energy left, she forced her arm out the door and waved.

See my arm. See I need help.

"Nora!"

In a flash, the sound of ripping came through the suffocating barrier, and a blast of wonderful oxygen filled her lungs; she gulped it in. Rush held her up. "Did you see him?"

She shook her head, coughing and inhaling deep breaths. "Keep this." He handed her the knife he'd used to cut away the plastic.

Rush shot from the bathroom and she slid down the wall, pushing back her sweaty, matted hair. She could have died.

It felt like an eternity before Rush returned and knelt in front of her. "What happened?"

She told him through ragged breaths. "If you hadn't shown up…"

He drew her to him and stroked her hair. "You said he wore a hard hat and had a nail gun." He looked around the bathroom, at the tools lying on the floor. "He must have taken it with him. I don't see either."

"Do you think he's working here or he followed us?" The thought froze her blood in her veins.

Rush frowned. "I can't say for sure. Either scenario is plausible, but I didn't notice anyone following us on the way here. Seems likely he's an employee. I'll get a list from Ward."

"You're going to interrogate a whole construction crew?"

"Just the ones who clocked in." He caressed her cheek. "You sure you're okay?"

She nodded. "How many do you think are here?"

"Thirty, maybe fifty. I don't know."

"That's going to take a lot of time." Time they didn't have.

Rush gripped her shoulders. "I don't care if it takes me till Kingdom Come. Whoever did this isn't going to get away with it."

His sober tone slid into her, melting away the fear until it waved again. "Rush, he wasn't trying to scare or threaten me. He wanted me dead." Tears stung the backs of her eyes. "He's going to strike again."

"I'm going to protect you, Nora Beth. I promise." Cupping her cheek, he forced her to make eye contact, to see he would do whatever it took to keep her safe. "Tell me you trust me."

He wasn't asking her to trust him with her heart. Just her life. "I trust you. To keep me safe."

"It's a start," he muttered. "I don't want you here any longer than you have to be. I'll get you back to Pine Refuge and I want you stuck to your daddy like glue, understand?"

Nora nodded and Rush escorted her outside and into the Bronco. He started the engine and blasted the heat; it blew cold so he turned it back down until it warmed. "Do you still want to keep looking into the past? I plan to continue investigating these attacks, but we don't have to pursue the past."

"Depends. You believe foul play was involved that night?" She didn't want to have to convince Rush that something sinister happened to Mom. She wanted Rush to believe it for himself. If he did, he'd work harder, be more aggressive in the investigation.

"We can't prove it. The striations on her skull are inconclusive. Even if you find the weather in all likelihood didn't cause the accident, there are a million other things that could have sent her into the lake. Deer. Bobcat. Dog. Not paying attention…"

She got it. The list was endless. "We can't prove anything. But if we keep poking around, someone will eventually tell us something or lead us somewhere. And we know the report is inconclusive, but no one else knows. We have leverage."

"Nora," he groaned.

"It's not illegal to bend the truth. It's not even entrapment. I've watched every legal show on the planet. I can google it and I will." She pulled her phone from her purse.

Rush chuckled. "Okay, Detective Livingstone. I see what you're saying. I don't like it, though."

"Of course you don't. But you have nothing to lose."

He gripped the wheel and his jaw ticked. Had she struck some kind of nerve?

Turning the heat full blast, he murmured, "Some of us already lost everything because of this."

Was he talking about losing her? What else could he mean? What could she say? Sorry didn't seem good enough for how much she'd hurt Rush.

Rush changed the subject. "Do you want the lowdown on Ward?"

"Yeah. I wanna know." Better to keep it from getting personal anyway.

"He thinks your mom was involved with someone else besides him—toward the end of their relationship."

Nora covered her face. The overwhelming humiliation set her cheeks aflame. What in the world was wrong with that woman? What if she'd passed down the cheating genes? Was that even possible?

"Nora," he said softly. "Do you want me to go on?"

She wanted a time machine to go back, change everything. "Go on. I'm fine."

"He fell in love with her, Nora. Wanted to marry her. Told his wife. It broke up their home but your mom wouldn't leave your dad."

Nora snorted. "What in the world was keeping her?"

"I don't know. I suspect your dad knew. I have no clue why he wouldn't give her the boot." His cheeks flushed. "Sorry."

"No, he'd have every right. How many times can one betray you until you walk away? How could he have trusted her? Yet he says he continued to put money in a personal account. I'd have put a tracking chip under her skin or something." Nora half laughed. What wasn't her dad telling her? Why would a woman not leave? Why would a man hang on?

"I think Ward's still angry over their breakup, but I'm guessing. And that doesn't mean he did anything that night."

"But so far he's our best suspect. Unless your dad knows something." She waited for Rush to respond, but his nostrils flared and he sighed.

"I said I would. I will."

"Today."

"Today. Now. Do you want to hear the rest of my conversation with Ward?"

She nodded.

"He said she visited a bar and grill outside of town. Mac's? Sound familiar?"

"I mean, I've heard of it but I've never been."

"He suspects she was meeting a man there. It's what caused the downward turn in their affair. Ward doesn't know who the man might be. Never saw her with anyone else during their time together."

"I guess we need to take a trip to Mac's after you get that list of construction workers from Ward."

Nora wasn't ready for what they might find. But she had no other options.

SIX

Rush glanced out his office window into the bull pen, where desks butted up against one another.

He'd nearly lost Nora this morning.

The memory sent a new wave of sickness into his stomach.

After he'd dropped her off at her dad's, he got the list from Ward McKay, went back to the site and did interviews through lunch. Fifty-two men and not one claimed to have done it. He hadn't expected them to. But it was still possible that they'd been followed or a worker not on that list had shown up. No one would have thought anything about him being on-site.

Rush had checked in by phone with Nora after lunch. She'd been searching weather maps and online sites to try to discover the weather that night along with helping her sister at the guest center.

Now it was nearly five thirty and he was hungry, but every time he pictured Nora with plastic nail-gunned across her face, he lost his appetite. He picked up his cell phone and called as he gathered his coat and keys. She answered on the second ring.

"Any news?" she asked.

"No. But we'll keep searching. Have you eaten?"

"Not since lunch. You?" Her tone had a hint of hopefulness.

"How about I stop by Rudy's and grab some Italian food and we can eat in. The weather is—"

"Going to get nastier around eight. Sounds good. I'm at the chalet with Dad."

"Okay. He going to eat with us?"

"No."

"Chicken Parm still your favorite?"

A beat of silence passed through the line. "Yeah. Yeah it is." Was that surprise he detected? There wasn't anything about her he'd forgotten. Not even the fact that she loved Christmas but hadn't put a tree up since her mother died. Now she'd been attacked multiple times and heard straight from the horse's mouth that her mother had been involved in several affairs.

"It'll be about an hour before I can get to you. That okay?"

"Sure. I'll be the one with the growling stomach."

He caught her humor but didn't miss the grief beneath it. "Sit tight, Nora Beth." By the time she fell asleep tonight, he might be able to make it a little better.

Sheriff Parsons met Rush at the main doors. "You callin' it a night, Rush?"

"Yeah. No news on the Livingstone case. You hear anything new?" Rush asked as they pressed into the frigid night, light snow but heavy, dry wind. Later, it was supposed to snow and ice again.

"Nope. How are things?" He gave Rush the inquisitive eye.

"With Nora?"

Troy chuckled. "Yes, with Nora. She's a sweet girl,

son. But I don't see her sticking around long. Don't get too tied up."

He wouldn't.

What he was about to do had nothing to do with personal feelings; it was about making a friend feel better—or trying to. "We're friends. Which is more than we used to be. I'll take it."

Troy clapped Rush's shoulder. "All right, Rush. All right." He climbed in his truck and pulled away as Rush slid into his Bronco and headed for his parents' house.

Inside, his mother sat on the couch knitting a pink-and-gray scarf. "Rush, what are you doing here?"

"Can't a guy come by and see his mama?" He bent and kissed her cheek. "I smell cookies."

She snickered. "Family will be here tomorrow. Wanted to get a jump start on snacks. But help yourself to some and take a few to Nora." She looked up at him. "How is she?"

"Worse for the wear, but truckin' on."

Dad stepped out of the hallway in his navy blue robe and moccasin slippers. "Nora home?" he asked.

He'd aged dramatically in the last decade. Frail. His hair, once dark blond like Rush's, now full of gray. "Yeah, she's home. Helping look into her mom's disappearance."

Dad's mouth pinched and divots formed between his eyebrows, but he offered nothing. Rush expected no less. Nora didn't understand who Dad was these days.

He turned to Mom. "Do you still have those extra boxes of ornaments up in the attic and the tree you used to put in the family room?"

She squinted. "I believe so. You putting up a tree?"

"That's my plan." At Nora's. Who would press him about if he'd questioned Dad or not. He'd promised. "Dad, while I'm thinking about it, do you remember anyone in particular wearing a Phantom of the Opera mask the night Marilyn went missing or anything that might be helpful for me in this investigation?"

"Can't say," he grumbled, and shuffled into the kitchen.

Can't or wouldn't?

A few moments later, he heard the cookie jar lid clinking. Rush sighed and climbed up into the attic, retrieving two huge boxes of ornaments, and then he brought down the tree. Christmas tree lots wouldn't be open this late. Artificial would have to do.

Fifteen minutes later, he was back on the road. Snow steadily coming down. The curves were rough to handle and slick, but he made it to Rudy's and then to Nora's chalet over an hour later. Living room lights glowed. Smoke puffed from the chimney.

He grabbed the to-go boxes and made it to her door, slipping only once. He knocked with his boot. "It's me, Nora Beth."

The door opened. "I'm starving."

"You're welcome." He stepped inside and greeted Joshua before he left. Rush locked the door behind him. The cabin quickly filled with Italian spices, onion and garlic. Nora had already set the table.

"Thank you for dinner."

He handed her the chicken Parm and piled the linguine on his plate. They made small talk while they wolfed down their meals and he gave her a brief update on the interviews and that his dad had no information to offer, but he didn't want to talk shop tonight.

"You want hot cocoa?" she asked.

"Actually, I was thinking about something else."

Nora's sculpted eyebrow rose.

Rush chuckled. "It's outside." He stood. "Be back." He braved the cold and brought in the two boxes.

"What in the world?" Nora said and retrieved the top box. "More pictures?"

"No. For the rest of the night, I kinda don't want to talk about the case." Rush set the box on the floor, then went back out and brought in the tree.

"Rush, what is going on?" she asked, confusion filling her face.

He plopped the tree box down and dusted his hands on his pants. "You've had a horrible day. And I thought maybe we could bring back some good times tonight." He paused, hoping this would be okay with her. "It's time to start putting a tree up, Nora Beth," he whispered.

She scanned the tree box and ornaments and shook her head. "I don't think I can."

"Yes, you can. You've pushed this case and been attacked but you keep going." If there was a time to tuck tail, this was it. But she hadn't. It shifted something inside him. "You can put this tree up. Remember the good times. Believe there will be more to come." He leaned down to catch her eye. "Let's do it together."

Nora gnawed her bottom lip and crossed her arms across her chest, her oversize red sweater swallowing her in a way that made her ridiculously appealing. She nodded. "Okay, Rush. You're right. I need some kind of goodness to end this night."

Rush's chest swelled with satisfaction and a Psalm came to mind. "'I had fainted, unless I had believed to see the goodness of the Lord in the land of the living,'" he quoted. "We'll see the goodness of the Lord in all this. I believe it."

Nora opened a box. "I'm glad you do, Rush. You've always had stronger faith than me." She hauled out glass ornaments in red, gold, green and silver.

Rush pulled out the three-piece prelit tree. He put the sections together, plugged it in and hoped the lights all worked. "I think your faith was pretty strong until that night." He and Nora had shared that—faith. Hope in the Lord.

He still hoped. Still believed, but sometimes he had doubts. When it came to finding a wife, having a family. He had to admit he'd been struggling to trust God in that area.

"It's too quiet in here," she said, and grabbed her cell phone. She set it on a small docking station on the counter and a Christmas music station belted from the speaker. "Rockin' Around the Christmas Tree" played, bringing the atmosphere back to an upbeat vibe. A few lights were out and he messed around until he got them working.

"You ready?"

Nora stared at the white lights casting a romantic glow on the cabin. Her eyes filled with moisture, and Rush couldn't help it; he closed the distance between them and laced his hand in hers.

"I forgot how much I've missed this. Mom used to

say colored lights were fun, but white lights were pure. Innocent. Clean. She was right."

Rush studied the lights. He'd never thought about it that way. In terms of innocent. Clean. Interesting for a woman who had multiple affairs. Something stirred deep within him. He couldn't put a finger on it, but all of a sudden, he felt sorry for Marilyn Livingstone.

Nora started trimming the tree with the glass ornaments and humming along with the music as "Blue Christmas" belted through the room. He'd had some pretty blue Christmases over the past several years.

"What are you asking Santa for this year?" He placed a gold glittery ornament on the tree.

"You know what I want, but since we aren't discussing that right now…a job would be pretty great. Bills won't pay themselves." She dug through the ornaments and retrieved a small wooden box. "What's this?"

"Oh, wow." Rush laughed, but his chest tightened. "Open it."

She did. Her eyes widened and she gaped. "I can't believe you still have this." Nora held up a ceramic hand, painted red and white like a candy cane. She held her own hand against it. Perfect fit.

Ought to be. It was hers.

She snickered until she found the acrylic painted inscription written on the palm, then she sobered. "Do… do you want me to put it back? Or…"

"Hang it," he managed, emotion choking his voice. "It was a good memory."

"You have the other three?" she asked.

"Somewhere." He turned away to get his bearings. She'd made that first hand in their freshman year of high school. The plan was to make one each year forever. And one day when they were old, their tree would be nothing but Christmas hands.

He read the black painted note.

You have my hand and my heart. Forever. I love you always.
Nora

The date was right under her name. Over twenty years ago.

He didn't have her hand. Or her heart.

"Silent Night" came on the music station. His favorite. Perfect song to match the atmosphere outside, where fat wet flakes fell. It was a winter wonderland.

The fire inside crackled.

Nora's candle smelled wonderful. Not as good as her, though.

"You want cocoa now?" Nora asked softly.

"Sure."

He continued hanging ornaments. At the bottom of the decorations, he found three more wooden boxes but he couldn't bring himself to open them, read the inscriptions or to hang them on the tree. "I'm gonna take these empty boxes out to the Bronco."

Without wasting time, he hurried outside and put them in the back of the truck. When he returned inside, Nora sat on the sofa, feet curled up underneath her as she watched the lights on the tree. By the firelight, she was breathtaking.

A smile tugged at her lips.

She was deep into memories. Fond ones. Which was what he wanted from the start. He wondered if any of those memories included him. The teakettle whistled and he motioned for her to stay put. "I got it."

"I put the cocoa mix in the mugs already."

He poured the water into the mugs—not his favorite kind of cocoa but it would do in a pinch. He stirred them and brought them to the couch, sitting beside her.

Nora wrapped her slender fingers around her mug and inhaled.

Curiosity got the best of him. "What were you thinking about just now?"

Nora's face glowed against the flames of the fireplace. "When I was little, Dad always let me put the angel on the tree. He'd say, 'Nora, you're my sweetheart.' But I haven't been a sweetheart. I left him when he needed me most. Left Hailey…" Shifting, she faced him. "You…" she whispered. "Sometimes I wonder what would have happened if I hadn't pulled away from you after Mom vanished."

Rush knew exactly what would have happened.

He'd have married her.

Nora peered into Rush's warm brown eyes, not sure what she hoped to see or hear from his mouth. They couldn't go back. Couldn't change the past, but he brought back her best Christmas memories with her family—decorating the tree by the fireside and drinking hot cocoa while listening to festive music. He did it because that's who he was. Compassionate, selfless and generous. He was going the extra mile to see to her safety, knowing he might be in jeopardy too. Not to mention, he probably had a life but he'd put it on hold—for her.

Seeing that ceramic hand had only brought back memories of two teenagers dreaming of a future together, when it seemed bright and full of hope, when it was like the white lights. Innocent. Pure. Untainted by mistakes, scandals and Nora's insecurities.

Rush ran his hand through her hair, brushing it from her face. "I wonder sometimes too." He held her eyes captive as the wind howled and rattled the window-panes. The smell of chocolate on his breath reached her as he slowly descended on her lips. "I think we would have made a great life, Nora Beth."

Would they have? Would Mom's scandals have hung over them like ice-encased branches, shattering over their happy homemade lives? Would Rush have gotten bored with Nora and cheated? Would Nora have cheated on him?

As his lips met hers, scraping on the roof drew her attention away. She drew back, almost thankful for the distraction. "What was that?"

Rush glanced up. "Probably tree branches." When he met her eyes, he sighed. "If you weren't okay with where this was going, Nora, you could have said so."

She wasn't using the noise to stop the intended kiss. Prickles ran along her skin. "I wasn't, but…we can't let the way we felt about each other in the past trip us up now. We're…we've been over a long time, Rush."

"Is this about what happened with Ainsley?"

"No." Maybe. Partly. "I'm leaving after Christmas. I can't stay here permanently. I don't want to. And I don't see you ever leaving. That kinda puts a halt on anything between us, don't you think?"

"I think—"

Crack!

"Get down," Rush hollered, and shoved Nora on the floor between the couch and the coffee table.

"Was that a gunshot?"

Rush drew his gun and crouched low, moving toward the window in the breakfast area. Nora curled into a fetal position watching, waiting.

Metal outside clanged. Rush turned the knob on the door. "Don't move. I'll be back."

Panic raced through her system. "Don't! Rush, you could get shot!"

He placed his index finger on his lips and slipped out the back door. She threw up a prayer that God would keep Rush safe.

Scraping on the roof continued. Snow fell like curtains of cotton blocking her view into the woods. She couldn't huddle like a scared rabbit and do nothing! Not when Rush was out there risking his life to keep her safe. Crawling across the living room, she made her way to the back door. The only weapon in her possession had been stolen. She was defenseless against someone with a gun, but Rush could be hurt—could use another pair of eyes at least. As she reached for the knob, the door swung open and a blast of cold air swirled with snow into the kitchen area.

Nora yelped, then realized it was Rush.

"What are you doing?" he demanded.

"I was coming to help you. Is he out there?" she asked and balled her fist to hide her trembling hand.

Rush eased her up to her feet, his nose and cheeks pink, hands icy. He'd hurried out without a coat. "A tree split on the north side of the house. Barely missed the roof. Sounded like a gunshot. But there are footprints out there. Fairly large. Work boots, possibly." He rubbed his upper arms. "I think the tree splitting scared him off, and he knocked over the garbage can. Must have been crouching behind it."

Lurking.

Nora shivered.

Rush led her to the fireplace and they sat on the hearth; he might be warming up cold bones from the weather, but no amount of heat could warm up the fear racing through Nora's.

"I followed the footprints into the woods, but without a flashlight it's useless. And with the snow coming down this hard, they'll be covered by the time I can get back out there," Rush said.

Nora rubbed her clammy hands together. "So the rustling on the roof actually was ice weighing down branches and dragging with the wind?"

He held his hands, palms open to the fire. "I suspect."

A gust of wind shook the door and whistled in the flue. The lights flickered. Ice, most likely, was encrusting power lines. Whoever was spying must be desperate to come out in this kind of weather. "If he was in work boots, could it be the same attacker from the hotel?"

"I don't know." Rush frowned. "When you're at work, do you keep your cell phone on to hear notifications?"

Where was this going? "Depends. If I don't mind interruptions, then yeah, I keep it on. Why?"

"It just hit me. Earlier when Ward got that text... I didn't hear it. Not even a buzz. The place was loud and noisy. Wouldn't he have it on to hear the ding?"

Nora's mind raced. "He checked it, then sent a text... Do you think he faked getting a text so he could send one to whoever attacked me? Let him know where I was? What better alibi than the Chief Deputy?"

"We come in and Ward knows what we're after. But that also means he's not working alone—if this speculation is correct."

At least this time, Rush didn't apologize for it. But the thought of more than one killer after her—a band or at the very least a pair of killers working in tandem—terrified her. "If he is working with an employee, then we can't rely on the list he gave us. He could have easily had his accomplice's name removed."

"Valid point. If it's an employee. We don't know anything concrete, so it's not like I can subpoena his phone records, texts." Rush faced the flames, eyes appearing even darker against the firelight. "His information on Marilyn meeting someone at the grill might be a rabbit trail."

"Best way to find out is to go to Mac's tomorrow and hope the owner can tell us something—or the manager if he or she still works there," Nora said. The lights dimmed, flickered and went out, leaving them with only the firelight and the candle she'd purchased earlier.

"Extra candles?" Rush asked.

"I think I saw some tea lights in the nightstand drawer." She used her cell phone flashlight to guide her into the bedroom. Retrieving the box of tea lights and a lighter, she lit them and scattered them throughout the house. In the living room, Rush peeped out the windows.

"Lights are on at the main house and lodge," he said.

"Generator. Chalets and cabins don't have them. I imagine Guest Services will be getting a boatload of calls tonight."

Rush's cell phone rang.

"Hey, Troy," he said. His face grew stern. "Okay, I'll

be there as quick as I can." He listened a few moments more, then hung up. "I need to take you up to the main house. Car accident on Route 5. Doesn't look good."

Nora's stomach knotted. "What if he comes back? To the main house?"

Rush laid gentle hands on her shoulders. "I can't say for certain, but I think you'll be safe. Between me chasing him off and the weather…"

But he couldn't say for sure.

"Can I come with you? I'll stay in the car. Promise."

Rush rubbed his earlobe—telltale sign he was thinking about it. "The weather is terrible. Let me take you to your father. I'll come back for you. Three hours tops."

"Okay." She slipped into her coat and Rush's Bronco, then called her dad to let him know she was coming home.

Rush walked her inside and squeezed her hand. He seemed to want to say something more, but instead he motioned a hand to the door.

"Lock this behind me. I'll call you when I'm on my way back."

She simply nodded and closed the door. Dad stood just inside the foyer in his robe and slippers. The backup generator had kept the lights on and the fridge humming. "Everything okay, hon?"

"Yeah. Wreck on Route 5. Rush had to go." She left out the scare from earlier. "Hailey here?"

"No, she's up at the lodge. I was going to head that way too, but Dalton's asleep."

"I can keep an eye on him."

"And who will keep an eye on you?"

Point taken. "I'm going to go lie down." She kissed Dad's cheek and retired to her old bedroom, but sleep wouldn't come. An hour later, she tiptoed downstairs for a cup of warm milk. The greenery on the banister poked at her fingers. Hailey had decorated in silver and gold with pops of red. Festive. Elegant. From the kitchen, she studied the tree. White lights like Mom loved. Childhood ornaments along with glass ornaments. Gold ribbon cascaded down the ten-foot tree. Stockings hung on the mantel. Four. Hailey, Nora, Dalton and Dad.

Dad dozed in the recliner, lightly snoring.

She'd rifled through the offices in the lodge, but she never searched Dad's home office. Tight-lipped meant keeping something hidden. He might be hiding it in his office. Hurrying quietly down the hall, she slipped into Dad's office and closed the door. The lamplight cast a soft glow over the dark wood. A sliver of guilt niggled at her, but she ignored it.

She rummaged through drawers and filing cabinets. Nothing that raised red flags or held secrets. Could his lack of words and pressing an investigation simply be the way he grieved? Privately? He might be able to let things go, but Nora couldn't, especially after Ward McKay's outright admission of guilt. It had lodged like a wet clump of dough in her stomach and grew until she couldn't find a single drop of peace, but only more questions.

Questions that wouldn't be answered here.

On her way to the door, she tripped over the area rug, peeling it back to reveal a small exposed bump in the hardwood. Had his flooring been warped? Kneeling to toss back the rug and leave everything as it was, she noticed the board wasn't uneven, it was raised. Using her thumbs, she pushed the board out of the groove and two more came loose. Underneath lay a small fire safe.

Her heart raced and she quickly pulled the safe from the floor.

No key. She hadn't seen a key while searching the drawers and cabinets.

Dad's set hung in the kitchen. Nora put everything back the way it was and carried the fire safe to her room, hiding it before going back down to retrieve Dad's keys.

He still snoozed in the recliner. She spotted them hanging on the hook by the back door. Without causing too much jingle, she gripped them and raced upstairs, then locked the door.

Chest pounding, she flipped through the keys until she found a small silver one.

It was now or never. She might find nothing but money and valuables, but at least she'd know.

She opened the safe.

Inside was a box lying on one lone manila file folder. She opened the box. Several legal papers were sandwiched inside; she scanned them and gasped.

Her blood ran cold.

SEVEN

Nora's eyes blurred with tears, as a pain, deep and raw, cut like a jagged blade through her heart. Dad had definitely been hiding something.

Like the fact that Nora wasn't his biological daughter.

Whose daughter was she? She could hardly breathe as she blinked away the tears and scanned the documents.

One stood out. A legal agreement.

This hereby states that Scott M. Rhodes relinquishes all parental rights for Nora Jane Cotter.

Cotter—her mother's maiden name.

Scott Rhodes.

Who was this man who fathered her but didn't want a single thing to do with her? She read on and gaped. No. This wasn't true. Couldn't be.

The only dad she'd ever known had paid Scott Rhodes half a million dollars and had agreed to pay him one hundred thousand dollars a year for the rest of Scott's natural life.

So that's what it cost to give her away.

Why would Dad even agree to that? Was this Rhodes guy so nefarious that he felt it necessary?

Nora continued to read, realizing that the document had been drawn up by her own father! Not Scott Rhodes. If the contract was breached by Scott, all agreed monies would be cut off and Rhodes's transgressions would be made public.

What transgressions? Nora? Had to be.

Nora snagged her phone and searched for Scott M. Rhodes.

Gaping at the image before her, a fresh wave of tears fell. She'd always wished for her father's eyes. Looked like she got her wish after all. She may have Mom's hair and lips, but her face shape, eyes and nose belonged to Mississippi senator Scott Rhodes.

Married for almost forty years. Three children. All a bit older than Nora.

Mom had said she was twenty-two when she'd had Nora, but according to the dates on the documents, Mom had been eighteen when she'd had Nora. Which meant she'd been lying about her age. Claiming to be older than she was. Was this one of his secrets too?

Nora continued to read the history on Scott Rhodes until her stomach roiled.

A man dedicated to wholesome values. An article about families eating meals together popped up with him sitting around a dining room table with his wife and children—minus Nora, who had been a mistake. Someone to throw away and forget about.

Who did this man think he was? That he could sail through life with Dad's money as if Nora never existed. Like red-hot bubbles, anger boiled over until Nora saw nothing but rage. Before she knew it, she was grabbing her coat, slipping on her boots and racing out the front door.

She couldn't handle any more. The walls were closing in on her. She couldn't breathe.

No one would give her answers. She'd take them.

This man who shared her eyes would look into hers and admit he'd abandoned her. Not even that—but had never even cared.

She drove all the way to airport, white-knuckling the steering wheel as she slipped and slid across the icy roads, hoping flights wouldn't be too delayed or canceled. Tourists were still making it into town. Surely she could make it out. When she got to the parking garage, she called a journalist friend with the news station she'd worked for to get an address for the great senator who focused on family values.

Nora needed answers. Clearly, she wouldn't get them from Dad.

But she would get them from her father. She bought the ticket, paced for the entire thirty-minute delay, then boarded the plane to Jackson, Mississippi. She managed to arrive around eleven fifteen. Her friend had texted her the address with no questions asked. She also had several missed calls, voice mails and texts from Rush. She ignored every single one. This was something she would do alone. Nora didn't need Rush standing by and trying to comfort her. She'd lose all resolve. Turn to mush. Maybe even fall apart.

She hailed a cab, climbed inside and rattled off the address. This man would have answers about her mother and if she woke him from sleep, so be it.

As the cab neared Senator Rhodes's antebellum home, some of the fury dissipated and fear burrowed into its place. This man could have had something to do with Mom being in the lake. She had a camera case full of money. He might have asked for more. Was that where Mom was heading? To take him money?

What if he was the one trying to kill Nora now? That wasn't possible. Mom's death would have made Tennessee news, but not national and doubtfully Mississippi. And he hadn't had time to get to Splendor Pines to spray paint her cabin, but it was possible he knew someone there who had seen the news and called him. But who? That seemed far-fetched.

The cab pulled to the curb and she told the driver to wait. Hopefully this wouldn't take long. She didn't have a ton of cash to spare. She'd maxed out her last credit card paying for the airfare. She stood at the black iron gates locking her out of stomping to the front porch and banging on the door. Gates would not keep her out.

She pressed a button on the intercom and waited silently.

A rattle filtered through the speaker. "May I help you?"

"Scott Rhodes?"

"Who's asking? It's nearly midnight."

"Your daughter. Nora Livingstone." That ought to jerk a knot in him.

The line went silent, but in a few moments, a figure appeared rushing toward her. As the man approached, the sight nearly knocked her breath away. Seemed it did the same to him. He stood staring through the bars, blue-green eyes mirroring hers.

"What are you doing here?" he hissed.

No happy reunion.

"My mom died."

"What do you want me to do about that?" he asked, eyes narrowed. There was no love here either. Not even an ounce. "Do you want money or something?"

Money. Oh, she had debt up to her eyeballs, but she wanted nothing from this man. Besides, her own dad had enough to pull Nora out of debt if she'd ask for it. "I don't want anything but answers. I found the agreement you made with my dad. It was in a safe I stumbled upon earlier this evening."

Scott glanced behind him. "My wife is in the house, upstairs asleep."

"I'm not asking you to wake her up and bring her to the party." Nora wanted to rip his head off. Instead, she forged ahead. "When was the last time you saw my mother?"

"Before you were born. She told me she was pregnant and I told her to get rid it of it." A hard edge formed around his lips.

"*It* is me." How could he stand here and talk about her like she was a thing and not a person?

"You, then. I told her to get rid of you. She said she would."

The man was a liar, but she couldn't tell if he was lying now. "Why did my dad draw up those papers? And did you ever meet him?"

Scott hugged his robe tighter around him. "He came to visit me right after you were born. Said he wanted to raise you as his own. I was concerned he might try to extort money from me—"

"Blackmail you for producing a child through an illicit affair with an eighteen-year-old girl who probably thought you loved her?" Nora nearly spit on the ground. "He is much classier than that."

Cocking his head, Scott studied her, then laughed. "You think she loved me? That I let on like I loved her?" He sobered and his eyes widened. "You don't know, do you?" He laughed again. "Oh, this is rich."

Dread pooled in her gut.

"Your mother was nothing but a high-end call girl. You were an oversight in a business deal gone bad."

Nora couldn't find a single word.

"She didn't want to keep you because she had any imaginings of me leaving my wife. But I didn't trust her not to try to blackmail me or ruin my career. When Joshua Livingstone agreed to pay *me* to have you, I knew he'd keep the secret and not come after me. So I took the deal. It wasn't my first choice, but it's worked so far." His smug smile sent her over the edge.

His first choice would have been to abort her!

"Well, the money stops right now. You won't be getting another penny and if you so much as contact my father, I'll come forward and tell the whole world. And they'll believe it. Because even without DNA testing, I look like you."

That changed his arrogant face. For the first time, he looked afraid of her. Not of getting caught but of Nora.

"And if I find out you had anything to do with my mom's death, I promise you, you'll go to prison. But not before the world and your family know what a piece of slime you are." She balled her fists to keep from shaking in front of him.

Scott hesitated, then spoke. "How do I know you won't come after my money? My career?"

"Because my father raised me better than that." Her father had paid quite a high price to have Nora as his own and was willing to pay until the man before her died.

Another taxi pulled behind hers, lights shining in the distance.

"What is going on?" Scott demanded.

Nora wasn't sure.

Until Rush stepped out of the backseat with fire in his eyes.

Rush stalked to the gate; anger boiled to his brain, but relief that Nora was alive and okay for the moment kept his head level. He'd finally left the pileup on Route 5 only to return to Joshua's and discover Nora wasn't there.

What they'd found on her bed told the tale. Joshua had revealed that he wasn't her biological father. The man who was looked livid and slightly nervous.

Rush approached. Pulled his badge. "Chief Deputy Rush Buchanan. I'm from Splendor Pines."

"Why are law enforcement involved in this?" Senator Rhodes demanded and glared at Nora. "You said you wouldn't tell anyone. Didn't want anything."

"I don't!" Nora's voice rose. "How did you get here?" she asked Rush. "I got the last direct flight and there were delays."

"That's not really what we need to discuss at the moment, now, is it?" He held his temper in check. "I have a few questions about Marilyn Livingstone."

"I already answered those."

Rush listened as the senator recounted his relationship with Marilyn—who he claimed to be a call girl. Joshua hadn't shared that. He might not know. "I'm done talking without my lawyer."

He gave Nora one last glance, turned his back on her—for the second time—and marched toward his home. Rush couldn't imagine the pain and torment she was feeling at this moment.

She'd opted into flying the coop. Hadn't called him, approached her father or stayed put. Nora had possibly put herself in further danger, though Rush didn't have a gut feeling the senator was behind the attacks on her. He wasn't sure if he'd had a hand in anything that might prove nefarious from the night Marilyn died. She did have a case of money.

Now that Nora had revealed everything, Rush couldn't be certain the senator wouldn't retaliate somehow. But the most important thing at the moment was Nora.

She stood gazing through the bars as if they would open up to her and a new story would unfold. Rush laid a hand on her shoulder. "Nora, it's time to go home."

She rapidly blinked, then inhaled. "Right. Okay."

Rush paid her cabdriver, then guided her into his cab. She gnawed on her nail and stared out the window. Lost in thought. There had to be thousands. "Do you want to talk about it?"

"No. You heard it yourself. There's nothing to say."

There was tons to say! She had to be dying inside, and more than anything, Rush wanted her to lean into him. To talk about her feelings. To know she could confide in and trust him. It was this barrier that had torn them apart and kept them apart. Rush had thought Nora might not be a runner anymore since she'd stuck around to look into her mother's past. But this heavy news had sent her heading for the hills. Physically and emotionally. Proving there were no more shots between them.

"Your dad knows you found the papers. You left them on the bed."

Nora nodded.

"Nora, I know this is a major bomb, but what really matters is that your dad loves you. And he's a good dad. Now you know what he's been hiding." Rush touched her hand, but she pulled away, then slowly she gave it back to him. The simple gesture warmed his heart. He laced his fingers with hers. "Please talk to me."

"If my dad was keeping quiet to protect me from the senator, then he must believe that the senator is dangerous."

Rush didn't mean to talk about the case but if that's all he was going to get, then so be it. "But he couldn't be behind the attacks. That first one at the chalet happened only hours after you arrived in town. Unless he has a connection to Splendor Pines and someone called him and he put out an order. Even then... I'm not sure it's Scott Rhodes."

"Me either. He was genuinely surprised to see me on his doorstep. Mom may have been going to take him money that night and something happened. Either done by him or someone else, but if it was him, why not take the money?"

The cab dropped them at a private hanger. Rush paid the fare and he and Nora crawled out of the cab. "This is how I got to you." He smirked. "When there were no more direct flights, I hit up Buddy Wilkerson."

"Ah Buddy. I didn't realize he was still flying planes."

"On occasion. And he's always been a bit adventurous, so the storm didn't affect him as much as a few extra dollars and doing me a favor did." Rush waved to him and they made small talk before boarding. Once they were buckled in and taxiing, Rush continued, "I agree with you. I don't think the senator is our present-day killer. I can't say for sure if he's involved in the past. But my cousin Hollister was in the navy with a woman who is now a private detective. Lives in DC."

"How would you remember that?" Nora asked.

"He brought her home a few times after you moved to Knoxville. They seemed pretty serious, but it ended. On amicable terms. She can probably look into the senator discreetly. See if we can find any airline tickets or hotels nearby on that night. It's a long shot, but it's all we have."

"Is she how you got Scott's address?"

"Yep."

"What's her name?"

"Theodora VanHolt. She goes by Teddy, though." Rush leaned back as they ascended. When the plane steadied, he sighed. She may not like what he had to say, but she was going to hear it now that she couldn't make a break for it. Unless she had a parachute. "Nora, you shouldn't have taken off like that. You could have gotten yourself killed. We were all hysterical. Do you not care about the people who care for you?"

Nora squeezed her eyes shut. "You weren't there when I read those papers. You have no idea how it made me feel—"

"And you won't tell me. Ever since your mom died, you've closed yourself off emotionally and physically. You didn't used to be this way. You used to trust me with your hopes, fears and dreams. You can't pin this one on Ainsley. It happened long before her."

Nora started to speak but closed her mouth. Finally, she spoke. "I can't explain what happened to me after Mom disappeared. Or I didn't want to because it would make me a horrible person. The last person I wanted to see me in a bad light was you."

Rush's chest ached to hold her. He cradled her cheeks. "Nora, I could never see you in a bad light. Not then. Not now." Though he was disappointed in her and her actions, there was no hiding the generous, kind and clever woman before him. More than anything he wanted to lean in and kiss her, but now wasn't the time or the place.

"I'm tired. Mentally. Emotionally. Physically."

Rush scooted closer and offered his shoulder. "Rest. We can talk later."

The turbulence didn't seem to affect her. Nora slept right through it all until they landed at Splendor Pines Airport. "How you feeling?" Rush asked.

"I don't know. It's been a lot to take in. Instead of answers I keep getting more questions."

Rush thanked Buddy and led Nora to his truck. They climbed inside. Rush shivered and found his gloves. "I'm going to take you back to the chalet."

Nora nodded and they inched their way toward the cabins. The heat kicked in and warmed the cab of the truck. When they arrived, Rush parked in the driveway of his cabin. "We'll walk over."

Nora only nodded. Her face was pale and her eyes tired, dark circles underneath. Snow crunched under their feet, and Nora leaned into Rush and he put his arm around her.

Crack!

Gunshot. Snow sprayed about a foot from them. "Run!" Rush hunched over Nora, shielding her, and ran behind a tree.

Another shot fired.

And another. Bark splintered. Which was safer—heading for her chalet or into the woods?

Woods. "Let's haul it through there and to your dad's." Someone had been lying in wait. Rush didn't have his radio on him to call it in. But he did have a gun. He fired back, hoping whoever was shooting might change his mind knowing they were armed.

The shooter returned fire.

Grabbing Nora's hand, he hauled her into the woods with him.

When they'd made it deep inside and almost to the stable, the firing stopped. Either they were tracking quietly or they'd given up.

Rush fired one more round to test and see. Nothing.

"Now what?" Nora breathed, air pluming from her lips.

The shooter probably expected them to make a dash to the main house, where he might be tracking to now. "Let's double back to the chalet and I'll call for backup. Make sure no one gets hurt here or at your dad's place."

Scott Rhodes could have called someone. But the better assessment was someone else had planned this attack. Maybe Ward McKay. Maybe anyone. Marilyn had a slew of deadly secrets, and one of them was out to get Nora.

EIGHT

The morning was overcast and full of snow and ice. Nora hadn't slept a wink. The weight of her mother's past had borne down on her heavily along with the adrenaline from the attack and confronting Scott Rhodes. She picked up her cell phone from the side table: 7:00 a.m. Now she was feeling the exhaustion, but there was no time to sleep. The smell of toast drew her attention to her stomach and it rumbled. Toast. Power must be back on. She plugged in her cell and the lightning bolt lit up.

After brushing her teeth and hair, she entered the kitchen. Dad sat at the table drinking coffee. Tired eyes met hers and for the first time in all her life she glimpsed a measure of uncertainty in them. Nora's stomach knotted.

Conversation time.

Rush cleared his throat. "Pot of coffee and toast. I'm going to go next door and shower. Call me when…" He nodded and grabbed his coat, then bolted.

Nora forced herself to pour a cup of coffee and take a piece of buttered toast from the plate by the coffeepot. "I'm not sure how to start," she said. Tears burned the backs of her eyes.

"Let me start, then." Dad stood. "I love you, Nora. I love you because you belong to me. I chose you to be mine. I haven't regretted it a day."

Nora's throat tightened and she gripped the counter as she felt Dad's presence move closer to her until she could hear him breathing behind her.

"I love you, Nora."

With trembling lips, Nora turned and faced her father. His deep, dark eyes gazed into hers and tears glossed them over. She fell into his arms and sobbed. "Were you ever going to tell me the truth?"

"No. Because the truth is you're my daughter. Nothing else matters and I wanted to spare you the pain you must have endured last night. I wish you hadn't gone to Jackson."

But she had and she was glad she did. She would have always wondered. Now she knew what kind of monster had created her, the way in which she'd been born. "He said some ugly things, Dad. I don't want to believe them, but I can't ignore them."

"Your mother came here looking for a job."

"At eighteen. I know she lied about her age all these years." Nora sat at the table, unable to stand. This was too much information. Too heavy. Too devastating.

Dad slowly nodded and sat across from her. "She was lost and looking for a place to belong and have you. Something about her moved me. I was way too old for her, and at first it was me giving her sanctuary and a job as a maid."

Her mother. A call girl and a maid.

"But I fell in love with her and I wanted to marry

her. I believe she fell in love with me, but her past was tragic." He choked on his own voice. "She was born into an abusive family and she was hurt in every way you could imagine, Nora. When she sought help at sixteen, that man took advantage of her so she ran away."

Nora's heart broke and she sobbed. Mom had been hurt so much, so often. No way to trust anyone. She must have seen the goodness in Dad. His compassion, kindness and generosity. It must have drawn her.

"She lived on the streets awhile in Virginia, where she was from."

"After the house fire that took her family and all the photos?"

Dad sighed. "Those were stories. Your mom didn't want to tell you about her horrific childhood or family. She escaped them."

"They never came looking for her?"

He placed a gentle hand on hers. "They weren't the kind that cared if she left or stayed, I'm sorry to say. She ended up in Jackson, where she met a girl who talked her into making a lot of money. Told her it was safe. Classy." Disgust hung on his words. "That's how she met Scott Rhodes."

Nora covered her face with hands, her mind reeling. "But, Dad, why the affairs? I mean, if she loved you. You were kind to her. You respected her."

Dad's lip trembled. "Sometimes, familiarity is comforting when you don't feel worthy of good things. Of love. Even if familiarity is like going into bondage."

Nora was reminded of the Israelites. Wishing for slavery because they at least got three squares a day and the wilderness seemed uncertain even though God promised to be with them. He'd given them freedom.

"I kept praying and hoping she'd see that I loved her unconditionally and she would change." He rubbed his face, exhausted. "I didn't turn a blind eye. I talked. I ranted. I begged and pleaded with God to let me walk away, to give up, but He seemed to always bring me back to the book of Hosea. Do you know how many times I read it? More times than I can count. Those pages are riddled with tears."

Nora could hardly imagine her dad wetting the pages of his bible in tears.

"But I stuck it out. I reminded myself of her past. The pain. The torment. I did everything I could to prove that she could trust me and was safe."

The bank account. Her own money.

"She struggled her whole life, Nora. But one thing she knew was that I loved her. That she could always come back. Because no matter how exhausted I became, how numb at times and furious at others...down to the bitter end, I loved her."

Nora's heart lurched into her throat. Dad had stayed the course. Kept loving. What if Nora had done the same with Rush? When things got tough. Far less severe than what Dad had experienced. "You knew all this time she was leaving us?"

"Nora, what do you think was happening when she left so many times before? Have you blocked that out?" He clasped her hand. "I told you she was gone on a trip, but, honey, she was leaving. She bolted when things got difficult, when she felt guilt over the affairs. It was hard for her to face me at times. But she always came home because deep in her heart, I know she loved me. And I have no doubt she loved you and Hailey."

Nora could hardly breathe. Mom had left on occasion. Sometimes a weekend. Sometimes a week. Maybe Nora had blocked out the truth to cope. "And Hailey? Is she yours?"

"You're both mine. It doesn't matter."

Hailey might be some other man's child too. But she couldn't be mad anymore. Not knowing the unimaginable terror and abuse her mother suffered from childhood.

She stood and came around the table and fell on Dad's neck. "I love you, Dad. You are my hero. And I'm sorry for being angry with you over the years. For not fighting to discover the truth." She looked him in the eye. "Do you think Scott Rhodes had anything to do with Mom's accident, that money that was in her trunk or the attacks on me? Is that why you kept so quiet?"

Dad touched her cheek. "Scott Rhodes threatened your mother. If she didn't get rid of you, he would get rid of her. She wanted you desperately so she ran and she feared he'd find her, find you and kill you both."

Nora couldn't fathom it.

"I don't know how much was truth or paranoia, so to put her and myself at ease, I met with Scott. I made the deal and I've honored it and so has he. I don't think he'd rock any boats now due to his upstanding career and the fact that the money was coming in. I have no idea why he might want more money from her. It makes no sense."

"He's not getting any more money. I made it clear. Dad, you're done paying him. But I'm grateful for the lengths you were willing to go to keep me safe. To keep Mom safe and give her a measure of peace."

Dad hugged her. "I'd do it again."

"What do you think will happen now? Do you think

he'll come after me?" Two possible killers coming for her? The thought weakened her knees.

"I think he's going to live in a huge amount of fear and paranoia. I think he tried to scare your mother into doing his will. I don't think he'd have ever actually gone through with it. At the end of the day, he's a coward, a liar and a hypocrite." Dad kissed her forehead. "We're all going to be okay."

She wanted to believe that. Wanted to come clean and tell him she'd racked up debt and needed help. After all he'd done for her she couldn't end this conversation with disappointing him. Her mother never had a voice. Never saw justice on earth. She died a victim. Something or someone had her running. "Did you two have any discussions or fights prior to that night that might make her take off?"

"No. Things seemed to be right with us and I'd like to remember that." Dad smiled. He didn't know about the male mask and cuff link in the car. Nora couldn't tell him. He needed the happy memories. She'd give him that. Besides, the mask and cuff link didn't prove she'd had another affair. Only that someone had been in there. Maybe Ward tried to woo her back and that had sent her into making a break for it out of guilt.

"I'd like you to remember that too. Should we tell Hailey? Last we talked she didn't want to know." Nora was sick of keeping secrets—though she was still keeping hidden what had truly brought her home. "I can tell her or we can tell her together."

They decided to tell her together. Not about the possibility that she might not be Dad's biological child either, but all the rest. Rush called and said he'd be over in five minutes. Dad left and Nora's cell phone rang.

She answered to the Tampa Bay news station and a job offer at the first of the year, which she accepted. A sliver of regret niggled its way into her chest. Even through the pain and the threats, Splendor Pines was once again feeling like home. But this job was necessary. Dad had forked out enough money on her behalf. She would pay her own debts.

After a few more pleasantries, she hung up and Rush knocked on the door. He wasn't dressed in his uniform but a red-and-gray sweater and dark denim jeans. "How did it go?"

"Better than expected. He doesn't believe Scott Rhodes is behind these attacks or what might have happened with Mom, but he can't be sure. None of us can. Did you get in touch with your private eye friend?"

"I did. She's going to check into it." He searched her face. "Anything else?"

Rush had been pushing her to open up, but she didn't even know where to start, and if she let all her emotions surface, the feelings for Rush would come flooding out too and she was leaving soon. "No. That's it."

The disappointment was visible. It hurt her to see it, but in the end she was sparing them all heartbreak.

"What's your plan today? Staying in your pajamas all day?"

Nora looked down at her reindeer fleece pants. "Wouldn't that be nice. I'm supposed to help Hailey with masquerade inventory. Never was my favorite. You on call?"

"Always. Thought I'd ride out to Mac's and talk to the owner and manager about who Marilyn might have been meeting with."

"I'd like to go with you if you can wait until I'm finished helping Hailey. I can't bail on her."

"No problem. I'll drive you up to the lodge."

Nora paused at her bedroom door. "There is one thing that might be relevant to the investigation. My dad said that during the time leading up to Mom's disappearance they were happy, which is why he wasn't sure why she'd want to run off. She usually did that when things got…difficult." Exactly what Rush said to her last night. She was more like her mother than she wanted to be.

"They were?" Rush asked with a hint of skepticism.

"Yeah. So, let's not tell him about the mask and cuff link. We can't be sure it was there from a man she had an affair with—could be from a man who had a former affair like Ward McKay."

Rush stayed silent.

"I mean, you're the king of not speculating or ruining reputations and lives. Has that changed?"

"No. Nothing's changed."

Except for the fact that she was leaving right after the New Year.

Rush stewed while helping Hailey and Nora unpack boxes. He was good for heavy lifting, but not leaning on for emotional support.

With each hour, the day grew darker, colder. Yet shuttles arrived one after the other with excited tourists chattering about the masquerade ball coming up and how wonderful a snowy Christmas would be. Icy more like it. Like the way Nora reacted to his prompts to open up to him. He couldn't deny feelings surfacing; they were like unwanted weeds in a garden. Rush would pull them but couldn't get to the root. He wasn't looking for a one-sided relationship.

"You ready?" Nora asked, and brushed her hands on her jeans.

"Yep. Might take a while with the road conditions." Rush led her to the Bronco.

"I haven't even thought about a dress and mask," Nora said as she buckled up. "You coming?"

"I'm sure I will. You're gonna be there, right?" Pulling onto the main road, he slowed. The snow had been dozed away but it was still slick. Barely any traffic. Good.

Nora chewed on her bottom lip.

"What's eating at you? And don't say it has anything to do with something to wear to the masquerade."

Nora wrung her hands. "I was offered the job in Tampa. I have to be there after the New Year."

Rush's heart sank. "I see. Well…good for you, Nora. I hope you enjoy the sand and sun. I'm sure you'll be great." He could feel her eyes on him, but he refused to look at her. He shouldn't be this upset about her leaving. "I imagine your family will miss you, especially since they've had you home longer than usual." More like he was becoming used to having her here. Knoxville wasn't too far away, but it wasn't like he could see her every day.

"Yeah. I'll miss them too."

Why did she need a change? What happened in Knoxville?

"Hey, I was thinking. Harvey Langston's wife moved with their daughter too. Remember how upset Dan was over that?" Nora asked.

If Tina Langston hadn't moved, Dan might be married to her and not Ainsley. He'd been crushed. Sheriff Parsons had been pretty worried about him, and let Rush spend a lot of school nights over at their house. "Yeah, I remember." Tina hadn't wanted to move away. "We can talk to Dan. But he's stayed close with Harvey over the years. I doubt he believes Harvey would have had anything to do with hurting Marilyn. And again—"

"We don't know she was hurt by foul play. We don't know she wasn't either. Look, maybe it was all an accident. I still want to know what happened that night. Who was in the car with her and why did she have all that cash? Where does Scott Rhodes fit—if at all?"

"I don't know, but Dan's office is on the next block. He works for Ainsley's dad." Rush pulled up next to Dan's Ford truck and went inside.

Lenora—the receptionist—gave a welcoming smile. "Hey, Rush. What can I do for you?"

"Dan in his office?" he asked.

"He is. Go on back."

Rush led Nora to the offices and knocked on Dan's door.

"Come in."

Rush entered, Nora behind him.

Dan stood when he saw Nora. "I heard you were back in town." He came around the desk and hugged her. "How ya doin', Nora? Heard you left the news station in Knoxville. Where you planning to go?"

"Florida. How are you?"

"Fair to middlin'. What can I help you with?" he asked and looked at Rush.

"Information hopefully. We're trying to trace Nora's mom's steps that night she disappeared. And the days before."

Dan frowned. "Dad said it was an accident. You find something new?"

"Nothing I can divulge, you know that. Did Tina ever talk to you about her dad having an affair with Marilyn?"

Dan shifted his gaze to Nora, discomfort twisting his lips.

"It's okay, Dan," she said. "I'm aware of my mother's indiscretions. Whatever you know will be helpful."

He rubbed the back of his neck. "Tina said her parents fought about it. Got real heated and her mom threatened Harvey and your mom, Nora. Just words, though. I seriously doubt Sheila Langston hurt your mom. She said Harvey promised to end it, but it was too late. Sheila filed for divorce and y'all know the rest."

Sheila might not have hurt Marilyn, but what about Harvey? "Do you remember seeing Harvey the night of the masquerade ball?"

"Yeah. Can't say what time or anything, but he was there."

"What did he have on? You remember?" Rush asked.

Dan laughed. "How can I forget? He tripped over his stupid cape on the stairs, spilled his drink and cussed. I don't think I'd ever heard him cuss before. Pretty funny."

A cape? Rush's gut twisted. "Mask?"

"White. Covered half his face." He shrugged. The Phantom of the Opera.

Harvey could be the man Rush saw kissing Marilyn that night. And now that Nora clung to the hope that Joshua and Marilyn were in happy at that time, Rush couldn't tell Nora the truth and ruin her last image.

"How long you in town for?" Dan asked Nora.

"First of the month."

"Well, don't be a stranger."

They left the office and climbed back inside the Bronco. Rush pulled onto the street. "Harvey could have been the man in the car."

"I know. He may have promised his wife it was over, but when she left him anyway it made him angry. Harvey may have at the least been in the car to have a heated conversation. At the most, he had something to do with the accident. I wish the striations weren't inconclusive! At least we would be piecing the night together to follow the money in the trunk, not possible murder."

If Harvey was the Phantom of the Opera, his mask and cuff link weren't in the car over a heated conversation. Keeping the secret needled him, but he remained silent.

Ten minutes later, they pulled into Mac's Bar and Grill parking lot, which was mostly empty. Inside there were only a few patrons at the bar. Three couples in booths. The air smelled of grease and smoke. Rush's stomach rumbled. He hadn't eaten since the toast. "You want to order. If we buy something the owner might be more apt to talk with us."

They sat in a red leather booth near the bar. A young girl with a swinging blond ponytail approached. "What can I get ya?"

"Is the owner in?"

"Mac? No. He's in the Bahamas for Christmas. Wish I was."

"Me too," Nora said.

She'd get warmer weather soon enough. They placed their orders—burgers and fries. "What about the manager?" Rush asked.

"Joe?" She laughed. "He's been around since the dinosaurs. He's in the back. You need him?"

"We do," Rush said, and she disappeared. "I hope she means he's been here for a long time and not that he's old."

Nora chuckled. "Same. After this, we should go see Harvey. I'd rather talk to him in person than over the phone. I want to see his face. Faces are so much more telling than voices."

"I agree."

An older man with a large bald spot and frail arms approached. "I'm Joe Rooney. Can I help you?"

Rush shook his hand. "I hope so. Did you by any chance work here seventeen years ago?"

"I've been here for almost thirty years."

Rush glanced at Nora. "Do you remember a woman named Marilyn Livingstone?"

His eyes softened and he shook his head. "Rotten shame to hear she's been gone all these years, dead in the lake. She was a lot of fun."

"What kind of fun?" Rush asked, hoping it wasn't the illegal kind.

"Lot of laughs. She always had a new joke. Cheesy but funny."

Nora remained silent, but Rush recalled all the jokes she'd tell him that her mother had told her. She had a big joke book Nora had bought her one year as a Christmas gift. He'd helped her pick it out. "Did she come in here often, and do you know who with?" Rush showed him his deputy badge.

"Yeah. About once or twice a week." He sniffed and pointed to the booth in the corner. "Sometimes alone. Sometimes with a friend."

"Any particular friend?" Rush asked.

Joe shifted from one foot to the other. "I don't like ratting out people, but I liked Marilyn and if something bad happened to her I want to help. Langston. Harvey Langston came in with her often, but he's not the only one."

"Who else?" Nora asked.

"I don't know…"

"It would be helping Marilyn, I promise," Rush said. "You can trust me to be discreet."

"Can I trust you to keep my name out of it?" Joe asked.

"I'll do my best."

Joe licked his lips and leaned down. "Right before she went missing she came in several times with… Troy Parsons. Your boss—the sheriff."

NINE

"Rush, my mom was seeing Troy! What are we going to do about that?" Nora buckled her seat belt. The hits kept coming.

Rush pawed his face. "I don't know. Let's not jump to conclusions. It could have been anything."

"Then why not admit it then or now?"

"It might not have been pertinent to the case."

"Or it might have. That would give him motive and a front seat to your investigation." Troy would have a lot to lose if he'd been involved with her and he'd have a lot to protect now to make sure it didn't get out. "Rush, I know he's a mentor to you."

"He's more than that, Nora." Rush leaned his head against the steering wheel. "He's been a father to me. Especially in the past several years."

Nora laid a hand on his back, soothing him. "What does that mean? You've been acting strange about your dad since you put off talking to him about the investigation, and he didn't go to church with your mom, which you never gave a real reason for. He isn't pastoring anymore. Talk to me, Rush."

He lifted his head from the wheel and laughed hard

and humorlessly. "You can't expect to bottle up every single emotion and hide things from me, then demand I talk to you. That's not fair."

"You're right. You don't have to share anything you don't want to." And neither did she, but she felt the sting and knew it was the same one Rush endured every time Nora refused to talk intimately with him.

Rush started to say something but his phone rang. "I gotta take this. It's my mom." He answered. "Hey, Ma. Everything okay?... Yeah." He grinned. "Okay. Can you give me an hour or so? I need to take Nora home... Uh..." He glanced at Nora, his neck flushed. "Sure." He hung up. "My family have made it in. I'm shocked they even tried. People don't have the sense God gave them."

She could testify to that.

"You don't have anywhere else to be, do you?" he asked.

"We have somewhere to be. The police station talking to Troy and finding out why he was meeting up with my mom outside of town. Don't let this slide, Rush. He could be impeding the investigation if he's guilty. From the weather to—"

"Not everyone can remember weather facts from twenty years ago." Rush's face soured. "And I never said I'd let it slide. But will a few hours kill us?"

"Maybe! Maybe they will." Nora's frustration rose to stroke levels. "Someone wants me dead. Every second is critical. But let's go have some Christmas festivities."

Rush ground his jaw. "I need to think about my approach, Nora. I need the time, and while I'm figuring it out, I'll keep you safe. You have my word." He headed onto the main road.

Nora studied his face. Rush wasn't just upset, he was

rattled and broken. She heaved a sigh, her heart reaching out. A small breather might do them some good. She'd needed time to process everything; Rush did too. "I'm sorry. For my actions and that someone you care about might not be who he lets on to be." She understood completely. "Let's go visit your family. Take a beat." And while she was there, she'd talk to Pastor Buchanan herself. If he had to look her in the eye, he might offer up information that he hadn't to Rush.

Rush nodded, his nostrils pulsing and jaw working overtime. As they neared Rush's family's home he slowed the vehicle. "My dad isn't the same man you knew." He bit his lower lip. "After you left for Knoxville, he counseled a congregant with an addiction to pornography, which had developed into soliciting prostitutes. But after a period of time, the man seemed to be healing and doing well. He had his family back."

Nora nodded for him to continue.

"One night Dad got a call about an illegal gambling and prostitution ring out in the woods near the end of the county line at a pool hall. They raided it and guess what? The man—Randy—was inside. He claimed innocence but refused to explain why he was there. Knowing his history, Dad arrested him for gambling and soliciting prostitutes."

Nora feared the rest of story but listened as Rush told of that arrest, which led to losing his family again. The rumors that spread.

"Randy hung himself but left a letter that stated, once again, he was free of the addiction, loved his family and wasn't guilty, but couldn't live with knowing his family and friends didn't believe him. Many heard about this terrible addiction for the first time. It was horrible."

Nora touched Rush's shoulder. "Was it true?"

"No." Rush's voice cracked. "The truth came out. Randy was trying to give back and help others bound by the same addiction. He found out a young man he was mentoring had gone and he went to get him out. The man had only been married two years and had a newborn. Randy didn't want to give him up and hoped that Dad would believe him. But he hadn't. Not because of the evidence. Randy wasn't actually with a prostitute or at the gambling table. But based on what he knew from pastoral counseling. He'd falsely accused a man and it wrecked dozens of lives, including my dad's."

"I'm so sorry, Rush." No wonder he was hypercareful to avoid rumors. Scandal. It had turned his own world upside down.

"The church board asked my dad to resign. If he was going to use what was said in confidence to accuse someone, they didn't think he could be trusted, and then there were remarks that he lacked discernment. It crushed him, along with the guilt."

Rush had been close with his father. It must have been terrible to go through.

Rush pulled into the driveway crowded with vehicles. "He hasn't healed. He's closed off to everyone. Lost all joy. We keep praying..."

Nora laced her hand in Rush's and squeezed, hoping it would bring comfort. "He'll get it back," she said. "I'll believe it with you." She hadn't believed in anything for so long. But she would believe in this with Rush. It was much easier to believe for someone else. "We'll do it together."

He stared at their hands, traced her finger with his index. Was he thinking of the ceramic Christmas ornaments like she was? The pledge behind that gift. To give him her heart. Always. Forever.

Snow had covered the windshield like a curtain, hiding them. Rush didn't bother to switch on the wipers. Instead, he brushed the thumb of his free hand across Nora's jaw, then let her cheek rest against his palm, calloused but strong, like Rush. He wasn't only physically powerful, he had an inner strength that drew her heart to him.

He met her eyes, held them.

She swallowed.

Slowly he met her lips with his. Familiar. Surprisingly new. At first it was soft as a whisper, as if asking permission to be more intimate. She granted it, allowing him freedom to set off a fire of a dozen suns within her, enough to melt away the ice outside. Unable to catch her breath, she didn't care. Even his kisses were powerful, yet tender like the man. He'd always been special, unique. His fingers slid into her hair. She touched his scruffy cheek before wrapping her arms around his neck as he took his time exploring and savoring.

The beating on the driver's-side window abruptly brought the kiss to a halt. Nora jerked back, her fingers pressed to her thoroughly kissed lips. Rush sighed, didn't bother to even turn and see who was pounding on the window.

"We're going to talk about this later," he said, his voice husky and breathless.

He opened the door and nailed his cousin Hollister in the shoulder.

"Oomph!" Hollister said through laughter. He hadn't changed much. Maybe got a bit better looking if that was possible. What was it with the Buchanan genes? "Didn't mean to interrupt." He cast amused eyes on

Nora. "Well, well. Nora Livingstone. I see you still got it bad for this loser."

She couldn't really defend herself after that kiss.

His sister peeped out from behind him. "I told him not to come out here messing with the two of you, but he doesn't listen." She came around to her side and Nora opened the door and hugged Greer Montgomery.

"How have you been?" Nora asked.

"Busy. Moved back to Alabama. And I'm a mom now."

No mention of a husband. Nora didn't pry. "Congratulations."

"Baby girl."

"Can't wait to see her."

"Come inside and you can. We'll leave these men to act like the apes they are."

Nora snickered and followed Greer. Maybe Rush would forget that kiss and they wouldn't have to discuss it. Doubtful. That wasn't the kind of kiss one forgot.

Inside, she was welcomed by everyone, the house crowded with family laughing, joking and eating an array of desserts.

In the corner of the living room, Pastor Buchanan sat alone. Time hadn't been kind to the aging process. She made her way over. "It's nice to see you again."

He patted her hand but didn't make much eye contact. "How you been, Nora?"

"Better."

"Me too. Me too." She couldn't bring herself to bombard him with questions and press him for answers that he might not even have.

Nora caught Rush's eye. His expression was tender

and emblazoned with an emotion she didn't want to put a name to. Couldn't. She was too afraid.

Rush stood in the bathroom staring in the mirror and still feeling that kiss. For a moment, it was just a man and a woman in that car. No law enforcer. No weather professional.

No past holding them apart.

No pain.

No fear of the future.

And he'd lost himself. In her eyes that had held longing. In her hands that had intertwined with his to bring comfort, companionship and hope. A woman who seemed hopeless herself was going to believe with him for healing for his dad. That kiss had been his wordless way of revealing how much that meant to him.

How much she meant.

But she was moving, and he'd be left once again watching with a broken heart.

Leaving the bathroom, he entered the festivities and after a few hours of eating and playing games—Nora right in the middle as if she'd always belonged—his phone rang.

Troy.

Stomach in knots, he answered and returned to the bathroom for some privacy. "Hey. What's going on?"

"Got the ballistics from a bullet in the tree the night you were shot at. They're from your gun."

The stolen gun from Nora's. Ballistics were easy enough to follow up on. No reason not to trust the report.

"Have you found any new information?" Troy asked.

Now would be a good time to ask him about his involvement with Marilyn. But Rush wanted to look him in the eye, see his face. "Not much. I'll let Nora know."

"Where are y'all?"

"My folks' place. Probably be here an hour or so longer. But I'm available if you need anything."

"I'll let you know. Bring me a slice of pecan pie." He chuckled and hung up.

"Rush," Nora said as the knock came.

He opened the door. "You need in?"

"No, just looking for you. I thought I heard you in here talking to someone."

"Troy. The gun used to shoot at us was the same one stolen from the chalet."

"What did he say about meeting my mom?" Her eyes drilled into his.

Rush's neck heated. "I didn't ask. I want to do it in person."

Nora's eyes narrowed and she poked a finger in his chest. "Rush, you need to talk to Troy. You've had time to process—at least all the time you can. If he's involved, he's trolling around with a badge and power to destroy evidence and who knows what."

Rush snorted. "You sound like a dramatic crime show. Troy has never once abused his power. I'm sure there's a logical explanation and I'll find out what it is."

Nora gritted her teeth and inhaled. "I've had every imaginable tragic thing thrown at me in a few days' time. When I found out Scott Rhodes was my dad, I went straight there, knowing it wasn't going to be pretty. It's your turn, Rush. Nothing about this has been logical. Nothing."

And what happened when he confronted Troy and found out he was wrong? What would that do to their friendship? Their mentorship? His run for office? No, that wasn't the most important thing, but it was a dream of his. Was he supposed to throw it away because Nora wanted to charge like a bull? "I just need my bearings in order. Figure out how I want this to go down."

"Be a straight shooter—"

His phone buzzed and an alert popped on-screen. He glanced down. "Nora, I gotta go. My alarm at the house is going off." He flew down the hall toward the front door. "Stay here with my family. I'll be back."

Hollister met him at the front door. "What's wrong?"

"Alarm going off at the house." Could be a glitch, a tree falling against a window or the roof, or it could be something else.

"I'm going with you," Nora insisted.

"No, you're not."

She grabbed her coat from the coatrack in the foyer. "Watch me!"

Rush growled. No time to argue. "I have to take the snowmobile." It would take too long in the Bronco.

"And? Let's go!"

"If you need me, call," Hollister said.

Rush ran out the door and to the shed, Nora on his tail. He opened the shed doors, grabbed two pair of goggles, tossed one and a helmet to Nora and they climbed on.

He raced across the snow like sailing over smooth glass. Nora tightened her grip around his waist, leaning into his back. The wind bit and sliced at his skin as they raced through the snowy woods and embankments to his cabin. They made it to the winding drive to his house and he slowed the snowmobile down, then stopped.

He removed his helmet, grabbed his gun. He wasn't sure what to do with Nora. Leaving her on the snowmobile gave her a fast way to make tracks if necessary, but if guns were involved, she was a sitting duck.

"Stay close to me," he said. Having her near meant he could protect her.

The front looked clear. The alert on his phone indicated the kitchen window had been breached, which was in the back of the house. Staying below the windows and scanning the surrounding area, he and Nora made their way behind the house. The window had been busted out and the door was open. "Looks like he went in the through the window and came out the door." Whoever *he* was.

"What do you think he was after?" Nora asked.

"The only thing I can think of is the box of photos. He tried to steal them from you so it's not a stretch." Rush toed the back door farther open, entered and cleared the kitchen. "Stay right behind me."

She did as he instructed and followed him through the downstairs as he cleared all the rooms, including the study where he'd kept the photos. They were missing. "Well, that tells us what he was after."

They cleared the upstairs and returned downstairs.

Rush massaged the back of his neck. "I think the intruder knows he can be identified. By the mask or the cuff links or both. Or maybe he's in a picture with your mom that I haven't found. I don't know."

"Now what?"

Good question. "Now I take you back to my family's house, and I'm going to go have a chat with Troy. I am a straight shooter, Nora. I'm just careful."

Nora threw her hands in the air. "I feel like I keep saying I'm sorry, but I am."

Rush tugged at her hair playfully. "I know. I'm going to leave the snowmobile here and take my truck. I don't like us being so open right now."

Nora agreed and they headed for the garage and climbed into Rush's personal truck. He hit the garage door and slowly backed out of the drive. The wind rocked the vehicle like their lives at the moment.

Mountains and forest flanked the road that narrowed around the curve. What little sun that had been peeking through had dipped below the horizon, and the moon was blocked by the heavy cloud covering.

"What if Troy tells you their involvement was romantic?"

"Doesn't make him a killer. Just a colossal disappointment," Rush said, and spied headlights coming around the curve behind him. He couldn't tell if it was a truck or SUV, but it had to be tourists. No local would go this fast and this close to another car on the road.

Rush pressed the gas, but he didn't want to go too fast with the road conditions.

The vehicle kept coming.

"Nora, hang tight. I think we have trouble."

The other vehicle made impact.

Nora yelped.

Rush's truck spun in circles across the icy road.

"Rush!" Nora hollered as they went over the side of the road and down the ravine.

TEN

Rush's truck plummeted over the side of the road, tail end first, banging them into rocks and tree branches. Metal crunched and scraped as he prayed and endured.

Nora knocked her head against the window and went limp.

Rush was helpless.

"God! Save us!"

He hit the emergency brake, hoping it would slow them down before they crashed to their deaths. The truck slowed minimally, and then it rocked and pitched onto the passenger side. Rush's seat belt cut into his skin as the flipping of the vehicle battered his body and knocked the wind from him. Glass shattered.

Tree branches poked through the pulverized windshield. Rush's face stung and burned.

The truck rolled again and again. If it continued down the mountain, they wouldn't make it. "Nora," he choked out. Blood trickled down her forehead. "Nora!"

She wouldn't answer.

It felt like every bone in his body was breaking; his head pounded and his ears rang.

Sudden impact jarred him, and he bit his tongue. Every nerve in his body screamed.

But they'd stopped rolling.

The truck was lodged in a huge pine. Snow dropped onto their bodies through the missing windshield. Rush's hands were cut up. It hurt to move. To breathe. But he didn't know how long the tree would break their fall.

They were a fourth of the way down the mountain if he guessed right.

"Nora," he choked out again and undid his seat belt while thanking God they'd at least landed upright. *God, give me strength*. He was nauseous and dizzy.

His driver's-side door butted up against the side of the mountain, and Nora's door hung open. Nothing but branches and evergreen.

The only way out was through the open windshield, and then they'd have to find a way to climb up the snowy terrain to the road.

It seemed hopeless.

A gale rocked the truck. No time to waste. He needed Nora to wake up this minute.

"Nora." He lightly shook her for fear of serious injury. If she was unable to move… How would he ever get her out and up a steep mountain with no climbing gear?

She stirred and moaned.

"Nora Beth, can you hear me?"

"Rush." She moaned again and shifted.

"Don't move, Nora."

Her eyes fluttered open, glassy at first, then they focused on him and panic shot through them. "Rush!"

"Don't move," he repeated. "We're in the pines and

it's not secure. We went over the edge of the mountain. How bad are you hurt?"

"My head hurts and…my everything hurts." She wiggled her fingers. Cuts and scrapes covered her face and neck.

"Anything major?"

"I don't know. I don't think so."

That in itself was nothing short of God's divine protection over them. "We have to get out through the windshield. Go first. Onto the hood, then grab on to those branches for support. We'll use rocks and stumps to anchor us as we climb."

Her eyes grew to the size of dinner plates.

"We have no other choice. We can do it." He hoped his confident words masked how he actually felt.

Rush had lost his phone from the console and Nora's purse was missing. No one to call for help. The Lord would be their very present help. That was a promise in the Scriptures he was going to stand on. In this case…climb on.

The night was bleak and dark. Only the headlights gave a soft glow. This trek would be one done blindly. Fear raced through him.

Nora unbuckled and winced. Groaned.

"Be easy. Go slow but fast," Rush said. "I'll be right behind you."

"I'm scared, Rush. I don't know if I can." Nora's faint voice shook with uncertainty and terror. He was scared too.

"You can do it, Nora. We've climbed mountains together before."

"We've had climbing gear and it wasn't in winter."

"Let's pretend we have them now. And light to guide

our way. It'll be a fun challenge. We'll look back on it years from now and laugh."

"Yeah, right." She leaned forward and the truck jerked; the cracking of tree branches tore through his heart. If the branch broke…

Nora paused, breath pluming in front of her.

"Keep going," Rush offered. If nothing else, he could at least get her out. Keep her safe and alive. He'd worry about himself later. Nora's safety was his focus.

Hopefully her leather gloves would protect her from the small shards of glass littered across the dashboard. With shallow breaths, Nora placed her hands on the dash and lifted herself from her seat, groaning in pain, but she managed to get her head out of the windshield and her hands onto the hood of the truck.

The wind shook snow onto her body and she flinched.

His truck shuddered again and she squealed.

Carefully, Rush helped her scoot all the way onto the hood. "Can you see a branch or rock or anything to hold on to?"

"I can't see anything, Rush! I'm gonna die out here!"

"No one is dying, Nora Beth! Find something! Once you have it, let me know and I'll come out next."

Nora turned and looked at him. "What if I can't? What if the truck falls when I climb off it?" Hysteria laced her tone.

"Listen to me," he pleaded. Fear would keep her glued to the truck and they'd both end up at the bottom of the mountain. "Climb on top of the truck and grab a tree branch."

She nodded and slowly stood, placing her hands on

the top of the truck. Wind battered her; she nearly lost her balance.

The branch splintered and cracked further; Rush's heart raced. "Go, Nora!"

Nora used her arms to push herself on top of the truck. The sound of metal above him told him she was reaching. "I got a branch… I'm on the mountain. Come out."

Now the tricky part. He had to move onto the console without kicking the gearshift sticking out beside his steering wheel.

He grabbed the lever to push the seat back so he could maneuver. The branch shook and the truck did too. He froze, didn't breathe.

"Rush!" Nora called. "Hurry up!"

Now that he had more legroom, he lifted his right leg and swung it carefully over the console, then using his arms for support lifted himself up and slid onto the console. Once he was in position, he made his way through the open windshield and onto the hood.

Wind howled through the trees and it began to sleet again, but his adrenaline chased away the cold.

About three feet up, Nora clung to a branch.

"I'm coming. Hold on." He didn't want her to get ahead of him. If she slipped, he wanted to be behind her to catch her. Again, using his arms, he lifted himself to the top of the truck, but his foot swung inside the windshield, kicking the steering wheel and turning the tires.

The branch cracked and the truck dropped farther down. Rush lost his balance and slid; his heart pounded.

He grabbed the door, holding on and thankful the window was no longer there. Feeling with his foot, he worked to find a solid hold.

Wood splintered at deafening levels, and his body screamed in pain.

His throat tightened and sweat ran in trickles down his temples.

The truck plummeted and he let go, catching a branch and hanging on by a thread.

"Rush!"

"I'm—I'm here," he called. He found footing and worked his way up, slowly, steadily—slipping every few feet. It was snowy, rocky, uneven ground and slick from ice, but he made it to Nora.

"That scared me half to death," she said through chattering teeth.

"Back at ya. Up ya go. Be slow."

She found another limb and used it for support as they made their way up the mountain. Nora stumbled and Rush caught her with one hand to steady her.

"Who—who do you think hit us?" she asked.

"Someone who knows how to drive on icy roads. Stop talking and concentrate on getting to the top."

Heaving, shaking and fighting for every step forward, they finally reached the top and collapsed on the shoulder of the road. Rush didn't care that he was lying in snow. But a chill would come and they couldn't afford to get sick. Nora lay beside him breathing heavy.

"How you doing, Nora Beth?"

"Well…let's just say 'over the hills we go' is no longer appealing to me."

Rush laughed. "Amen." Time to get out of the elements and dry. "Come on." He pulled her to her feet. "We're hoofing it."

"I'm not sure I can walk very far, Rush."

He wasn't either but they had no plan B. Nora had

been brave and resilient. She could make it a few miles more. Gently wrapping his arm around her shoulders, he coaxed her forward. "You can do it. I know you can."

Hunching from the snow and sleet, they trekked about a half a mile when headlights came into view.

Rush's stomach knotted.

Blue lights flashed.

"The cavalry."

Nora bristled against him as the window rolled down.

Inside, Troy Parsons eyed them and smiled.

"Y'all look like you've been rode hard and put away wet. What happened?" Troy asked.

Nora clutched Rush's arm. Mighty convenient Troy being out on the road on this side of town an hour or so after they'd been sent over a mountain. Nora didn't trust him. Not even a little, and she hoped Rush didn't either. Not after what they discovered earlier today.

"Someone sent us over the cliff. 'Bout a half mile back," Rush said with steely eyes. Looked like he had the good sense to suspect Troy. "After we left Mama and Dad's."

Troy sobered, and he shone a flashlight in their faces. "Get in! I thought y'all just broke down. You need a hospital."

Nora didn't want to get in the vehicle with Troy. What if he was lying? Rush glanced at Nora and patted her hand. "All right." He opened the back door of Troy's Bronco. "Get in, Nora Beth." He urged her to get in the backseat, but she wasn't sure that was a smart idea. "We have to," he whispered in her ear.

He was right. The cold was catching up to her. Sweat had turned to chills. The crashing of adrenaline had her shivering on top of the cold. Their hair was soaked with sweat, snow and sleet. Reluctantly, she eased into the backseat. Her body was aching and stiff everywhere.

Rush closed her door and hobbled to the passenger side. He got in the front seat and strapped in.

Troy glanced in his rearview. "I'm taking you to the hospital. Don't even start, Rush."

Nora touched the cut on her head. She wouldn't turn down some heavy meds, but mostly she wanted warmth and a cup of hot tea.

"What exactly happened?"

Rush told him the gist of the story as Troy drove them to the ER. "I can't help but think it came on the heels of us visiting Mac's today." Rush studied Troy. Nora couldn't see Troy's face from the backseat, but she didn't miss the tightened grip on the steering wheel at the mention of Mac's.

"Oh, yeah?" Troy asked. "Find out anything important?"

Yes! Tell him, Rush.

"Mac's in the Bahamas. We didn't get to talk to him."

What? *Rush!* Why was he not questioning Troy? This man might have information, and the fact that he wasn't coming forward with it meant he wanted it to stay a secret. He'd already been adamant it was an accident, lied even—possibly—about the weather conditions that night. Nora had been checking into it, but she hadn't had the proper time to access the many different sites necessary for the research. Not with all the attempts on her life.

Exhaustion was setting in and she didn't have time to be tired. There were too many unanswered questions. Too many puzzle pieces that didn't fit. Pieces Rush should be asking about.

"Shame," Troy said. "Guess you'll have to wait."

Wait? He didn't seem too upset about that.

"Nora, hon, do you think all this investigating has been worth the pain? I'm worried about you," Troy said. "Maybe it's best if you leave this to the professionals and back off."

Someone knocked her down a side of the mountain. Quitting now was never going to happen. "What if it was someone you loved? Would you give up?"

"I'm not asking you to give up. I'm asking you to step down. Difference."

She closed her eyes and trembled. "I can't do that, Sheriff Parsons. I'm not breaking any laws."

He grimaced and moved from her line of sight in the rearview. "You're blessed to be alive right now. I don't want to get a call in the night saying I have to come out to your homicide scene."

She wasn't so sure she believed that, but he was taking them to the hospital. He could have run them over. "Then I suggest you do more than what you've done so far. I didn't see you fighting hard to find my mom seventeen years ago, and I haven't seen you do much of anything now," she spouted as he pulled up to the hospital.

Troy's tone turned hard. "What am I supposed to do about an accident, Nora? The coroner ruled it one. Not me. And I have other things to do besides look into why she left the party, got in her car and had an accident. You may not have closure, Miss Livingstone, but *this* case is closed. I've only let Rush work on it as a favor to you because of y'all's history. But it's put him in danger."

"Troy," Rush warned.

"No, it's true. Your life has repeatedly been in danger—"

"Which proves something sinister is going on!" Nora cried. "Why would someone want me dead if something bad didn't happen that night?"

"Maybe it did, Nora. Maybe someone from that night doesn't want you digging up an affair and ruining a family that may or may not have gotten back on track. And I'm not being passive on the attempts on your life—I'm making sure bullets have tests run and prints are taken. That is an open investigation. What went on seventeen years ago *is not*!"

Nora bounded from the car, the pain in her muscles protesting. But she slammed the door anyway and stalked inside.

Rush followed and they said nothing while doctors attended to their wounds and stitched the cut on Nora's head. Two hours later, Hailey picked them up and brought them back to the chalet. After changing into dry clothing, Nora eased on the couch with her laptop.

"Before our pain meds kick in, what was that?" he asked. "Back in Parsons's car?"

"That was someone being proactive. That was someone taking matters into her own hands because…well never mind or I'll end up having to apologize again later."

"Ah, so you want to call me names and hurl insults at me again." He huffed.

"You had the chance to question him, Rush. You caved. You're too afraid of hurting his feelings. Or maybe you're afraid to find out the truth—that he isn't the man you thought he was. Well, guess what, Rush

Buchanan…no one is! I've learned that." She slammed her laptop on the couch and stood, enduring the pain in her joints. "At least I'm doing something to get the truth for my mom."

Rush inhaled sharply and ran his tongue along the inside of his cheek, his nostrils flaring. "First of all, don't for one second think I believe you're doing all this for truth for your mother. She's gone. She doesn't care about the truth. She doesn't need answers. You want answers to prove she wasn't running, but you already know that she was. This is about you. Answers you won't and can't get." He stalked to her and stood toe-to-toe, his gaze drilling into hers.

"But I've risked my life over and over to make sure you stayed alive and safe while on this hopeless quest because it's what you want. Like I *always* have done whatever you wanted. Because I loved you!"

Nora shrank back from the truth giving her another pounding. Rush was right. Again. As always. She tried to intervene, but he was on a tangent and he rightly deserved it.

"I've kept quiet about what I saw that night. I've given in to all your whims," he yelled. "I've watched you walk away twice! Twice, Nora. Twice you've killed me. And here I am doing what you want—for what? You to yell at me, tell me I'm not doing my job?"

She'd killed him twice. Those words. This whole tirade wasn't fully about the investigation but Rush's heartbreak at Nora's hands. Hands she'd promised to hang on a tree to show her love for him year after year. She was a horribly selfish person.

"And for your information, I didn't question Troy because if he is involved, why would I call him out on it when we were at his mercy? I had no weapon. No control of his vehicle—and things might have been different if you hadn't been inside. But you were, Nora. And I was afraid if he is the bad guy, showing him my hand could have put you in danger."

Nora hadn't thought of that. She'd been too focused on nothing but what she wanted. Answers.

"And as steaming mad as I am right now at you, I'd do it all over again. Because, Nora, I *still* love you! I doubt I'll ever not love you."

What? He…loved her? Now? In the present? "Rush," she whimpered.

He thrust a hand up to halt whatever she might be about to say. "Before you go reminding me that I'm a cheater and you're moving to Florida and all the other excuses, let me tell you all the reasons I'm not going to act on it. You're a runner, Nora. When things get difficult, you take off. Figuratively and literally. And I won't be with a woman who can't open up to me. Who will run from me and not *to* me. So, this time, you don't get to leave me. You don't get to hurt me. You don't get to say things aren't going to happen between us, that we're over. *I'm* saying it."

She blinked back tears, every word crushing her with the weight of its truth and Rush's own pain in every syllable. She'd hurt him. Time and again. She hadn't meant to. Didn't want to, but she had.

"We're never going to happen. And I hate it. I hate having to voice that out loud. Because all I've ever wanted is to love you. To make you happy. To be happy with you. But I don't trust you, Nora. You think you can't trust me because of all those years ago when I was dating Ainsley. But I can't. Trust. You. I can't trust you not to leave. How is that for irony for someone who didn't want to be anything like her mother?" He shook his head, raked a hand through his hair and exhaled an exhausted sigh.

Nora couldn't form a word. He was so right it was scary. Talk about tough love.

"I'm tired, Nora Beth. If Troy isn't the bad guy here, then someone thinks we're dead. I'm going next door to have a minute to myself and I'll be back to bunk on your couch in an hour or so."

He slunk to the front door.

"Rush," she called. "I'm sorry."

"It's kinda too late for that, don't ya think?" He closed the door behind him.

Nora stared at the door for several long beats, then she locked it and leaned against it until she slid to the floor, tucking her knees under her chin. Burning tears exploded from behind her eyes and erupted in sobs.

She *was* like her mother. In more ways than she wanted to admit. What was she going to do with that? *God, I don't know what to do.*

Her world had been crumbling around her for years, and now it was falling faster than she could breathe in and out. Everything was being stripped away and what was laid bare wasn't pretty. She wasn't who she wanted or needed to be.

Nora had lost herself so long ago, she wasn't sure she would be able to find her true self again.

One thing she did know. It was time for a change.

Inside out.

ELEVEN

Rush sat on the couch in Nora's chalet with a cup of coffee warming his hands. He'd popped several meds throughout the night, and this morning he had a dull headache and body aches from yesterday's events. His truck was totaled. Tow truck company was hauling it out this morning. Cell phones were gone. He'd have to get a new one today at some point, talk to Troy and deal with the aftermath of last night.

When he'd returned, Nora was in her bedroom. He'd gone to the door to knock and hoped to apologize. He'd been angry and gruff. Not that what he said wasn't true, but he could have said it with more constraint and compassion. But he'd heard her crying and he couldn't bring himself to knock. Not when she'd called his motives into question about his hesitation to address Troy.

Because it was true.

He'd had plenty of time to talk to his mentor before they went over the side of a mountain. But Rush was afraid of what Troy might say—or what he might not say. When he'd brought up going to Mac's he'd hoped for a better response. He'd known Troy a long time. His boss was hiding something—possibly an affair with

Marilyn, which would wreck his marriage and relationship with Dan.

The bedroom door opened and Nora entered the kitchen and living room looking bruised and battered. And beautiful. She left her hair down—likely to hide some of the bruises and abrasions. Her eyes were red rimmed. He stood and rubbed his hands on the sides of his jeans. "Hi," he murmured.

"Hi," she said. "Coffee left?"

"Yeah." He motioned toward the pot. The silence was deafening. Awkward. Uncomfortable. "How you feelin' this morning?"

"Sore. You?"

"Same." His neck muscles were tight and not just from the wreck. "I'm sorry, Nora, for the way I came at you last night."

She paused, then put the carafe back in place and slowly stirred cream into her coffee. Her cherry scent wafted his way.

After sipping her coffee, she turned toward him. "I'm sorry too. I hadn't realized what you were doing and I was... I was scared. But it's not an excuse for accusing you of not doing your job. You're the most honest man I know. Full of integrity and compassion. You'd never lie." She sighed over the coffee cup. "And if I'm being honest... I was scared all those years ago when I found out about Ainsley. Yes, I was mad about what it might do to my reputation, but mostly I was afraid. So I used my anger as a reason to go."

"Afraid of what?" He wasn't expecting this. Nora was opening up a measure.

"That if we got back together—at some point down the road—I'd end up hurting you. And even with us not together, I have. I've hurt you terribly, Rush. And I'm sorry. It's not too late to say it."

Rush wasn't sure what to say or even if he could, not with the lump clogging his throat.

"I've hurt myself too," she said. "I don't share the truth about me or how I feel because I hate the truth. I hate a lot of things about myself. For one, I'm a hypocrite." She set the cup down, hand trembling, but then she raised her chin. "I'm up to my eyeballs in debt. I went to Knoxville to escape this place. Escape being Marilyn Livingstone's daughter. I didn't want that. I made this new life, made connections with the elitists and tried to be someone new, but that someone couldn't keep up with those people—I don't have my dad's money."

Rush stepped forward to go to her, to comfort, but she shook her head and he paused.

"I didn't quit my job. I lost it to someone else. But I didn't want anyone to know that either. You're right, Rush. I've been selfish. And you're also right...you and I...we had something once. We did. But too much has happened between us. We can't ever get that back. I'd hurt you. Like I always do. You're right to have stopped it before it started."

Rush's eyes burned and he clenched his teeth to hold back a dam of emotions.

"And one more truth for today." She inhaled and let out a shaky sigh, but she looked him square in the eye. "I love you too. I don't think I'll ever not love you."

She repeated his words from last night, but instead of filling him with joy it only brought a stabbing pain and ache. There was nothing left to say.

Nora returned to her coffee cup and paused, then

straightened her shoulders. "Now. Moving on. Last night, you said something. It didn't hit me until this morning."

Rush mentally trekked through their previous conversation. "I don't know what you're talking about."

"You said, 'I've kept quiet about what I saw that night,' and then kept going. As I replayed that conversation it dawned on me... I have no idea what you were talking about."

Rush's stomach landed at his feet. In the heat of the moment, he'd blurted it. So much for trying to spare Joshua and Nora peace about Marilyn at least being faithful in the end.

"Rush? What are you keeping me from me?"

Rubbing his forehead, he turned around, his back to her. "Nora, I was trying to spare you then and I was going to tell you early on in the investigation but you were still in denial...and then your dad thought everything had ended well—"

"Rush!" Nora grabbed his forearm and spun him around. "What do you know?"

"Your mom was kissing a man with a Phantom of the Opera mask that night. In your dad's office."

Nora gaped, then her eyes lit up. "That's why when I got to the basement, you hurried me away. Said you wanted to exchange presents somewhere else. My mom was in the office with a man! Possibly the man in the car. Probably so."

Rush nodded. "How mad are you?"

"Yesterday, I might have gone off the deep end. But I've been a vault of secrets so I can't really be angry. I'm sorry you had to see that. Sorry you carried that with you all this time."

"I didn't want to hurt you."

Nora's eyes turned watery. "I've done all the hurting, Rush."

They remained silent. No words to be said. Only regret and pain.

Nora gave a tight-lipped smile. "I've almost finished my research. While it's not one hundred percent accurate, it is likely the weather didn't contribute to my mother's car accident. Troy was either lying or he remembered poorly. After what we've discovered, my guess is he was lying."

Rush nodded. "I'm going to talk to Harvey Langston today. I can't be sure he'll tell me the truth, but it's worth a shot."

"I'd like to come with you."

"I know." His phone rang. "It's Teddy VanHolt." He answered and put her on speaker. "Hey, Teddy. It's early."

"Not for you. And I'll sleep when I'm dead."

"I suspect you have news."

"I do. My friend Wilder Flynn at Covenant Crisis Management had his computer analyst do some research for me. I can confirm that Scott Rhodes has been receiving payments from Joshua Livingstone. I cannot confirm the purchase of plane tickets on or around the Christmas Eve in question. Nor did I find any paper or digital trail of him making a road trip to Splendor Pines or any town or city within a day's drive. It appears he isn't directly involved now or in the past."

Rush and Nora had a hunch he wasn't. No, Scott Rhodes had the sweet end of the deal. A lot of money every year his entire life to leave Nora and Marilyn alone. Why rock that boat?

Teddy continued, "I have enough to expose him for soliciting prostitutes and using high-end call girls. I'm always up for leaking anonymous info to the press. Say the word."

Rush looked at Nora and she shook her head. He silently agreed with her. If Scott Rhodes wasn't out to hurt Nora, better to leave him alone. Not that he condoned what Scott Rhodes was doing, but that wasn't for him to expose. Besides if the press dug, they might find Nora and who knows what kind of backlash that would have. "No. Sit on it. Anything recent? Trips here? Any way to know if he hired muscle to come deal with Nora?"

"I don't think so, Rush. Seems your problem is local. Anything I can do to help? Happy to take a trip to the mountains."

"The weather is treacherous. You're safer where you are but thank you."

"No prob. How's Hollister?" Teddy asked.

"He's same old, same old. Is that why you really wanna make the trip?"

Teddy laughed. "If I wanted to know what Hollister was up to, I'd know."

That was the truth. "Merry Christmas, Teddy."

"Merry Christmas, Rush."

He hung up. "What do you want to do, Nora? I think we can safely rule out Scott Rhodes."

Nora nodded. "I agree. Let's pursue the leads we have now, see where they take us."

"Let's start with Harvey Langston."

Harvey Langston hadn't coughed up anything other than admitting he had been involved with Nora's mom for a brief time and it had cost him his marriage. Nora couldn't be sure if he was lying or not, but she still had her sights on Ward McKay. He was shady. He had motive and opportunity as well as connections to hire someone if he wasn't actually doing the dirty work.

But what had Nora up in arms at the moment was the phone call from Hailey. Dalton was sick and she couldn't get away with all the preparations for the masquerade ball. Nora didn't mind picking him up; it was nice to be needed and feel useful.

But the elementary school connected with the middle school, and there might be a chance Nora would encounter Ainsley Parsons. She didn't want to bump into her even if bygones were bygones, according to Rush.

"I can't believe the kids have school," Nora said.

Rush chuckled. "As long as they can keep power and water going, the kids are stuck having to attend and pining for snow days."

"I loved snow days. Poor Dalton won't be enjoying anything."

"You want me to come in with you? Help out if he needs carried or something?" Rush asked.

The idea of him swooping in to carry out a sick little boy sent flutters through her middle. Rush would make a wonderful father. "That's sweet but…but I'd rather go alone." She was dreading bumping into Ainsley. Having Rush with her would be even worse.

"I understand. Text if you need me."

"Will do." She went inside and straight to the office. A fresh-faced brunette sat behind the reception desk. "I'm here to pick up Dalton Gladwell."

"Name?"

"Nora Livingstone," a voice said from behind.

Nora swiveled and shrank inside. "Ainsley. Hello." Well, of course she'd see her right off the bat.

"Miss Livingstone," the receptionist said, "I'll need your license for checkout."

She showed her the photo ID and the receptionist called the nurses' station for them to bring Dalton to the office.

"You can wait in here or on the bench in the lobby."

The lobby. "Thank you." She hurried by Ainsley and into the lobby, where she perched on the bench and prayed Ainsley wouldn't approach her again.

Didn't look like the prayers had reached Heaven yet. Ainsley returned, flaming red hair, dark eyes and a file folder in hand. "How've you been?" she asked as she approached.

"Good. You?"

"Good." She blew a tuft of hair from her eyes. "How about we not let this feel awkward. Chalk up the past to young adult drama."

Nora relaxed. Rush had been right. "I'd like that."

"So you know, I never went blabbing like I said I would. I was hurt, but Rush and I..." She shrugged. "I started seeing Dan a few weeks after that. The rest is history."

"You got a great catch."

"I did." She sighed. "I'm sorry about your mom. That can't be easy."

"No, it hasn't been. But thanks. And I'm sorry about your dad's hotel. We stopped by there the other day to talk to Ward and I couldn't believe it." She also couldn't believe she was sitting here chatting with Ainsley Parsons. The insecurity in her past had made her paranoid. What if she hadn't gotten out of Dodge but stuck around?

"Dad's had some hard knocks but he always gets back up."

"Aunt Nora!" Dalton feebly cried. His little face was pale and his lips cherry red and cracked. "I'm sick."

"I heard, buddy. We're gonna get you home and all snuggled up. Sound good?" She rubbed his head, the heat radiating against her palm. "Has he had any Tylenol?" she asked the nurse.

"No, we're not allowed to administer medicines without a prescription." She smiled apologetically. "His temperature was 101.2 thirty minutes ago. I gave him a Popsicle and a cool rag."

"Thank you," Nora said.

"Where's my mom?"

"She's covered up right now on the big masquerade ball stuff so here I am. That okay?" Poor kid. When Nora had been young and sick, all she wanted was her mother. She'd have to suffice for now.

"Will you be in town for the ball?" Ainsley asked.

"Yeah. First one in a while."

Ainsley patted Dalton's head. "Feel better, little man. You can't be sick at Christmastime. You have too many sweet treats to eat!" With that, she waved and went back inside the office.

"Flu's going around. I'd have him tested," the nurse said. "Feel better, Dalton."

Nora bundled Dalton into his coat and wrapped her scarf around his head. "Come on, buddy. Mr. Rush is waiting outside, and he's in the sheriff's Bronco. Maybe he'll switch the sirens on for you. That would be fun, huh?"

"Yes, ma'am," he said, and trudged along beside her. She helped him into the backseat, buckled him up and grabbed the flannel blanket from the floorboard, covering him with it.

"I don't know what meds are at the house. Can we stop for some?" she asked Rush as she climbed inside the toasty warm Bronco.

"Of course. Hey, Dalton. Sorry you feel bad." Rush switched on the sirens and Nora's insides turned to marshmallow. She hadn't even had to ask. Dalton's glassy eyes lit up.

"Cool!" he said.

They stopped off at the convenience store for medicine and a few other items. "I'll be right back," Nora said.

She hurried inside, but carefully—the parking lot was slick. Christmas music played over the speakers, and the store smelled like pine cleaner and vanilla. The cashier—who seemed bored to death—greeted her.

Nora strode down the aisle and found the Tylenol. If it was the flu, what else might make an six-year-old feel better? She perused the shelves. Hairs rose on the back of her neck. She glanced up. No one was in the aisle with her. But she had the distinct feeling she was being watched.

She went back to hunting items that might make him feel better. She'd filled her small cart with Popsicles that had electrolytes in them, chicken noodle soup, crackers, 7 Up and a pack of Pokémon cards. No one seemed to be lurking, but Nora couldn't shake the feeling that someone was.

After paying for the items, she hurried with her plastic bags to the vehicle.

"Did you see Ward McKay?" Rush asked as she climbed inside.

"No."

"He left a couple of minutes ago."

Could Ward have been spying on her? Hiding from her, then making his exit before she got to the check-out line? "I won't lie. I felt watched in there, but I never actually saw him. Did he see you when he came out?"

"I'm hard to miss in this vehicle, but he didn't pay me any attention. Didn't wave."

"My tummy hurts, Aunt Nora."

Nora hurried and emptied a plastic bag—just in case. She handed it to him. "We're almost home, buddy. Hold tight and you can crawl in bed soon."

"Main house?" Rush asked.

"Yeah. His movies and bedding are there. Thanks for running errands for us." Rush made it a point to go out of his way for others. She admired his giving spirit and it wasn't only at Christmastime. This was Rush all year long.

Nora opened the Tylenol and poured a dose in the cup. "Here, buddy. Go ahead and take this."

She caught Rush smirking.

"What?"

"Nothing," he said.

"Something."

He chuckled. "I was thinking you'll make a great mom, Nora Beth." His voice became hushed, almost reverent. "You still want kids?"

"I do." She'd dreamed of baby names since she was a little girl. Dreamed of having Rush's last name. "Someday."

"Someday feels out of reach, doesn't it?" Rush murmured. Was he reading her mind or was he speaking quietly for himself?

Hope for them was lost.

Hope for Rush finding love again wasn't.

Nora wasn't sure she'd ever find anyone as special as Rush. She might as well be doomed to live alone forever.

Hope had disappointed her time and again.

The Lord is my portion, saith my soul; therefore will I hope in Him.

The verse from *Lamentations* that hung on the wall in her father's office struck her heart. Had her hopes been in Jesus or in the things she'd longed for and wanted? She glanced at Rush. She'd placed her hope in him as a young girl. When Mom vanished, not even Rush could fill the void and ache.

And she hadn't turned to the Lord for her strength, to soothe her sore soul.

She'd run.

"You okay, Nora Beth?" Rush asked as he pulled into the snowy drive of the main house.

Turning her head to wipe a few stray tears that had escaped, she nodded. "Yeah. Let's get this little man inside and to bed."

Poor little Dalton was looking even more feeble. "I got him," Rush said and scooped the boy in his arms. Tears stung her eyes at the sight. Nora grabbed the plastic bags and they entered the house. "Where's his room?"

"Upstairs. Second on the left. I'll be up after I call Hailey."

Rush started up the stairs with Dalton. He was talking to him, but she couldn't hear the words. Dalton giggled. She sighed and called Hailey.

"How is he? I feel so guilty for not picking him up myself, but these invoices won't get entered by themselves and Nathan couldn't leave work... Don't get me started."

Being a single mom wasn't easy. Nora wished there was more she could do. "I could come enter the invoices for you. Leave me a list of codes and I'll get the hang of it."

"Thanks, Nora. But I'm almost done."

"Okay, well he'll probably go to sleep. I gave him Tylenol on the way here and bought some stuff for him. Rush is putting him in bed now. The nurse said it could be the flu and he'll need to be tested for it. If you can't take him to the doctor, I can." It was the least she could do to help her sister out.

"I'll do it. I'll call now and let you know. Thanks for helping me, Nora. I miss having you around—not for favors but because I just miss you. I wish you weren't taking the job in Florida. Hank always needs help at the radio station."

The original job she'd been coming home to interview for before the fiasco with Rush. "I don't want to work in radio, Hailey. But I do miss you and being here, even though it hasn't been easy. It still feels like home." Unfortunately, Nora couldn't bear to live so close to Rush knowing they could never be together. That felt like punishment.

"I understand. Dalton will be thrilled to come visit you and get beach time in. There are definitely perks." She snickered. "I could use some soaking in the sun on the beach, reading a good book. I can't tell you the last time I had the chance to enjoy a delicious story. Way too long. I'm gonna call the doctor and finish up the invoices unless he can get us in now. I'll text you." She hung up.

Rush leaned against the kitchen door. "He's in his pajamas, TV is on his favorite superhero movie and he's already asleep. Poor kid."

"Thank you. Hailey is calling the doctor. You want coffee?"

"No," he said. "Dispatch called. Semi jackknifed. Hazardous material. I have to go. I hate to jerk him out of bed again to take you to the resort."

"I'll be okay. Besides, Hailey will be here soon to take Dalton to the doctor and I'll ride along for moral support." She gave him an encouraging smile. "I'll be fine. You be careful out there, though."

"Always." He gently clipped her chin with his knuckles. "Lock the door behind me, please."

Nora walked him to the door and watched him get inside his vehicle, then she closed her door and locked it. Coffee didn't sound as good as tea. Calming tea to soothe her nerves.

She headed into the kitchen, straight into a dark-clad figure.

TWELVE

Nora froze at the sight of the man standing in the kitchen, dressed head to toe in black. He came at her and it jerked her into motion.

She pivoted and ran from the kitchen into the living room, heading for the front door. Not to escape but to lure him out of the house and away from Dalton.

Reaching the sofa, he tackled her and they crashed on top of the coffee table, knocking magazines and a vase of flowers to the floor. A searing pain shot up her back, already sore from the car accident.

He shoved her face into the rug as he sat on her back like a weight. She struggled for the crystal vase as the attacker's hands wrapped around her throat and squeezed.

She got her fingers around a broken section and stabbed it into her assailant's gloved hand gripping her throat.

He howled as she ripped through the material, hitting flesh, and he released his grip. She slashed his other gloved hand. Managing to wiggle out from under him, she shot to her feet and raced to the front door. She couldn't leave him here alone with Dalton. Couldn't stay in the house with the child upstairs.

She paused and faced him.

"Is that all you got? Because you're going to have to put me in a snowy grave to stop me!" Hoping her false bravado didn't show the real fear burning through her, she looked her attacker dead in his dark eyes. Dark eyes!

He pulled a hunting knife and acid lurched into her throat. He bounded toward her like she'd intended but now this plan seemed futile. She slid across the porch, leaped down the steps to avoid ice, jarring her back and feeling every move in her stiff muscles. Bolting through the snow, Nora pressed toward the tree line. If she could get into the thatch of woods, she might be able to lose him, and once she broke through to the other side, the resort and lodge wouldn't be that far off. The stables were close and sleigh rides would be in full swing. Someone would see her. Help her.

But she had to make it there first.

Mr. Dressed In Black was hot on her heels and wielding a really big knife.

Wind whipped and stung her face, her lungs burned from gulping eight-degree air. Adrenaline kept her moving, kept her from paying too much attention to the pain in every stride.

She made it to the tree line but tripped over a log and face-planted in a drift of snow. Fighting to get up, she stumbled again and righted herself, barely dodging her attacker.

Screaming for help and continuing to zigzag through the evergreens, Nora felt the man closing in on her. *God, if You can save me from plummeting over the side of a mountain, You can rescue me now and keep Dalton safe!*

Hopefully, her prayers would be heard. Hanging

a sharp right, she slipped between the narrow trees, squeezing through. He might have to go an alternate route and if so, Nora would make it to safety.

Ella Fitzgerald crooned, "Sleigh Ride" on the wintry air. She was close to the stable. She could taste freedom.

A hand grabbed the back of her shirt and pulled her to the ground so hard she bit her tongue.

He raised the knife.

She grabbed a gnarly branch.

As he brought it down, she whacked him in the head.

The knife fell from his grasp and he toppled over, unmoving.

She hadn't knocked him out, only stunned him.

Move. Move. Move. Nora forced her exhausted, protesting body to get up and get going. Before she bolted, she grabbed the knife, then fled for safety at Pine Refuge.

Tourists laughed as they imbibed hot cocoa, listened to Christmas carols and climbed into sleighs with quilts and foot warmers, never once realizing a woman had been screaming and running for her life in the woods only yards from them.

She made it to the stable and stumbled inside. A phone on the wall would give her a direct line to Dad's office. Picking it up, she rang him.

"Yes," Dad said.

"Daddy. Daddy, it's me. Come…" She dropped the phone and collapsed on the stable floor. When she awoke, she was in her bed at the chalet and Dad was sitting beside her. Rush stood behind him, worry in his eyes.

"Hey, hon. How do you feel?"

Confused. Exhausted. Hanging by one little thread. "Dalton?" she asked, her throat gritty.

"He's fine." Rush handed her a cup of water that was on the nightstand. "Here, drink this."

She accepted it, feeling the warmth of his fingers discreetly brushing hers and giving her security. "What happened?" The last thing she remembered was calling Dad from the stable phone.

Dad patted her leg. "You called me and said, 'Come,' then the line went dead. I ran out to the stable and found you passed out. John was with you."

The stable hand.

"You had a knife and blood on your hand. I sent John to Dalton. Brought you here."

Nora scooted up in bed and sipped her water again. "Someone was in the kitchen, Rush. When you left I went to make tea and he was there." She finished telling them what happened and how she led the attacker away from the house to protect Dalton. "I'm so sorry. I shouldn't have come back to the main house. I should have brought Dalton to the offices—"

"He's safe. You were very brave, hon. And Hailey is grateful. She's with Dalton right now."

Grateful? She ought to be fuming. Nora had inadvertently put her nephew in danger. "I didn't see his whole face, but his eyes were dark."

"Good. That's good," Rush murmured.

"Ward McKay has dark eyes. Troy Parsons has dark eyes too," she said.

"Troy Parsons?" Dad asked and looked at Rush. "What is going on?"

Rush frowned. "A lot of men have dark eyes. Your

dad for one, and do you think he attacked you? Let's not go off half-cocked again just yet."

"Why would Troy Parsons want to hurt Nora?" Joshua asked.

Rush scowled again, then gave Nora a "now what are you going to do" look.

How to explain? Nora was going to have to wound her father. She should have kept her mouth shut and not been so open with her opinion like Rush had been insisting.

"He...he was seen meeting with Mom a few times before she disappeared. At Mac's."

Dad's eyes narrowed. "Hmm..." Standing, he shook Rush's hand. "Keep me abreast of the situation, Rush. And keep my baby safe." He stalked out of the room, blinking too fast and nostrils flaring.

"You see why I'm careful with my words, Nora? Now he has that image along with so many others to battle through."

Nora closed her eyes. "I'm exhausted, and I should have thought first, spoke second."

Rush sighed and sat on the side of the bed, taking her hand and kissing her knuckles. "Nora, you could have been killed."

"While you were called away by Troy. Convenient."

"Possibly. But we don't know for sure."

She wasn't up for another argument. "Give me my laptop. I need to finish my weather research."

"Right now, you're going to sleep, and I'm going to keep watch. End of story."

He had the no-nonsense face her dad used to have when she asked to go somewhere that wasn't going to bring anything good. "Fine."

Rush eyed her, suspicious.

"What? I said I'd sleep. I'll sleep," she insisted.

His smirk was like a tickle to her ribs, and she grinned. "If I come back in here and you're not sleeping…"

"You'll what?" she flirted. After all that had happened and knowing they were a lost cause, she couldn't help it.

His smirk slid into a full-on lady-killer grin. "I'll—" he seemed to be hunting for a punishment that might fit the crime "—be disappointed."

She half laughed. "I've been living with disappointment most of my life, Rush. You can't scare me."

He leaned in as if he were going to kiss her. His lips were mere inches from hers, his hands resting on either side of the fluffy pillow she was propped up on. Panic sent her heart thrumming. He searched her eyes. "You look scared right now."

She swallowed, couldn't find her voice.

His warm, minty breath filled her senses with anticipation and a heavy dose of alarm. If he kissed her again she'd never recover.

"If I come back in here, Nora Beth, and catch you doing anything but sawing logs…" His eyes revealed exactly what he'd do, what he wanted to do right this second. He slowly came closer. One pucker and they'd make contact. "Just give me a reason," he whispered.

Her brain screamed, "Run." Her heart shouted, "Do it! Kiss me!"

"You'd regret it," she murmured back.

"Probably, but not until it was too late to take it back."

This was not the way to make her sleep. This was a

great way to keep her awake for days! Months. Years. It wasn't only that Rush was an amazing kisser; he'd had years to practice it to perfection on her. They'd been each other's first kiss.

This felt like a first kiss kind of anticipation mixed with a measure of fear and excitement. It would do wild things to her physically, but what had her stomach in butterflies was what she'd feel emotionally. The way Rush would pour out his love and affection for her. Like he had so many times before. It had made her feel like she could be anyone. Do anything. That she was his alone. Those kisses had been full of beauty and promise.

Right now, something crackled between them. More than attraction. Enough to make her want to cry. Hope mixed with the tragic reality that they no longer had hope for a future and it was surely the only thing suspending Rush from dipping lower and exploring her lips.

It would be excruciating on them both when she left. Rush would have to deal with the heartache of watching her leave again—he'd said it himself. But he seemed willing to risk the pain of the future for the joy of the present.

A kiss wouldn't last. It would be over too soon, and they'd be met with waves of confusion. She was already confused enough. Rush loved her. She loved Rush. And love—well love wasn't enough to hold them together. It never had been.

"We were good at this once," Rush whispered.

"We were, but we weren't good at the rest of it." She wasn't good at the rest of it. Opening up. Sticking around when things got tough. "I wasn't. I'll own up to that. I may never be." She knew she needed a change.

But she'd run and cocooned herself for so long, she wasn't sure change could be made. And she refused to hurt Rush in the trying process.

His cloudy brown eyes cleared and pain pulsed in them. He tipped up his lips and gently placed a kiss on her forehead. "Get some sleep."

Yeah, right.

He turned at the door. "I'm sorry, Nora. Knowing you were out there being chased by a man with a knife...in the cold. Alone. You could have died and I... I lost it because I can't imagine a world where you're not in it. Even if you're not with me... I want you around for a long time." Emotion clogged his voice, and tears bloomed in her eyes. She didn't have anything but a nod in her.

He quietly closed the door. When she was sure he was in the kitchen and not coming back, she snatched her laptop and powered it up. She had a few weather sites she needed to browse and sleep was not going to happen no matter what he said, or how hard she tried.

Rush collapsed on the couch, staring out the window as the snow fell, leaving a fresh, untouched surface. A clean slate. Any mud, tracks, divots had all been covered with a sheet of white as if nothing lay beneath it. Nothing dark, nothing muddy.

Like God's mercy.

New every morning.

And yet they all lived as though there was none. As if their own lives weren't like fresh fallen snow, pure and white each and every morning they woke. Dad still hung on to his guilt for mistakenly accusing Randy of soliciting. Nora still clung to the belief that she couldn't truly be herself to be loved wholly. Rush's love hadn't been enough to convince her. *God, may Your love do that. Please open her eyes to see that there's nowhere she can go, nothing she can do that will keep You from loving her.*

What about Rush? Was he showing mercy? Man's mercy—yes. The kind where Rush offered enough to make things civil between him and Nora, but that was it. He hadn't forgotten how much heartache Nora had inflicted in the past. He wouldn't attempt to ask for a chance at something new. He couldn't risk it. But how was that new mercy? How was that fresh grace like new snow? His grace, his mercy still had faint footprints of pain, reminding him that it could only be doled out in small measures.

Did that mean he was being cautious or fearful?

Did that mean he wasn't trusting God with his heart? Was he leaving whether he found joy or sorrow up to Nora—up to himself?

He wasn't sure, and he didn't want to dig further or allow God to reveal any truths. If Rush let God do that, he'd be responsible for working through it. And Rush wasn't ready to deal with working through his feelings for Nora. He wished it would stop snowing. That he wouldn't have to keep seeing it laid fresh. That he wouldn't have to fight tooth and nail to keep his heart safe.

Everything was piling up. Work. Troy's possible involvement. A relentless killer bent on shutting Nora up for life. Did this guy realize if he murdered Nora, Rush would never stop coming after him? He'd make it his life's mission to find him and put him away until he stopped breathing. Did this killer think he was so cunning that Rush wouldn't find him? That he would get away scot-free? Because he wouldn't.

Rush glanced at Nora's bedroom door. He didn't for one second think she was sleeping. No, she was probably on the internet right this moment searching past weather conditions and digging around social media sites for clues. But he couldn't go in there. He'd told her what would happen if he did.

And he'd follow through if he walked in there.

Rush would kiss her, pour out his heart, and it would hurt because she'd pour hers right back. She could never withhold her feelings from him—not in a kiss. Thinking about it was only going to drive him mad.

He jumped up and put more wood on the fire, the wood smoke comforting him some. The flames warming him, but only so far. A knock on the door came. He drew his piece and looked out the window.

Troy.

The last person he wanted to see. But the one person he needed to see most. Rush was afraid of the truth. Afraid that another mentor and man he considered a father would disappoint him. Nora said she'd been disappointed so much she was used to it. So was Rush. But he didn't want disappointment to be the norm. Didn't want to expect everyone and everything to let him down. That was no way to live. But to choose the other meant exposing himself and being vulnerable.

Rush holstered his weapon and opened the door. "Troy. What are you doing here?"

"I heard what happened to Nora. Thought I'd come by and check on her. On you." He peeked inside. "Can I come in?"

"Sure." He motioned Troy inside. "Have a seat."

Troy looked around. "I've never been to the chalets before."

"They're state-of-the-art," Rush said.

Sitting on a wingback chair by the hearth, Troy leaned forward. "What can you tell me about what happened? Did she see who did it?"

Rush wasn't sure if Troy was asking as a concerned friend, the sheriff or someone working against them. "He was wearing all black, including a ski mask." Did he tell Troy about the knife? The attacker was wearing gloves but they might be able to get prints. He hated not knowing if he could trust this man. If he accused him of sinister things, Rush would not only lose Troy's endorsement for his run for sheriff, he'd lose a friend and mentor.

But he had to know.

"Troy, did you have any kind of relationship with Marilyn that you might not want to admit?" Rush's stomach knotted.

Troy's bushy eyebrows rose, and then he frowned. "Are you asking me if I betrayed my wife of thirty-two years? If I put my family at risk of falling apart over a fling with a woman who had flings with just about anyone? You really want to ask me that?"

Rush sighed. "I don't want to believe it. But I have to ask. Because the manager at Mac's said he saw you in there with Marilyn on a few occasions before the masquerade ball. It's my duty to follow up."

The sheriff rolled his signature toothpick around his lips. "I didn't have an affair with Marilyn Livingstone. You have my word on that. I love Betty. I'd never do anything to hurt her or Dan."

Troy held Rush's gaze. The chalet was quiet except

for the wind outside and firewood popping in the fireplace. Rush wanted to believe him. "Then what were you meeting with Marilyn about?"

Sighing, Troy stood. "I wasn't. The only thing I'm guilty of is going out of town to have a beer. That's my only betrayal where Betty is concerned. Her father was an alcoholic, and she didn't want me having a drink. Not even one beer after a rough day, but some days... some days called for an ice-cold glass of relaxation. I'd go to Mac's and have it."

"And Marilyn?"

"Marilyn was there often. Did I ever sit down and chat with her? Yes, because she was actually a nice person, and she didn't judge me sneaking around to have a drink, but then why would she? She was there sneaking around, I suspect, too. I saw her a few times with Ward McKay. But that wasn't new information."

Rush wanted desperately to trust Troy's explanation. "Then why did the manager say you were with her?"

"I was. Sitting at a table for a while. I suppose like other men who met her there. But I promise nothing untoward happened, and I was probably wrong to do it. Clearly, it gave the impression I was one of her side-suitors. I wasn't. Marilyn wasn't a pariah. I don't know what she was or why she stepped out on Joshua so often."

Troy driving up after they went off a cliff had to be coincidence. He'd done nothing to thwart the investigation. It made sense not to put all their manpower into investigating what the coroner had signed off on as an accident. If Rush were sheriff, he would have done the same thing.

"Nora has been working on the past weather reports

and it's looking like it wasn't wet, snowy or even icy that night. But you remembered it raining and snowing."

"Are you accusing me of something, Rush?" His voice held a hint of anger but mostly surprise and a splash of hurt and offense.

"No. Just trying to get answers."

"I do remember it raining and snowing that night, late, not during the party. But it was seventeen years ago. I barely remember what I ate for breakfast yesterday. I could be wrong. I'm not saying I can't. But that doesn't mean I'm lying on purpose. And to a woman I know is a forensic meteorologist and could prove me wrong or right? Why would I do that?"

Why indeed?

Nora's paranoid suspicions were messing with his head. Troy wasn't guilty of murder or attempted murder. "Do you think Ward McKay could be behind these attacks on Nora? Him or Harvey Langston?"

"I don't like Harvey for it."

"When Nora was attacked at the hotel, Ward was with me."

"Doesn't mean Ward didn't have someone do him a favor. I wouldn't put anything past him. He's double-dealing in business. Why not in his personal life as well? But I stand by my call and the coroner's. If he's after Nora for digging into the past it's not because he hurt Marilyn. Could be about that money, though."

"Why would Marilyn take him that kind of money? And since she never gave it to him, it's dead in the water, pardon the pun. Why come after Nora now? What could she dig up—with my help—that would expose him?"

Troy held his toothpick and used it to point at Rush.

"That's the million-dollar question, son. I'd do a little hunting around his business deals. But if that's where the answers lie, then expect even more backlash. And be discreet."

He could count on that. "I'm sorry, Troy, if it seemed like I was interrogating you—"

"Seemed?" His eyebrows twitched skyward. "Hey, it's good work. You'll make a mighty fine sheriff, Rush. I've always thought so. You don't need my endorsement to beat out Jack Thomas, or anyone." He hugged him, clapping him on the back.

"You heading back to the station?" Rush asked.

"I am. Whatcha need?"

Rush lifted his coat off the table and took the gallon freezer bag holding the serrated knife. Nora had cut the attacker and it had some blood on it. Possibly prints. "He came at Nora with this. She cut up his hands and there's some blood. Can you enter it and get it to the lab? I don't want to leave her."

Troy accepted the bag, inspected the knife. "Hunting knife. Not uncommon. Good thing Nora's quick. She may not have made it, and this would be an entirely different conversation."

"Agreed." He was beyond thankful for God's protection of Nora.

Troy headed for the door, turned back. "Give her my best, though I doubt she wants it if she's labeled me a criminal."

"She's confused."

"I'll keep you posted." With that, he closed the door. The lights flickered. The power had been going on and off for days.

He walked to Nora's door and knocked, giving her

time to put that laptop away and pretend sleep, ultimately giving her and himself an out.

"Nora," he called. Maybe she was asleep. He cracked the door and saw her lying on her side. He walked in and noticed the laptop on the floor. Touching it, he felt the warmth.

Faker. He grinned but went along with the facade. "Wake up, Nora Beth. We gotta talk."

Now to make her believe that Troy wasn't the enemy.

But someone was. He'd been brazen enough to get into the main house. He was desperate and reckless.

And that meant unstable.

Unstable meant unpredictable.

Unpredictable meant Rush was at a disadvantage, and that terrified him.

THIRTEEN

It was already Christmas Eve and Nora hadn't even thought about a ball gown or masquerade mask. Seemed like a silly event to attend when someone was trying to kill her, but Rush had insisted on some normalcy—not to mention he had to be at the ball.

She stood inside Hailey's room staring at the gowns lying across her bed.

"Pick any one you like. I should have put them in consignment, but I figured I'd recycle them. Glad I did." Hailey sat on an empty space on the bed that wasn't covered with sequins, silk and satin. "I'm behind on the event since Dalton's been sick."

"Hey, at least it wasn't the flu." Two days and his fever had broken. He was still a bit lethargic, but his appetite had returned with a vengeance and he would be well enough to stay with Nathan tonight.

"Yeah. It's going to be weird not having him at all on Christmas Eve. We used to bake cookies and open one present that day, then come to the ball. I suppose he and Nate will go to his parents'. They never liked the ball anyway." Hailey shrugged and held up a strapless red silky dress with a large red sash and a rhinestone pendant on the side. It was gorgeous. "I think you should wear this one." She rummaged through the pile on the bed. "And this mask."

A black-and-gold mask on a gold stick. Ornate. Touch of glitter for shine. Classy and elegant. "Okay. I like it." Red and Christmassy. "Now that my costume is picked out, how can I help you catch up?"

"It's mostly overseeing what's going on in the ballroom. Ice sculptures, caterers, decorators. Sound guys are supposed to be here at two for a sound check." She sighed. "I need the crew to come back through and shovel the snow from the chalet drives and roads leading up to the resort, and the parking lot."

Nora peered out the window. It had been coming down hard all morning. "I don't think it'll do any good, sis. The overnight temps were low with high relative humidity and low winds…high pressure system. Black ice is coming. People need to stay indoors and off the roads."

"Nothing is going to keep people from this masquerade ball."

The power flickered.

Died.

"Great," Nora mumbled.

"Generator will kick on in a minute." Hailey checked her cell phone. "I have to get to the resort. And you can't be left alone."

Nora felt like a helpless child.

"I've got the snowmobile. It's easier than trying to deal with a vehicle. Grab your things. I'm gonna call and check on Dalton right quick."

Nora nodded and headed for the kitchen to collect her purse, coat and gloves. Black gloves. Reminded her of the attacker from a few days ago and the knife he'd come at her with. Rush had given that piece of evidence to Troy. Nora hadn't been thrilled to hear about Rush's conversation with Troy, but it did make sense. Why lie about the weather knowing she had the skills to prove him wrong? And she had.

She'd scoured the National Climatic Data Center, co-op sites, which were a notch above Weather Underground but she'd checked there too, collecting what data she could. She'd studied the weather information for that Christmas Eve as well as five days prior and after. In all likelihood, there had been no ice, no black ice. Not even wet roads. Weather was probably not a factor in Mom's accident. Troy may have made a mistake. And Nora was hunting for a culprit to pin this on.

She caught a shadow at the living room window; her heart lurched and she clutched her chest, then exhaled and relaxed. Rush. She opened the door and shivered. The temperature was in single digits. "Hey," she said.

"Hey," he said as breath plumed in front of his face. His nose and cheeks were pink. "It's crazy out there. Northern half of town is shut down. No power. Pipes are frozen in many homes and businesses, meaning no water. It's going to get even worse tonight. I don't think anyone local should be driving."

"Locals won't drive. They'll bring snowmobiles." She laughed. "And freeze in ball gowns and faux fur coats."

The blustery winds rattled the window and whistled. "It's gorgeous, though," she said. Trees looked made of glass. Hints of evergreen peeked through. Nothing but a white winter wonderland.

"I told Mom I'd come by and eat a bite. She can't stand me not being there for festivities, and they're hurrying it up in case they lose power. You mind riding along?" he asked.

"No. I'd like to see Greer again. When is she going back to Alabama?"

"Supposed to be the day after Christmas, but I don't see that happening. Not if we get two inches of ice tonight and another one tomorrow. Weather is calling for it and another two feet of snow."

Nora smirked. "I'm well aware of what the weather is supposed to be doing."

"I suppose you are."

"Hey," Hailey said as she came into the living room, snug as a bug in her winter gear. "I'm leaving. You with me or going with Rush?"

"Rush."

Nora spotted the knowing look. Rush was protecting her. That's all.

"See you tonight?"

"Yeah. But I may have on boots with my gown and not heels."

Hailey snickered. "You'd think bad weather would keep folks away. But Christmas brings people together no matter what storm is raging." Sadness flickered on her face. "Well, most people are brought together."

She hurried out and Rush turned to Nora. "Nathan's a real jerk."

Nora nodded. "Ready?"

Rush guided her outside and into the vehicle.

"We probably shouldn't be out in this either."

Rush started the motor. "Well, I have chains and, hey…we've made it over the mountainside once. We can do it again."

Nora frowned.

"Too soon?"

She laughed. "Little bit."

Inching along the roads, it took almost thirty minutes to arrive at Rush's childhood home. Festive lights wrapped around the porch rails. "Lights are new."

"Hollister was bored I think."

Inside, the fire blazed and Nora welcomed the warmth. The dining room table was still covered in sweets galore and the smell of cinnamon and Christmas ham set her stomach rumbling. Nora loved the Buchanan ham. Cured and cooked for nine hours. She would be up all night gulping water from so much salt intake, but it was worth it. The tree twinkled with colored lights and tinsel. Bing Crosby's "White Christmas" played in the background. Kids ripped and tore through the house and adult laughter helped drown it out.

"Merry Christmas, Nora." Mrs. Buchanan took her coat. "Come in, out of that terrible weather." She pointed at Rush. "You don't need to be driving in this."

"Yes, ma'am." He kissed her cheek. "I can't stay long, Mama."

"You work too hard, and it's Christmas Eve. Eat. Make merry," she teased, and patted his cheek.

Rush was nothing if not a mama's boy at heart.

"Yes, ma'am," he said again, and Mrs. Buchanan bustled away.

"You hungry?" he asked.

"Starving, and I smell Christmas ham."

He chuckled and led her to the kitchen. Hollister leaned against the refrigerator, mischief in his eyes, as they came in. He pointed upward.

Mistletoe.

"Kiss her or I'll come under and do it," he teased.

Rush frowned and glanced up again. "Well, it is tradition."

"It is that," she murmured. And Hollister would make good on his word—the insatiable flirt. The last thing she needed was Rush punching him like he had when they were sixteen.

Her stomach fluttered, and her heart sped up as Rush descended on her lips. Soft. Chaste, but lingering long enough to send a serious zing through her middle.

Hollister opened the fridge and pulled out a soda. "Pitiful, Rush. Pitiful." He cracked open the can, wiggled his eyebrows and strode out of the kitchen.

"I didn't think it was pitiful, Nora Beth. Did you?" His eyes held mischief of their own. "I can try again if you did."

"I—"

"Nora, good to see you again." Pastor Buchanan entered the kitchen, eyed the mistletoe. "Am I interrupting?"

"Not at all, Dad," Rush said, and backed a foot away from Nora.

"Rush, can you bring the card table in from the craft room?" Mrs. Buchanan called.

"Yes, ma'am." He tossed one last glance at the mistletoe and winked at Nora. That was not fair. Not holding up to his words. Words like they could never be together. Rush wasn't one to lead her on. He must be as confused as she was. Her head told her it was futile. Her heart said something else.

"Will you be staying long?" Pastor Buchanan asked.

"No. I took a job in Florida. I leave at the New Year."

"I thought maybe you and Rush might be…" He

shrugged, but a hint of amusement danced in his eyes. He seemed more like the man he used to be.

"It's complicated."

He pursed his lips, started to leave, then stopped. "Love usually is."

No one said anything about love. Oh, who was she kidding? "I don't know if we could ever get past our heartbreaks, Pastor Buchanan."

His eyes widened. "It's been a long time since I've been called that."

Nora used to call him that all the time. He had been her pastor. A mentor. A role model. "I don't think one mistake should cost you the honor of being one."

"And one or two mistakes ought not cost you a chance at being with someone you love."

Nora's chest cracked a little. If that were only true. "To be honest, he's made it clear that we're nothing but friends. We have too much bad history. I'm sure you know that."

A flicker of light came into his eyes. "Love covers a multitude of sins, Nora."

"Not sure it covers fast enough to Mach speed racers like me." She swallowed the emotion clogging her throat as it dawned on her. "I suppose you and I are similar."

"How's that?" he asked quietly.

"Hiding away, keeping things inside and not letting anyone in. Rush calls it running—physically and metaphorically. And he's not wrong."

When he looked at her, moisture filled his eyes. "This is why he...why he wants to keep things platonic?"

"It's why he should," she whispered. "I can't promise not to do it again."

Pastor Buchanan looked longingly into the living

room; more moisture sheened his eyes and he wiped them. Slowly, he turned. "Love does cover a multitude of sins. It reaches far and wide. And fast, Nora. Love moves fast when it needs to." He glanced back at his wife and sucked his trembling bottom lip into his mouth. "The question is, do we let it blanket us or do we stand out in the cold and keep shivering unnecessarily?"

Was that rhetorical or was he asking himself?

Suddenly, he inhaled and squeezed her shoulder. "Thank you."

For what? She didn't get a chance to ask. Rush came into the kitchen with a card table in his arms. "Where am I supposed to put this?"

"By the laundry room," his mother said. "I know it's early but you're leaving, so will you come and read the Nativity story before you go?"

Pastor Buchanan had always done that in years past. Guess Rush took up the mantle after all that happened. Pastor Buchanan caught Nora's glance. The flicker in his eyes had turned into a bright and shining flame, as if life had suddenly come back into them. He grasped his wife's hand. "I think I'd like to do it."

Tears filled Rush's mom's eyes. "I'd like that, darling."

"Let me get my Bible." He paused next to Nora, kissed her cheek. "Thank you, dear one." Then he disappeared into the living room.

Rush gaped. "What just happened?"

Nora wasn't sure. "I don't know."

Dad hadn't read the Nativity story since he lost the church. Now Nora waltzed into the house and, all of a sudden, he was offering to go and get his Bible and read it aloud? Rush hadn't seen his dad with the worn, black leather-bound Good Book in ages. She had to have done something. His father had thanked her!

"Well," his mother said, "I don't know either, but I'm thanking you also." She patted Nora's cheek and left Rush alone with her.

"What did you talk about?"

"Complications. And love."

Rush cupped her face. "What about love?"

"That it covers a multitude of sins."

Nora had been believing for something wonderful at Christmas. Was this it? A turning point for Dad?

"Everyone, gather round," his father called.

"Well, whatever you did or didn't do…it shifted something loose in my dad. Come on. Let's hear the story of our Lord's birth."

"I'd like that."

Rush laced his hand in hers and led her to the living room. The reading of the birth of Christ the Lord never failed to move Rush to tears. It reminded him of how frail and flawed he was and how gracious and merciful and loving God was.

Dad finished his reading and paused, then he prayed.

Rush could hardly stand upright. His father. Was praying. For peace. For joy. For hope.

Mom leaned against Dad and cried.

They were witnessing answers to prayers that had been going up for a decade. On this holy eve, God was giving them the greatest gift.

Rush was getting his father back.

Mom was getting her husband back.

What about Rush's prayers? Would they be answered anytime soon? Would he ever find love that would work out, have a family of his own?

After prayer, the family piled plates full of ham, potatoes, casseroles, deviled eggs and homemade yeast rolls. Nora sat beside Greer at the kitchen table, talking and laughing.

"Son, can we talk a minute?"

Rush set his plate on the counter. "Sure." He followed Dad into his study and shut the door.

"I owe you an apology."

"For?"

"The last ten years. And for keeping you from the woman you love."

"Dad, you didn't keep me from Nora. We did that all by ourselves." Rush leaned against the desk and crossed an ankle over the other.

"Fear has kept you from going after her. Fear she's like me. Like what I've become. It's true. I've been wallowing in guilt for what I did, in bitterness for what happened, anger at God for allowing it. I thought I'd lost everything, but I didn't. The most important things to me were still here, still covering me with love, and I ignored it to be selfish. To be resentful and fearful."

Rush swallowed the lump in his throat.

"You see me and what I've done to this family in Nora. For that I'm sorry. Because tonight I saw the love you have for her. And the pain. I've been afraid to live for ten years. Don't be me. Don't think Nora is me."

Dad hugged him hard and tight. "She helped me see that tonight, and it hit me that my son is miserable because of me and I can't have that. Your mother has been miserable because of me."

"Dad, I love you."

"I love you too, son."

"But it doesn't change anything with Nora. She won't

confide in me. Open up to me. I can't be with a woman who won't give me all of her heart. All of her dreams and fears and everything. Even if you hadn't changed... I would still feel the same way about her. I would still want it all. And she can't give me that."

Dad nodded. "Love covers a multitude of sins."

But what did that mean? Was Rush to love her and hope she wouldn't leave him again when things got tough? He'd barely recovered from the last time.

"I don't know if love can cover distrust. And I can't trust her not to leave me when things get rough, and it's no secret marriages aren't perfect. I want someone like Mama."

"I'll pray for you, son."

Rush hadn't heard those words in so long. Tears stung the backs of his eyes. "I'd like that."

"And I suspect you'd like some answers on this case."

Dad may have answers and was willing to help him, to divulge information. This was beyond anything Rush could ever imagine. Proof God had been working to soften him over the years. To bring him to this point. Rush could hardly speak. "I would if you have any. Did you see anyone in the Phantom of the Opera mask that wasn't Harvey Langston or Ward McKay?"

Dad sighed and rubbed the back of his neck. "After I accused Randy of that crime... I promised myself I'd never speak about another person again no matter what. But Nora's life is at stake. And so is yours. I do know of one man who wore a Phantom of the Opera mask that night. And I know he was involved romantically with Marilyn because I witnessed him kissing her the night before, near the lake, when I was on patrol."

Rush couldn't believe his ears. "Why didn't you say anything after she disappeared?"

"Because I promised him as a pastor that I wouldn't. I felt guilty about it, which is why when Randy was in that old pool hall in the woods, I didn't hold back because I'd done it before. I had to be honest."

"Who did you see kissing Marilyn?" It was undoubtedly the same man Rush saw kissing her the next night in the offices.

"Gary Plenk."

The words knocked the breath from him. Gary had been a deacon in Dad's church. But more than that—he was the county coroner. "Is that why he stepped down as a deacon?"

"It was our deal. He stepped down, and if Marilyn returned they would break it off, and I wouldn't say anything to Troy about it. Besides, I never believed for a second he had anything to do with her disappearance. In fact, I thought he might be getting ready to leave his wife and go with her, but when I approached him he was confused. Upset. He didn't know what happened to her. And we made our deal."

Rush's mind reeled. "Thank you for sharing that information. It's helpful. Beyond helpful. I need to find Nora."

"Go on. Be careful."

"I will." He gave him one more hug and found Nora where he left her. Sitting at the table with Greer's baby in her arms. "Hey."

She glanced up and must have read his expression; she passed the baby back to Greer and stood. "Ready?"

"Yeah."

Once they were back inside the Bronco he told her everything his dad shared.

"Rush. What if he was lying about the striations being inconclusive? If he was kissing my mom one minute, and then the next she was leaving town without him…?"

"A fight could have gone down. We can send the reports and photos to a coroner outside the county and get a second opinion. Be sure."

"He's still with his wife. Me digging around might have turned it up—it did turn it up. He has a lot to lose. Besides his reputation."

"His family. His marriage. Before we approach him, let's get that information emailed to someone else."

"Okay. I need to change and get ready for the ball tonight."

"We can do that as soon as I swing by the station and email an outside coroner. I know someone in Shelby County that's a friend."

"Memphis area?"

"Yeah. We went to summer camp together."

The tires rolled over packed snow and ice, and the vehicle rocked. Branches clanked like ice in glasses as the wind hurled through the trees. They slid a few times, Rush righting them, but his face was grim, jaw working.

He pulled up at the station. "Sit tight. I won't be but a minute. No point in us both having to get out and freeze." He left the Bronco running and hurried inside. The station was quiet since most deputies were out helping on the roads, due to downed power lines and car accidents. It was a nightmare out there. He rifled through the box of evidence, scanned the photos and report, then emailed it to Walt Brudebaker. Then he sent him a text telling him he had mail and it was of utmost priority.

Back inside the Bronco, he shivered and turned the

heat back up to full blast. "I can't believe we're going to a party."

Nora snorted. "Well, believe it."

"I want coffee by the fire and that's all."

"You'll look good in a tux."

"But I'll be cold."

"My dress is off one shoulder so I don't wanna hear it."

He'd like to see it. And he would in a few hours.

"Are you going to tell Troy about Gary Plenk?"

"As soon as I hear back from Walt. If it is inconclusive, then I'm going to approach Gary with some questions." He didn't want to be the bearer of bad news again, but... "Nora, you have to know that if we don't find some kind of solid evidence or if someone doesn't outright admit they were with her that night and know what that money was for, then we may never know the details."

Nora smeared ChapStick on her lips. "I know. But what if this Walt person says otherwise about the marks on my mother's skull?"

"Then we know Gary has lied and that implicates him in foul play."

"But you still have no hard evidence."

"No." That was the worst part of this. The killer could go free. Yeah, Gary might lose his license. But even if he had a silver cuff link and Phantom of the Opera mask, that was all circumstantial and wouldn't convict him in a court of law. Not of murder in any degree. And no one seemed to know what the money was for and probably never would.

FOURTEEN

Gold and glass-beaded chandeliers hung in rows from the ceiling of the ballroom. Buffet tables with black tablecloths held silver warmers and white china plates rimmed in gold. Savory garlic and onions wafted from the magnificent dishes underneath the heavy lids.

Sparkling cider flowed down a mountain of champagne glasses, creating a beautiful amber waterfall. The center of the room held a Nativity ice sculpture that was breathtaking. The round sitting tables dotting the massive room were covered in black, gold and silver with pops of red. A live band, including a string quartet, was already faintly playing Christmas carols. It was glorious.

Nora had changed and Dad had brought her to the resort to oversee a few things for Hailey so she could dress in her gown.

The twenty-foot fir was trimmed in crystal icicles, glittery ornaments and dazzling gold beads. Nora gazed on it with fond memories. This had been her favorite night growing up. Families would come and dine together, then staff took children under twelve back to the kids' corner, where they watched Christmas movies, made crafts, ate cookies and drank cocoa until parents arrived for them before midnight. At midnight, masks would be removed and everyone sang, "We Wish You a Merry Christmas" with the band and toasted Christmas morning in.

Nora couldn't stay in Splendor Pines, but she had to admit she didn't want to go. She had no job here. Debt to pay.

And there was Rush. Staying was too hard. But maybe there was a way.

A throat cleared and drew her attention from the band and the tree.

Rush stood at the doorway in a black tux, black vest and tie. He'd never been a fan of bow ties. The gold flecks in his hair were magnified by the twinkling lights in the chandeliers. He'd shaved, and a dimple on his left cheek was visible. Broad shoulders carried that jacket well. But the black mask with pewter designs brought out his amber eyes. Her mouth turned dry.

He swaggered toward her. When he reached her, he gave her an admiring appraisal. "You look amazing," he murmured.

She held her mask over her eyes. "Oh, this old thing," she teased, and snickered, but his open approval of her appearance did wild numbers on her heart.

He held out his hand and motioned with his chin to the string quartet practicing. "Can I have the first unofficial dance of the night?"

The first. The last.

Would he want her to be his last dance? She curtsied, and he chuckled and took her hand in his, guiding her against him and placing his other hand on her upper back, drawing their intertwined fingers to his chest.

Then he glided her across the floor in a waltz like a contender in one of those reality dancing TV shows. "Been practicing, have you?" she asked.

"Maybe. Or maybe I remember those horrid dance classes my mother made me go to before I was stuck escorting Greer to her cotillion."

"You'd think 'coming out' parties would have been banned long ago due to women's rights efforts."

"Some things never go out down South. You know this." He turned her effortlessly and grinned. "Did I mention you look amazing?"

"I don't think you did," she teased.

"My apologies. You look amazing." His lips met her ear. "You smell amazing too."

His breath tickled her sides.

"You look quite handsome yourself."

He drew her closer as they danced in front of the Christmas tree to the sounds of violins, viola and cello playing the "Christmas Waltz."

Could they possibly be more? Have a fresh start? Even with a killer out for blood and finding out she wasn't Dad's biological daughter—in all that mess and pain, for once in a long time she felt hope. Dinner at Rush's, seeing his father read the Bible and pray had done something. God hadn't given up on Rush's dad. Even when he'd turned his back on God. Finally, the hope and love had broken through.

Could it also break through for Nora? For Rush?

"Rush?"

"Yes," he said and gazed into her eyes.

"What if I didn't go to Florida? What if I stayed here?"

He faltered in his perfect dance steps. "Are you being serious right now?"

"Yeah. I could… I don't know…find work." Somewhere. Somehow. "Spend more time with Hailey—be here for her while she goes through this tough time. Be here for Dalton. Help with the resort, even." It was the family business. "And…then there's us."

"Us," he murmured. "I—I want you to stay. If you want to stay. But…"

Nothing about his earlier words had changed. His dad's breakthrough hadn't reached him. He didn't feel the same hope as Nora, and the rejection slid into her lungs, deflating them like a popped balloon. A balloon full of hope. "You know what? It was just a thought." Humiliation racked her every nerve.

"Nora, I—" His phone rang.

"Better take that." She slipped from his embrace and scurried through the tables. She needed some time to compose herself. She beelined it to the elevator and took it down to the offices. Inside Dad's office, she laid her handbag on the desk and slumped in his chair and cried.

The case was closed. Rush's hesitation, his lack of enthusiasm, said it all. He didn't trust her. Didn't want her. Had all this investigation on her mother shown him the probability of what his future might look like? She wiped her eyes, leaving trails of mascara on her hands. The last thing she needed was guests and Rush seeing she'd been crying. Seeing she was heartbroken.

She hurried to the office entrances and was met by Harrison on the golf cart. "I need a ride! To the main house." She slid in with Harrison.

"Everything okay?" he asked and sped up.

"No, it's not." Nothing felt okay. She'd made an attempt to change, to open up like Rush had wanted, and he'd shut her down.

Harrison pulled up to the house. "Be careful, Nora. Weather ain't gonna get no better."

"Thanks for the ride." She froze. She'd forgotten her keys. Her purse was in Dad's office. "Wait! Harrison! Do you have a set of spare keys on you?" He'd been there in a pinch several times over the years when Nora or Hailey had locked themselves out.

"Some things don't change, Nora." He chuckled and unlocked the front door. "If you need a ride back, call the security line."

"Thank you." She shivered and entered the house, then switched on the light.

Nothing but darkness.

The generator must have run out of gas or something. Suddenly, the darkness crept up her spine, leaving cold chills. With her hands stretched out in front of her to guide the way, she maneuvered through the living room and down the hall to her old childhood room. Once inside, she dug through the nightstand drawer and found a battery-operated Christmas candle. She turned the plastic flame and brought a tiny orange glow to the room.

Now what? What did she do next?

She collapsed on her bed; her hand hit something soft and silky. Sitting up, she squinted in the dark and raised the pitiful candle.

Her mouth fell open and the scream rising from her gut wouldn't make its way from her lips.

Hailey lay next to her, in her evening gown and masquerade mask.

Blood covered the bed.

Covered Hailey's middle.

Hailey didn't move. Her chest didn't seem to be rising and falling with breath.

"Nooo!" She felt for a pulse, didn't find one. She picked up the receiver on the phone by the bed but there was no dial tone. Power lines must be down. Her phone was in her purse in Dad's office.

Tilting Hailey's chin back, she began CPR. Every muscle in her body shook; her lips trembled.

This was all her fault. Someone had mistaken Hailey in her mask and gown for Nora and put a bullet in her.

Please, breathe, Hailey.

In this moment, she wished she had listened and stayed out of it. Rush and Hailey were right. There might never be answers and the ones that came would have emotional and physical consequences. Nora had ignored it all for the need to feel loved and not abandoned by Mom.

But wasn't that exactly what had happened that night? Mom was deserting them. She might have come back like other times.

Or she might not have.

Hot tears slicked down Nora's cheeks until they turned to sobs. "God, please! Please!" She repeated it over and over.

How would Nora tell Dalton that his mama was dead, and it was all Nora's fault?

"Please!"

One and two and…

Breathe. Breathe.

And one and two and…

Rush pinched the bridge of his nose. He'd just hung up with Troy. Another car pileup had occurred and the power was now out on most of the south side of town too. But more important, once again, Nora had taken off. And that's why he'd hesitated when she'd brought up them as a couple and her staying. Nothing would make him happier than to be with Nora and live right here in Splendor Pines. But she wouldn't even wait around to have an adult conversation about why he'd paused.

She'd taken his words as complete rejection and instead of listening, she let her assumptions send her out into the night where it wasn't safe. They needed some space and air, but with a killer out there, she should have waited until he was off the phone. But she'd taken advantage of his need to be on that call and thrown all caution to the wind. Did she not care one iota what it might to do him?

No. She didn't think about anyone but herself sometimes. Like now. And as much air and space as Rush needed away from Nora to think things through, he couldn't give it to her because he couldn't leave her alone. He'd already searched the main hall and offices, calling out her name. She wasn't on the property.

Without her car, she wouldn't have gone far. Security was on golf carts. She probably caught a ride to the main house. Or the chalet. Both dumb ideas with everything going on.

His phone rang.

Walt, his coroner friend.

"Hey, Walt." Rush hunched in the weather and dashed for his vehicle.

"I know it's Christmas Eve but it didn't take long to look at those photos and come to a conclusion."

Rush hopped inside his truck. "And what conclusion is that?"

"It's clear that Marilyn Livingstone was murdered."

Faltering to get the keys in the ignition, Rush paused. "Say that again. How so?"

"I don't know why it wasn't ruled a homicide."

Rush had a few ideas. Gary Plenk. Where. Was. Nora? Rush's blood turned to ice.

"Go on," he said, and cranked the engine. *Please let her be at the main house or the chalet.*

He could barely swallow, barely hear Walt speaking.

"The markings on her skull have indentions that match a crowbar perfectly—if you know what to look for, which I do. Someone hit her, and hard enough to leave those impressions in the bone."

Sliding on the ice, he tightened his grip on the steering wheel and made his way down the road that cut up to the main house. The snow fell in fat flakes like white ash from a volcano. "Would she have been alive long enough to drive a car into the lake?"

That at least had to have been an accident—otherwise someone had thought their tracks were covered. No wonder someone was bent on killing Nora. They'd never expected to have that car found. Gary hadn't expected that. But he was in a prime position to lie. He knew Rush would look at that report. See the indentations, not be able to identify it as a layperson and therefore putting all his trust in Gary's lie.

"No. That kind of blow would cause immediate death. If her car was found in the lake with her in it, then it was put there after the blow to the head."

"Walt, thank you for getting back to me so quickly. Merry… Merry Christmas," he mumbled, and hung up as he pulled into the drive at the main house.

Gary Plenk had mountains to lose back then and now.

Rush bounded up the steps to a wide-open front door; his knees turned to water and his heart jumped into his throat. He grabbed his flashlight, drew his weapon and raced inside. No sign of a struggle. He ran down the hall and into Nora's bedroom.

Was that— Was she—

As he came closer he realized the dress wasn't red, but black.

The hair a darker blond and longer.

Hailey.

Blood.

Where was Nora? He checked Hailey's pulse.

Faint. But there. He used his cell phone and called it in. Gunshot wound to the abdomen.

"Hang on, Hailey. We're gonna get you help." But where was Nora? Had the killer shot Hailey and abducted Nora? Had she even been here at all?

Or did the killer mistake Hailey for Nora in the dark?

"Rush?"

"Back here, Troy."

Troy entered. "Just got back from the pileup. Drove by. Saw your vehicle and the door wide-open. What happened? Where's Nora?"

"I don't know. Nora took off about thirty minutes ago. I came looking for her. I found Hailey like this. Could you check the chalet for me? I'll stay here with Hailey."

And hope she didn't die. Hope that Nora was out there and safe.

Nora entered the ballroom as the power died. She'd thrown on boots and run through the snow and ice to the party to get help for Hailey. Throngs of people gasped and moaned and groaned over the inconvenience of the power outage. Candlelight from the tables illuminated the rooms. Why wasn't the generator on? Where was Dad?

Hailey needed medical attention, but Nora feared she was already dead. She had no pulse that Nora could find.

Nora pushed through the people, looking for Rush or Troy. Someone who might be able to help her, but she couldn't find anyone. Her mind raced as panic took over.

Her purse was in the office. She'd get her phone and call Rush. Call 911. Something! Anything! She hated leaving Hailey there all alone and bleeding, but she also had to get some kind of help.

She headed for the stairwell leading to the offices. As she opened the door to the stairs, a hand grabbed hers. Dan stood dressed in his tux. "I've been looking for you."

"Dan, I don't have time to talk right now. Hailey's... Hey, is your dad here? Do you have a radio by any chance?"

His eyes clouded over and he seemed to be agitated. "Dad? No... I mean yes, he's... Nora, we have to talk."

"Fine, but talk fast." She bounded down the stairs, Dan right behind. "What's going on?" She raced for Dad's office.

Inside, she flipped on the light out of habit. No power. Only a trace of moonlight filtering through the windows. Dan grabbed her arm.

"Hey!" she yelled. "What is wrong with you?"

Dan's face turned eerie in the low light. Nora got a sick feeling in her gut. "Nothing. It's... I... I have to talk... I'm..."

"Dan, you're scaring me. Let go of my arm. Right now."

The lights flickered.

Flickered again.

Stayed on! Landlines might be working now. She grabbed the phone and Dan yanked it from her, slamming it back on the cradle. "I need to talk to you! Are you not hearing me?"

Sweat slicked Dan's face; his glazed eyes darted around the room.

All Nora wanted was to get help for Hailey. "Dan, my sister is hurt. I need to call in some help." She held her hands up, every bone in her body trembling. "Calm down. We can figure this out."

"That's the problem, Nora. You have to try to figure everything out." His eyes darkened and he stepped toward her. Fear iced her heart. "Why did you have to go digging into your mom's death?"

FIFTEEN

Rush held pressure on Hailey's wound and prayed she would make it. This was his fault. If he'd sped up the investigative process like Nora wanted, if he'd pressed Dad for information like she'd asked sooner and more often, they might have found out about Gary Plenk earlier. But he hadn't. He'd been too afraid of stepping on toes and making mistakes. How would Nora ever forgive him for this?

"Hang in there, Hailey. You have a little boy that won't be ready to see his mama go. Fight."

Sirens signaled the arrival of ambulances and Troy bounded into the bedroom. "No sign of her in the chalet, Rush."

Either she'd been taken or... He couldn't think of what might be the worst-case scenario. "By any chance have you been up to the ball?"

"Earlier, why?"

"Did you happen to see Gary Plenk?" *Hang in there, Hailey.* She was too pale. Too still.

"Saw his wife, so I assume he's up there. Why? You want to call him down here or something?" Troy glanced toward the front of the house as the sirens grew louder.

"No." His dread grew. Gary was here. He had access to Nora. "He doctored the death certificate, and he might have Nora right now. Hired someone to take her—hurt her."

Troy's eyes narrowed. "And how would you know that? You talk to him? He admit it?"

"No. I found out before I arrived. I sent the report to a friend in Shelby County."

First responders entered the house. Rush stepped aside and let them do their job. Fear coursed through his veins. Putting her on a gurney, they took her from the home.

"Why would you do that?"

"Because Nora still wasn't sold on the fact that you aren't the one coming after her." Rush's cheeks heated even saying it.

"Nora or you?" Troy demanded.

Rush shook his head. Right now, all that mattered was Nora. "Put a BOLO out for Plenk."

"And what if he's not the man who has her? You put out a BOLO, people are gonna talk."

"Let them talk." Rush wasn't going to let his fear interrupt his job or stop him from finding the only woman he'd ever loved ever again. "I'm heading up to the ball. Call it in, Troy. Now."

Troy licked his upper lip.

"Troy, what is it? I don't have time. Nora could die!"

Raking a hand through his hair, Troy dropped his head. "Gary Plenk did doctor those records."

Troy knew? "Why didn't you say something?"

He raised his head, met Rush's eyes and nothing but

shame filled them. "Because I told him to do it, or I'd expose the fact that he'd had an affair with Marilyn."

Rush felt the weight of his words, the betrayal, and it knocked him back a step. "Why?" It made no sense. Unless Troy had lied and did have an affair with Marilyn. Had he seen her kissing Gary Plenk that night and killed her? "What did you do, Troy?" He slowly placed his hand on his holster. "And where is Nora?"

"Don't go getting trigger-happy, Rush." Troy held up his hands. "I didn't hurt Marilyn."

"But you were having an affair with her. You lied." And he hadn't responded to the question about Nora. It was a like a nest of merciless wasps had descended on him.

"I didn't lie. I never had an affair with her, but I knew the truth about her. She'd had too much to drink one night at Mac's and she'd been crying. She told me she had escaped from a man who wanted her dead. Sometimes she got scared and bailed, but she always came back. I told her I could help her, but she clammed up. That night at the Christmas Eve Masquerade Ball I went to talk to her about it again. I found her in the office."

"With Gary Plenk?"

"No. Alone. She was crying."

Before or after Rush spotted her kissing Gary?

"So what happened?"

"I hugged her. Told her whatever had happened would be okay and that it was time for her to come clean about everything, that I'd help her. She promised to come see me the day after Christmas. But she vanished."

"Why blackmail Gary then, Troy? Why didn't you tell what you knew about Marilyn back then...or in this investigation? You never even tried to find the man you thought was after her?" Which was Scott Rhodes. "How could you? They have the right to know that Marilyn was murdered. And where. Is. Nora?"

"Because I was protecting my son, Rush."

Protecting Dan?

Troy's eyes brimmed with tears. "He made a mistake, Rush. That's all, and I couldn't let it ruin his life forever. What kind of dad would that make me?"

Rush's blood turned cold. "What kind of mistake?"

"That night, he caught me embracing Marilyn in the office. He got the wrong idea and instead of confronting me, he followed Marilyn. Confronted her at the lake. They got into a heated argument. He didn't want her wrecking his family—he'd already been broken by Tina moving away. He blamed Marilyn for that as well."

The stunning reality hit Rush. "He hit her with the crowbar."

Troy sadly nodded. "When he realized he'd killed her, he panicked and sent her car into the waters with Marilyn inside."

What was Marilyn doing at the lake in the first place? "The cuff link and mask we found in the car?"

"Dan's."

Too much of the mask had been unrecognizable, or Rush would have known earlier. "You let it go?" Rush hollered.

"I didn't even know for about a month. It ate him up until he had a breakdown and confessed it. By that time, she wasn't going to be found and no one was asking questions anymore." One shoulder lifted in an apologetic shrug. "I let it go to save my boy. I had to."

"You broke the law. You're an accomplice after the

fact. He was seventeen. He could have been tried as a child, Troy, and you know it!"

"Marilyn ruined lives and probably had a criminal past—fleeing from some dangerous man. She was gone and people were glad. Even Joshua didn't do much to find her!"

Rush gaped at his mentor. "Are you saying Dan has done all of this and you've been helping him?" He balled a fist.

"I haven't hurt anyone and I wasn't sure it was Dan at all until recently. He's been acting just like he did after he…after he did what he did."

What he did was second-degree murder.

"I don't want anybody else to get hurt."

A little late for that. "Where is Dan? Does he have Nora? And don't lie to me!"

"I don't know."

With Nora out of the way, and if Rush believed every word Troy said, Dan would have once again skated by with murder, and Troy would have once again been an accomplice after the fact. Without them discovering the truth about Gary Plenk, Troy would have never confessed.

He was thankful Nora hadn't given up.

"Where is Dan? I won't ask again."

"He's here at the party with Ainsley. Nora is safe."

"Nora hasn't been safe since she set out to discover the truth. And Hailey has been shot. Clearly, you're wrong. You and I will deal with this later, Troy. For now, find Joshua and tell him his daughter has been shot and is at the hospital. And if Dan's so much as laid one finger on Nora, I won't hesitate to put him in the ground and you too if you try to stop me." Rush flew from the house and jumped inside his Bronco. He'd deal with the hurt and betrayal later. At this moment, all he could think about was Nora and getting to her before it was too late.

"Dan, you want to talk. Let's talk." Nora backed toward the desk, hoping to get her cell and dial 911 while keeping Dan calm in the process. Fear zipped up her back, leaving a wake of chill bumps, but she found her clutch with her phone inside and slipped it into her hand. Dan didn't seem to notice. "What do you mean by asking why I dug into my mom's murder?"

Dan peeked out the door as if someone might be coming to interrupt him.

The power flickered again.

"Help me understand." Could Dan be involved? "Did you see my mom the night she died, Dan?" She crept toward the credenza by the door. If she could get to the door, she could bolt. Dan was unstable, unhinged. Warning bells rang in her head.

"I didn't mean to, Nora," he mumbled.

"You didn't mean to what?" Fear paralyzed her.

"I didn't mean to kill your mama. I just... I got so mad. I was in love with Tina and when her mom moved away with her, you know how hurt I was."

Dan admitted to murdering Mom. Nora's jaw dropped, but she recovered quickly. Anything to survive what might be about to happen. Admission meant he had no intention of letting her live. "I did know how hurt you were. I was so sorry about that. I liked Tina."

"It was your mom's fault, so when I saw my dad hugging her that night... I lost it. I mean... You can understand that, right?"

Troy did have an affair? He lied? "I can. Yes." She barely inched toward the door.

"I just wanted to talk to her. To tell her to leave my dad alone but she kept denying that they were involved. But I saw it with my own eyes! I grabbed the crowbar from the back of my truck and I..."

Nora didn't want to hear another word. Couldn't.

"I didn't mean it."

She took another small step.

"Where are you going?" Dan asked, and moved toward her. "You can't go anywhere, Nora. You can't leave this office. You don't understand."

The power flashed again and died.

Dan lunged.

Nora shrieked and grabbed a crystal paperweight on the credenza, bringing it down on Dan's head. He went limp and crumpled facedown on the floor. She only hoped he wasn't dead but knocked out. She wasn't planning on sticking around to find out, though. Once she found Rush, they could call an ambulance if it wasn't too late.

She tore from the office and into the hallway. "Lord, help me!" she whispered and kept running, tripping over her ball gown and boots.

She yelped as a figure appeared in front of her.

Dressed in a glittery midnight blue gown and matching mask, Ainsley Parkwell-Parsons stood with a gun in hand. "Where do you think you're going?"

Nora froze. "I— Ainsley, Dan—" Was she protecting Dan?

"Dan is an idiot," Ainsley said. "He's made one mistake after another. I'll deal with him. Right now, I'm going to deal with you."

"Rush knows!" Nora lied through her teeth hoping Ainsley would be too scared for whatever her intentions might be.

Ainsley gave her a look that stopped Nora in her tracks. "Rush might know Dan murdered your mother, maybe. And he might think that Dan's been coming after you to shut you up. Which means Rush only knows a half-truth. Give me that purse."

Blood whooshed in Nora's temples and her skin froze over, but she complied and tossed her clutch.

What was the half-truth?

"You make me sick. You have everything!" Ainsley used the gun to motion Nora back toward the offices. "The perfect life. Did you know that my dad owned this property before your precious savior of a father rescued him from debt and purchased it? I should be living on this mountain! I should have been the bright and shining star, not the girl always struggling financially."

"I—I didn't know."

"Of course not. You were too busy living a perfect life. With the perfect father. The perfect boyfriend. You should have never come back. I had what I wanted and you took him."

Rush? She wanted Rush? And a perfect life? Seriously?

"Where is Dan? I know he came after you. To warn you."

Warn her? Nora pointed toward Dad's office. "He's in there. He's…unconscious."

Ainsley forced her into the office. The sliver of moonlight only gave them a silhouette of Dan. He lay on the floor, blood surrounding his head, but he moved. He was alive! *Thank You, God!*

"He needs medical attention, Ainsley." Maybe she'd help her husband, forget Nora for a second and give her a chance to escape.

"No, he doesn't." She aimed the gun and fired, shooting Dan in the head.

Nora opened her mouth but a scream wouldn't leave her lips. Ainsley murdered her husband in cold blood, then she turned the gun on Nora. "Out the office exit. Now."

"You just killed your husband!" Nora held her hands up and walked on shaky legs toward the office exit that led up the steps and into the employee parking lot.

Ainsley forced her into the blizzard. Snow barreled down; the wind whipped against her dress. Ainsley didn't seem to be affected in her ball gown and ballet flats. Rage and homicide must be keeping her warm. Nora's teeth chattered.

"See that red car? Move."

"I don't understand," Nora said through trembling lips. "Why did you kill Dan? Why do you think I have a perfect life? Did you ever meet my mom?" The irony wasn't lost on Nora. "You have no idea how hard I've fought to not be the daughter of Marilyn Livingstone. You don't know how I feel. You only see what's on the outside and it's all been a lie, Ainsley. I'm not perfect. I'm an impostor." But she didn't want to be.

Ainsley pulled her keys from a hidden pocket on her evening gown and pressed a button. The trunk opened. "Get in. We're going for a ride."

"Where? Why? Rush is going to know that Dan didn't do this to me when they find him in the office. He's dead."

Ainsley's smile turned vile and malicious. "No, dear, he won't."

Nora looked down and gasped. Another body was already in the trunk. Dressed all in black. Nora recognized the coat and ski mask and build. "Who is this?" This man was the one who had repeatedly attacked Nora. "Dan didn't try to kill me?" Confusion wrapped around her brain, turning it foggy.

"No. Dan didn't try to kill you. He trusted his dad to keep things quiet and make this go away, and he would have if you hadn't shown up once again wrecking it all—wrecking my life. You had my childhood life. You had the man I wanted. And now you want to take my husband!"

"You just killed your husband!"

"I had to." Malicious eyes bore into Nora's. "You made him so crazy with your snooping, he went off the rails. Was going to confess to what he did all those years ago. I've learned if you want something, you have to take it. Make it happen. But when I started making things happen, he figured it out and he wanted to turn me in too!"

That's what Nora didn't understand according to Dan. He wasn't trying to kill her. Ainsley had been doing it all this time. He was there to rat her out and reveal his crime also. The guilt had been too much for him to bear.

Ainsley's long red hair whipped across her face, but she didn't shiver. "I'm about to make everything good that should have happened to me then, happen now."

Nora shook her head, confused. She stared at the man in her trunk. "Is this man…is he dead?"

"Do you see him breathing? Get in."

Ainsley wanted her to get in the trunk with a dead man. No.

"I can shoot you right here, Nora, but I find it poetic to make it happen where it all started. Where I found you in Rush's arms. You're no better than your mother. You don't deserve the perfect life you've been given. You don't deserve Rush. And when this is all over, when they discover that Dan hired this guy to kill you, he turned on Dan and killed him, then killed you, Rush will need comforting and so will I."

Ainsley. She hired this man to threaten Nora. Then to kill her when the threats wouldn't work. At first to help keep Dan's secret. But then… Revenge?

"You need a straitjacket not comfort!" Nora screeched. Her words were returned with a slap to her face.

"Get in!"

Nora slowly eased beside the corpse of the man who had once tried to murder her. "Who is he?"

"A brother of one of my students. Low-life drug dealer. No one special. But he botched the job mistaking your sister for you. Imagine my disappointment when I saw you alive and well heading for the stairwell." She put her hand on the trunk to close it. "So again. If you want something done, you do it yourself. Here I am."

She slammed the trunk shut and Nora heard the car start, then it moved. She could lie here and cry and re-main confused or she could figure out how to stay alive. First off, she needed protection from the elements. The cold already worked through her bones, creating a stiff-ness in her joints. She rolled on her side, facing the dead man. Overcoming the fear of being next to him, she whispered an apology and rifled through his pockets.

Pocketknife. She took it and slid it down the top of her dress, then she removed his gloves and ski mask, his lifeless eyes staring back at her. She jerked and closed her eyes but used his ski mask as a hat and donned the leather gloves that had once wrapped around her throat.

Rush wouldn't let her out of his sight for long. Already, he had to be searching for her. Maybe he'd found Hailey, gotten her help. If she was actually alive. He'd find Dan dead and know someone had taken Nora when she was nowhere to be found.

Once they discovered this man, they'd connect the dots between Dan and him. No matter what scenario played out, no one would suspect Ainsley.

She'd be the grieving widow.

And Rush would be a grieving man. He'd feel guilty and responsible.

The horrifying truth smacked into her.

Nora's and Dan's deaths would bond Rush to Ainsley. Which was exactly what she wanted. To grieve together, comfort one another, form a new relationship—one she hoped would turn into a romance.

I've learned if you want something, you have to take it. Make it happen.

Rush would never suspect Ainsley. He'd dated her once. So there had to have been some kind of attraction there in the first place.

Tears filled Nora's eyes. Rush would always remember her leaving him. He'd always remember her back not her face.

God, help me. If I make it through this, help me change. Help me...help to run to You. Then give me the strength to go through the hard times, to hear the hard truths.

She had run. Away from God. From the people who loved her. Over and over. And all for what? So she could die alone in a blizzard because some crazy woman thought Nora had a perfect life. Perceptions were dangerous. She'd falsely perceived the way others thought of her and it had kept her insecure and hiding. There were so many things she wished she could go back and change, but it was too late.

Too late to tell Rush she'd made a dozen mistakes. If he were here now, she'd open up and tell him anything and everything he wanted to know. He was right about that too—two people had to communicate and be open and honest with one another.

She'd unlock everything she'd locked away after Mom died. She wouldn't bail. God would help her stay. Help her stick it out.

The car stopped.

The trunk opened and the barrel of the gun pointed at her head.

SIXTEEN

Rush blew through the main doors and into the ballroom. Candles illuminated the room. The band played and guests danced as if there wasn't a blizzard outside, and like the power wasn't totally out.

If Dan had hurt Nora…

He pushed his way through the crowd.

Gary Plenk.

Rush's fury burned hot. He'd deal with him soon enough. He asked locals if they'd seen Nora. Gary's wife spoke up. "I saw her going toward the stairwell earlier tonight. Dan Parsons was with her."

No.

"Thank you." He raced into the stairwell and hurtled down the stairs, then sprinted to Joshua's office.

Dan lay on the floor with a bullet wound to the back of the head.

Oh, no. Wait. Nora wasn't a killer and didn't have a gun. Someone else must have done this and taken Nora. But who?

Troy burst in behind him. "Joshua is at the hospital with Hailey. What can I do? I have to help do—" His sight landed on his son and he sank to his knees. "Dan!

Oh, Dan!" He felt for a pulse but Rush knew what Troy surely deep down did. Dan was dead. If Dan wasn't the masked killer who had been attacking Nora, then someone else was in on it with him and somehow a struggle or something had taken place.

Troy continued repeating Dan's name.

Rush used Troy's radio on his shoulder and called it in, though it was far too late for an ambulance.

"I'm so sorry, Troy. Do you have any idea who might have done this?"

"No. Dan murdered Marilyn and he's been acting antsy lately. Especially the past couple of days. I had a hunch he was the one after Nora."

"But you never confirmed it with Dan?"

"No. He called me earlier this morning and told me he needed to talk to me, to tell me something. Get some advice. I assumed it was to confess what he'd been doing. I told him I'd take care of it and I thought I had. I guess he got scared."

"So who would do this? Because it wasn't Nora. Does anyone else know what Dan did all those years ago?" Gary was here; couldn't be him. Dan could have hired someone to do the dirty work and he killed Dan. But who? Was there anyone who might know anything? "Does Ainsley know?"

"Doubtful."

Dan was dressed in a tux, which meant he'd come to the party as a guest. "Troy." He laid a hand on his shoulder. "I'm sorry. I have to find Ainsley." She might know something Troy didn't.

"Go," he whispered. "I'm gonna stay here with my boy." His voice faltered. His sobs echoed through the quiet hall.

Inside the ballroom, throngs of people danced and milled around in masks. He had no time to waste. He went straight to the stage and took the microphone. He paged Ainsley but she didn't respond, didn't come forward. He left the stage. Who had Nora? Where would he have taken her?

Rush's heart pounded until it nearly beat out of his chest.

Gary Plenk approached. "I saw Ainsley earlier."

"You sure? Because we both know you're prone to lying." He glared until Gary had no way of denying that Rush now knew the truth.

Gary's face blanched. "I was backed into a corner, Rush. I made a mistake. I got back on the straight and narrow patch and haven't so much as looked at another woman. It would kill my wife to know."

"I don't care why you did you what you did. You're going to answer for lying about documents, but right now, tell me where you saw Ainsley."

"She was looking for Nora. My wife told her she was with Dan, like she told you. I haven't seen her since."

Maybe this crazed killer had Nora and Ainsley!

Or…

A more chilling thought grabbed him by the throat.

Could Ainsley be behind this? No. No way. But then he never imagined Dan would be a killer either. If Ainsley knew Dan was a killer, she'd have done whatever to help protect him. But who killed him?

"Rush." Troy ran toward him. "I found this outside the office." He held up a midnight blue mask with silver sequins. "It's Ainsley's. She drove separate tonight. I had two deputies check the lot for her car. It's not here."

Either the killer took them both hostage in Ainsley's

car or Ainsley wasn't so innocent. "You think Ainsley has Nora? You think she killed Dan? Why?" Rush couldn't quite make the puzzle pieces fit.

"I know she didn't like Nora. Talked about her on occasion."

Then she hadn't put the past behind her.

If she took Nora, she couldn't have gotten far. Not with these weather conditions.

"Get everyone on the roads. We have to find them." *God, help us find her. Show us where to go.*

Ainsley stood over Nora, gun in hand. "I see you've warmed up. Don't you know dead bodies never stay that way? Out."

Nora climbed from the trunk of the car, her legs nearly numb from the weather. She glanced around. They were at Lookout Tower, which opened up to the Great Smoky Mountains. Any other day it would be breathtaking.

"You're going to shoot me? You can sleep at night knowing you're a murderer?"

"I'm counting on Rush's warm arms to keep me safe. I'll sleep like a baby."

"You're underestimating Rush. One, he will figure it out, and two, he was going to break up with you long before we had a thing. But go ahead and think otherwise—most delusionals do."

She was aggravating the situation, but if Ainsley thought Nora was going to roll over and go out without a fight—even a verbal one—she had another think coming.

Ainsley put the barrel of the gun to her head again. "I'd watch your mouth. Now, get him out of the trunk.

You can do it. If I could get him in, you can get him out."

"Why?"

"Because he brought you here to kill you. You struggled. You shot him. But he got the gun before he died and he got you. You both died. It's tragic. Really."

Nora dragged the man to the lip of the trunk and struggled, but got him on the ground. As he landed something fell from his waistband.

A phone!

She bent to get a grip under his arms and snatched the phone. It was an older model. If she could find a way to call Rush without Ainsley noticing the light of the phone, he might be able to make it in time, and if not, he'd at least know she'd tried. The wind cracked a branch on a tree and Nora ducked as a limb fell.

Discreetly, she removed her right glove as she dragged him along the gravel. Tucking the phone in the folds of his heavy shirt, she dialed. Thankful his number was ridiculously easy. Sliding her thumb along the side of the phone, she turned the volume down so Ainsley wouldn't hear. The wind helped with noise control as it howled and whistled through the trees, bending them in odd angles. Any minute one might come down on them. Snow covered her hair, fell onto her eye lashes.

"Now what?" she asked and glanced down. Rush answered! "Why kill me at Lookout Tower, Ainsley? Shouldn't this be a reminder of what you lost? Don't you think Rush will figure out your plan?"

Hear me, Rush!

"Billy will take the fall for the murder. Are you a dunce, Nora? What am I thinking? You left a man like Rush not once, but twice, and if you weren't going to die tonight, third time's a charm. You're the dumbest woman I know."

"Billy. So that's the name of the man you hired to kill me. Well, at least I have a name to a dead face."

"Drop the body there."

Nora released the body to the ground in a way that kept the phone from being exposed.

This was the end. Rush wouldn't be able to get to her in time. And she couldn't hear him if he was speaking on the other end of the line.

Headlights shone in the distance.

Ainsley whipped her head in that direction.

Nora pounced on the open opportunity and charged her, grabbing for the gun.

The lights came closer.

Nora struggled to get the gun, the wind not helping as it knocked her off balance. She and Ainsley fell to the snowy ground.

A car door slammed.

"Ainsley!" Rush called.

Ainsley turned.

"Run! Run, Nora!"

The gun went off, startling Nora. Then Ainsley kicked her and she slipped over the edge of the mountain, screaming.

Rush watched in horror as his future tumbled over the mountain, unsure if she'd been hit with a bullet. He raced to the edge. A splitting noise cracked through the night and before he could be sure what was happening a tree branch fell, knocking him down and his breath from his lungs, pinning him in the snow.

Nora! He had to get to Nora. To see if she was even

alive. Moisture burned behind his eyes. What if she was lying down there bleeding out? Bones broken.

Legs. He couldn't feel his legs. Couldn't move anything but his arms. He pushed on the huge limb but it wasn't budging.

Nora had found a way to call him. He'd only been about five minutes from Lookout Tower when the call came.

He'd heard Nora loud and clear but she hadn't heard him on the other end of the line. Hadn't heard his promise to come for her. To rescue her. That he loved her.

He hadn't rescued her. He hadn't been in time.

Rush fought and struggled but it was no use. He couldn't get the monstrous branch off his body.

"Hello, Rush."

Ainsley stood over him.

"Ainsley, help me."

"Why are you here?" She blinked as if they were chatting over lunch.

"Why do you think?"

Her eyes narrowed. "And that's why I won't help you. You're a liar and a cheater and the only reason you want out from under that tree is to see if you can save your precious Nora. Well, guess what? You can't. She's lying down there dead as a rock. But don't worry, you'll meet her soon."

"And what exactly will you tell Troy?" His gun was out of reach. If he could get her closer he might be able to get a hold on her, choke her out, but that didn't help him out from under the tree.

"That Billy Arnold kidnapped me and Nora. Killed Nora, shot me. I'll have to shoot my leg or something, I guess. You showed up and this tree fell on you and he shot you too. I'm the lone survivor. For once I'll be in the spotlight and beloved by all and not Nora. High time."

Rush didn't have the fight to tell her how many plot holes were in that story. Troy wasn't stupid, just blinded by love for his son. He'd sniff the truth out before Ainsley realized she'd have gun powder residue on her hands.

"I loved you, Rush. I've loved you since seventh grade when you climbed a tree to rescue my cat. Kinda fitting a tree is between us now. Did you ever love me?"

Rush closed his eyes. Here came the kill shot. Because he wasn't going to lie. He couldn't.

Nora's lungs burned and she was pretty sure she'd broken more than one rib. Her entire body convulsed in pain. She tasted blood in her mouth but she was alive and bullet-free. Ainsley had missed. But she thought she'd heard another gun go off.

Which meant Rush might be dead, but Nora wasn't going to lie here and do nothing. She wasn't going to burrow into the snow and let it rob her of her life. She wouldn't cut loose now. Army crawling toward the side of the mountain, she gripped a tree branch and pulled herself up, clawing and struggling to make it to the top.

Soaked hair, clothes and feet, her fingers and toes numb, she kept fighting to reach Rush. She'd take a bullet, a knife, being mowed over by a car even; it didn't matter. All she could think about was falling into his arms.

Dead or alive.

God, let him be alive.

She had skidded and slipped down the mountain,

losing a boot and ripping her dress, her skin frostbit and everything that wasn't numb ached, but she forged ahead until she made it to the top.

Ainsley stood over Rush.

A tree! He was pinned down.

Wind howled. Trees swayed until they nearly touched the ground. She hunted for something. Found a large piece of wood and snatched it up as she fought for every step; every breath felt like knives stabbing her as she inched closer and closer to Ainsley. But she would not leave even if he'd begged her to go. She'd die fighting for Rush. For them.

For love.

"No, Ainsley. I'm sorry," Rush said. "I've always loved Nora. It's always been her. It will always be her." It didn't take much light to see the fire in Ainsley's eyes at his rejection. At his truth. Maybe he should have lied. But Ainsley would have seen that too.

A shadow behind Ainsley caught his eye.

"I hoped your answer would be different."

She aimed.

The shadow from behind raised its arm and brought something down hard on Ainsley's head. She toppled into the snow, unmoving.

"Rush!" Nora cried, and fell to her knees beside him.

"Nora?" She was alive. She was the shadow. "How? Wait…get the gun, Nora Beth."

She scurried through the snow and grabbed Ainsley's gun. "Tell me what to do, Rush." She studied the tree. "I don't know if I can move it. But I'll try."

This woman had climbed half a mountain bloodied

and broken for him. Instead of making herself scarce like he'd told her to, she'd saved him. On her own.

"Get my radio. It fell." She felt under his legs until she found it lodged in the snow. She gave him the radio and he called it in. Nora ran her hands through his wet hair. "Go get in the car, Nora Beth. Turn it on and try to get warm."

"No," she protested.

"Nora, you're injured. It's freezing. Go get in the car."

"No!" She stroked his cheek. "I'm not leaving you again. No matter what. Understand? I'm. Not. Leaving."

"Not even for Florida?" he asked and tried to smile, but even that hurt.

"Not even for Florida. I want to stay. If you can forgive me. If you love me enough to try one last time." She sniffed. "Because I love you. I don't want to keep secrets or hide things away. And I don't want to run. Not anymore. Not even to your car. I'm done running from everything. From you, especially."

He grabbed her hand and kissed it. "I love you, Nora Beth. Don't go to Florida. Stay here. With me. For always."

Sirens wailed.

"For always."

"Nora Beth?"

"Yeah," she whispered, and tottered.

"Merry Christmas, love."

"Merry Christmas," she said, and collapsed in the snow.

SEVENTEEN

Nora stood in Dad's kitchen. Tomorrow was New Year's Eve and Nora was thankful that in this new year she would live and so would Rush and Hailey.

Hailey had emergency surgery, spent several days in the hospital, but she was home now, resting in bed. Nora carried a cup of tea to her, limping with the lovely black boot she was stuck with for a while. They'd taped up her ribs, given her pain meds and diagnosed her with a mild concussion. But she'd made it.

So had Rush. Broken leg. Bruised femur. But alive and recovering.

Nora knocked on her sister's bedroom door.

"Come in."

She opened the door. Hailey lay in bed, pale but smiling. Nathan sat next to her. He kissed her forehead and scooted off the bed. "I'm going to check on Dalton. Make sure he's not sitting in cold bathwater. Him and his boats." He patted Nora's shoulder and left.

"I brought you tea."

"Thanks."

"I'm sorry," Nora said.

"You say that every time you look at me. Stop. It's

over, and the truth is that while I'm not thanking God I got shot and almost died, I am thanking Him for causing some good to come from it. Nathan has been by my side since I woke up from surgery. It was a wakeup call for us, and we're going to work things out. We love each other, Nora. I'm not sure we would have let ourselves feel that again had I not almost been gone for good. So stop the sorry bit. Okay?"

She handed Hailey her tea and squeezed her hand. "Okay."

"Nathan told me that Gary Plenk admitted his affair to his wife. She left him. I hope they can work it out."

"I do too."

"And the money in Mom's trunk. Will you be okay not knowing why it was there, Nora?"

Nora sighed. "I've had to learn the hard way that not every question comes with an answer. Some things we have to carry through life not knowing, but trusting that God does and He's got it. Was she blackmailed? Was she taking it to vanish? To abandon us? I don't know. I have to find peace there. We all do. And even if that was what was happening, I know God never leaves us. Never abandons us. He loves us so much. I'm going to rest in that knowledge. Find who I am in the light of who Jesus is. I've never attempted that before."

Hailey snickered and moaned. "What about Billy Arnold?"

"His parents have been notified of his death and that he was being blackmailed by Ainsley. Everyone is grieving in one way or another. But it's a new season. A New Year is upon us."

"And you're staying."

"I am." She'd confessed her debts to Dad and he'd

canceled them. Paid it all for her. No strings attached. Nothing but grace. "I think I'm going to do some private meteorology work. For mountain climbers, et cetera, and I'll keep up the forensic meteorology. Dad said I can stay in the chalet as long as I'd like."

"And Rush?" Hailey asked.

"Rush and I haven't talked turkey yet." She laughed. "We love each other. So far that's enough. I didn't used to think so." She stood.

"What changed?"

"I learned that love truly does cover a multitude of sins—not condones but covers. It can cover faults, flaws and mistakes. God's love. And if His love can do that and He can continually stick with us, then His love can do that through His people to one another." Nora blew Hailey a kiss. "Get some rest."

"Ditto."

Nora left and entered the living room. Rush stood by the hearth. "You feel like a sleigh ride?" He motioned with his chin to the front door. Nora spotted a sleigh outside.

"If you're going, I'll go anywhere with you."

His eyes lit up and he hobbled over. "We're peas in a pod, aren't we?"

"We're something." She grabbed her coat and they managed to get outside and into the sleigh, laughing at their injuries and lack of grace.

Rush covered them with a blanket and took her hand. "Troy's going to have to go to prison, Nora. I know what he did was wrong, but it kills me."

She leaned on his shoulder. "I'm sorry, Rush. What's that mean for you and the department?"

"I'm going to be interim sheriff until it's time to run in the fall."

"You'll make a great sheriff."

He shifted and looked deep into her eyes, stirring an old longing and dream in her heart. "You think I'll make a great husband?"

She swallowed as he reached into his pocket.

"I think you'll make the greatest husband. And father."

He raised an eyebrow playfully. "Oh, yeah?"

"Yeah."

"Nora Beth, I've loved you my whole life. I want to finish it out loving you. Would you marry me?" He opened a velvety box to reveal a round solitaire diamond with small diamonds on each side.

Nora gasped at the beauty of the ring, but more so at the love Rush had for her and the journey it had taken to bring them to this point. "It's all I've ever wanted, Rush. Yes."

He placed the ring on her finger, kissed her knuckle, then framed her face. "You're all I'll ever want." He claimed her lips, gingerly, then more possessive. Pouring into her promise and hope. Like a guarantee of their future together. No running away. Only to each other and to God.

He nuzzled her nose. "I was thinking a Christmas wedding."

"I don't want to wait one more year, Rush. I don't even want to wait another day."

Laughing, he kissed her nose and cheeks. "What I meant to say was, I was thinking of a New Year's Eve wedding. Me, you, our family outside under the pines and my dad officiating. If we can get a license that fast."

"It's Tennessee. Got a valid picture ID?" She laughed.

A few poinsettias around the glorious snow. Family surrounding them. "It's how I want to start the new year, Rush. Married to you. I don't care if we're in boots and bruised. We can have a reception at the lodge in a few weeks and take pictures then. I just want to be your wife. Finally."

"I can't think of anything I want more. I've been praying for this day. Can't say I loved the waiting period, but it was worth it. So worth it."

He gazed into her eyes. The love shining in them reached deep into her soul, warming it like a cozy fire. Life wouldn't always be sunny skies and warm breezes. Storm clouds would roll in. Cold fronts. Maybe even hailstorms.

But Nora would remember when storms came. When the cold crept up, she had a place to run for shelter. In the arms of God.

And into Rush's arms.

For always.

* * * * *

Liz Shoaf resides in North Carolina on a beautiful fifty-acre farm. She loves writing and adores dog training, and her husband is very tolerant about the amount of time she invests in both her avid interests. Liz also enjoys spending time with family, jogging and singing in the choir at church whenever possible. To find out more about Liz, you can visit and contact her through her website, www.lizshoaf.com, or email her at phelpsliz1@gmail.com.

Books by Liz Shoaf

Love Inspired Suspense

Betrayed Birthright
Identity: Classified
Holiday Mountain Conspiracy

Visit the Author Profile page
at Harlequin.com for more titles.

HOLIDAY
MOUNTAIN CONSPIRACY

Liz Shoaf

For the love of money is the root of all evil: which while some coveted after, they have erred from the faith, and pierced themselves through with many sorrows.
—*1 Timothy* 6:10

This one is dedicated to both of my wonderful sisters, Donna Wright and Sherri Stout. You're beautiful, inside and out, and I'm so blessed God chose you to be my sisters here on earth. Growing up was such fun with the two of you. You bossed me around, but you also protected and loved me like no one else ever could. That still holds true today. I love you with all my heart.

And a BIG thank-you to my editor, Dina Davis, who always catches my mistakes. What would I do without you? I don't want to find out. :) And to her boss, Tina, who has final approval of all books. There's a host of people at Harlequin who work on a book from beginning to end. I don't know all your names, but I want to thank you for the hard work you do to make the finished book possible.

ONE

Mary Grace Ramsey breathed out a puff of frigid air as she slogged through the deep, freezing snow. *Treacherous* didn't even begin to describe this mountain located in Jackson Hole, Wyoming. She prayed she'd be able to find the person she was searching for—a mysterious and elusive man known as Mountain Man. Her thoughts came to a screeching halt when a loud muffled sound resonated from down the mountain behind her. Snow flurries swirled in the air as she slowly turned around, trying to make as little noise as possible. She winced when the snow crunched beneath her hiking boots. In the hushed quiet of the forest, the breaking ice under her feet sounded like a cannon shot.

"Tink, did you hear that?" she whispered.

A tuft of white fur, followed by a pink nose, popped out of the nylon dog carrier she had strapped to her chest. Tinker Bell sniffed the air before ducking back inside her cozy quarters.

"Some help you are," Mary Grace grumbled affectionately, but she didn't blame her dog. Mary Grace's own nose felt like an icicle and her toes were freezing to the point of pain. She owned decent outerwear, but nothing in her closet would have kept her warm in this brutal weather.

She strained to hear something, anything, but the vast forest remained quiet. She turned and slowly moved upward, praying earnestly that she was headed in the right direction. Huge pine trees heavy-laden with snow-covered limbs towered above her like skeletons in the waning daylight. Shivering inside her ski jacket, she prayed she'd find Mountain Man soon—and what kind of a name was that?—because there was a real possibility of her and Tink freezing to death if she didn't locate the cabin Sheriff Hoyt had described.

It was her stepbrother's fault that she was in this untenable situation, hiking into the wilderness in the dead of winter. The day after she found the note Bobby had left her, telling her she was in danger and needed to find the Jackson Hole Mountain Man, she'd sensed someone following her. On the way home from a press briefing at the White House that evening, a car tried to run her off the road. It was no accident. She was afraid to contact the police because of the warning in Bobby's note, advising her not to trust anyone inside the Beltway.

She'd tried repeatedly to get in touch with her brother, to no avail. It was as if he'd fallen off the face of the earth. His boss at Langley would only say that Bobby had requested a leave of absence, but as she well knew, the CIA was in the business of keeping secrets. And as a White House press correspondent for FBC, Future Broadcasting Company, it was her job to uncover them.

Mary Grace stopped, took a deep breath and scanned the area. Visibility had dwindled even more. Nothing but snow, ice and trees surrounded her. A deep, scary-looking ravine dropped off to her left. There was no cabin in sight and she was chilled to the bone. What if once she found the cabin, Mountain Man wasn't even there?

With no signal for GPS, she pulled her compass out of her pocket and checked it once again. According to what the sheriff had said, she should be close to her destination.

Tinker Bell popped her head out of her carrier and barked, and a split second later, Mary Grace heard the loud report of a rifle shot echo on the mountain. Before she even had a chance to run, fire ripped through her right side and she was thrown toward the deep ravine.

Her eyes closed as she floated soundlessly through the air. It was an ethereal experience. She wondered if this was what heaven would feel like, all light and buoyant. Pain ricocheted through her body when she forcefully hit the side of the mountain and was once again thrown into the air. Time seemed to slow before she finally landed on her back in a deep snowbank. After she caught her breath, her dire situation came flooding back. She was alive, but the killer was still out there. Slowly, she wiggled her arms and legs to see if anything was broken. Everything was stiff, but no bones screamed in pain. Her dog! She'd only bounced off the mountain once and she prayed her precious baby was okay.

"Tink! Tink? Answer me. Are you okay?"

When she tried to push herself up, pain seared her side. She gently dropped back down and ran her hands across her chest. She breathed a sigh of relief when she identified the dog carrier still attached to her body. She dug inside the nylon bag and grabbed Tinker Bell. Her side burned like fire when she lifted the Chihuahua toward her face, but relief overwhelmed her when Tink snorted and growled.

"You're okay," she breathed and hugged the dog close to her chest. But for how long, was the question. She touched the clothes covering her right side and groaned when her hand came back covered in blood. The reality of their situation was grim.

She and Tink were stranded on a freezing mountain in the middle of winter. She had been shot. No one knew where they were besides the sheriff. She had no way to call him, and there was a killer out there who wanted her dead. The worst thing was that she didn't even know why. *What has my brother gotten me into?*

She tried to push herself up again, but almost passed out from the pain. She fell back into the snow as darkness blanketed the area. At least she and Tink were no longer easy targets with the night shadows and the huge snowbank somewhat hiding them. Maybe the shooter would leave, thinking she was dead.

Time passed, but instead of feeling cold, a circulating warmth enveloped her body. In the recess of her mind, she knew this wasn't a good sign, but her eyelids grew heavy and she didn't seem to care. She wondered if she would soon meet her Maker. Her grandmother's face swam across her mind. Who would take care of the proud, independent older woman if Mary Grace died? Certainly not her own mother and stepfather with their gambling addiction. She didn't even know where they were most of the time.

As she lay there, halfway between sleep and wakefulness, she thought of her latest romantic fiasco. She'd dumped John Stiles after three months of dating. She couldn't seem to make a relationship work, or rather she didn't have a desire to after growing up in the dysfunctional household of her youth.

Now she'd never get married and have a family of her own. She and Tink would die on this beast of a mountain in the middle of nowhere.

A noise pierced the deep slumber she was descending into. It sounded like Tink barking. But maybe it was a dream. Or maybe the killer had found them, after all.

Nolan Eli Duncan, known to the world only as Ned, woke abruptly from a short nap in a cold sweat, fragments of the familiar, recurring nightmare lingering in his mind. The stench of blood and betrayal filled his senses. A soft bleep, bleep sound in the small cabin swept away the remaining splinters of his past, and with minimal movement and sound, he slipped out of bed and pulled on his holey faded jeans. He ignored the sting of the cold wooden floor against his bare feet.

Opening a drawer in the kitchen, he pressed a hidden button. A well-oiled portion of the counter automatically lifted and his laptop and security cameras rose to counter height.

Krieger, his long-coated, old-fashioned giant of a German shepherd, padded softly to his side.

"Security breach. Probably a bear," he grumbled, but his eyes narrowed when he brought up one of several security cameras and went to live feed. A large person dressed in winter fatigues wearing a ski mask came into view. "Or maybe," he whispered, satisfaction flowing through him, "the person who betrayed me and Finn has finally come calling."

He tensed when the guy wearing the fatigues lifted

a high-powered rifle to his shoulder and scanned the woods through the scope. "He's tracking something… or someone, on my mountain."

Krieger went on full alert, ears pricked, ready to move on command. Ned's breath caught when one of the roving security cameras slowly swept past a huge snowbank. Was that blood on the snow? It was getting dark so he switched to night vision. He typed a command on his computer and operated the camera manually. There! He stopped the motion and zoomed in. There were large splatters of blood on the snow. He followed the trail, but the snowbank blocked his view.

Motionless, he stared at the blood, then glanced at the other camera, showing the guy in fatigues creeping closer to the ravine. He turned on the camera's sound.

When a sharp bark pierced his ears, he glanced back at the monitor showing the snowbank. His brows lifted when the smallest rat of a dog he'd ever seen popped onto the top of the snowbank. At least he thought it was a dog. It was solid white and had tattered limp Christmas bows attached to its ears. And if he wasn't mistaken, the dog was also wearing a Christmas sweater. He shook his head at that bit of nonsense and focused on the matter at hand. That meant a person was stranded in the snowbank and his assumption was that the guy in fatigues was an unfriendly.

"Krieger, protect the civilian and dog. I'm right behind you."

With barely a whisper, his dog flew out of the hidden dog door and took off down the mountain. Ned donned his inner and outerwear quickly and opened a concealed panel on the cabin wall. It was all legal, but he'd compiled a small arsenal, waiting for his enemies to come after him.

He slung a long-range rifle across his chest, stuffed a handgun into his pocket and shoved a large knife inside the holster strapped to his calf. He grabbed a first-aid kit and was out the door.

The action wasn't far from his cabin. He didn't know if that was accidental, or if someone was searching for him, but he'd find out soon enough. His long legs and steady tread covered the quarter-mile distance with ease. He'd been living on this mountain off and on for several years and knew every nook and cranny. He'd spent a fortune on security. He had enemies, dangerous enemies.

But that wasn't the only reason he'd holed up on his mountain for months. He had somewhat become a recluse after the betrayal, much to his family's dismay, and he no longer liked, or trusted, most people after everything he'd been exposed to during his clandestine missions. Everyone had an agenda and many would do anything to get what they wanted. He'd be content living by himself on his mountain after he rooted out the worm who had betrayed him and Finn.

He picked up his pace as the thrill of the hunt coursed through him. After all this time, he hoped the carefully laid bread crumbs he'd left several months ago for the betrayer to follow had finally led the person to his mountain for a showdown. Although in reality, he knew the odds were low that the person who originally set the trap would do his, or her, own dirty work.

When he closed in on the coordinates, he slipped his fingers under the cross-body strap and lifted his rifle into his hands. It was second nature and the weapon felt like an extension of his arms. He hid behind a large tree and listened. The soft crunch of boots came from a one o'clock position. He moved, following the sound. Experience had taught him how to walk in the snow without making any noise.

Ned caught sight of the person several hundred yards ahead. He speculated, based on size, that it was a man, but in his line of work, it paid not to make assumptions. He wanted to subdue the person so he could question them, but someone was injured—maybe dying—in that snowbank, and he couldn't take any chances.

At least he had that much humanity left in him. Lifting his rifle—armed with a silencer, he scoped the guy. Even though Finn had lived through their nightmare, a gory vision of Ned's best friend and comrade going down from a gunshot wound flooded his mind. For a split second, he aimed the gun at the man's head, then lowered the barrel and pulled the trigger.

The bullet soundlessly puffed the snow up at the man's feet. The guy's head snapped around and Ned moved from his cover into an open position, his rifle pointed straight ahead. The man's eyes narrowed from behind the slits in the ski mask. Through the scope of the rifle, Ned snapped a mental picture of those blazing violet-colored eyes. He'd recognize them if they met again unless the man was wearing contacts. The guy lifted his own weapon and moved backward, keeping his gun trained on Ned. No question, the guy was a professional. Was he after Ned, or the person lying in the snowbank?

Krieger popped his head over the top of the ravine. Ned gritted his teeth as he allowed the man to get away and followed his dog. He'd probably just blown two months of a carefully planned trap because of the person who had fallen into the ravine.

He scooted down the steep hill and approached slowly. Krieger stood on alert at a caved-in portion of snow, but gave no indication of danger. As Ned stepped closer, the tiny rat dog he'd seen on the security camera at the cabin popped out from behind the freshly disturbed snow. The small dog barked ferociously at Krieger and Ned's fierce, highly trained giant of a German shepherd went into a down position and whined. Ned did a double take. His dog never whined. The little mutt growled when Ned brushed away a mound of snow and discovered what had caused him to miss a possible golden opportunity to get a lead on his betrayer.

He huffed out a frustrated breath. It figured it was a woman. A beautiful woman whose eyelids fluttered open after he jerked off a glove and touched her neck with his cold fingers to see if she had a pulse. In past missions, he'd met women who looked soft and vulnerable, but turned out to be killers in disguise.

Her golden eyes widened in fear seconds before they flooded with determination and fury. "Go ahead and kill me if that's your plan, but you better not lay a hand on my dog."

The woman passed out using the last reserve of her strength to protect the rat. An unexpected ping resonated near the region of Ned's heart, but he ignored it. He pulled his glove back on and started gathering the woman in his arms, but the tiny dog ran toward its owner and buried itself inside the pouch of some kind of dog carrier, similar to a backpack, strapped to her front.

Ned picked her up as if she weighed nothing and started climbing the steep hill. He didn't know how long she'd lain in the snow, but he hoped she wouldn't die. That could complicate matters. He ignored the small flame of hope that had sprung inside his heart when she'd opened her eyes and fiercely tried to protect the dog. Maybe she loved the animal, but there was a reason she'd shown up on his mountain, and it couldn't be good. Everyone had an agenda and he didn't trust anyone outside his family and Finn. Humanity, in his eyes, was a lost cause.

TWO

Mary Grace slowly awoke from that wonderful, murky place somewhere between sleep and wakefulness and winced as she stretched. Her limbs were stiff and her right side burned like fire. She vaguely remembered being on the mountain... The mountain! She'd taken a bullet and had fallen into a ravine.

She shot upright in bed, sucked in a startled breath at the pain in her side and popped her eyes open. She screamed when a large creature that looked way too much like a wolf opened his mouth and big sharp, gleaming white teeth came toward her. She threw up her arms to protect her face, but instead of razor-sharp blades piercing her arm, she felt a rough tongue gliding against her skin.

The ache in her side left her gasping for air and it was in that helpless, vulnerable state that she noticed a bear of a man sitting in a chair facing her, a roaring fire burning in the stone fireplace behind him.

Was this the elusive Mountain Man she'd been trying to locate, or was he the person who shot her on the mountain? Or were they one and the same? Bobby trusted Mountain Man, but she'd rely on her own gut when she figured out who he was. Not that she was in any condition to defend herself or get away if it came down to it.

Her heart racing, she quickly scanned her surroundings and wasn't at all happy with what she discovered. There were two doors in the small cabin. One appeared to be the front door and the other smaller door probably led to a bathroom.

She took a deep breath and locked a steady gaze on the man. She did her best to achieve what Gram Ramsey always advised in that strong, independent, proud Georgian tone of hers, *Always use proper manners, but don't ever let 'em see you sweat. Look like you're strong and know what you're about, even if you're quivering inside like Jell-O.*

She prayed she'd make her grandmother proud and lifted her chin. "Where's my dog?"

The man just sat there and kept staring at her like a knot on a log. The keen observation she was known for in her chosen profession as a journalist went active. The man appeared to be a throwback from mountaineer times. He was huge, really huge, with dark bushy hair that brushed the collar of his plaid shirt. An unkempt beard covered most of his face. Unblinking, razor-sharp green eyes stared back at her. He wore holey ancient jeans. She noticed a heavy fleece jacket hanging on a coat rack placed next to the front door.

He was large, like in a mountain-man-horror-film type of big, which directly opposed the odd tendril of attraction she felt when those green eyes flickered with a small degree of warmth. Her body ached, her side felt like an inferno and testiness quickly replaced any lingering terror.

She ignored her unreliable feelings where men were concerned and blurted out, "I said, where's my dog?" There! That came out sounding firm and in control. At least she hoped it did.

A sound came from a lower wall beside the kitchen counter and a portion of the wall lifted inward, allowing Tinker Bell inside the cabin. Mary Grace's fingers tightened on the plaid blanket thrown over her and she was really wishing she'd brought the gun safely tucked away in her Arlington town house with her.

Her eyes widened when Tink approached the bed and the big wolf dog moved to the side so her baby could hop up beside her. She held Tinker Bell to her chest, closed her eyes and said a quick prayer, asking the good Lord to keep her safe, then took a deep fortifying breath and lifted her lids. She subdued the nervous laughter bubbling up inside her as she wondered if the man had even blinked while her eyes were closed. He hadn't moved a muscle since she'd woken up.

"Who sent you?" His words sounded gruff and rusty, as if he didn't talk much.

"Are you Mountain Man?" She inwardly rolled her eyes. Thus far, they had exchanged a few two-and three-word sentences. Her colleagues would find her situation amusing because she was widely known as a shark disguised as a soft-spoken Southern woman. She had a talent for squeezing every tiny bit of information out of the politicians on Capitol Hill without their even realizing it. She attributed her success to her Southern upbringing, and she didn't think those particular attributes would work on this big, solid mountain man, but she'd give it her best shot.

She dug deep and dredged up a sweet, soft smile. He

couldn't have been the person trying to kill her on the mountain. He'd had plenty of opportunity to do away with her and hide her body while she was unconscious. Her fake smile wavered as she felt the bindings on her side pull and she wondered if this crazy mountain man had patched her up, but she kept her smile in place.

"Why don't we start over. My name is Mary Grace Ramsey, and no one sent me. Well, that's actually not true. My brother did send me, but that's a long story and I need to find a man everyone refers to as Mountain Man. The sheriff in Jackson Hole said people around here call him Ned. He's supposed to help me. But then I got lost on the mountain and someone started shooting—"

"Stop!"

His bellowed word sounded pained and he rubbed his forehead.

"Do you have a headache? Maybe you should take some aspirin. I've always found that—"

"Stop!" he bellowed once again. "Just be quiet for a moment."

Her chattering was already working. This wasn't a simple mountain man. Under duress, his short verbal gruffness had revealed a sophisticated speech with an underlying Scottish brogue.

He closed his eyes for a minute, then blinked them back open. "Are you for real?"

Mary Grace rubbed Tink's head. Time to make good use of her famous interview skills. "I'm not sure how to answer that question, but if you're Ned, then we definitely have several things to discuss, and sooner would be better, considering someone shot me earlier."

Seeing the stunned look on his face, she gave him a big, warm Georgian smile.

He attempted to smile back, but it looked more like a feral grin, throwing her game back in her face. "Who's your brother?"

He had picked out the key part of her chattering, which shouted of intelligence. She'd have to tread carefully around this man.

"Well, technically, he's my stepbrother, but I refer to him as my real brother because we're very close."

His chair slid back as he stood and walked to the side of her bed. Her fingers tightened on Tinker Bell as he towered over her. He was even larger than she had originally thought, but she forced her hands to relax.

"Your brother's name?"

It really made her mad when her hands shook. "Bobby Lancaster."

His eyes narrowed, and his large hands fisted at his sides. Deep, abiding fear sliced through Mary Grace, but she gallantly lifted her chin and glared at him.

He leaned over her and Tink and his long beard tickled her chin, he was so close. "Where is he?" he breathed in an ominous tone.

Fury filled Ned when Bobby Lancaster's name rolled off her lips. It didn't help his disposition that he found the irritating woman beautiful, either. She had light brown hair with sun-kissed streaks winding through the strands, and those golden eyes of hers were enough to bring a man to his knees. He imagined her soft-spoken Southern accent encouraged people, both men and women, to spill all their well-kept secrets.

He refused to fall into her trap.

"Where's Bobby?" Anger made his words sound harsh. He almost regretted his question when she scooted away from him, toward the wall that the bed was pushed against, but he didn't move.

The rat growled, but Ned ignored it until his own dog pushed his way between Ned and the bed. He was stunned. Krieger was protecting the woman and her dog. He growled at Krieger and his dog growled back. He couldn't believe this little slip of a woman had turned his trusted companion against him.

Ned knew his mother would have been appalled at the way he was treating Mary Grace Ramsey, and his dog might have decided to trust her, but that little ping he'd felt in his heart right after she spoke for the first time and defended her rat dog went still. A dark wall of mistrust replaced any minute tender feelings he had allowed himself to feel.

His gut clenched when her lower lip quivered, but he felt justified in his wariness when she pasted on another warm smile.

"I take it you know my brother, and that must mean you're Mountain Man, or rather Ned. I'm so glad I found you. You wouldn't believe what I've been through—"

"Stop!"

Ned backed away from the woman and winced at the expression of relief on her face. Maybe he did need an aspirin. He grabbed the wooden chair from in front of the fireplace, flipped it backward close to the side of the bed and straddled it. He nudged Krieger out of the way, leaned forward and folded his arms across the back of the chair.

"Let's start over. Yes, I'm Ned. I want to know exactly why you're on my mountain and I would highly advise you to tell the truth."

She scrunched up her pert little nose. "My gram would have something to say about your manners and hospitality."

He leaned back in his chair, crossed his arms over his chest and waited. It took less than two seconds. The woman could probably talk the hair off a dog.

"Fine. You know my name. Bobby is my brother, and two days ago I found a note from him that someone had slipped into my tote bag. It said he's in big trouble, but that he's innocent and for me not to trust anyone inside the Beltway or I might get myself killed. That's where I live, you know. Well, not actually inside the Beltway. I have a sweet little town house just outside the city in Arlington—"

Ned couldn't help himself, he released a low growl and she quickly got back on track.

"Sorry, anyway, he told me to contact you, that you're a big part of whatever is going on and that you could protect me. I'm really glad I found you, because besides getting shot here, I'm pretty sure someone tried to run me down in the city. I was afraid to call the police because of Bobby's warning, so here I am."

"Where's Bobby?" Ned now wanted to wring her stepbrother's neck for several reasons. He'd planned to personally interview Bobby if his carefully laid plan to draw the bad guys to his mountain didn't work out, and he'd also wondered if Bobby had been coerced to do what Ned had proof he'd done. Either way, Bobby was involved in the mission that left Ned's best friend in a wheelchair for life and now he'd placed his own sister in danger.

Unless Bobby had sent her to Ned's mountain to finish the job someone had botched in England—to rid the world of Ned and Finn. Another startling question begged to be answered—how had she found him? Only a handful of people knew where he'd holed up.

She picked at a thread on the plaid blanket. "I, um, don't know where Bobby is." She lifted her head and started gabbing again. "And that's the honest truth. I tried calling him and even called his boss at Langley. They said he was on leave. I'm really worried. Bobby and I are pretty close. You see, he was only eight years old when my mama decided to marry his daddy—"

She stopped talking when Ned raised a hand in the air.

"I'm not interested in your life story." He leaned forward again. "How did you find me?"

He could almost see the wheels turning behind those sharp golden eyes. She might act like a silly Southern debutante, but Ned had learned long ago how to cut through a ton of garbage and grab the nugget hidden inside. His gut screamed that she was smart as a whip, and he seldom read people wrong. The question was whether she was telling the truth or planned to slit his throat the first chance she got.

She pulled the thread completely out of the plaid blanket and tossed it to the floor. The fact that she didn't have a ready answer told him she was carefully weighing her words.

"The note Bobby slipped into my bag said I was in serious danger and that I'd be safe with *Mountain Man*, who was currently residing in Jackson Hole. The sheriff gave me directions to this mountain, and I was afraid Tink and I were going to freeze to death before I found you."

She rubbed a hand across the quilt and stared at the unique coloring. "Is this some kind of a special design? Kind of like the tartan colors they use in Scotland?" She glanced around the cabin again. "And speaking of colors, you don't have any Christmas decorations."

Based on the hideous Christmas sweaters the woman and her dog were wearing, Ned assumed she was a big fan of the holiday, but he made sure his expression revealed none of his hidden thoughts. He hadn't celebrated Christmas in a long time.

He studied her a moment longer and a facet of her personality settled in his gut. Her chatter and speech slowed down when she went on a fishing expedition, and she was trying to find out more about him, hence the question about the quilt. She must have picked up on his Scottish accent, which proved her power of observation was keen, but he didn't have time to play games. The man he had allowed to get away was still on his mountain because the perimeter alerts would have gone off if he'd left.

He had to determine if the intruder was after him or Miss Ramsey. Speaking of which...

"Are you married?"

Her head jerked up and her light brown eyebrows scrunched together.

"There's a killer out there and you want to know if I'm married?" Her voice raised several octaves higher.

He didn't see anything wrong with the question. It always paid to know whom you were dealing with. He denied the tiny niggle in his chest telling him he wanted to know for personal reasons. That was preposterous.

This was about finding Bobby Lancaster and dealing with the people who wanted him and Finn dead, and that was it.

He stared at her without blinking.

"Fine, I'm not married, nor have I ever been."

He couldn't stop the next question that shot from his mouth. "Boyfriend?"

She sniffed. She actually sniffed, reminding him of a little old lady.

"Not that it's any of your business, but I don't have a boyfriend. At least I don't have one at the moment."

The tightness in his chest eased and he had no idea why. Her incessant chattering must have scrambled his brain.

"Forget the chitchat. We have a big problem on our hands. I need all the information you can give me. The man who tried to kill you is still on the mountain, and I need to track him down, but first you have to tell me everything."

Those golden eyes narrowed, reminding him of a mother panther getting ready to strike while defending her young.

"Do you think that's why Bobby's in hiding, because someone is trying to kill him, too?"

"You're sticking to what you've told me? You know nothing more?"

Exasperation filled her voice. "I've told you everything. Bobby somehow got me that note, telling me to leave DC and find you. Someone tried to run me down in Washington, and then they tried to kill me on this atrocious mountain."

Ned's mind worked furiously. He tried to think of a way to rid himself of Mary Grace Ramsey, but her brother had pulled her into this mess, and Ned's best opportunity of finding the possible traitor was to keep Bobby's sister as close as possible. Whether major or minor, Bobby was part of what had happened to him and Finn. Whether by choice or not was another matter. Now that Mary Grace Ramsey was in the picture, his plan to lure those responsible to his mountain was trashed. Her brother had now become his only lead and he had to find him.

He rose from the chair, crossed the room and reached for his jacket.

"Where are you going?"

He didn't hear a speck of fear in her voice. It was more of a demand. He had to give her credit, the lady had guts.

He shoved his arms into the sleeves and strapped the high-powered rifle to his chest.

"I'm going hunting."

She winced as she threw her legs over the side of the small cot. "But you can't just leave me here. What if he comes back?" She held out a hand. "Give me a gun." At his lifted brow, she added, "I know how to shoot."

He didn't respond and she lifted her chin. "I'm from Georgia. I know how to handle a weapon."

"I just bet you do, Miss Mary Grace Ramsey. Do you know how to use a knife, too? Do you plan to slit my throat the first chance you get? Are you and your brother working together to get rid of me and Finn?" He didn't really think she was there to kill him, especially after she'd been shot trying to find him, but he threw out the question to gauge her reaction.

Her mouth dropped open and Ned wanted to believe she was innocent in all of this, but he'd learned a long time ago that an innocent face could hide a host of danger.

"You're a very rude man, Ned."

His lips curled upward at the corners. It was an odd sensation. One he hadn't felt in a long time.

He placed his hand on the latch to open the solid wooden door, but stilled when Krieger released a low dark growl. Ned sprang into action. "Krieger, to the cellar," he commanded. He was by Mary Grace's side within a few strides. He scooped her into his arms and ran to the back of the cabin.

"Wait," she screeched. "I don't know what's going on, but you have to get Tinker Bell, the dog carrier and my backpack."

Ned shifted Mary Grace to his left side, holding her like a football, wincing when she gasped in pain, and in one fell swoop he ran his arm through the straps of both packs on the floor, grabbed the dog by the scruff of the neck and kicked a lower panel on the back inside wall of the cabin. A portion of the wall lifted just as a huge explosion rocked the small structure.

Ned practically dove into the yawning darkness below as a bright orange detonation took place at the front of the structure and his cabin shook under the force. The woman was screaming and squirming in his arm and her rat dog bit his hand while he was trying his best to save them. He had a sinking feeling in his gut that this whole mess wasn't going to end well.

THREE

Throwing up became a real possibility for Mary Grace. She gritted her teeth against the pain in her side as Ned held her tight with one arm while running down a flight of stairs into total darkness. She couldn't believe someone had bombed the cabin. Was there more than one man following her on the mountain? She was used to reporting the news, not being part of it.

"Hang tight. We should be okay. The cabin is built with reinforced steel under the wood."

She couldn't respond. Air hissed through her teeth until he gently placed her on the floor. She took a deep breath as a lantern flickered to life. The light reflected on Ned's fierce, concerned expression and she took another quick breath to calm herself. A mass of emotions roiled through her. Fear and—she couldn't believe it under the circumstances—still that annoying attraction to the man currently hovering over her. It wasn't possible. She barely knew the guy and he had the manners of a warthog, but there it was, the tiniest little flutter in her heart. She ignored it.

Tink whimpered and Ned's big dog trundled over to offer what Mary Grace assumed was comfort. It worked because Tinker Bell quit shivering and growled when the massive dog licked her on the face. The limp and tattered Christmas bows had disappeared and her sweet little dog looked like a wrung-out dishrag in her previously pristine doggy Christmas sweater.

Tentatively, Mary Grace reached out and laid a hand on the large animal next to her little one. "Sweet Krieger. Nice doggy." He allowed her to pet him. His fur was long and felt wiry to the touch.

"Mary Grace," Ned said in a soft tone, "I'm going to have to recon the area. I bandaged your wound before you woke up, but I need to check and see if it started bleeding again."

Mary Grace didn't want to talk about the explosion and the men who had just tried to decimate them. Not just yet. She needed a minute. "When we get through this, you'll have to tell me how you and Krieger met. He seems like a sweet dog, once you get to know him."

Ned kneeled in front of her and placed the lantern on the hard, cold dirt-packed floor.

"I was wrong about you."

Her hand stilled in Krieger's wiry, comforting fur. "What?"

"I thought you were tough, but here you are, wimping out on me at the first sign of trouble."

Her nostrils flared at the insult. "You don't know anything about me, so how dare you accuse me of being a wimp."

He grinned and she realized he had done the same thing to her that his dog had to Tinker Bell.

"I can check my own wound," she said, embarrassment threading through her words.

Mary Grace lost her train of thought when he smiled

again, revealing a set of perfectly aligned, sparkling white teeth. The man definitely wasn't what he appeared to be and her reporter's curiosity was roused. Maybe she'd do a piece on him once they were out of this mess. He had a closet full of secrets and she could literally smell a story.

"I didn't know you were modest." He actually chuckled. "Don't worry, the bullet went straight through the fleshy part of your waist. Even though you bled a good bit, it's not a serious wound."

"Easy for you to say."

He stood and towered over her before reaching for something under the staircase. He came out with a pistol and handed it to her. "You said you knew how to use one of these."

She grasped the gun and looked it over. "SIG Sauer P38. Perfect."

He chuckled one more time before climbing the stairs. Over his shoulder, he issued a command. "Krieger, protect the woman and dog."

Before she could protest, he disappeared silently through the hidden doorway.

Her hand shook as she checked to make sure the gun was locked and loaded. She had done her best to hide her true emotions from Ned. She was not only terrified at the situation she found herself in, but worried sick about Bobby. As far as she knew, her brother was a simple computer analyst with the CIA. They had lured him in straight after school by offering to pay off his college loans if he'd work for them for five years. Mary Grace had advised him against it because she knew how naive Bobby was and how political the CIA had become. She offered to help him until he got established, but he was determined to make it on his own.

After rubbing a hand over her wound to make sure it wasn't bleeding, she picked up the lantern and held it high, checking out the cellar. It wasn't very large—about half the length of the cabin. Both the walls and floor were constructed with hard-packed dirt, but the interesting thing was the canned food and water stored on crude shelves built against the wall. Matches, several more lanterns and a first-aid kit were there if needed.

Settling her back against the wall, she kept the gun in her hand and her ears peeled for any sound coming from upstairs. Both Krieger and Tink snuggled beside her, and she decided to review the information she had so far. It helped to keep her calm and her mind from wondering whether Ned was okay out there on that freezing, fierce mountain with killers running loose.

She knew next to nothing about the man living on this mountain in the middle of nowhere. Was Ned his real name, and what was his last name? What did he do for a living? Her reporter's curiosity had been roused and she knew from experience that she wouldn't stop until she found out everything there was to know about the man.

In her mind's eye, she went over what she'd seen of the cabin, searching for clues. The place itself wasn't much to look at. Log walls. A tiny kitchen/living area. The bed she'd lain in was pushed against the wall and there was one door, besides the obvious front door, that probably led to the bathroom.

What struck her was the neatness of the place. It made her think of military precision. An old couch with a ratty afghan folded across the back sat in the middle of the living area. A coffee table squatted in front of the couch, but there were no side tables. No computers or TV anywhere. Mary Grace's eyes narrowed as she remembered seeing a large landscape painting hanging on the wall beside the bed. She had only glanced at it, but the quality seemed out of sync with the cabin, so she filed the information away. In the past, she'd broken stories wide open by taking note of the smallest details.

She shivered and both dogs snuggled closer. She knew she should do a better check on her wound, but she didn't want to lose the warmth of the animals.

Chewing her lower lip, she tried not to worry about Bobby, but she couldn't stop herself. He was the only family that counted outside of Gram Ramsey. She still prayed for her mother and stepfather, but had pretty much given up hope of them overcoming their gambling addiction. She smiled as she thought of her grandmother. The older woman was a spitfire and Mary Grace knew this time of year the old historic house would be traditionally festooned with Christmas decorations—a lot of them made by Mary Grace and Bobby when they were kids—and a huge live tree. Gram stood about five feet two inches in her stockings, but her strong will and absolute faith made her seem ten feet tall. She had withstood the tests of time with an elegance that Mary Grace could only aspire to.

A scratching noise upstairs jerked her out of her musings. Krieger got to his feet and quietly stood at the foot of the stairs. Reacting quickly, Mary Grace clamped a hand over Tinker Bell's snout before the dog could bark. She held her breath and heard a shuffling noise that sounded like someone walking through the remains of the cabin. Whoever it was stopped at the top of the stairs.

She held Tink up to her face. "Shh. Don't bark. Please."

Slowly, she released her hand, and when she was sure her dog would stay quiet, she scrambled to her feet, ignoring the pain in her side, and crossed to stand beside Krieger. She willed her hands to stay steady as she lifted the gun and held it with both hands toward the small hidden door at the top of the stairs. It hadn't been long since Ned left, and it could be him returning, but what if it wasn't?

The panel started to open, and she tightened her grip on the gun, ready to stop the killer.

Standing from his crouch over the footprints he'd discovered circling around to the back of the cabin, Ned's head had snapped up and his body tensed when he heard a snowmobile coming toward the front. Sound carried differently in the mountains and there was no way of knowing how close it was. By the time he raced around the structure, someone had already entered the cabin.

His pulse pounded as he called on years of training and forced himself to relax. He slowly mounted the steps, then sidestepped the front door, which hung by the top two hinges.

"Uncle Ned?"

The tentative, fear-filled words froze the blood in his veins.

He'd warned his family to stay away from the cabin until he notified them, but his niece, Fran, was an intelligent, determined twenty-four-year-old woman currently working on her master's in advertising. What scared him was that his niece was on the mountain at the same time as the killer. He stared at her, standing in front of the open panel that led to the hidden basement. He didn't know if Mary Grace would realize Fran was friendly, but before he could control the situation, Krieger bounded out of the opening with the woman on his heels, the rat dog tucked under one arm and the gun in the opposite hand. He was relieved to see the weapon quickly lowered to her right side.

Fear stamped on her face, Fran glanced between the two of them, then dropped her gaze to the gun in Mary Grace's hand.

"Uncle Ned?"

"Aye, niece, I'm here. Everything's okay."

He opened his arms and Fran flew against his chest. She shivered for a few minutes, then pulled away. Propping her hands on slim hips, she attempted to show bravado, but Ned could see the fear lingering in her eyes.

"It looks like you've gotten yourself into a real mess this time." She slanted a questioning look toward Mary Grace. "Wait till I tell Mom and Grandfather."

Ned shook his head and went along with her stab at courage. "Ye and yer mother canna seem to stay out of my business. 'Tis embarrassing."

With a triumphant glint in her eyes, Mary Grace scooted forward and he gently took the gun from her hand when she got close enough to get in his face.

"I knew you had a Scottish background. I just knew it."

She appeared very pleased with herself until Ned cut a sharp glance toward Fran, sending her a message to keep quiet about his private life.

Mary Grace took a step back, folded her arms across her chest and tapped her foot. "I saw that."

He ignored her astute observation and addressed his niece. "Sweetheart, I know you're a grown, independent woman, living at home while you work on getting your master's, but does your mother know you're here? You know she worries." Fran might be twenty-four years old, but she still managed that sweet, pleading look that always turned his heart to mush. He lifted a hand.

"Never mind. We have to get off this mountain. I'm pretty sure the guy who bombed the cabin is gone, but there's no way to be certain."

Both ladies tensed, and he could almost smell their fear return. He mentally shook his head. How, after meticulous planning and patiently waiting, had these two women ended up in his cabin at the exact moment his enemy had decided to attack? If it was indeed his enemy and not Mary Grace's. It was implausible, at least concerning Mary Grace. But she was connected to all of this through her brother.

He had to track down Bobby Lancaster and he needed Mary Grace to make that happen.

"Did you check your wound?" Her hesitation answered his question. "Do it now and do it fast. We're leaving in ten minutes." He turned to Fran as Mary Grace flew back down the stairs to the basement. "Did you see anyone on your way up the mountain?"

Fran's eyes widened. "Y-you mean like the person who did this to your cabin?"

Ned nodded. "Didn't you hear the blast?" He felt bad about scaring her, but she needed to know the gravity of the situation.

"N-no. I couldn't hear anything above the noise of

the snowmobile." She glanced toward the darkened stairwell. "Was she hurt in the blast?"

"Her name is Mary Grace Ramsey. I found her in a ravine with a gunshot wound well before the bomb was detonated." He rushed out an explanation when Fran's face paled. "She's fine. Just a flesh wound."

His niece lifted big blue eyes full of love that sent an arrow straight to his heart. "Uncle Ned, are you in trouble? I couldn't stand it if anything happened to you."

"Aw, come here, lassie." He folded her in his arms, then placed his hands on her shoulders and pulled her back, looking straight into her eyes. "Now havenae I always come back home in one piece?"

She grinned, and he was glad to see it. "Your accent always shows itself when you're emotional."

"Aye, that it does." He grinned and stepped back. "Now, let's get off this mountain."

Mary Grace cleared the top step. The dog carrier was strapped to the front of her body and she winced as she slid the straps of her backpack over her shoulders. "I'm all for that," she said, and gave him a look, practically daring him to mention her wound. "I'll be fine and I'm ready to leave. I left my car at the base of the mountain."

Ned led the way to the front door, but came to a grinding halt when he heard a sharp bark behind him and his niece squealed. "You have a dog! What a precious little thing."

Waiting for both women to come up behind him on the front porch, Ned scanned the frozen tundra surrounding them, but he didn't sense the presence of another human being. He'd checked a half-mile perimeter around the cabin and at the front of the structure found the remnants of a simple bomb. It had an attachment that appeared as if the device had been detonated remotely. Whoever tried to kill them had left the mountain. He felt it in his gut.

"Stay close."

He heard Mary Grace grumble to Fran behind him. "Your uncle is certainly a man of few words."

Fran whispered, "He wasn't always this way."

Ned sent her a sharp look over his shoulder and Fran zipped her lips. He pulled the shed door open and started checking his snowmobile.

Mary Grace sidled next to him. "What are you doing?"

"Making sure no one has tampered with my equipment."

Her eyes rounded and she didn't ask any more questions, which suited him just fine. He'd talked more since meeting her than he had in a long time.

"Fran, you'll take your snowmobile. I'll strap Krieger in behind you. Mary Grace can ride with me. I'll take the lead, but you stay close. I want to get you back to your mother safe and sound."

"But, Uncle Ned—"

He interrupted what he knew was coming. Fran and Sylvia were always at odds these days, and normally he would try to help, but now was not the time.

His voice was loving, but firm. "We'll talk later."

Everything checked out, so he fired up the snowmobile and motioned for Mary Grace to hop on. He didn't miss her wince of pain as she threw her leg over the seat.

"Hold on tight."

She placed her arms around his waist and Ned felt an unfamiliar warmth at her touch. He attributed it to the fact that he hadn't dated or even been around many women in the last few years. Ignoring the sensation, he pulled in front of the cabin. Fran was already seated on her snowmobile and ready to ride. She'd strapped Krieger in herself.

Ned took two helmets from the side of his snowmobile and handed one to Mary Grace. When they were both ready, he took off and Fran followed closely.

If he were still a praying man, he would have sent up a quick prayer for their safety, but he'd learned not to trust anyone but himself, and that included a God who allowed good people to get hurt.

It didn't take long to reach the bottom of the mountain, but fortune wasn't on his side. They pulled to a stop beside Mary Grace's car and there stood Sheriff Jack Hoyt, his arms crossed over his chest. Ned cut the engine and helped Mary Grace off the back of the sled. Fran was already off her snowmobile and came to stand beside Ned.

Ned nodded at the lawman. "Sheriff."

Sheriff Hoyt nodded back. "Ned."

He heard Mary Grace grumble. "What is it with this town? Do all the men speak in one-syllable words?"

Ned ignored her and watched the sheriff. He didn't have time for any delays or long explanations. He hoped the mountain and snow had muffled the blast enough that it hadn't been heard in Jackson Hole.

Hoyt's brows lifted as he nodded at Fran, then focused on Mary Grace. "Saw your vehicle on the side of the road and figured you'd decided to try to find Ned."

To her credit, Mary Grace pasted on a friendly smile and her explanation didn't leave any openings for questions. "I sure did, and I appreciate all your help."

Hoyt turned to Fran. "Didn't know you were familiar with Ned."

Taking her cue from Mary Grace, Fran grinned at the sheriff. "I've seen him around a few times."

Ned slowly released the breath he'd been holding. His family understood he didn't want anyone in Jackson Hole to know he was related to them for their own safety. One day his past might catch up with him.

Hoyt leveled a disbelieving look at the three of them, but cracked a grin when Mary Grace's dog stuck its head out of the pouch and barked. The sheriff moved close and rubbed its fluffy white head.

"Aw, what a cute dog. I have one of my own. Left him at the station today."

Hoyt stepped back and gave them all a hard look. "So everything is okay here?"

Ned's gut clenched when Mary Grace gave the sheriff a wide, welcoming grin.

"Absolutely," she said, "and I'm sorry for leaving my car on the side of the road. Ned's driveway was impassable, so I hiked to his cabin. Well, we'll just be on our way now. I'm sure you'd like to get back to the station where it's warm."

Hoyt gave them one last lingering look, nodded and folded his long frame into his patrol car.

Maybe living alone on his mountain hadn't been a good idea, because when Mary Grace gave that warm, gracious smile to the sheriff, Ned wanted to strangle the guy.

Maybe he'd been isolated for too long and it had affected his brain.

FOUR

Mary Grace hunched over the steering wheel in her rental car as she followed the two snowmobiles in front of her. Ned had said Fran lived several miles away.

She checked the heater to make sure it was on full blast. She'd never been so cold in her life. She'd take the sticky, sweet humidity in Georgia any day over these bone-chilling temperatures.

She couldn't imagine Ned living all alone on that isolated mountain. But maybe not completely alone. She now knew he had a sister and a niece. They evidently visited periodically. When she awoke that morning, she assumed he was all alone, because why in the world would anyone choose to live sequestered in complete isolation?

Tinker Bell growled when Krieger stuck his massive head between the bucket seats.

"It's okay, Tink. Krieger just wants to be friends."

Tink growled one more time for good measure and Krieger disappeared into the back seat. The dogs reminded Mary Grace of her and Ned. Uptown girl meets gruff mountain man. She chuckled at the comparison, but sobered when she remembered riding on the snowmobile with her arms wrapped around his waist. Something had stirred deep inside her. It was attraction and that was ridiculous. She didn't even know what his face looked like. It was almost completely covered by a beard that appeared as if it hadn't been groomed for months. Her grandmother would have been horrified by his appearance. About the one thing she was sure of so far was that the man calling himself Ned apparently loved his niece and, judging by his reaction, loathed Mary Grace's brother.

He was an enigma. She had to find out everything about Ned's connection to Bobby so she could protect her brother. She had no idea what was going on, but she'd find out. It was her gift—ferreting out secrets and information.

Outside of his negative reaction at the mention of her brother's name, the only thing Ned had actually said about Bobby was when he asked if she and her brother were working together to get rid of him and Finn.

Who was Finn and why would someone be trying to get rid of both men? But the most disturbing question was how her brother was involved in this situation. The people after Mary Grace and Bobby weren't playing games. Even though she finally felt warm, she shivered at the thought of the recent attempts on her life. She prayed Bobby would be safe until she could resolve this situation.

Her reporter's curiosity piqued once again when she made a right turn behind the snowmobiles onto a long driveway that appeared manicured, even beneath the snow. After making several soft turns, a large house loomed at the end of the driveway. A sizable fountain stood in the middle of the circular drive, complementing the wood and stone structure. She wouldn't classify it as a mansion, but it definitely came under the heading of mini mansion.

She cut the engine and flung open her car door. This was her best chance to find out more about Ned. There was no name on the mailbox and she needed information. She'd always had great rapport with other women. One mention of their cute kids or their pets or their boyfriends/husbands and they were usually off and running. Politicians would be the exception to that rule. She had to break out the big guns for those interviews.

She had one leg out of the car when Ned silently appeared and halted her momentum with a big bear claw on the door, stopping her from reaching her goal: to talk to his sister.

"You stay here. I'll be back."

His quiet but firm order really burned her. The terror she'd experienced on the mountain had melted away and she was more herself now.

She jutted her chin out. "Why should I?"

His expression didn't change, but she noted the twitch in his left eye, the only thing that remotely revealed what he was feeling.

"Because I'm the only one who can protect you while we look for your brother."

Like she was born yesterday. "For all I know, you want to kill Bobby. Why should I trust you?"

Her heart palpitated when he grinned for the second time since she'd met him, and her gut clenched. No, no, no, she absolutely refused to be attracted to this bear of a man. He hovered over her open door like a caveman. He had to be at least six and a half feet tall. She considered herself of average height at five feet six inches, but he towered over her. He wasn't skin and bones, either. She briefly wondered how much muscle was hidden beneath those layers of clothes.

"Because your brother sent you to me."

Well, that took the wind out of her sails. He was right. Bobby had sent her to Ned. With little grace, she jerked her leg back inside the car and grabbed the door handle. It'd serve him right if his hand got caught in the door, but that wasn't to be. He showed his superior strength by holding on to the door until he was ready to release it. She gritted her teeth and pulled hard. He let go suddenly and the door slammed shut, rattling her hand.

Fuming, she crossed her arms over her chest and watched as Ned met Fran at the sidewalk and together they walked through the front door, firmly closing it behind them.

"Tink, I don't trust that man, not with Bobby's life on the line."

Tink barked and Mary Grace jerked when a big, rough tongue licked the side of her neck. She turned her head and looked at Ned's dog. "If only you could talk." The animal's eyes were full of intelligence and she remembered how Krieger had followed Ned's orders right before the explosion. She sat upright in her seat. Was Krieger military or police-trained?

As happened when she came across a vital piece of information while pursuing a story, her adrenaline took a sharp spike. She reached across the console and grabbed her backpack from the passenger floorboard of the car. Dropping it onto her lap, she dug through her belongings until her fingers wrapped around her cell phone. She lifted it triumphantly in the air.

"Ha! Got it." Tink barked her approval and Mary Grace held the smartphone close to her chest. "Now, if I can get a signal, I'll be in business."

She turned on the phone and fidgeted in her seat, willing the phone to power up fast. She wanted to do a quick search on Krieger before Ned came out of the house. Her heart beat faster when two bars appeared. Opening the search engine, she typed in Krieger—military dog and pressed the search tab. The blue line at the top had never taken so long, but when it finished, she grinned. There were several articles that popped up immediately.

The first one caught her attention and her nose actually twitched. She was in what she called her "reporter zone," a place where her gut told her she was on the right track.

It read: *Old-fashioned, giant German shepherd musters out with handler after six years of service in Army Special Forces.*

Mary Grace quickly skimmed the article, looking for a reference to the handler, but it never gave a name. She checked several other articles, but nothing. They did list all of Krieger's achievements and they were quite impressive. She glanced over her shoulder.

"I appreciate your service to our country, Krieger."

Tink growled again, but Mary Grace ignored her and scanned the house and grounds, searching for anything that would give her a clue she could follow to find out Ned's true identity. Then an idea popped into her head. She opened Google Maps on her smartphone and a map popped up. She got the address of his sister's house from there and was just following up on that when the driver's door whooshed open.

"Move over, I'll drive."

Mary Grace scooted over the console into the passenger seat and quickly sorted through all her options. She could probably, eventually, find Bobby on her own, and she was uncertain why Ned wanted to find her brother. Was it for information, or had Bobby inadvertently done something to anger this quiet, lethal mountain of a man? On the other hand, there were people trying to kill her and she wasn't quite ready to meet her Maker. Ned could protect her. She'd stay with him for the time being and try to figure out what was going on. If he would bother saying more than two words, she could make faster progress. She was a whiz at research.

"Fine, but you're going to have to start talking or I'll find Bobby on my own."

For a moment, Mary Grace had amused Ned. Through her eyes, he could almost see her brain rapidly processing her options, but then she smirked. She was up to something.

As he pulled out of the driveway, he glanced at her and considered her demand for answers. She was staring out the window and the rat dog—he really should call it by its name, but Tinker Bell just didn't feel right slipping past his lips—was glaring at him. The small dog and its name were enough to unman a guy. Concentrating on TB—that's what he'd call the animal—helped him to ignore the unwanted pull of attraction. Instead of answering her questions, it was time he asked a few of his own and got back to the task at hand.

"Do you have any idea where Bobby might be hiding?"

She turned her head and glared at him, much like her dog.

"Why do you want to find my brother? Bobby said you were a big part of *this*, whatever *this* is."

He stopped the car at the end of the driveway and turned toward her. Her jaw was set at a stubborn angle and her lips were pressed together. He had to give her something or she might bolt, and Mary Grace Ramsey was the only lead he had at the moment. His gut told him Bobby could lead him to the people who were after him and Finn.

All the evidence he had accumulated so far involved Bobby Lancaster, but the geeky young man just didn't fit the profile of a killer, which is why Ned had been trying to lure the bad guys to his mountain.

He'd soon find out where the CIA's computer wonder boy had holed up. At this point, he didn't care who he tipped off. Bobby had gone on the lam recently, and the ambush had happened six months ago, but it had taken Ned four months to get Finn settled, make sure he was okay and then lay his trap for their enemies. Prior to this, he'd stayed on his mountain between missions. No one in town knew when he slipped away and returned because of his hermit-type lifestyle, and he'd made sure no one knew he was related to his sister and niece because danger might follow him from current or previous missions. As far as the townspeople and anyone he worked with knew, he was all alone in the world.

Bobby must have been alerted by something, or found himself in a tight spot and took off. His gut told him that Bobby had to be involved because he'd fed Ned and Finn the bad intel that placed them in danger.

Whether it was voluntary or involuntarily, well, that was yet to be determined.

"It's classified." She snorted, and he rushed to add, "Fine, I spent some time in the military a while back. You can trust me."

She didn't even respond to his admission of a small part of his past, instead she started typing on her phone.

"What are you doing?"

She lifted her head and gave him a challenging grin. "It's over two thousand miles to Georgia. You wanna drive or fly?"

He was onto her game. To fly, a person had to present identification. He grinned back and whipped out an encrypted satellite phone. He tapped in a number and held the phone close to his ear. There were two clicks, and he knew his contact was listening. "I need the private plane in Jackson Hole, pronto, headed to—" He looked at Mary Grace and almost laughed out loud at the stunned expression on her face.

"Waycross, Georgia," she answered through gritted teeth.

"Waycross," he repeated into the phone. "We'll be at the airport in thirty minutes. No paperwork."

He put his phone away and turned left out of his sister's driveway.

Mary Grace settled into her seat and kissed her dog on top of the head. He felt a mood shift in the car. It was almost as if he could sense her switching gears in that agile brain of hers. He liked the challenge of matching wits with her. He'd always appreciated beautiful women, but it was the smart ones who held his attention, and Mary Grace had proven to be very intelligent.

"Why Georgia?"

"That's where we grew up for the most part, at my grandmother's house." She turned toward him, as much as her seat belt would allow. "Unlike you, I have nothing to hide. Bobby and I were both born and raised in Georgia. My father passed away when I was twelve. My mom remarried quickly—way too soon for decency— and Bobby became my little brother. I was a little over thirteen and he was eight years old at the time. I helped take care of him."

She twisted back around and became interested in the passing scenery as she continued, "Bobby and I spent most of our youth at Gram Ramsey's house. We had what everyone now refers to as a dysfunctional family. Our parents were, and still are, pretty much gambling addicts. They traveled a lot and we stayed at my grandmother's house."

This time the chatter was laced with an undertone of hurt and regret and it made Ned even more curious about Mary Grace. But he clamped down on the sudden protective instinct that rose to the surface as she matter-of-factly discussed a childhood that had to have been fraught with heartache.

He empathized with her pain more than he wanted to and it was time to get the conversation back on track. He had to find Bobby.

"Why would Bobby go to Georgia? If his family lives there, that's the first place anyone would look for him."

Relief hit him full force when he glanced at her. The right side of her mouth kicked up and the challenge was back in her eyes.

"You ever been to a swamp, Mountain Man?"

He had fought the enemy plenty of times in a swamp, but decided to let her win this round. For some foolish reason—a reason he didn't examine too closely—he wanted to see the now-familiar smirk back on her face.

His hands relaxed on the steering wheel as he turned onto the road leading to the airport. "There's a first time for everything."

After waving his hand at the guy at the gate, he pulled onto the tarmac right up next to the plane.

Mary Grace gave him an incredulous look. "You can't just drive onto the tarmac without permission, and don't we need to go inside and see about the car return and go through security?"

He grabbed her hand, stopping her. "The car will be taken care of and we don't need to go through security. Stay close to me until we're on the plane."

She stared at him for a full minute, then pulled her hand away, her eyes narrowing. "Is this legal? Am I going to end up in jail?"

He couldn't help it, he grinned through his beard. "Everything is legal, and no, you won't end up in jail."

She stared at him a moment longer. "Who are you?" she asked, then grumbled, "Never mind. I'm sure it's classified."

She didn't sound as if she believed him, but after he called Krieger, she and TB did follow him onto the tarmac toward the plane. He stopped halfway there when the fine hair on his nape rose. Mary Grace ran into his back and he pulled her under his arm. Smart woman that she was, she didn't fight the maneuver.

"What is it?" she asked, her voice muffled under his heavy fleece jacket.

"Stay close to me and run when I say go."

The instinctual warning system that had saved his life on more than one occasion was screaming a red-hot alert. He took two more steps, moving them closer to the plane before he gave a quiet command. "Go. Now."

Mary Grace shot out from under his arm, clamored up the steps and barely got through the door before Ned heard a ping on the steps leading into the plane. He took a giant leap forward and slipped into the plane before the sniper could take another shot. Unfortunately, he still didn't know whom they were shooting at—him or Mary Grace. The bullet could have been meant for either one of them. But the one thing he was sure of was that they needed to get out of there before the sniper found a way to ground them…and finish the job.

FIVE

Mary Grace's heart thundered ominously inside her chest as she cleared the open door of the plane. Someone had shot at her. Again! A dangerous mixture of fear, adrenaline and fury had her whirling around as soon as she got safely away from the door. She released an undignified oomph when she hit a rock-solid wall of muscle. Ned hissed out a frustrated breath as she slammed into his chest, then caught her by the arms when she bounced off.

Tinker Bell yelped inside the dog carrier strapped to Mary Grace. Horrified she might have injured her dog, she lifted her from the pouch and held her high. Krieger whimpered at Mary Grace's feet and the tiny dog responded with a half-felt snarl.

Assured her dog was okay, Mary Grace took a relieved breath and placed her on the floor of the plane, then allowed both the dog carrier and the backpack to slide off her shoulders onto the carpet. Jerking her gaze toward Ned, she looked up, way up, and snarled herself. She felt as tiny as her dog standing in front of the six-and-a-half-foot giant and she wasn't used to feeling intimidated.

Still shaken up from the close call, her words came out sharper than intended. "Don't you think we better get out of here before whoever is out there shoots the fuselage?"

He nodded curtly and disappeared into the cockpit.

Mary Grace put on a brave act for Ned, but the seriousness of their situation shook her to the core. She prayed that Bobby was someplace safe and that no one was trying to harm him.

The loading stair door closed and Mary Grace took a deep calming breath and glanced at her surroundings for the first time. Her breath caught in her throat when she took in the luxurious interior of the plane. Or maybe it was a private jet.

Her eyes narrowed at the oversize leather seats placed strategically in groupings throughout the plane. Each area had an oblong table in the middle, and if she wasn't mistaken... Tromping down the center aisle, she lightly ran a finger over the top of a highly polished table. Yep, it was definitely teak wood and very expensive.

She walked to the back of the plane, jerked open a door and slowly entered a huge bedroom with a king-size bed sitting smack-dab in the middle. She stalked around and discovered a super fancy bathroom. Gold faucets gleamed from a sink surrounded by a green marble countertop. Teak cabinets completed the look. She slid open the shower door and discovered gold fixtures matching the ones in the sink.

Mary Grace mentally slapped her forehead. She was a seasoned reporter and she had made assumptions about Ned that she shouldn't have. Everything she'd learned pointed at him being in the CIA, or the military, in some form or fashion, but good ole Uncle Sam didn't provide rides as nice as this one.

She had a ton of questions, but she was mesmerized by the gold fixtures in the shower, wondering if they were made of real gold. Leaning over, unable to help herself, she took her fingernail and started scratching the faucet to see if it was real.

"You're a real snoop, you know that? And you shouldn't be leaning over like that with the wound in your side."

The low, gruff voice startled her so bad she jerked up from her bent position and heard an oomph from behind her as the back of her head slammed into his chest. If he weren't so tall, she could have clipped him on the chin, and wouldn't that have been a shame.

She whirled around. "Who owns this jet, and shouldn't we be taking off? Have there been any more shots from the gunman? We were fortunate the first shot only hit the steps."

He ignored her questions, turned on his heel and whispered out of the room. It was uncanny how such a large man could move so quietly, which demanded even more answers.

She followed him but came to a dead stop when he disappeared into the cockpit again. Surely he wasn't going to fly the plane. Was he?

She stuck her head through the small door and there he sat in the pilot's seat, flipping a bunch of switches.

"Um, where's the pilot? Are you planning on flying this plane?"

"Yes."

Mary Grace shivered. She was getting more nervous by the second. "Don't you have to file a flight plan?"

He did look up at that question and his white teeth sparkled from beneath the messy beard. "A flight plan has already been filed, but we're actually landing at a small, relatively unknown airfield in Georgia, near Waycross."

"What about when we don't land at the planned destination?"

"There'll be records showing we landed where we were supposed to." He refocused on the controls and waved toward the copilot's chair. "Take a seat. We'll be leaving soon."

Slowly sliding into the chair, Mary Grace closed her eyes in frustration. Bobby had gotten her into this mess, and now she was worried about her own safety, as well as her brother's. Just *who* was Ned, and how was he mixed up with Bobby?

There were too many unanswered questions, and she wasn't sure she could trust Ned.

"I see you agree with me."

The question snapped her out of her unsettling thoughts. She blinked her eyes open and stared at Ned as the plane rolled down the runway.

"Agree about what?"

He grinned, but kept his eyes straight ahead as the wheels of the jet left the ground.

"Trust no one."

Ned's own words reverberated in his mind. He didn't trust anyone, and that included the woman perched in the seat beside him. Oh, he might be attracted to the feisty little scrapper from Georgia, but he would never act on it. He preferred a simple life these days, free of emotional entanglements and betrayals.

But that didn't mean he wasn't concerned for her welfare.

"How's your wound?"

She slid him a sideways glance and he didn't miss the suspicion shining out of her eyes. Well, welcome to his world.

"It's fine. Like you said, it's a flesh wound. It'll be okay in a couple of days."

Ned rolled his shoulders to get the kinks out. Even working for the CIA, before he'd taken a leave of absence, he'd lived in something vaguely resembling peace until he decided to bring the enemy to his mountain, but then Mary Grace had shown up and turned his life upside down.

"Why don't you make use of the shower." He flashed her a grin. "And to relieve that curious mind of yours, the fixtures aren't solid gold, but they are gold-plated."

Her stubborn chin jutted out. "I'm not going anywhere until you tell me who owns this plane, and it better not be a two-bit dictator from some obscure little country."

"You don't have to worry, the plane is aboveboard, legally owned by an upstanding citizen of the United States." It was time he got some answers of his own. "We haven't had time to discuss you. Are you risking a job with your disappearing act?"

She turned her head away and stared out the small side window. "When I realized what was happening, I took some personal time. I had a lot of vacation time coming and I requested that first." Without looking in his direction, she stood to leave the cockpit and glanced down at her tattered Christmas sweater and dirty jeans. "I think I will take that shower."

Ned grabbed her arm as she swept past him and forced her to look him in the eye. "Two things. One, don't ever lie to me, and two, there's different sizes of women's clothes stashed in one of the bedroom closets if you need anything."

She tried to jerk her arm away, but he held fast.

"I haven't lied to you about anything."

"Good. Let's keep it that way. What do you do for a living, Mary Grace?"

A muscle in her jaw ticked and her eyes shifted away. He waited, wondering if she would tell the truth. Deep down, in a place he had protected for a long time, he really wanted her to be who and what she appeared to be. A sister afraid for her brother's life. Finally, she looked him straight in the eye again, this time of her own accord, and his gut told him she was being honest.

"I work for FBC, Future Broadcasting Company, as a White House press correspondent."

A big invisible fist punched Ned in the gut. A good chunk of his adult life consisted of secrets and clandestine operations. Secrets that could get people killed if they were ever exposed. He hid his unsettling reaction behind a carefully constructed mask.

Mary Grace leaned one shoulder against the doorjamb and crossed her arms over her chest. "Yeah, I didn't think you'd appreciate that little piece of information. You're a man with a belly full of secrets." She pulled away from the door frame and smiled.

Ned held his breath while he waited for the ax to fall. That smirk of hers always meant trouble.

"Do you believe in God, Ned?"

The question threw him completely off guard. He

hadn't seen that one coming, but he was quick on the uptake. "Why do you ask?"

The smirk changed into a full-blown grin. "You asked me not to lie, and you better take your own advice when we get to Georgia."

He found himself intrigued, and that hadn't happened in longer than he could remember. "And why is that?"

"Because we're stopping at Gram Ramsey's house before we go to the swamp shack and my grandmother has a way of getting people to spill their guts." Her smile slid away and her eyes softened. "She's the best Christian woman I know, but—" she smiled again "—she's also one tough lady. She'll have you confessing your sins and sitting in a church pew before you can blink."

Ned scanned the cloudless day outside the front window as Mary Grace left the cockpit. The conversation left him…unsettled. He grew up in a Christian home, but he no longer believed in a God who could allow his best friend to have to live in a wheelchair for the rest of his life.

Relaxing into his chair, his lips curled into a grin as he thought about the woman he was traveling with. Maybe one day he'd tell her he owned the plane. His "hobby" as a landscape painter paid a thousand times better than the money he made working for the CIA. He put the plane on autopilot, laid his head back and allowed himself a few moments to wonder what if. What if he'd never taken that first phone call from the CIA after he left the army? What if he'd retired from the CIA and he and Finn hadn't gone on that last mission? Everything would have been different now. He might have even been interested in asking Miss Ramsey on a date if he were a normal man, but he wasn't normal, so it was a moot point.

Opening his eyes, he switched back to manual and focused on the task at hand. It was wasted time wondering what if. A person could never go back and that was life.

Pulling out the plane's secure satellite phone, he made a call.

"'Bout time you checked in. I was starting to get worried."

Ned experienced a host of mixed emotions every time he heard Finn's voice. They had grown up together, and Ned loved him like a brother, but guilt always accompanied the affection. Ned had trusted the wrong people and Finn would pay the price for the rest of his life.

"Everything's fine. How's the new wheelchair? It's state of the art, not even on the open market yet."

A pause. "The chair's great. I appreciate it." Another longer pause. "Something's happening, isn't it? Have you caught whoever set us up?" Finn's voice was tinged with anger and hurt. Ned knew why, but it wasn't going to change anything.

"Finn, we discussed this. I don't want you involved in this hunt. You've lost too much already, and I have to live with that every day of my life."

A sulky voice responded. "You could at least tell me where you've been holed up for so long. Have you been staying on that mountain of yours?"

He no longer had to keep his location a secret, now that he was on the move. "Yes, I've been at the cabin.

I recently set it up so they'd come after me, but things changed."

He could almost feel the energy crackling to life on the other end of the phone. "What things?"

"Let's just say Bobby Lancaster went on the lam and I now have a lead on him. We've both always agreed that was the best place to start if I wasn't able to root them out without alerting them by contacting Bobby."

"Where do you think he is? Ned, please don't keep me in the dark anymore. Let me help. I have just as much invested in this as you do." He let the words linger. "Maybe more."

Ned wanted to include Finn, but his best friend had already lost too much so he ignored the heavy weight of guilt that Finn so expertly threw his way.

"I'll keep you posted and I'll have my accountant send you more money. Let me know if you need anything. Anything at all," he said, and ended the call.

A shroud of guilt lingered over him for a few minutes, but he put it away. He was doing the right thing by protecting Finn. He had stashed his best friend in a place where no one would find him until Ned discovered who wanted them dead.

The only problem was his dependence on a journalist to help him do this. If she ever got wind of some of his secrets, his life could literally blow up in his face.

SIX

Mary Grace checked out a variety of women's clothing in the huge walk-in closet in the bedroom. Either the owner of the plane was a womanizer of vast proportions or it was outfitted to carry different people. Maybe some sort of rescue transportation carrier. Her reporter's intuition indicated the latter. Just another layer of mystery surrounding Mountain Man.

Thankfully, she had an extra outfit in the backpack she'd grabbed on her way to the bathroom and had no need of the clothes. She smirked when she unzipped the pack and pulled out another Christmas sweater. She hadn't missed Ned's wary expression whenever he stared at her sweater. It only made her more curious about the man. Didn't he like Christmas?

She grinned when she passed by the king-size bed on her way to the shower. Krieger and Tink were curled up together sleeping, as if they didn't have a care in the world.

She took a quick shower, dressed and left the bathroom, dropping a kiss on her sleeping dog's snout before heading back into the main cabin. She wasn't quite ready to face Ned yet, so she started snooping around the living area. On a luxury craft like this one, there had to be hidden technology somewhere. Her heart accelerated when she plopped onto one of the buttery soft leather chairs, stared at the oblong table and noticed a thin pullout drawer beneath.

Leaning forward, she slid out what could probably also serve as an eating tray, and there sat her heart's desire. A silver gleaming laptop. Glancing toward the closed cockpit door, she opened the lid and prayed a password wasn't needed. It was already booted up, so that wasn't a problem.

She quickly typed in the home address of Ned's sister that she'd gotten off her GPS and searched the county public records for the owner's name. When the name popped up, she sat back in disgust. What in the world was RBTL Corporation? She'd never heard of them. She searched for the name on the internet but failed to get any hits. Legitimate companies usually had websites.

Pushing the laptop back underneath the table, she decided it was time to beard the lion in his lair. She snickered. Speaking of ugly beards. Her humor evaporated when she opened the door and slipped into the cockpit. A sleek little laptop, similar to the one she had just been working on, sat on the console between the pilot and copilot's seat. The screen was turned toward the door revealing the address she had just visited on the other computer. Avoiding eye contact, she slipped into the copilot's seat.

"Snooping again, Miss Ramsey?" he asked after eyeing her sweater with something akin to horror.

A streak of anger shot through her system, along with a bit of embarrassment at getting caught red-handed, but then she shrugged. She was a reporter, after all. It was her job to snoop.

"You only call me Miss Ramsey when you're aggravated. The name's Mary Grace."

She slipped him a glance. He had a smile on his face and it disarmed her. No! No way was she allowing herself to be attracted to no-last-name Ned—a man with the word *secret* emblazoned on his chest.

Back to business. "I assume there's a sat phone onboard?"

He reached down, opened a hidden compartment and handed her the plane's phone. She gave him a sharp look, but grabbed it out of his hand. "I thought I'd try my brother again. I doubt I'll get an answer, but it's worth a try."

He gave a slight nod. "Just don't reveal our destination."

She nodded and punched in the number from memory, counting four rings before the voice mail recording came on. "Bobby, please, if you get this message, call me. I located Mountain Man." She wanted to say more, tell Bobby that even though she wanted to kill him, she loved him more than anything, but since Ned was listening to every word, she ended the call.

Lost in thought and worried sick about her brother, Mary Grace stared out the front window of the plane. She prayed Bobby was holed up at the swamp shack. When they were kids, they'd trekked through the woods to the abandoned cabin hidden a little ways into the Okefenokee Swamp. As far as she knew, no one was aware of the place. In all the years they went there, nothing indicated anyone else hanging around. Anyone visiting the swamp tended to take the offered tours and stay within the strict, designated pedestrian areas. In the past, people had disappeared in the 438,000 acres of wetland.

Lost in her thoughts, it took a moment for Ned's question to penetrate her brain.

"What?"

"If he's on the run, do you really expect Bobby to answer his phone? If we're right, I'm sure there are people trying to track him."

A picture of her blue-eyed, fair-haired brother formed in her mind and she shuddered at the thought of him on his own, trying to outrun a bunch of killers. "He is in cyber intelligence. I was hoping he could figure out a way for me to get in touch with him."

"I know a thing or two about technology and I don't think your brother would take a chance by using his phone. That's the first thing he would have ditched."

Mary Grace slumped in her seat. If Bobby wasn't at the old cabin, she didn't know where else to look. They would have to wait for him to contact her. That didn't sit well because she was used to plowing forward and making things happen.

"You know I'm a reporter." It wasn't a question.

"An unfortunate circumstance, but yes, you shared that nice little tidbit of information with me earlier."

She cut him a sharp look. "My job is not a crime and there's no need to be sarcastic."

"I apologize. Now, why did you bring up that disturbing information again?"

A small twinkle in his eye revealed that he was baiting her. She refused to give him the satisfaction.

"My point is that I'm very good at what I do, and I have quite a few contacts in Washington. If you'd tell me what you think Bobby has done to you and your friend, Finn, maybe I can help. You know, dig up some information."

The twinkle disappeared and his green eyes took on the unyielding substance of emeralds. "If the situation turns out to be explosive, will you write a story and tell the world what is happening, even if it disrupts and maybe even places people's lives in danger?"

"You go too far, Mountain Man. I would never knowingly place someone in danger."

From one second to the next, Ned's body relaxed and he nodded at the sat phone in her lap. "I suggest you call your grandmother. Let her know we're coming and make sure she's okay."

Mary Grace's heart almost exploded inside her chest when the meaning of his words sank in. "What do you mean, *make sure she's okay*?" But deep down she knew what he meant and reprimanded herself for not thinking of it earlier. If the people after her and Bobby went to Georgia looking for them, they'd find Gram Ramsey.

Fumbling, she almost dropped the phone before she got the number dialed. Her grandmother answered on the third ring and Mary Grace's heart settled back into a regular rhythm. Gram was safe. For the moment.

Ned hardened his heart against Mary Grace's apparent love for her grandmother. Just because she adored her gram didn't mean she wouldn't use him and his circumstances to further her career. He'd never been exposed to many reporters because he'd always stayed as far away from them as possible. He had a cache of hidden secrets, in both his personal and professional life, and he never ever wanted them exposed to the world.

He only halfway listened to Mary Grace's conversation with her grandmother and waited until she disconnected the call. "Everything okay?"

Her tortured gaze met his. "For now. I tried to talk her into staying with one of her bridge partners until we arrive, but she wouldn't hear of it. Said she'd spent every night in that house since Grampy died and no ill-mannered thugs were going to force her to leave."

"Sounds like your grandparents loved each other."

Her lips curled into a half smile and Ned wasn't happy that his heart pinged in gladness when the worry lines on her forehead disappeared. Not a good sign.

"They did. In their own way. Gram is the epitome of Georgian hospitality and tradition. I think my grandfather somewhat resented Gram's family. She inherited her family home—the Hubert House—and they lived there after they got married."

"The Hubert House?" Mary Grace was turning out to be a fount of information. He grinned and it felt good. Too good.

"Only the historic houses have names, and Hubert is Gram's maiden name—the house has been in her family for generations, but back to Grampy. He wasn't as high on the social ladder as Gram, and all those years ago, that was a big deal. It didn't help that he couldn't handle money well. Gram still lives in the house, but she really doesn't have enough cash to keep it up as it should be."

Mary Grace went quiet for a moment and Ned caught a look of nostalgia on her face.

"You still worried about your gram?"

She shrugged, but Ned could tell something was bothering her. She peered out the side window of the plane and continued talking. "Gram was an only child. My mother was her only child and I'm Gram's only blood-related grandchild."

"And?"

When she turned around, the sadness in her gaze caught him off guard. He wanted to slay dragons if that's what it took to remove that emotion.

"Gram is leaving Hubert House to me. She doesn't trust Mom not to sell it. She hopes I'll get married one day and fill it with children and happiness."

His gut clenched at the thought of Mary Grace married with children, but he gritted his teeth and spoke as if no emotion had touched him. Something he was good at.

"Maybe that'll happen."

She turned away again. "Let's just say I come from the epitome of a dysfunctional family and it hasn't helped in the relationship department. But you don't want to hear about my sordid childhood. All you're interested in is locating Bobby and attaining whatever information he has." She turned and gave him a hard look. "Right?"

His heart wanted to protest her statement, but his brain conquered the momentary glitch.

"Right."

"Well, hopefully we'll find Bobby, you'll see that he is completely innocent and I'll be out of your hair for good."

Silence filled the cockpit and Ned's curiosity got the best of him. He tried to convince himself that the more he knew about Mary Grace and Bobby, the better his interrogation of her brother would go, but he also had a burning desire to gather every tidbit of information he could muster from the woman sitting next to him.

"You want to know more about me? How about we trade information?"

Her golden eyes reflected the intensity of a tiger on the hunt and he almost regretted the offer. Almost. But he was a master at revealing vague information that could never be researched and analyzed.

She fired a shot at him immediately and the question surprised him.

"Which side of the family did you get your height from? You're what, six and a half feet tall?"

He held back a grin. At least she wasn't worried about her grandmother for the moment.

"Got my height from Dad's side of the family, and yes, I'm six feet six inches. My turn."

She leaned back in her seat and grinned, anticipation of the verbal battle lighting her eyes. It was the first time he'd seen a genuine smile and he took a hard punch to the gut, but quickly tamped down the emotion.

"Go for it. Unlike you, I have nothing to hide."

He fired a volley. "Exactly how many relationships have you tried that went bad?" He wanted to sew his mouth shut after the question passed his lips, but he really wanted to know why her relationships never worked out.

"Three."

Ned didn't miss the dispassionate way she answered. He detected a world of hurt hidden behind her short, clipped response.

It was her turn to ask, "You don't wear a ring. Are you, or have you ever been, married?"

"That's two questions, but the answer is no, and no. What made you want to become a journalist?"

She paused and a thoughtful expression blanketed her face. He liked that she didn't give a status quo answer.

"I found my niche in high school when I joined the school newspaper. We published it once a month and I quickly became hooked. I discovered that the pen actually is mightier than the sword. I exposed bullies and all sorts of injustices that teenagers have to live with. I also got to report on the happier achievements of students. I loved it and still do."

Ned heard and greedily absorbed every detail of what she said, but he caught movement in the sky out of the corner of his eye.

"We have company. Go to the back and buckle yourself into one of the seats."

"No can do, Mountain Man," she said as she tightened the buckle on the copilot's seat. "You might need me."

It didn't surprise him that the spirited woman sitting next to him refused to take orders, but he didn't have time to worry about it.

"In that case, brace yourself. There's a drone closing in on us and it's locked and loaded."

Instead of doing what any normal person would have done to protect themselves, she chose to argue. "That's impossible. I recently did a story on the rights of private citizens to shoot down drones that hover over their house, which, by the way, several states have now allowed, but there aren't any drones on the market, even military ones, that can keep up with a jet."

Ned banked the jet hard to the right and gritted his

teeth. He had no doubt the thing was going to shoot at them. "That's because they've kept it a well-guarded secret. The Pentagon is close to releasing what they call the UTAP-22. The thing can fly seven hundred miles an hour and is loaded with a lethal mix of weapons. Looks like someone either stole the specs and built their own, or this thing we're involved in goes all the way to the top of the food chain."

The drone caught up with them and was keeping pace with his side window. "Hold tight!" he yelled.

SEVEN

Mary Grace's hands clenched the arms of her seat when the drone came alongside their jet. The thing was large but had a toylike appearance, at least until the bottom doors opened and a small bomb fell into the air.

"Ned?" she choked out.

He didn't answer, but kept one hand on the yoke while typing furiously on the still-open laptop on the console with the other.

"Ned!" she shrieked. "What are you doing? You're typing and we're about to be blown to smithereens."

"I have this," he said calmly.

She stared, mesmerized, as the small bomb chased them through the air and Ned banked the jet sharply to the right. The missile came within inches of hitting the plane before suddenly making a sharp turn back toward the drone. She held tight as Ned shifted their plane once again, and then understood why when the drone exploded into tiny little pieces.

Everything happened so fast it took Mary Grace several seconds to come out of her frozen state. "Wh-what just happened?" She gazed into his electric green eyes, alive with the excitement of battle, and shivered again.

"Who are you?" she whispered.

He sighed and gripped the yoke of the plane harder. "I'm just a man trying to survive and see that justice is done. Listen, I own this plane. I hacked into the drone and turned the missile back on itself."

Mary Grace closed her eyes, said a prayer of thanks for the good Lord sparing their lives, then turned and looked at Ned. It was time to play hardball. "Here's the deal. We're going to part ways when this airplane lands if you don't tell me what's going on, and I mean everything." She held her breath and allowed her words to linger in the air.

He stared at the clear blue sky in front of them before shifting his gaze to hers. His hands finally relaxed, as if he had come to a decision.

"I'll tell you everything on two conditions."

She took a hard swallow. This was going to be a tough one, she knew it in her gut. "I'm listening."

"First, anything you find out about my personal life and identity is to be kept private, and if your brother is culpable, in any way, you won't interfere while I make sure he's prosecuted to the fullest extent of the law."

This was the warrior she'd caught glimpses of while at the cabin. His voice had hardened to a degree she hadn't heard before and she knew he meant serious business. Well, so did she.

"I have two conditions of my own," she snapped back. "Before any authorities are called in, I insist you have rock-solid evidence that Bobby did something wrong. Also, if, and this is a big if, Bobby was somehow involved in what happened, someone could have set him up. I want you to listen to what he has to say, if we find him, and follow up on all the information he gives us before you make that final decision. And I also want your identity verified by someone official. Someone I can trust."

His lips curved upward at the sides and it threw her off guard.

"I like your style, Mary Grace, and I admire your loyalty to your brother. I'll give him every opportunity to prove his innocence." He took the satellite phone from her hands and grinned before pressing a button. "This is Ned. I need to speak with her."

Curiosity was eating Mary Grace alive, but she stayed quiet and waited, a professional journalist at her best.

Someone on the other end of the line must have picked up. "It's Ned. I'll fill you in later. I need you to verify to someone that I'm one of the good guys. You know her. Mary Grace Ramsey. She's a White House press correspondent for FBC."

Mary Grace heard the person on the other end of the phone line raise their voice and she leaned close, straining to hear.

Ned grinned at her and she snapped back in her seat.

"She won't be a problem. I'll make sure of it."

He handed the phone to her and she grabbed it out of his hand before placing it close to her ear.

"This is Mary Grace Ramsey," she said in a crisp, professional voice.

A woman chuckled on the other end of the line and it stunned Mary Grace for a moment. "I can tell from your tone you've been around Ned for too long. The boy has the social skills of a bull in a china shop."

A herd of wild horses kicked up a storm in her gut and Mary Grace swallowed the lump in her throat when she recognized the voice on the other end of the line. She had thrown more than her share of questions at CIA Director Madeline Cooper in her role as a journalist.

"Ma'am I apologize for interrupting your day, but I'm in a situation here and I need to know I can trust the man sitting next to me."

A weary sigh reached her ears. "I have no idea what's going on, but yes, you can trust Ned with your life." Madeline Cooper cleared her throat and transformed into the powerful, no-nonsense leader she was widely known to be. "But I want to make one thing clear. There will be no cooperation from this department on a story unless it's approved by me first due to potentially classified information. Do we have an understanding?"

Mary Grace backed down, but she had one more question. "Yes, ma'am. Understood. One more thing. What's Ned's full name?"

The CIA director laughed out loud. "You're a journalist. I'll leave that for you to discover," she said, and the line went dead.

Mary Grace mimicked Tinker Bell when she was in a bad mood, giving Ned the whale eye. "You could have warned me it was Madeline Cooper."

He laughed, and for some reason, Mary Grace got a toasty warm feeling because she had been the one to make him smile.

"And spoil all the fun?" He glanced at her. "You satisfied?"

She grinned back at him. "For the moment. And now that negotiations are complete, it's time for you to fess up and tell me everything that's going on."

That wiped the smile off his face. She mourned the

loss for a moment, but reminded herself that Bobby's freedom, and both their lives, were at stake.

"Aye, it's time." He hesitated, then gave her a rueful grin. "I'm not used to sharing information, so bear with me."

Mary Grace snorted. "You're a regular vault, all locked up tight as a drum. Just tell me already. It's not going to kill you." Her curiosity was on overload.

"You already know about my time in the army. After two years, I ended up in Special Forces and four years later, I'd had enough of the seedier side of human nature, so Krieger and I mustered out."

A thousand questions were already racing through her mind. "Did you have any trouble getting the dog out? I know a trained military dog is expensive."

The ferocious expression on his face had her leaning back in her seat.

"I had to jump through a dozen hoops to get the dog released into my custody, but Krieger was coming home with me, regardless. He saved my life multiple times."

Ned's love, passion and respect for Krieger shone in his eyes. Mary Grace didn't doubt for a second that he would have done just about anything to keep his dog with him.

"Let's just say, I agreed to make a hefty donation to the dog training program and let it go at that."

She nodded and he went on. "My best friend, Finn Lachlan, joined the army when I did, and we worked well together. We were assigned to the same unit. My team made a name for ourselves within the military and political community. We handled a lot of dicey international situations the government wanted kept quiet.

About six months after we both got out of the army, I received a call from the CIA director asking if Finn and I would come to work for her. We agreed as long as we could work together. Over a period of several years, we slipped in and out of places and gathered information. Nothing really dangerous."

"Why did she want you and your friend, Finn, so badly?" She was almost sure she heard his teeth grind.

"I have dual citizenship. My mom is American and my dad is from Scotland. Due to my family's vocation, we traveled all over the world and I learned to speak many languages. I can move in and out of a lot of countries with ease."

That could mean anything from his being a military brat to the son of the rich and famous, which, by looking at him, she highly doubted, but the luxurious plane confused things. His appearance and presentation didn't mesh with the jet.

"And your family's vocation is?"

He raised a bushy brow, ignored her question and kept talking. "The last job Finn and I handled went bad. It took me a while to piece together what happened, but I finally realized we were set up. I have absolute trust in Madeline Cooper, who has nothing to gain by setting us up. We were given bad intel and were ambushed." He gave her a dark look. "Intel, in part, given to us by your brother."

Shock reverberated through her. "Bobby doesn't work with field agents. He's a computer analyst. He gathers information and passes it on to his superiors."

He would wear his molars out at the rate he was grinding his teeth, but then he shot her a look of pity. Mary Grace seethed. She had gotten enough of those glances growing up when all the other kids in school teased her about her mother and stepfather.

"Sounds to me like your sweet, innocent brother hasn't shared everything with you."

Fury tore through her and her professionalism plummeted. Now *she* was gritting her teeth. "Maybe, just maybe, the CIA didn't allow him to tell me what he was doing. You ever think of that? Bobby is innocent and I'll prove it. Now tell me why Finn joined you at the CIA. Seems to me after years in the army, you both would have had enough of warfare."

He cast her a wary glance, then shrugged nonchalantly. Maybe a little too casually? Her gut told her he was only planning to reveal parts of the story, but she waited for his answer. She had learned a long time ago to give the interviewee time to trip themselves up, but it was obvious that Ned measured and weighed every tiny morsel of information he begrudgingly parted with.

"Finn and I were a team. If she wanted my services, they included Finn, and Finn needed the money."

So now she knew Finn was financially insecure. She briefly wondered if Ned needed the income, too, but quickly discarded the idea based on what she knew of him.

"It was supposed to be an easy in and out. Our job was to attend an art show at a famous gallery, pose as art dealers, get into the owner's office and download everything on his computer. The owner of the gallery had political ties and shipped art worldwide. He was suspected of hiding state secrets and information in the shipments. Our government wanted a list of his shipments."

"Why not just hack into his computer and get what they wanted?"

"In today's environment, people with something to hide usually have two systems. One for their normal work, and the other they never connect online. It's for their eyes only."

Mary Grace had to admit she'd never thought of that. "So you and Finn went in to download whatever was on the second computer. What happened, then?"

His hands tightened on the yoke again and Mary Grace rubbed her throat. She could easily visualize those large strong hands wrapping around someone's throat and squeezing the life out of them, but then she remembered how gentle and kind Ned had been with his niece and she dropped her hand and relaxed.

"It was an ambush. Finn went in to do the download and I waited just outside the door to make sure no one came down the hall. I heard a scuffle and entered the room, but it was too late. There was an open window in the office and a man dressed head-to-toe in black disappeared through the opening. I barely got a glimpse of him. I couldn't pursue because Finn was down."

He stopped for a moment, but Mary Grace knew better than to offer the comfort she so desperately wanted to. He thought her brother was somehow responsible for this horrific event. But that was impossible. Wasn't it? No, Bobby would never do anything like that.

"The guy used a silencer and the bullet hit Finn in the spine, disabling him for life." Her heart went out to him. She didn't want to ask the question burning a hole in her gut, but she forced her lips to move. "And what makes you think Bobby had something to do with the ambush?"

He looked at her and his emerald eyes turned molten. "Because Bobby was responsible for monitoring all movement and information of the enemy. He gave me the all-clear signal. There were cameras inside the office and he had hacked into them. He had to know those two men were lying in wait. I couldn't do two things at once and had to rely on the CIA team members to do the hacking and monitoring."

Ned's explanation shook Mary Grace to the core. She kept her expression even, but her heart was about to pound out of her chest. She breathed slowly through her nose until she calmed down enough to think. Pushing aside the churning, turbulent emotions connected to her brother, she forced herself to think like the reporter she was.

Mary Grace knew Bobby inside and out, but since working at the CIA, she noticed he'd become quieter, which she'd chalked up to maturity. She closed her eyes and let her mind rest for a second, clearing her thoughts. She popped upright when possible explanations presented themselves.

"You said yourself that Bobby hacked into the cameras in that man's office. What if someone else overrode Bobby's computer and the picture showed the room clear?" She gave a thoughtful pause. "Sounds to me like there might be some corruption going on."

He cut her a sharp look. "Aye, the corruption might begin with your brother, but there's someone more powerful behind him, pulling the strings. He should be able to lead me to them."

EIGHT

Ned only had a moment's respite before Mary Grace surprised him with her next question.

"Tell me about your friend, Finn."

"His name is Finn Lachlan. He's a natural born American citizen with a Scottish heritage. My family traveled a lot, but our home base is in the States. Finn and I were best friends growing up. He followed me into the army, and after that, as I told you, we joined the CIA."

"You feel responsible for his injury."

He took a deep breath and calmed the emotions churning in his gut.

"I don't see how that's pertinent to our current situation." His words sounded gruff and irritable, but he didn't really care.

She wouldn't find much information on his old friend because he'd made sure both his and Finn's operational backgrounds were buried deep. She might be a good, even great, reporter, but with his experience he had no doubt he could run information rings around her.

But he was curious. "Why ask me about Finn?"

She casually peered out the side window, but the tension in her body told a different story.

"Curiosity. That's all." The tone of her voice said differently.

"Tell me." It came out as a command, but at this point he really didn't care. He wanted to know what was going on in that active, inquisitive mind of hers.

She turned toward him and looked him in the eye. "Do you trust Finn?"

His gut rolled over once before the anger hit him. "What are you implying? Finn was the one left disabled for life. I grew up with him. Of course I trust him."

"Sorry to hit a nerve." She shrugged. "I'm a reporter. My job is to ask questions. If you say you trust Finn, fine, I believe you. Just covering all the bases."

He forced himself to calm down. She was right. It was her job to ask questions and probe for information and he'd do well to remember that. He needed a break from her inquisition and realized he could smell himself. He stunk.

"Listen, I'm going to take a quick shower and change clothes. I'll put the plane on autopilot. Call me if anything buzzes or sounds wrong." He grinned to himself as he pushed out of the pilot's chair and headed toward the door. Mary Grace didn't know he had a plane-wide computer system that would alert him if there were any problems. That included notifications of any unwanted visitors like the drone that had visited them earlier.

A big grin split his face and he kept walking when she screeched at his back.

"What? You can't just leave me here. What if someone tries to attack us again? What am I supposed to do? What if we have engine trouble?"

It got even worse when she realized he wasn't coming back. "I'm never flying with you again, you hear me? You're a crazy mountain man."

He scratched the scraggly beard covering his face and decided it was time to get rid of it. It had been functional on the cold mountain, but they were headed to Georgia. As he passed the plush seats in the middle of the plane, he wondered what Mary Grace would think of his clean-shaven face. Not that it mattered. As soon as he ran Bobby to ground and squeezed every morsel of information out of him, Ned would disappear. He wouldn't be seeing Mary Grace again.

His heart missed a beat at the thought of never peering into those intelligent golden eyes again, but he had a personal mission. Ned wanted to find the person responsible for putting Finn in a wheelchair and destroying his friend's life.

He shook his head when he entered the bedroom and spotted Krieger protectively curled around TB. The unlikely friendship between two such different dogs reminded him just how different he and Mary Grace were. He had tons of secrets and she was in the business of revealing them.

He grabbed a pair of worn comfy jeans and a soft blue jean shirt, but paused with the clothes in his hands and stared at the neatly laundered khakis and starched shirts. He threw the clothes back into the closet and removed a pair of pants and a shirt from their hangers. Mary Grace's grandmother sounded old school and he wanted to make a good impression. He had a gift for being able to fit into any environment and social situation.

He headed toward the shower and worked hard to convince himself that shaving his beard and dressing nicely had nothing to do with Mary Grace. Nope, this was all about information gathering. It didn't have a thing to do with the gorgeous, terrified, sassy woman currently sitting in the copilot's seat of his plane.

Fuming, and somewhat terrified to be the only person in the cockpit of a large airplane—although she'd never admit that to Ned—Mary Grace sat there and stared at the panel full of instruments, her fingers gripping the armrests. Every one of them was completely foreign to her. If something happened, they'd just have to crash while Mr. Mountain-Man-No-Last-Name-Ned took his leisurely shower.

Loosening her grip on the armrest, she started tapping her fingers against the leather while her brain began functioning again. She relaxed when she realized that a plane this equipped most likely had a computer system that would alert Ned if any problems presented themselves. No pilot on a commercial plane would ever leave the cockpit, except to use the bathroom, and they had copilots.

She grinned. Ned had a warped sense of humor and she liked it, maybe a little too much. He cared about and helped his friend, Finn, and had a burning desire to root out the bad guys. The only problem was that it might be at her brother's expense. Her momentary fuzzy feelings took a sharp nosedive at that thought.

Mary Grace would protect her brother with her last breath and Ned was convinced Bobby had something to do with the ambush the two men experienced.

Her nails tapped harder against the arm of her seat as she thought through everything Ned had shared. He'd been very careful to keep his personal life concealed.

He'd told her about the ambush, who he and Finn had worked for and that was it. What interested her the most outside of Ned's unknown personal history was the fact that Ned and Finn worked for the CIA.

That type of story was right down her alley, but her first priority was to find and protect her brother. Lost in her own thoughts, she jumped when Ned spoke from the entrance of the cockpit.

"Man, that shower felt great. I didn't realize how filthy I was."

"Yeah, well, I wasn't going to say anything, but..."

Her words fell away and her chin dropped when she swiveled around in her seat and got her first real look at Ned. The nasty beard had disappeared, only to reveal a granite-sharp jawline. The skin on the lower portion of his face was lighter than the upper portion due to the beard, but the man could easily be on the cover of a sports magazine, any sports magazine. He had on khakis and a starched button-down shirt with the sleeves rolled up, revealing muscled forearms.

The man was drop-dead gorgeous, and before she could clamp her lips shut, the words popped out of her mouth. "Are you sure you're not married?"

Those intelligent emerald eyes sparked with humor and Mary Grace wanted to crawl under the seat.

"That's not what I meant to say," she blurted out again. This was going from bad to worse. She took a deep breath and pasted on a false smile.

"I meant to say you clean up pretty good."

Grinning, he slid into the pilot's chair and checked all the controls. She wanted to smack the smile off his face because it was at her expense. She looked away, but couldn't stop from sneaking another peek. Mountain

Man really was too good-looking for his own good. The guy probably had a woman stashed in every country. He certainly had the means to travel extensively with his expensive plane.

"I'm really glad you didn't touch anything while I was gone."

An explosion welled up inside her, but he grinned at her again before she had a chance to erupt.

"And once again, no, I promise I've never been married."

With stiff shoulders, she shrugged in embarrassment.

Immense relief hit her in waves when he changed the subject.

"We'll be landing within twenty minutes. Buckle yourself in."

Mary Grace pulled the seat belt across her chest, her mind shifting to her grandmother. She prayed that the older lady was safe and the killer hadn't decided to pay her a visit, trying to find Bobby. Gram Ramsey might be tough, but she wouldn't stand a chance against the people after them.

NINE

After a perfect landing, Ned guided the plane behind a large building, which effectively shielded the aircraft from unwanted eyes. He flipped a bunch of switches and the engine rumbled off. He bit back a grin when Mary Grace slowly relaxed the death grip she had on the armrests.

"I didn't know this airstrip was here and I've lived in this area all my life." Those golden eyes of hers gazed at him, full of curiosity and suspicion.

He shrugged. "It's a privately owned airstrip. There's hundreds of them across the United States. Most owners will allow usage for the right price."

The gold band around the brown in her eyes burned bright with righteousness. "Does that mean bad, as well as good, people can pay for usage?"

He shrugged again. "If you don't like it, do a story on it."

Standing, she straightened her sweater and Ned winced. Most Christmas sweaters weren't very pretty, but this new one was much worse than the previous one she'd been wearing. It was green with a triangular Christmas tree on the front. Sewn in ornaments were placed all over it and yarn tassels flowed free from the top of several of them.

"I'll do that. We should get going. I'm worried about Gram Ramsey."

He understood her concern. He had a crotchety old grandfather he worried about all the time. Angus Duncan, laird of their family clan in Scotland, did his best to interfere in Ned's life, but he loved the old man dearly.

By the time he left the cockpit, Mary Grace and the two dogs were impatiently waiting on him by the exit door. She had her backpack slung over one shoulder and TB was safely ensconced in the dog carrier strapped to her chest.

She caught his scowl as she looked up from fiddling with the straps of the dog carrier. "What?"

"You shouldn't be carrying all that gear with the wound in your side."

She shot him a feral grin and the backpack slid from her shoulder and plunked onto the carpeted floor. "I'll be happy for you to carry my stuff."

He scowled again for good measure. Aye, the woman was as surly and stubborn as the pony he'd had as a kid. "Let me grab my gear and we'll be on our way."

He strode to the back of the plane to the bedroom, opened a hidden closet panel and grabbed the duffel bag that was always packed and ready to go at a moment's notice. He was back at her side in moments. He pressed the release hatch button and the stairs lowered to the ground.

He grinned at Mary Grace's back as she quickly scaled the steps and took a relieved breath when her feet hit the ground. His scowl returned when Krieger followed along behind, instead of in front of, the woman and her rat dog like a mutt in love. He was trained to leave the plane first and check the perimeter.

"Krieger, perimeter." He snapped out the order and Mary Grace frowned over her shoulder, her gaze following Krieger as the dog disappeared around the corner of the building.

Carrying his duffel and her backpack, he took the steps two at a time and stopped at her side, waiting for his dog to give the all-clear.

TB stuck her head out of the pouch and Mary Grace soothed the rat dog by stroking her gently on the head and making nonsensical noises when the dog started whining. She looked up at Ned with amusement lighting her eyes and his heart expanded in his chest. It disgruntled him that a mere look from this woman—a journalist at that—could make him react in such an unsettling fashion.

"What?" he snapped, then felt like a fool for allowing emotions to get in the way of the important task at hand.

She grinned wider and he felt as if she could somehow see inside him, past the gruff exterior and hard shell he'd grown.

"I think Krieger's in love with Tinker Bell."

"What? That's preposterous."

Mary Grace tilted her head and her eyes became mere slits. "You think just because Krieger is a fully trained dog that he's too good for my Tinker Bell?"

Ned became very wary. His grandfather always said that women would say one thing and mean something else entirely. That a man had to pay close attention to figure out what was really going on. He was terrified that she wasn't talking about dogs, but alluding to something much more personal, so he took a relieved breath when

Krieger came loping around the corner of the building and sat in front of him, giving the all-clear signal. He ignored her question and moved forward. "Let's go."

Handled by his contact, an empty car sat in front of the small building that manned the airport, waiting on them. A man inside the building threw his hand up but turned away when they approached the car. Mary Grace pinned him with a look brimming with questions, but opened the back door for Krieger, closed it and loaded herself and TB into the passenger seat.

He held her backpack out to her, which she took and placed on the floorboard, then tossed his duffel into the back seat. She didn't say a word until he pulled out his phone and asked for the address of her grandmother's house. He input the information she relayed, backed the car out of the parking space and they were on their way. He didn't have to wait long for the explosion of questions.

"I don't see how we were able to land at that airstrip without filing a proper flight plan. And how we were able to bypass security at the airport. We've probably broken a ton of laws, and if I get into trouble, it's going to be your fault. And why didn't you use the GPS in the car?"

His head pounded as her questions peppered him like a round of gunfire. "Everything we've done has been legally authorized. You won't get in trouble." Then understanding dawned. "You're a stickler for the rules, aren't you?"

She sniffed in disdain. "Rules are there for a reason. What would society look like if we didn't have rules?"

He snorted in disbelief. Mary Grace was a White House press correspondent. She was exposed to the underbelly of Washington politics on a daily basis. She should have known better.

"In a perfect world, if everyone played by the rules, then the government wouldn't need people like me. Someone has to be there to clean up the mess everyone else makes of their lives and their countries."

"You're very cynical, you know that?"

His lips twisted in the parody of a smile. "Yes, I'm cynical to the core, and with good reason. Someone, likely from my own country, betrayed me and Finn and I'll not rest until I track them down and they're rotting behind bars."

Ned ignored the fact that Mary Grace had reiterated what his own family had been telling him. He refused to let anything get in the way of justice, and that included the woman sitting closed-mouth—for the first time since he'd met her—in the seat beside him. Nothing more was said until they pulled into the driveway of her grandmother's house.

With the car still idling, Mary Grace instructed Ned to crack the windows for the dogs and then sat staring at the house that became a refuge during her turbulent teenage years. Not only for her, but for Bobby, too. Just like the old house, now decked out in Christmas finery, Gram Ramsey had wrapped both of the lonely, bewildered kids in her loving arms and practically raised them herself while her mother and stepfather were gambling their way to destitution. And now she and Bobby had possibly placed her in danger.

After removing Tinker Bell from her pouch and placing her in the back seat with Krieger, she reached for the door handle.

"Impressive place."

Trying to see it fresh, through Ned's eyes, Mary

Grace stared at the historical Greek Revival–style home, supported by four large round columns holding up the front porch ceiling. Two expanded windows were placed on either side of the half-glassed front door, and six regular-sized windows marched across the top. A set of six steps, sided with brick and flared out on each side, led to the porch.

The swing she had sat in as a teenager, dreaming about her future, still hung by two chains attached to the two-story porch ceiling. Gram Ramsey had shared many pearls of wisdom with Mary Grace in that swing. Two huge Christmas wreaths adorned each side of the tall historical two-door entrance. Greenery lovingly wrapped itself around the columns, each one with a big red bow at the top. Mary Grace had inherited her grandmother's love of Christmas adornment, but Gram made sure she and Bobby understood the true meaning of Christmas and everything it represented. Mary Grace had decorated her town house, but it never felt the same as Hubert House, the only place that was truly home.

But if a person bothered to look closer, and she had no doubt that eagle-eyed Ned would, there were small signs of neglect. A little paint peeling here and there, shrubs that needed trimming. Her heart clinched at the thought of the grand old place going downhill due to lack of funds, but her grandmother was a proud woman. Mary Grace had offered to help as much as she was able with the upkeep, but Gram Ramsey wouldn't hear of it.

Mary Grace turned the car door handle and pushed open the door. "Yeah, well, if I have anything to do with it, it'll stay that way, at least until Gram Ramsey goes to meet her Maker."

She heard the smile in his words when he asked, "Goes to meet her Maker?"

She twisted around, filled with comical anticipation. "Oh, I'm sure by the time we leave you'll understand all about meeting your Maker."

His grin slid away, replaced by a frown, but she swung her legs out of the car and landed on her feet. She wanted to see for herself that Gram was okay. She heard the driver's car door shut behind her, but she ignored Ned's order to wait on him and ran up the steps she'd run up hundreds of times. He caught up with her, grabbed the front door handle before she could reach it and shoved her behind him.

"It's safer for me to go in first."

Raising both hands in the air, she grinned. "By all means, be my guest, but I'd be careful if I were you."

He was still turned, staring at her, when the door jerked inward and out of his grasp. Mary Grace's grin widened at his expression of sheer amazement when he froze at the sound of a shotgun being cocked with the experience of a seasoned hunter. Without taking her eyes off Ned, she said, "It's okay, Gram, he's with me."

When the trigger made a sound, releasing the hammer and uncocking the gun, Ned let loose a pent-up breath and shot Mary Grace a dark look, silently promising retribution.

Mary Grace slapped a hand over her mouth to stop from laughing and sidled around him so she wouldn't miss anything as Ned slowly turned to face his adversary. He had to keep lowering his chin until he caught sight of her proud five-foot-two-inches-tall grandmother. She probably weighed in at a whopping ninety pounds, but she held the rifle with authority.

With gentility and grace, Gram Ramsey propped the rifle against the foyer wall and greeted her guest with all the aplomb of a Southern belle, as if she'd never pointed a rifle in his face.

"Mary Grace, child, you get over here right now and give your grandmother a big hug, then you can introduce me properly to your young man."

She stepped forward and hugged the small woman fiercely. A sense of peace and love enveloped her. Gram Ramsey had been the only stabilizing force in Mary Grace's life and she loved the older woman with all her heart. Pulling back, she studied Gram closely. She visited as often as she could, but it was never enough. Her grandmother looked a little older every time she came home. She'd been joking with Ned, but she couldn't stand to think of Gram *actually* meeting her Maker.

Feeling a huge relief that her grandmother was okay, Mary Grace waved a hand toward Ned. "He's not my young man. We only recently met. This is Ned. As I explained on the phone, we're looking for Bobby and some disreputable people are trailing us."

Gram gave her a sharp look. Mary Grace knew what it meant and she shrugged her shoulders. "He won't tell me his last name, so I can't introduce him properly." Inwardly, she smiled. She doubted Ned had ever met anyone like her grandmother. With a warm Southern smile and gracious manners, Gram could perform an interrogation that would make the military sit up and take notice.

Gram stepped closer to Ned and touched his arm in a friendly fashion, but the light of battle and determination lit her eyes in a way Mary Grace hadn't seen in a long time. There was something else in her grandmother's eyes. Something Mary Grace would put a stop to as soon as she got her grandmother alone. Gram Ramsey was envied in the community for her matchmaking skills, and Mary Grace didn't want her to get anything in her head about her and Ned.

"Well, then, Ned, my name is Athena Hubert Ramsey. Athena comes from my mother's side of the family, you know. I'd like to welcome you to Hubert House and I'd dearly love to know your surname so I can address you properly."

It was almost comical watching the hulking man hover nervously over her tiny grandmother, but he finally grimaced and spouted forcefully, "Nolan Eli Duncan, ma'am, and I would appreciate it if you wouldn't spread that around." He glanced at the plethora of decorations and a small Christmas tree that Gram always placed in the foyer before his gaze landed back on Gram, and he said in a nervous rush, as if trying to make conversation, "I see where Mary Grace gets her love of Christmas."

Ned stole a small piece of Mary Grace's heart when he nervously addressed her grandmother, and her heart warmed when her grandmother patted his large muscular arm. Then it dawned on her, Nolan Eli Duncan was long for Ned.

"Now that wasn't so hard, was it?" Gram said, then started spewing orders like a miniature drill sergeant. "Mary Grace, bring young Eli into the parlor to meet the ladies, then you can show him to his room. I'm sure you two would like to freshen up."

Mary Grace quickly moved past the fact that she now knew Ned's name—if that was his real name—and grimaced before laying a hand on her grandmother's arm. "Gram, we can't stay. I came to make sure you're okay and to ask again if you'd be willing to stay with one of your friends until we find Bobby and get this matter resolved. This is the first place the people after us will come looking for him. It's easy to find out Bobby and I pretty much grew up here."

Gram reared back and assessed Ned from head to toe. "Eli, I won't ask about the particulars of this situation, but can I trust you to keep my granddaughter safe?"

Mary Grace stifled a grin when he bobbed his head like a schoolboy being caught with his hand in the cookie jar. "I'll do my best, ma'am."

Gram nodded. "That's all I can ask." She turned toward Mary Grace and held her arms wide. "Come give an old lady another hug." Mary Grace walked into her arms. "I'll be praying for you, child," she whispered into her ear. "And I like your young man. The good Lord brought him into your life for a reason only He knows. Have patience."

Mary Grace didn't have a chance to ask what her grandmother meant because the older woman pulled away and marched toward the parlor.

"Eli, Mary Grace, I'm staying here and I'll be fine. Let me introduce my friends before you leave."

"Eli" looked none too happy as he motioned Mary Grace to precede him into the room. They both came to a dead stop once over the threshold and Gram chuckled as they surveyed the room full of Gram's bridge partners.

Three older ladies sitting at the bridge table each had a pink lipstick stun gun, the lid off, ready to use, placed within easy reach. Mary Grace recognized the stun guns because she had bought her grandmother one the previous Christmas. Gram must have ordered them for all her friends. The scene didn't surprise her at all. Every good Southern father taught his daughters how to protect themselves from an early age.

They all murmured the appropriate greetings. Mary

Grace introduced Ned as her friend and then backed out of the room as fast as possible. Gram followed them to the door.

"So you see, I'll be fine here at Hubert House." Her chin lifted and her eyes turned to steel. Ned took a step back. "In the past, Hubert women have weathered far worse than a few thugs who think they can run over an old woman." She gave a short nod to Mary Grace and spoke with intelligence that showed the sharpness of her mind. "Your old swamp boots are in the shed out back. I assume that's where you're headed. Let me know when you find Bobby. I need to have a talk with that boy. He's always getting into all sorts of trouble. And I expect you to be back in time for Christmas."

Mary Grace grabbed her grandmother in another fierce hug. "Thanks, Gram. We'll be careful and I'll find Bobby. Please take care of yourself. I couldn't stand it if anything happened to you."

They headed out the door, but Ned surprised Mary Grace by turning back. "Ma'am?"

"Yes?" her grandmother answered with patience and graciousness.

"Out of curiosity, why did you choose to call me Eli instead of Nolan?"

Gram had a sparkle in her eye. "Why, didn't you know? In the Bible, Eli was the high priest of Shiloh, the second-to-last Israelite judge succeeded by Samuel."

Ned paused a moment, as if pondering her answer, then moved to leave, determination in his stride. Mary Grace followed him with an equally determined stride. They had a killer to catch before anyone else got hurt, and that included her feisty, adorable grandmother.

TEN

Rounding the corner of the house after helping Mary Grace grab her gear out of the small storage building, Ned heard Krieger barking furiously from inside the car. He took hold of Mary Grace's arm and used the house as cover when she tried to run toward the vehicle.

"Get inside and take care of your grandmother and her friends. Go in the back way. Now!" Her eyes held terror and his heart pounded in his chest. He wouldn't allow anything to happen to this feisty woman who loved Christmas, her rat dog and her sweet grandmother.

His eyes on their car, he spotted movement behind the bumper.

"Go now," he said quietly.

To his relief, she tore off back the way they had come from and Ned pulled his pistol from the waistband of his jeans. When he glanced around the corner of the house, a guy was crawling out from beneath the car. Ned lifted his gun and moved into the open when the guy stood up. "Don't move or I'll shoot," he shouted in warning. The guy had a ball cap pulled low over his brow and Ned failed to get a good look at him. The man stood frozen for a moment, then glanced toward the house with surprise written on his face.

Ned's heart almost pounded out of his chest when a loud rifle report sounded from the front porch and vibrated in the still air. He almost had a heart attack when he heard Mary Grace's voice.

"You leave my dog and my grandmother alone or the next bullet is gonna make you limp for life."

The guy ran off and darted into the woods farther down the driveway. It took everything Ned had not to go after him, but he didn't dare leave Mary Grace alone. The guy might have a partner somewhere close by.

Shoving the pistol back into his jeans, he took several long strides toward the car. He opened the car door and released Krieger. "Krieger, search." Crawling underneath the vehicle, he spotted a simple bomb attached to the car. With steady hands, he examined the device, then carefully pulled a wire free to disable it before removing it from the vehicle. He slid out from under the car, stood and took a deep breath of relief.

He jogged to the front porch, gently pried the shotgun from Mary Grace's fingers and herded her inside. His anger at the risk she'd taken softened at the deep fear reflected in her eyes.

"Everything's okay, but we really need to convince your grandmother to stay somewhere safe. The guy planted a bomb underneath the car."

Gram Ramsey stepped into the foyer and smiled at Ned. "Don't worry, Eli, I'll be safe here. You two go on and find Bobby. I'll be praying for your safety." Her eyes hardened. "And take care of my girl."

He opened his mouth to argue, but she had already turned to go back and join her bridge partners. Ned could hear the nervous twitters coming from the other ladies over the recent excitement.

Mary Grace gave him a weak smile. "You heard the lady."

There was nothing else to be done, so he opened the door and there sat Krieger in his all-clear position.

"Okay, let's go to the swamp shack and get this thing done."

They got in the car and Mary Grace sat there for a few minutes, worry written on her face. "I couldn't live with myself if something happened to Gram."

Ned started the car. "We'll check out the swamp shack and get back as soon as we can."

"Well," she said with a nervous laugh, "at least now I know your name."

Ned breathed a sigh of relief. He disliked bursting her bubble, but after what had just happened, maybe a different subject would snap her out of her worry over her grandmother. "Your grandmother reminds me of my grandfather and I've found it's just better, in the long run, to go ahead and answer their questions. But I'm afraid you won't find any information on me if you go looking. I don't exist."

She shrugged, when he really wanted her to dig into him. "I get it. You don't trust me, and I'll never know who you really are. Fine, let's just find Bobby. I'll prove he's innocent and you can crawl back to your lonely mountain and I'll be out of your hair for good."

His chest, close to the region of his heart, rejected the idea that he'd never see Mary Grace again. The woman talked too much and poked around in places better left alone, but for some strange reason he wanted her to stay around. He started the car and berated himself.

He couldn't afford to trust anyone outside of the chosen few. His and Finn's lives might depend on it.

Back to the task at hand. "Where to?" His flat question had her stiffening in her seat and that was just as well. He had no business becoming attracted to a woman he didn't trust. He couldn't allow himself to forget that she had shown up on his mountain—a place few people even knew existed—to ask for help concerning her brother. A man who had conveniently gone off the grid.

He stopped at the end of the driveway and waited patiently.

She glared at him and motioned to the right. "Go up the road for a mile and we'll park the car in the Okefenokee Swamp public parking lot. Most of the time Bobby and I trekked to the old swamp shack from the back of Gram's house, but sometimes we went in this way because it's easier."

He swiftly turned the wheel and started driving. Within minutes a large wooden sign with some kind of cypress tree carved into it on the left announced the entrance to Okefenokee Swamp Park. A huge red bow was pinned to the top. He turned in and parked the car between two large campers.

Mary Grace opened her door and grabbed the muck boots she'd retrieved from the shack behind her grandmother's house. Using her open door to steady herself, she shed her shoes and pulled the boots on. TB had jumped into the front seat and Mary Grace slipped the dog carrier over her shoulders, stuffed the tiny mutt inside and grabbed her backpack.

Krieger whined from the back seat and Ned felt as if he were living in the twilight zone. His fiercely trained German shepherd had never whined in his life. After slipping on a jacket, she leaned into the car, her fighting face back in place.

"Okay, Mountain Man, let's see how you fare in a swamp. You'll need a jacket. It might be December, but we're in Georgia so you don't have to worry about getting frost bitten like you do on that mountain of yours."

He folded himself out of the car, slipped on a pair of well-worn hiking boots and grabbed his duffel. He shrugged into a light jacket, even though it was hovering around fifty degrees. Compared to Jackson Hole, this felt like springtime. The jacket was mainly to conceal the pistol in the waistband of his jeans. The gun wasn't only because their lives were in danger. He'd been in swamps more times than he cared to remember, places that housed far worse things than a Georgia swamp could ever dream of, but there was still plenty of danger in any swamp. He called Krieger to his side and met Mary Grace at the back of the car. She gave him a haughty stare.

"Dogs are supposed to be on a leash if they aren't being carried."

"Says Miss Rule-Stickler," he mumbled.

"What did you say?"

"Nothing." He shook his head and swept his hand in front of her. "I can control my dog off-leash. Lead the way."

The Georgia princess sniffed and started walking toward an area marked as the park entrance to the swamp. They followed a short path, then stepped onto a planked walkway with a small cable strung through square wood that disappeared into the murky depths of the water.

Mary Grace spoke over her shoulder. "We'll stay on the designated path for about half a mile, and if the old canoe Bobby and I sometimes used when we entered the swamp from this direction is still there and floatable, we can be at the shack fairly quickly."

Ned stared at the lowering sun. "It better be fast or we'll get caught in the swamp after dark."

Mary Grace threw him a challenging grin. "You afraid of a few swamp critters, Ned?"

He gave a mock shudder. "Aye, I'm a mountain man, not a swamp rat like you." He knew how to survive in a swamp, but his words were still true. He much preferred mountain lions and bears to gators.

She marched ahead and soon they stepped off the planked walkway and onto a path. Mary Grace led him into the woods off the designated public pathway and shortly after that they arrived at a slight embankment shouldering a wide expanse of murky water. She muttered under her breath while she searched an area next to a cypress tree, very close to the swamp. The woman never stopped talking. Ned kept a close eye out for gators. They were known to hide right below the surface and strike hard and fast.

Ripping away some undergrowth, she whipped around and pumped a fist in the air. "It's still here, after all this time. If it's floatable, we're in business. If Bobby is at the shack, he had to have gone in from the back of Gram's house."

Ned put Krieger in a Stay and helped her pull the canoe from the clutches of the forest. Green, peeling paint adorned the outside, and it looked water worthy, but Ned pulled it to the edge of the bank and pushed it in to make sure. He let it float a few minutes and, when it didn't take on water, deemed it safe.

They climbed aboard and he grabbed the only set

of oars. Mary Grace raised a questioning brow, but he only grunted and started rowing. He had always appreciated nature and found a small measure of peace among the huge cypress trees flourishing in the swamp. Lily pads floated aimlessly in the water and plant life was abundant.

"How far?"

Holding on to both sides of the canoe, she twisted around. "Such a conversationalist. Do you just sit there and grunt when you're on a date?"

Since he hadn't been on a real date in years, he only grunted again.

"It'll only take about ten minutes in the canoe. It's pretty far from civilization. Even if whoever is after us and Bobby found out about this place, it's doubtful they'd ever be able to locate it."

Mary Grace was still twisted toward him in the canoe when Ned saw TB stick her head out of the pouch and her ears prick. He followed the dog's gaze, but before he could make a move or say anything, the rat dog popped out of the pouch, landed on Mary Grace's leg and dove into the water. TB evidently spotted movement and decided a chase was on. Her dog definitely wasn't swamp savvy. As Mary Grace stood screaming in the canoe, threatening to overturn them, Ned muttered out loud, "Not again," right before he told his dog to stay, slid out of the canoe and prepared to fight a gator. He was right, the woman and her rat dog were nothing but trouble, he thought as he pulled the sharp blade from his boot and placed himself between a hungry gator and his next meal.

Horrified at the scene playing out in front of her, Mary Grace stood frozen in the canoe until Krieger's half growl, half whine broke her trance. She quickly plopped back down, but found herself unable to tear her gaze away. A huge alligator with beady eyes was silently gliding through the water toward Ned. He pushed Tinker Bell toward the canoe.

"Grab your dog out of the water if you can."

His calm words broke through her haze and she went into action, frantically calling Tinker Bell toward the canoe. She recognized the moment her dog realized she was in a precarious position and started paddling her tiny legs as fast as she could. Mary Grace scooped her out of the swamp water, hugged her precious baby close before placing her in the dog carrier, then yelled at Ned, "I have her. Get back in the canoe."

She thought she heard the words *too late now* right before the gator's large mouth yawned wide open in preparation for an attack. Ned dodged the powerful jaws after they snapped shut and grabbed the beast around the mouth, preventing it from attacking again. The water was chest high on Ned, but it looked like he'd found his footing. Her heart in her throat, she sat, mesmerized, as he pulled the gator through the tall grass and onto the embankment. With quick, efficient movements, he released the animal and jumped out of the way. She could now see it was a young alligator as it slithered back into the water, evidently deciding to search for a less troublesome snack elsewhere. It didn't look nearly as dangerous as it had in the water and her breath left her lungs in a giant whoosh when she realized Ned wasn't hurt.

Dripping wet, with his big hands propped on his hips, he stared at her sitting in the canoe. "Now I see why the park requires dog leashes."

She ignored his taunt, so happy no one was hurt, and grabbed the oars, paddling as hard as she could to get to the embankment. She made sure the young gator was long gone before pulling the canoe on land and lifting Tinker Bell from the carrier and placing her on the ground, then racing toward Ned. She reached up high, grabbed his head, pulled it down and planted a big kiss right on his lips.

"I'm so, so sorry. I never dreamed Tinker Bell would jump into the water. I can't believe you risked your life to save her from an alligator. You're a hero, that's what you—"

Her words stopped abruptly when he wrapped his long arms around her waist, lifted her off her feet and kissed her into silence. Only after he dropped her back down did she come to her senses. It took her a moment to assimilate what had just happened. They'd kissed each other, and she liked it. A lot. But that wasn't possible. She knew next to nothing about the man's personal life, and he thought her brother had betrayed him.

"Let it go, Mary Grace. It was only a spur-of-the-moment thing. I can see your thoughts running a mile a minute through that pretty head of yours. It was only a kiss. We need to find the shack and get out of this swamp before dark."

He thought she was pretty? She shook off the fanciful thought. He was right. It was only a we-made-it-through-that-terrifying-ordeal kiss, and she needed to find her brother. After that they would part ways. If the idea left her feeling more than a tad gloomy, she ignored the emotion as she scooped up her dog and climbed back into the canoe. Krieger followed Mary Grace and Tinker Bell. Ned pushed them off and climbed aboard.

He rowed and she forced her racing thoughts to silence. All that mattered was finding her brother alive and getting answers. She wouldn't allow anything else to get in the way of that.

As they approached the tree with an upside-down sign reading Mirror Lake that appeared upright in the water's reflection, she motioned for Ned to pull over. She was surprised to see someone had attached a tattered Christmas bow below the sign. Ned hopped out and pulled the canoe onto the bank. Mary Grace stepped out, followed by Krieger, and led them into the wilds of the Okefenokee Swamp. Ned told her to be as silent as possible and let him approach the shack first in case someone had gotten there ahead of them.

On foot it took them fifteen minutes and she breathed a sigh of relief when she spotted the rusted tin roof of the shack. A good portion of the small structure had been taken over by undergrowth. If possible, it looked even worse than it had when she and Bobby used to play there as kids. Gram Ramsey never worried about them in the swamp. She taught them about snakes and alligators and how to avoid them.

Silent as a gentle breeze, Ned gave Krieger a hand signal that she assumed meant to stay put. Ned slipped past her and moved into the woods to her right. Mary Grace remained hidden behind a huge tree and jerked in surprise when Ned silently appeared on her left. She hadn't even heard him. He must have been really good at his job when he was in the military.

He whispered into her ear, "Looks clear now, but someone has been here." She stiffened and he added, "But I think they're long gone."

She whispered back, "How can you be sure?"

"I found tracks leading to and from the shack, in the opposite direction of the lake."

Mary Grace whipped around in horror. The tracks were from the direction of Gram's house. She closed her eyes and prayed out loud. At the moment she didn't care whether Ned believed or not. "Dear Lord, please, please protect my grandmother."

After a few more seconds, she opened her eyes and leveled a stare at him. "We have to leave right now. What if those prints belong to the bad guys and not Bobby? I can't take that chance because whoever is after us might be headed back to Gram's."

Ned placed his large hands on her shoulders, ignored Tinker Bell's warning growl and looked her in the eye. "Listen, the footprints could belong to your brother. Maybe he holed up here for a while and then left. We're here, so let's check out the cabin and see what we can find."

Mary Grace said another quick prayer and swallowed hard. "Fine. But then we're heading back to Gram's as fast as possible."

He whispered a command to Krieger and the big German shepherd crept through the woods, then reappeared close to the sagging front porch of the shack. The dog slipped inside, and a minute later came back to the front porch and sat.

"All clear, let's go," Ned said.

Mary Grace sent up yet another prayer, asking for direction and information. She hoped Bobby had left a message of some sort and she knew exactly where he would hide it.

Memories assailed her as she stepped through a front door that was barely hanging on by one hinge. It was a one-room shack. No bathroom, no kitchen, only the old table and two chairs she and Bobby had placed there. Her nose wrinkled in distaste. Over the years an entire host of animals had taken refuge in the shack. There were animal droppings everywhere and one corner held a little skeleton, no doubt another animal's dinner.

After prowling the small space, Ned approached the table and picked up an envelope. "It's addressed to you," he said, before tearing the letter open.

"You're rude, you know that?"

"Many people have told me that over the years."

While he studied the letter, Mary Grace casually roamed the room. Precious childhood memories assailed her, but she chided herself to stay focused. With her back to Ned, she quietly pulled the end of a rotten board from the wall and slipped her hand inside. Her heart beat rapidly as her fingers touched something solid. An envelope. One meant for her eyes only.

Mary Grace and Bobby had concealed childhood treasures in their secret hiding place all those years ago in case anyone else visited the swamp cabin, and now she thanked their ingenuity.

Slipping the letter into her jacket pocket, she lightly pushed the board back into place and slowly turned when Ned started talking, his eyes focused on the letter in his hand.

"Your brother is implicating a very powerful person."

Mary Grace rushed to Ned's side, her investigator's nose twitching up a storm. "What does it say?" She grabbed the letter out of his hand, quickly skimming Bobby's words. She went into journalistic overload when his accusations settled into her mind. If what Bobby was saying were true, and she had no reason to doubt him, she was looking at the story of the year. A possible Pulitzer Prize winner.

Her pulse quickened and she looked at Ned. "I can't believe it. Bobby is pointing a finger at Chief of Staff Hensley. He thinks someone overrode his computer the night you and Finn were in that gallery. Ned, he didn't know someone was there waiting for you. This proves he's innocent."

Mary Grace was so filled with joy at proving her brother's innocence she grabbed Ned and gave him a big hug. Mortified to the tips of her toes, she pulled back, but at the same moment, on the fringes of her mind, she heard a noise very similar to the one at Ned's mountain cabin. In a split second, she found herself hefted into Ned's arms while he speared them toward the open front door. Just as they reached the edge of the porch, an ear-splitting explosion rocked the foundation of the shack and the powerful force lifted them into the air.

ELEVEN

Ned twisted his body midair so he would take the full impact of the landing. His breath whooshed from his chest and out of his mouth. He'd have a few bruises on his back, but overall he was convinced they had fared pretty well. The warmth of Mary Grace's body in his arms diverted his attention from their dangerous circumstances. He had grabbed her from behind in the cabin and her soft back was snuggled close to his chest. For a mere moment he allowed himself to consider how different things would be if he could allow himself to trust someone. Mary Grace, with her smart mouth and incessant talk, could easily slip past the protective barriers he'd painfully erected over time.

With years of practice, he compartmentalized any tender emotions and gave a sharp whistle for Krieger, hoping his faithful companion had been outside during the blast. He scrambled up from the ground, placed Mary Grace on her feet, grabbed her hand and guided her toward the nearest trees, keeping them both low. Tree bark stung his face as a bullet hit a tree nearby. It was close, way too close for comfort. Pulling Mary Grace in a zigzag pattern through the woods, he finally got them to the canoe. She clamored aboard and Krieger came tearing behind them and jumped into the craft. Ned pushed them away from the bank as fast as possible and started paddling with all his strength. Thankfully, there was a bend in the river and they lost the shooter. At least for the time being. She was most likely in shock, but he was thankful Mary Grace stayed quiet while he placed some distance between them and the shooter. It was going on full dark now and the enemy could be anywhere, but the darkness was to their advantage.

Mary Grace finally came alive and Ned was glad to see it. Her voice trembled, but he was proud that she was trying to be brave. "What are you doing? Where are we going?"

"Right now I'm putting some distance between us and the shooter. My gut tells me he, or they, will come after us. A swamp is a great place to leave dead bodies. Nobody around to witness the killing, and the swamp critters would most likely take care of the carcasses."

She grimaced, and he almost regretted his words, but he wanted her to realize the extent of the danger they were in.

She slumped her shoulders. "I can't believe someone tried to blow us up again. This is crazy. You'd think someone as powerful as Chief of Staff Hensley could come up with a more inventive way to get rid of us. I can see why someone is trying to kill you, but why me and Bobby?"

Ned had been thinking about that and there was only one reason why they would want Mary Grace dead. "Your brother is up to his eyeballs in this and you're a reporter. Maybe they're afraid Bobby told you something, which he did—he sent you to me—and they know you'll never give up on a juicy story." His last words were filled with sarcasm, but that's how he felt.

Ned kept rowing with quiet efficiency and waited for the storm but was surprised at her insight when she finally spoke.

"Ned, what if they set up Bobby to take the fall, knowing he would run and then contact me? Maybe they were aware Bobby knew where you were and was hoping I would lead them to you."

Ned didn't answer. Night had fallen and the moon was hidden behind a host of clouds. Creatures of the night were awakening with a loud ruckus and Ned had no doubt that there were many gators gliding silently through the swamp, hunting for their next meal.

"We can talk after we set up camp."

"What?" she shrilled.

He grinned when Mary Grace reacted just as he had thought she would. He loved her feistiness. Most women would be in a complete panic after everything that had happened.

"We can't spend the night in the swamp," she insisted. "It's too dangerous and I'm not spending the night alone with you."

"Unless you want to announce our position to the enemy, I suggest you keep your voice down."

Her voice lowered to a furious whisper. "I have to check on Gram. What if someone tries to hurt her. I'd never forgive myself."

Ned knew he had to allay her fears. He loved his grouchy grandfather as much as she appeared to love her gram.

"We'll get there as soon as we can, but it's not safe to

travel through the swamp right now. The shooters are probably still out here, and there's always the danger of the swamp critters. We'll wait until daylight before we try to make our way back."

Mary Grace faced forward in the canoe and he heard soft murmurings as she soothed TB. He hadn't thought about how upset the tiny dog would be. Krieger was military trained and gunshots and bombs didn't bother him. It was shocking how drastically Ned's life had changed in such a short period of time. He'd gone from hunting his enemy to protecting a spirited woman and her puff dog.

He steered the canoe toward one of the few solid-looking banks and hopped out, pulling it onto land. Krieger leaped out and Ned held out a hand to Mary Grace. A flash of annoyance crossed her face, but it was accompanied by the barest spark of vulnerability visible in her eyes before she pulled herself together and took his hand.

"Fine, I'll find us a safe spot to sleep," she said quietly. "We probably shouldn't build a fire in case they were able to follow us. At least we didn't take our backpacks off at the cabin. We'll be fine."

It sounded as if she were trying to convince herself, so Ned kept his mouth shut and went about preparing for a night in the swamp. He gathered the largest tree limbs littering the ground and formed them in a circle.

Mary Grace started chattering softly and Ned allowed the soothing cadence of her voice to wash over him. For some unknown reason, her incessant speech was having the oddest effect on him. Instead of getting on his nerves like it had at his cabin, her voice reached a place deep inside him. A place he had closed off long ago, even from his family.

"Ned." She kept her voice at a whisper. "Did you know we only have access to the Okefenokee Swamp today because in the 1800s loggers tried to drain the swamp so they could cut the huge cypress trees?" She chuckled and his heart warmed. "It didn't work, but they did create eleven and a half miles of canals before they were stopped. The canals have been expanded to one hundred and twenty miles."

He took note of the slight tremor in her voice and his respect for her courage slid straight to his heart and sidled up against the warmth he'd received earlier.

She stopped talking, propped her hands on her hips and glared at him. "What, exactly, are you doing?"

He left a small opening at the front of his hastily built fortress and motioned her forward. "This is to keep the gators at bay, at least long enough for us to protect ourselves if they breach the walls. A raised platform would have been better, but this is all we have available."

A myriad of emotions crossed her face and he could almost read her thoughts, she was so transparent. He knew the second she figured it out. Her nose scrunched up and she marched straight up to him. TB popped out of her pouch but ducked back in quickly when she caught sight of Mary Grace's angry expression.

"You lied to me," she whispered fiercely. "You do know how to navigate a swamp."

He grudgingly gave her points for standing up to him, but she wasn't as innocent as she was pretending to be. She had secretly slipped something into her jacket pocket when they were at the shack, and she had yet to share what it was with him.

"You're right, I've fought in much worse swamps than this, but my intent was not to deceive. It was more in jest." He gazed deeply into her eyes, his heart pleading with her to be honest with him. With every fiber of his being, he wanted to be able to trust her.

Casually, he asked, "Have you ever lied by omission, Mary Grace? Have you been completely honest with me?" He held his breath as he waited to see if she would come clean with him.

Mary Grace's heart began to beat triple time. Had Ned seen her slip Bobby's letter into her pocket? No, it was impossible. He'd had his back to her in the shack, reading the letter Bobby left on the table. She gazed into Ned's contemplative eyes. He looked as if he were waiting for her to make a momentous decision and a quick jab punched her gut. This felt like one of those odd turning points in one's life. A moment that could never be taken back or replayed over.

She found herself wanting to slip her hand into her pocket and share the letter with Ned. She believed with all her heart in Bobby's innocence, but what if Bobby had written something private that might appear incriminating to Ned? Ned had promised to bring the full force of the law down on Bobby if he proved his guilt. She couldn't take that chance. She wanted to read the letter so badly, she was burning with curiosity, but she'd have to wait until she had some privacy.

"I appreciate your little joke, but it's time to stop playing games. Now that Bobby has named one of the players in this mess, we have to plan our next move so we'll be ready when we leave the swamp."

She looked away and swallowed hard when something akin to regret and disappointment filled his eyes. Realization dawned like a light butterfly flittering around her heart that she really did care what this few-worded mountain man thought of her. He was slowly penetrating past the heartache of her dysfunctional youth and failed relationships. Almost of its own accord, her hand slowly moved toward her pocket, then fell away.

He gazed at her for a long tense moment, then gestured toward their makeshift fortress. "Let's settle in and we'll make our plans for tomorrow."

Mary Grace scuttled into their small fortress and lay down on the pile of leaves Ned had gathered. Sliding her backpack to the ground, she lay on her back, lifted Tinker Bell from her pouch and pulled a doggy snack from a zippered side compartment. Her dog accepted the treat with the delicacy of a true lady. Krieger bounded inside their temporary home and sat at her feet, a mournful look in his eyes as he gazed adoringly at Tinker Bell. Mary Grace sighed wistfully, half wishing Ned would look at her like that. It wasn't his looks that made her wish for the impossible—although the clean-shaven mountain man was much too handsome for his own good—it was the way he had treated her grandmother. With respect and reverence for her years of wisdom. Pulling out another snack, she offered it to Krieger and was surprised when the dog didn't take the food.

Ned stepped through the opening and gave a curt command. "Okay."

Much to Mary Grace's amazement, the dog gently took the treat from her hand and lay down, eating it slowly, as if the dog biscuit would have to last him a long time.

Mary Grace gave Ned a questioning glance and he shrugged.

"In the past, we've been in situations when we had to go without for days at a time. He's learned to savor it when it's easily won. Most of the time he has to work for it."

Ned got comfortable on the bed of leaves and Mary Grace did the same. She turned her head and stared into the heavens, thinking about what he had said.

"Ned, you have as many layers as a good Southern woman."

"Excuse me?" His startled statement made her smile.

"Just what I said. You're a man of many layers and you have a trunk full of secrets. Southern women are like that. We have our own language and codes."

He snorted and Mary Grace smiled wider, then went digging. "So, do you have any siblings besides your sister?" He stayed quiet so long she didn't think he was going to answer.

He kept his voice in a low whisper. "I have a brother and a sister."

"Will you see them at Christmas? It's only a week away, you know."

She held her breath, waiting to see how much he would reveal. He stayed so still she turned her head to look at him, but it was so dark she couldn't make out his expression.

"I haven't seen my brother in a while. It might be time to go back home."

Mary Grace heard a world of weariness in his voice and she wondered if he was close to his siblings. She knew he loved his niece, but that might not extend to other family members.

Dead leaves rustled and crackled as he shifted position. "Go to sleep. We'll check on your grandmother in the morning, get something to eat, then head to Washington."

So much for sharing personal information. Mary Grace stared into the inky darkness and pondered the future. Was Bobby safe? Was Gram okay? Would she and Ned make it out of the swamp alive? She closed her eyes and prayed that everyone she loved would be safe and they would all be together for Christmas.

"Don't worry, go to sleep. I'll keep watch for both human and animal predators. Your thoughts are almost as loud as when you're talking."

His disgruntled words had her smiling again. "Don't worry, Mountain Man, I'll say a prayer for you, too."

They quit whispering and the night creatures of the swamp were a comfort in one sense, due to growing up in Georgia, but she wouldn't have allowed herself to drift off if Ned hadn't been there. She knew he'd protect her, and in her sleepy haze, she realized she trusted him to watch over her. Tinker Bell snuggled against her chest and Mary Grace curled onto her side, almost asleep when Krieger, who was lying across the entrance of their mini-walled shelter, released a low, vicious growl.

TWELVE

Ned winced when Mary Grace sat upright and whispered loudly enough to draw anyone hunting them to their location. "What is it? Is something out there? Ned! Do you hear me?"

It was so dark beneath all the cypress trees loaded with hanging moss, he could barely see her pale face. Instead of answering, he reached out and laid a hand on her shoulder. Leaning in close, he whispered in her ear, "It's probably a wild animal. I'll check the perimeter. It'll only take a few minutes."

But it wasn't an animal. Krieger had been trained and the growl he released portended trouble, of the human kind. Ned admired her quick assessment of the situation when she grabbed his hand on her shoulder and squeezed it tight, lowering her voice even more.

"We can't stay here. You would have left the swamp earlier, but I know you were worried about my safety, so you chose to spend the night. I don't know if the person who blew up the shack and shot at us has found us, but we're sitting ducks. It's been a long time, but I know this swamp pretty well. I can get us out of here. I know several shortcuts to Gram's, but we'll have to go slowly and watch out for sinkholes." Ned could barely make out her anticipating grin. "If whoever is after us gets caught in the swamp mud, they'll have to remove their boots to get out and that'll slow them down."

Ned assessed her hasty plan. A swamp was dangerous at night, which is why he had decided to stay put with a woman and fluff dog in tow, but a swamp in Georgia was far different than some of the places he had fought while in the military.

"Can't you at least trust me on this?" she hissed quietly.

The annoyance in her voice made him smile—something he'd done more of since meeting Mary Grace than he had in a long time. He knew the heavy guilt he carried over Finn had pretty much taken over his life, but he was so close to finding the culprit, or culprits, he could almost smell it. But to answer Mary Grace's question. Did he trust her? She still hadn't told him what she'd found in the shack. But in the end, did it matter? After this was over, they would go their separate ways.

"Maybe." He grunted when a sharp elbow jabbed him in the side. Not many people would've had the courage to do what she had just done, much less argue with or tease him. And that included his own family, at least since the incident with Finn.

"Just for that I might let you fall into a bog and leave you there."

"You wouldn't do that," he surprised himself by saying.

She sniffed. "Well, at least you trust me that much. Let's grab our gear and go."

"Let's get out of here," he agreed.

"Fine by me. I'll lead the way. Stay close. I have a flashlight in my backpack, but I won't turn it on until we reach the dangerous places. We're taking the short-cut to Gram's."

She stuffed the mutt back inside the dog carrier, then tugged on his sleeve. He and Krieger allowed her to lead the way. He had no problem allowing a person, man or woman, to take charge of a situation if they were more knowledgeable about the current circumstances. Hyperalert, Ned scanned the area as they moved quietly through the swamp. They were heading away from Mirror Lake at a fairly rapid pace, but they didn't get far before Krieger released another low growl, indicating someone was right on their heels.

Mary Grace must have understood what was going on. She dropped back a couple of steps and whispered in his ear, "I have a plan. Stay right behind me and try to step exactly where I do." Ned's instinct was to circle around and surprise their company from behind, but he couldn't risk leaving Mary Grace.

"Lead on," Ned said, surprising himself. Mary Grace might know the swamp, but Ned was an expert at guerrilla warfare. If he were still a praying man, he would have asked for help, but the Almighty hadn't seen fit to help Finn and Ned's faith had taken a nosedive. He'd learned to take care of himself just fine.

Ned gave a hand signal to Krieger and the dog followed him closely from behind. He did his best to step where she did, but it was hard to see. It had gotten even darker the farther they traveled into the swamp. She slowed to a stop in front of him and he placed his lips close to her ear.

"Why did we stop?"

"Shh, wait and listen. Just give it a moment. I want to make sure my trap worked, then we'll move on."

Ned stood behind her, not moving a muscle. He could stay motionless for hours if need be. He'd done it plenty of times in the past, but he almost failed to hear the quiet commotion behind them because the cinnamon smell in her hair had assailed his senses. The woman was a walking Christmas card, ugly sweaters and all.

The night creatures suddenly went still and frantic whispers floated through the air.

"I need help. I'm buried in the mud up to my calves," one guy hissed.

"I'm in the same situation," a calm, authoritative voice answered. "We'll have to leave our boots behind. Lift one leg out slowly and try to find firm ground, but make it fast."

"Why?" the first guy asked, a slight tremor in his voice.

"Because there's a gator headed our way and I don't plan on being his next meal."

The first guy gave up all pretense of keeping their location a secret and belted out, "This is not what I signed up for. I was only supposed to accompany you. The boss wanted to make sure you did the job right."

Humor laced the second man's voice. "Well, now, if you make it out of the swamp alive, you can report everything to your boss."

Ned heard a pft, pft, double rapid suppressed fire, and knew some gator had probably met his death. Either that or the professional hit man had just rid himself of his employer's tattletale appendage.

Ned nudged Mary Grace forward. He didn't have time to round up the two men behind him for questioning. His first priority was to get Mary Grace to safety.

* * *

After hearing the muffled report of the gunshots, Mary Grace stumbled forward when Ned nudged her from behind. As a reporter, she'd been in some dicey situations in her life, but nothing compared to this. She prayed the man with the calm, icy-sounding voice had shot a gator instead of the whiny man accompanying him. She had known they were in danger, but actually hearing the two men in the swamp somehow made it much more real. And personal. Very personal.

She led the way out of the swamp, but with every step she took, anger replaced her initial fear. How dare someone set up her brother and try to kill her, Bobby and Ned. She became very determined to expose everyone involved in this mess. And at Christmas, of all times. It was the birth of Christ, a time for people to come together with good cheer.

About thirty minutes later, she stepped into the clearing at the back of Gram's property, but Ned grasped her arm.

"Let me check the area, see if anyone is watching the house."

She nodded her assent and sighed when he commanded Krieger to stay with her and Tinker Bell. Ned always seemed to protect everyone in his care, but she briefly wondered if anyone protected him. Was he close to his family, or had the mission with Finn changed him? She jumped when he soundlessly appeared at her side.

"Stop doing that," she whispered jerkily.

"Doing what?" he asked, all innocence.

She ignored his taunt. "Can we approach the house? I want to check on Gram."

"We're clear. I'm sure your grandmother is okay, but I don't want to take any chances that someone else might be in there. Do you have a key? I can jimmy the lock if you don't."

Upon hearing his words, Mary Grace scrambled around the side of the house and up the steps leading to the front porch. Going to the bench swing, she took hold of the left chain connecting the swing to the ceiling and crimped it, pulling the links apart. Ned crowded behind her and watched as she removed a spare key that had been interwoven with the other links.

"Ingenious," he exclaimed as he followed her, breathing down her neck, to the front door.

"Thanks. It was Bobby's idea."

Anxious to make sure Gram was safe, she turned the key in the lock, and wished she hadn't mentioned her brother because she literally felt Ned stiffen behind her. Well, that was too bad. She loved Bobby and had no doubts of his innocence. She would always protect her brother.

She cringed when the lock clicked as she turned the key. The letter from Bobby tucked away in her pocket probably proved his point about the trust issue. She hadn't exactly been honest with him, but she had to read the letter before she'd even think about allowing Ned to see it.

Ned pulled her behind him when she pushed the door inward and slid in front of her, entering the house first. Irritation rippled through her. She was used to taking care of herself, but memories of the sounds of muffled gunfire in the swamp made her shiver. She decided having six and a half feet of muscle go in front of her to make sure the house was safe didn't make her any less independent or strong.

She wanted nothing more than to check on Gram, but she silently followed Ned and Krieger through the downstairs, checking every room. She had to shush Tinker Bell a couple of times. They circled back to the foyer and she pointed toward the beautiful double stair-case leading to the second floor. They took the one on the left and slowly made their way up the steps. On the landing, Mary Grace pointed left again and tugged on his shirt when they reached Gram's room. She stepped around Ned, cracked the door open and assured herself that Gram was still safely tucked in. A soft, gentle snore reached her ears and she grinned. Being a gentile South-ern woman, Gram would have been horrified if she knew she snored. Mary Grace pulled the door closed.

"I don't want to scare her. There's no one in the house and I'm hungry. Why don't we go downstairs and raid the refrigerator?" She desperately wanted to read the letter from Bobby, but her empty stomach had decided otherwise.

He nodded and they retraced their footsteps to the kitchen. Mary Grace flipped on a light and the two-hundred-year-old patina oak floor shone dully in the reflection. Like everything else in the house, the floor needed resurfacing.

After pulling Tinker Bell out of the dog carrier and placing her on the floor, she immediately went to the pantry and pulled out a small bag of dog food.

"Gram always keeps a bag of food here for Tinker Bell in case we pop in for a visit."

Ned eyed the tiny bag askance, probably thinking Krieger could eat the whole bag in one meal, and Mary

Grace giggled, then closed her mouth in horror. She never giggled. She definitely wasn't a woman who giggled. She was a White House press correspondent, not a Georgian debutante, although her grandmother had done her best to turn her into one. She felt her chosen profession was a gift from God. She'd always stood strong for the underdog. She slid a sideways glance at Ned as she took two dog bowls from a lower cabinet. He didn't appear to be an underdog, but she'd do her best to help him find justice. *After* proving her brother was innocent.

She poured food into the bowls and Tinker Bell pounced, but Krieger sat on his haunches, his gaze on Ned and saliva stringing out both sides of his mouth.

"Eat," Ned commanded, and the dog slowly approached the food.

Mary Grace filled the bowl twice more before the dog finished and went to lay down beside his new best friend. Tink growled, but allowed Krieger to snuggle up against her small dog bed.

Opening the refrigerator door, Mary Grace's stomach rumbled and she clapped her hands together when she spotted leftover lasagna. "Yes! We're in business." Pulling out the casserole dish, she made quick work of placing food on two plates and sticking them in the microwave one at a time. The aroma of Gram's homemade meat sauce titillated her nose and she placed both plates on the kitchen island after they heated. Grabbing silverware out of a drawer in the cabinet near the sink, she tore off two paper towels and motioned for Ned to sit. "Dig in while it's hot."

He slid onto the stool beside her and tucked into his food.

Mary Grace spoke between bites. "I can't believe I'm so hungry, but if you think about it, I haven't had anything substantial since before climbing your mountain. I had snacks for Tinker Bell, but only a few energy bars for myself, and those don't really count." She stopped chewing when he just stared at her.

"What? Haven't you ever seen a woman eat before?"

He raised a bushy brow. He might have shaven all that hair off his face, but his brows were still bushy.

"I like a woman with a healthy appetite." He then lowered his fork to his plate, rose and placed the plate in the sink, his broad back to her. "We should get some rest. It's going to be a long day tomorrow."

Her stomach plummeted. In the past, Mary Grace had been accused of acting like a dog with a bone, never giving up until she had ferreted out every tiny piece of information there was to be found on a story, but somehow Ned had become more than a story.

She slid off the bar stool and placed her plate in the sink next to his. They stood shoulder to shoulder, staring out the small window overlooking the side of the house.

"I'm sorry," she said softly, regretting what could never be. "Your private life is none of my business. We'll catch whoever is trying to kill us and then you can go back to your mountain and your privacy."

He moved so fast, she was startled when he turned, wrapped his arms around her waist and pulled her close. She melted into his arms when his lips gently touched her own. For a man so large and gruff, he was gentle as a lamb. Pulling back, he dropped his forehead against hers, as if deep in thought. She had no idea what was going on in his mind.

She smiled weakly and pulled away, her heart saddened. She could never date a man who was convinced her brother had betrayed him, and then there were the trust issues.

Avoiding his searching gaze, she headed out of the kitchen. "We should get some sleep. There are plenty of bedrooms. You can take your pick."

As soon as she had Ned settled in his room, Mary Grace wearily made her way to her old room. Sitting on the quilt-covered mattress, she snapped on the table lamp and pulled Bobby's letter out of her pocket.

Running her finger along the sealed edge, she pulled the handwritten note from the envelope. She skimmed it once, then slowly read it again and closed her eyes, her heart saddened beyond belief. "Dear Lord, please, I'm asking that You help Ned through this impossible situation." She opened her eyes and read the note a third time. Bobby pretty much repeated the same thing as he did in the letter Ned had read—about Chief of Staff Hensley—but he added one more important, earth-shattering piece of information that Ned didn't know about. If Bobby was right, Ned's world, and faith—if he had any left—was getting ready to be blown to smithereens, right here at Christmas, because Bobby mentioned a second name in her letter: Finn.

THIRTEEN

Throwing his duffel onto the floor next to the bed, Ned pulled out his cell and checked the time. Three a.m. in the States meant it would be eight o'clock in the morning in Scotland. Finn should be awake. Before he made the call, he sat there, weary to the bone while memories assailed him. He'd met Finn in Jackson Hole when his family spent part of the school year in the family home where his sister and niece, Sylvia and Fran, were now temporarily residing. Ned had tutors when they traveled, but his parents wanted him to spend time with other children and made sure they were in Jackson Hole for at least half of the school year.

He and Finn had pretty much grown up together, then they both joined the military and served the country that had been so good to them.

He stared at the phone in his hand and thought about his best friend. The reason Finn always tagged along to Scotland with him was because his childhood family life had been less than ideal. His father drank a lot and there was always dissension and quite a bit of yelling in his household.

With a short sigh, Ned made the call. He'd love a hot

bath, but that could wait until morning. Finn answered on the third ring.

"Where have you been? I've been worried sick about you."

"Good morning to you, too."

"I can't believe you're not keeping me in the loop. I should be helping you, not tucked away safely in Scotland where no one can find me."

Ned rubbed his tired eyes with his free hand. "Finn, we've been over this before. I can't be worried about you while I'm trying to find the people responsible for putting you in that wheelchair."

"I'm not helpless, you know."

"I realize that. I can share a few things. I'm with Bobby Lancaster's sister. I'm hoping we'll be able to find Bobby. He's gone off the grid, but we'll catch up to him. Hopefully he'll have some answers."

Ned chose not to tell Finn about the letter Bobby had left at the shack. He didn't want his friend to worry because this thing went to the top in Washington. Ned assured himself Finn was safe in the cottage he had rented for him but cautioned him, nonetheless.

"You're staying out of public view?"

"Yes, Daddy," Finn said snidely, "but I'm going stir crazy. It's time to wrap this up so things can get back to normal."

Ned overlooked Finn's testiness. He'd have been irritated, too, if the situation were reversed.

"Did you get the money I sent?"

"Yes, thanks," he replied grudgingly.

Ned rubbed his forehead. He knew it was hard for Finn to take money from him, but after he caught their betrayer, Finn could find a job and his ego would be restored. At least Ned hoped that would be the case. Finn had always been good with technology. He shouldn't have a problem finding work.

"So this sister, Mary Grace Ramsey, what's she like?"

Ned stiffened. He was exhausted and just wanted to crawl into bed. He didn't want to discuss Mary Grace, but if it would give Finn something else to think about, he'd share a few details.

Ned smiled for the first time during the call. "The woman's a pistol. She chatters a lot and owns a rat dog named Tinker Bell."

"What does she do for a living?"

Ned gripped the phone harder. This wasn't going to go over well. "She's a reporter, a White House press correspondent."

"What?" Finn practically screamed into the phone. "Ned, you have to dump her. Most of what we do in the CIA is classified. If she finds out about some of the stuff we've done, it'll be all over the news. You can't let that happen."

Ned stiffened again. He was tired and Finn was grating on his nerves. "I'll handle it. You don't need to worry."

Finn paused. "You like her. I can hear it in your voice. Ned, you can't have a relationship with a reporter."

Ned rubbed the bridge of his nose and closed his eyes. "I know. Listen, it's 3:00 a.m. here. I'm going to bed."

"I'm sorry, buddy," Finn said, sounding contrite. "Life sometimes throws us curveballs and we just have to learn to deal with them."

Guilt weighed even heavier on his shoulders. Finn

was in that wheelchair because of him and would be for the rest of his life.

"I'm sorry, Finn." He'd apologized a hundred times, but it would never be enough.

"Don't feel sorry for me," Finn snapped. "Just catch these guys so we can move on."

"I'll do my best," Ned said and ended the call.

He had one more uncomfortable phone call to make before he could rest. He needed help and there was one person he trusted more than anyone. He punched in the number and waited. It rang twice.

"Aye," a smooth Scottish burr answered in his ear. The butler's all-too-familiar voice placed a yearning in Ned's heart for the home of his forbearers. Over the years, he'd spent more time in the United States than in Scotland, but his ancestry sometimes called to him, like now, when he was confused and tired. Tired of carrying the guilt over Finn and confused over the woman sleeping several doors away from him.

He stretched out on the bed and grinned. "Aye, Alfred," he said, slipping into his comfortable Scottish burr. It felt right. "'Tis the middle child calling." Alfred had been with the family since Ned's father was young. No one knew exactly how old the man was, but Alfred always knew everything that went on inside Dundar Castle.

"Is Angus taking care of himself?"

Alfred sniffed. "Nay, ye grandfather is a stubborn man. He won't adhere to the special diet the doctor placed upon him for the touch of diabetes he's developed. Would ye like to speak to him? I believe he's breaking his fast."

Ned would love to talk to the old man, but that would

have to wait until later. "Nay, let him eat in peace. I'll speak to Ewan if he's available."

A pause, then, "Aye, he's in the library. I'll get him for ye, and, Ned, it's time for ye to come home."

Ned waited on the line for his brother to answer and smiled, thinking about his grandfather eating break-fast. The old man had probably bribed the kitchen staff to serve him something that would make his doctor scream and yell in frustration. He'd visit the castle when this was over and encourage Angus to eat better. Ned wanted his grandfather to stay healthy for a long time to come.

"Yes?" a curt voice answered.

"Hey, bro, didn't Alfred tell you it was me?"

Ned heard the old office chair creak as Ewan leaned back. The furniture in the castle was almost as old as the castle itself. The place was loaded with antiques and art.

"No, he said it was a surprise. What's wrong?"

That was Ewan, straight to the point. "What? I can't call my brother to say hello?"

"No, not since you decided to carry the weight of the world on those broad shoulders of yours." Ewan paused again. "Listen, Ned, it's not your fault that Finn was injured."

"Stop! I don't need a lecture." He paused and sorted out his thoughts. "I'm close, Ewan. I'm going to catch these guys, but I need a little help. I need use of the po-litical connections you've made through the art gallery and that Machiavellian mind of yours to help me come up with a plan. I heard your last bestseller made quite the stir in Germany."

"It's all fiction, Ned, you know that."

"Aye, if it's fiction, why did the German chancellor lose her position?"

Ewan signed. "Tell me what's going on."

Ned caught him up to speed and they started working on a plan to trap Chief of Staff Hensley. Ned ended the call when Ewan got a little personal, asking questions about Mary Grace.

He lay there a minute, going over both conversations in his mind. Something niggled at the back of his brain, but he was too tired to figure it out. Sitting up, he pulled his boots off and lay back on the bed without even removing his clothes.

Waking up the next morning, the first thing Mary Grace noticed was her dry mouth. She grimaced when she realized she'd been so tired the previous night, she hadn't even brushed her teeth, much less taken a shower. At some point she'd crawled beneath the quilt, but when she tried to move, she found herself completely penned in.

Lifting her head off the pillow, she laughed when she realized Krieger was laying across her legs and Tinker Bell was snuggled against his back. She tried to pull her legs out from under the huge dog, but it was useless until he roused and stood, stretching on all fours. The massive dog padded his way to her head and licked her on the chin. Not to be outdone, Tink barked and scooted up and over Mary Grace's body to take prime position.

Mary Grace loved on both the animals before shoving them aside. "I'll take you both out in a few minutes. Let me at least brush my teeth." She made her way to the bathroom and smothered a scream when she glanced in the mirror. Her hair looked like a rat's nest and she had a huge pillow crease on her cheek. Thankfully Gram had remodeled when they still had a good bit of money and installed private bathrooms in all the bedrooms. Before that, there had been a shared bathroom at the end of both halls that housed the bedrooms. There was no way she wanted Ned to see her like this.

She eyed the shower with acute anticipation, but Tink barked and Mary Grace knew she'd have to let the dogs out first. Maybe Ned was still asleep and wouldn't see her looking so horrible, but then again, what did it matter? Yes, the man had kissed her, but when she shared Bobby's letter, that would never happen again. She was sure of it.

With that depressing thought in mind, her untied robe flapping around her legs, she left her bedroom and trotted down the left stairway with the dogs on her heels. Just as she reached the bottom stair, Ned stepped out of the kitchen with a steaming cup of coffee in his hand. He was clean-shaven, had on jeans and a khaki shirt, and his hair was much shorter than it had been.

She stopped in front of him and scrutinized the new look. It was a little jagged on the ends and Mary Grace grinned. "I see Gram got her scissors out."

He grimaced, then shrugged. "I was due for a trim."

It tickled her how a woman as small as her gram could wield so much authority over such a large man, but then she became aware of the way she looked.

"Yes, well, I have to let the dogs out."

She turned to go, but Ned gently grabbed her elbow. "I'll handle the dogs, go take your shower."

They stood frozen, gazing into one another's eyes. For a moment in time, Mary Grace mourned the loss of what would never be—there was too much standing between them. He was a man full of secrets and she was a journalist—a person who revealed secrets to the world. And most of all, there was Bobby. She doubted Ned would ever fully trust her brother, even after she had proven his innocence.

On her way to her bedroom, she thought about Bobby's letter. She really wanted to show it to Ned—be completely honest with him—but maybe she should do some research first and find out more about the other name listed in her private letter. Even Bobby admitted he could be wrong, which is why he hadn't mentioned Finn in the letter left on the table at the shack.

She knew Ned would never forgive her for not being completely upfront, but if Bobby was wrong, she had a chance to prevent a lot of heartache for Ned. By the time she had whirled into her bedroom, more than ready to grab a shower and wash off the swamp stink from the previous day, she had formed a plan and knew whom she could call for help. A man who'd done work for her in the past.

She almost skidded to a stop when she saw her gram coming out of her bathroom. Dressed in slacks and a silk blouse, with perfect hair and a full face of makeup, her grandmother looked horrified when she lifted her head as Mary Grace stopped in front of her.

"Young lady, I was looking for you. Please tell me you didn't go downstairs without dressing first. Did Eli see you looking like something a stray dog dragged up?"

Mary Grace loved her gram, but the older woman really was steeped in outdated traditions. Then again, Mary Grace's love life was in the pits, so maybe she should listen to her grandmother. Make some changes. It sure couldn't hurt.

She did her best to appear abashed. "Yes, ma'am. The dogs had to use the bathroom. I know that's no excuse, but it's the only one I've got."

Her grandmother smiled and opened her arms. "Come here, baby, give your gram a big hug."

Mary Grace flew into her arms and all the fears and frustrations of the last couple of days came tumbling out. "Oh, Gram, I'm so worried about Bobby, and Ned thinks Bobby may be mixed up in what happened to him and Finn. And Ned kissed me, but it can't come to anything because Ned thinks Bobby is partially responsible for putting Finn in a wheelchair and the whole thing is just awful. There's some powerful politicians involved in this mess and it's dangerous. I really wish you would move in with your friend Sadie until this is over."

Her grandmother pulled back, took her by the arm and they both sat on the edge of the bed.

"Now, let's put things in perspective. I don't know all the details, but we both know Bobby would never do anything immoral. I helped raise that boy and I know he's innocent of whatever Ned thinks he's done." Gram smiled wryly. "But that's not to say Bobby wasn't used in some way without his knowledge. For a genius, the boy doesn't have a lick of common sense when it comes to devious dealings."

Gram rubbed Mary Grace's hair like she used to when she was a kid and it soothed her senses.

"Now, I want to know how you feel about Eli."

Mary Grace swiped the tears from beneath her ey and smiled sadly. "It doesn't matter how I feel ab him. There are too many things keeping us apar

I've known him for less than thirty-six hours. I'll not make the same mistakes my mother made. She rushed into marriage twice and both times were a disaster."

Gram placed both hands on Mary Grace's cheeks. "Sweetheart, I've told you this many times. Your mother has a disease. It's called gambling." She sighed and removed her hands. "I've prayed for her and it's now in God's hands."

She took Mary Grace's hand and held it with both of her own. "My sweet baby girl, you can't let your mother's mistakes rule your life. You have to trust that God knows best. If you do develop feelings for Eli, don't allow your past to ruin it for you."

Mary Grace dropped her head on her grandmother's shoulder. "Thanks, Gram."

Feeling much better, she stood up and grinned, wanting to lighten the mood. "Oh, well, after seeing what I look like in the morning, I probably scared the man off, anyway."

She hugged her gram and headed for the shower. Twenty minutes later, dressed, her hair pulled back in a wet ponytail, she followed the scent of bacon to the kitchen. Her stomach rumbled even though they'd raided the kitchen the night before.

She walked into a picture of domestic bliss, judging by the expressions on Ned's and both the dogs' faces. Mary Grace headed to the coffeepot, poured herself a cup, then leaned her backside against the counter and stared at her grandmother.

"Eggs and ham for the dogs, Gram?"

Sitting across from Ned at the small table placed in of the bay window, Gram sniffed. "I don't get to see Tinker Bell very often and it's my pleasure to spoil her while she's here."

Mary Grace took that as a subtle reminder that she hadn't visited as often as she should. You had to listen close to Southern women to catch the nuisances of a conversation. She blew on her coffee and took a sip.

"What about Krieger?"

Gram beamed across the table at Ned. "Eli explained that Krieger has faithfully served our country in the past, so he deserves a good hot meal."

Mary Grace was just getting ready to grab a plate when suddenly, without warning, one glass panel of the bay window shattered and a barrage of bullets tore into the wall across the kitchen. Before she could move, Ned had shoved Gram down onto the seat. Krieger started growling fiercely. Shaken to the core, Mary Grace dropped to the floor and crawled toward Gram. Gently taking her arm, she helped the older woman out of the seat and to the floor.

Ned had already ducked under the table and was standing away from the window.

"Take care of your grandmother and stay away from any windows. I'll find the shooter if he decided to hang around." The calm authority mixed with solid fierceness in his voice stilled her trembling. She nodded, and he and Krieger left the room.

Mary Grace pulled her grandmother to a safe area away from the window and helped her to her feet. She hugged her gram fiercely and tears came to her eyes. Pulling back, she peered into brave, wise old eyes. "Gram, please, for my sake, go and stay with one of your friends until this is over." Mary Grace choked on her next words. "I can't stand the thought of something happening to you."

Gram raised a hand and gently wiped away Mary Grace's tears. "My dear child, only God knows when it's my time to go. But for your peace of mind, I'll do as you ask."

Mary Grace hugged her again. "Thanks, Gram. I hope it won't be for long."

The front door opened and closed, and Mary Grace pushed her grandmother behind her, but it was Ned. She sent him a questioning glance and he shook his head.

"Whoever took the shot is long gone. Krieger and I cleared the area. He didn't try again, so I'm assuming he's by himself now and doesn't want to take a chance on getting caught." He looked at Gram. "You alright, ma'am?"

Gram stepped forward and lifted her chin. "I'm fine, Eli. Thank you for asking. I've decided to stay with a friend until this is over. Now, I want your promise that you'll see no harm comes to my granddaughter."

Ned nodded grimly. "Yes, ma'am. I'll do my best."

Fifteen minutes later, after saying a tearful goodbye to her aging grandmother when her friend picked her up, they gathered their stuff to leave.

The letter she'd stuffed back into her pocket was at the forefront of her mind now that Gram was safe. At some point, she'd have to tell Ned what Bobby wrote and it saddened her heart to realize that this may very well be the last time she and Ned would be even somewhat in accord.

FOURTEEN

Overnight one of Ned's contacts had someone pick up the car they'd left in the Okefenokee Swamp parking lot and deliver it to Mary Grace's grandmother's house, so they could make it back to the airstrip without relying on a taxi driver to lose a tail. Now Ned's plane was lifting off, heading to DC.

Suspicious about the item Mary Grace had found in the shack and still hadn't shared with him, Ned waited until she excused herself from the cockpit on the premise of checking her emails. He logged on to the server, hoping to slip into her email through the onboard Wi-Fi, but she was password-protected. He could have hacked in, but his heart wasn't in it.

The conflicting emotions of attraction and mistrust warred constantly with each other, but he had good reason. She'd lied to him by omission and he couldn't live with that. Maybe he should demand to see what she'd found, but another part of him wanted her to trust him enough to volunteer the information.

He shook his head. He never wavered like this. He had been trained to be in control of every possible scenario and situation. His life sometimes depended on it.

Gram's words of faith and prayer had hit their mark, but he pushed them aside and concentrated on the task at hand.

Pulling out the satellite phone, he called his brother.

Ewan answered with a clipped, "Yes?" His older brother was fighting his Scottish heritage by not using the brogue he had grown up with. Ewan and their grandfather butted heads all the time and this was Ewan's way of rebelling against the expectation of being named laird of the clan. It amused Ned. In the States the title sounded outdated, but in Scotland it was still very real. Much like the aristocracy in England. Not what it once was, but still there.

"Ewan, it's Ned. We're in the air and I'm on a secure line."

"About time you called. I've been busy."

"Tell me."

"I made a few calls to friends with high connections in Washington who like to chat. I casually dropped the information that you're dating a journalist who is very interested in your and Finn's story. That should be enough to prompt the chief of staff to do something rash and reveal himself."

"Ned, I don't have to remind you that you're playing a very dangerous game. If Hensley is involved, things are going to get very dicey. He won't take this lying down. He'll come after you. Do you trust the information Mary Grace's brother left you?"

Ned gripped the phone hard, but slowly relaxed his fingers. "Not entirely, but it's the only lead I have at the moment and someone is after me, anyway," he said wryly. "I think they want to get rid of any loose ends and Finn and I are loose ends. Mary Grace's brother is a loose end, too, even if he's in it with them."

Mary Grace's laughing golden eyes flashed in his mind. He didn't like that she was in danger, but her brother was responsible for that.

"You told me she got shot on your mountain. I know her brother is involved, but why would they come after her?"

Ewen's question was a good one. "Aye, why would they? Maybe her brother got in too deep and realized the error of his ways. Then he got worried about his sister and sent her to me. I really don't know the answer to your question, yet, but they have to know she's a reporter and they would only use her as a last resort, through her brother, to try to find me since Bobby went off the grid."

The thought didn't sit well with Ned and he was ready to get off the phone.

"Be careful, brother. You do know if anything happens to me, you're next in line for the position of laird." Laughing into the phone, Ewan ended the call.

Ned grinned, despite himself. In the old days, long, long ago, the position of laird would be highly coveted, but in these modern days, no one wanted it. Ned grinned wider, thinking how slick his own father had been. He had removed himself from the role. To keep the old castle and grounds up, he claimed he had to spend his time running the family's art galleries, which was pretty much the truth. The old castle took a lot of money to operate, but it was the family seat and the community also depended on them in a lot of ways.

Staring at the onboard computer, Ned could see that Mary Grace was still online, even though he couldn't see what she was working on. He halfway lifted himself out of his seat, thinking he should demand to see what she had found in the shack, but then he slid back down. He really wanted her to fully trust him and share the information herself.

He gave a gruff snort. He didn't trust her, so how could he expect her to trust him? He'd let it go until they reached Washington, and if she hadn't shared by then, he'd demand to see what she was hiding. He had to have every scrap of information if they were going to beat the sly politicians in Washington. And he had a gut feeling that things were going to move fast as soon as they hit the ground.

His sat phone rang and he answered with a gruff "Aye." Very few people had the number.

"Ned, it's Madeline."

"Ma'am, good to hear from you." That's all he said. As was his customary response, he waited patiently.

She sighed into the phone. "You never were one to chitchat. I take it this is a secure line?"

His lips curled at the edges. "You have to ask?"

She chuckled. "No, but it's always smart to make sure. I wanted to check on you. I was a bit surprised by our last conversation and concerned that you were dealing with a journalist."

Ah, so that's what this was about. "Don't worry, I can handle Mary Grace."

A slight hesitation, then, "Well, that's good to hear."

He waited again.

"Listen, Ned, I know you want justice for what happened to Finn, but what will it gain you? Finn will still be in a wheelchair."

Ned stiffened. Was the CIA director—his boss, or

maybe his previous boss if he chose not to return after his leave of absence—warning him off? He trusted her implicitly and she should trust him to handle the situation. "Is there something you're not telling me?"

She quickly backed down. "No, no, you've served your country honorably and I just thought you might want to get on with your life. Is Mary Grace Ramsey still traveling with you?"

Interesting that she'd ask about Mary Grace, but also plausible. He was spending time with a woman who exposed others as a profession.

"She's still with me. We're heading to DC, and let me assure you, you don't have to worry about anything."

She accepted his assurance and ended the call.

Settled on a plush leather seat with the laptop on the tray in front of her, it took quite a while for Mary Grace to read her emails from work.

After she finished, she looked down at both dogs curled on the floor near her feet. They were giving her accusing stares.

"Hey, don't look at me like that. I haven't done anything wrong."

But she felt as if she had. Hiding the letter from Ned was the right thing to do, but she still felt like a heel. She glanced back at the dogs. "Okay, here's the deal. If Bobby is right about Finn, I'll tell Ned immediately, but if he's wrong, Ned won't ever have to know or live through the pain it would cause."

She rolled her eyes. "And why am I sitting here talking to two dogs?"

Pulling up a new draft, she started writing an email

to a private investigator she knew. A man she trusted and one who had done a lot of work for her in the past.

She asked him to check into Finn and went for the full service. Background, financials, personal life. The works. She also wanted the information ASAP. She hit Send and it didn't take but a minute or so to get a response: This is gonna cost you.

She smiled and ruefully thought of her bank balance. She made good money, but wouldn't be able to get reimbursed unless she wrote a story connected to the request.

She typed in I know, and hit Send.

Sitting back in her chair, she gazed at both the dogs, thinking for a moment before returning her gaze to the computer. She hunched over the laptop and sent Bobby a fairly inane email, one that wouldn't mean anything to anyone watching the account, but would tell him she was alive and well if he was able to sneak in and check.

She sat back again and pondered everything that had happened. This was the first time since this whole thing began that she'd had time to relax and really process all the events.

In her private letter, Bobby didn't go into detail about how he had gotten involved or set up. She'd have to wait until they found him to get that information.

She laughed when Tinker Bell hopped into her lap and Krieger whined because the love of his life had abandoned him. Mary Grace ran a hand over the silky fur of her dog's back and spoke to the big German shepherd. "Don't worry, Krieger, I'll get Gram to make you a Christmas sweater to match Tinker Bell's."

The image of the proud, well-trained dog wearing an ugly Christmas sweater made her chuckle.

Mary Grace thought of all the times she'd tracked down Chief of Staff Hensley and stuck a microphone in his face. She was known on the Hill as a shark when she was after a story. She had always thought highly of him and just couldn't imagine him doing something as heinous as selling state secrets to the enemy. But then again, she had exposed other politicians for things that surprised her after uncovering the truth. Most politicians were good actors, but Hensley had a sterling record. No blemishes that she could find in the past when dealing with him on various other issues.

She glanced over her shoulder toward the cockpit—the door was still closed—then back at the laptop. Her reporter's gut was telling her that Hensley may be a pawn, much like Bobby, but if she did what she was thinking about doing, Ned would probably strangle her.

Her gut had never steered her wrong, so she started typing an email. She'd send it to Hensley, giving just enough information to motivate him into meeting with her privately. That way she could study his reactions in person. She vaguely mentioned that she had come across information that could destroy his career, and if he wanted to talk, he could contact her at home later this evening. She sent the email and sat back, wondering just how bad Ned's wrath would be. Well, no time like the present to find out.

She stood, opened the door to the cockpit, took a seat in the copilot's chair and stared out the front window. His low voice startled her when he spoke.

"You've been up to something."

She immediately took offense, even though she *had* been up to something. "You have absolutely no reason to say something like that."

He stared at her until she squirmed in her seat.

"Let's just say I got the ball rolling before we land in DC. We never really came up with a plan and I know this town and the people on the Hill better than you do. I work here."

She couldn't hear his teeth grinding, but he looked ready to break a tooth, his jaw was so tight.

"Let's hear it," he ground out.

She shot him an exasperated look. "It's not as if you have a better plan. As far as I remember, we really hadn't made any plans at all except to head to DC and stomp in the middle of the hornets' nest and see how many wasps come flying out."

His jaw relaxed and his lips curled at the corners. He seldom smiled and her heart opened just a little wider every time it happened. It made her happy to see him happy, and wasn't that just about as sappy as a girl could get?

"Stomp on a hornets' nest?"

She shrugged. "It's a Southern saying. Anyway, I decided to poke the bear, so to speak." She stopped talking when he gave her a sideways glance. She cleared her throat. "Sorry, I'll try to stop using euphemisms. Anyway, I got to thinking about Hensley. I've interviewed him on the Hill and decided to send him an email, insinuating I've come across something that might have a negative impact on his career."

She waited for his reaction and he didn't disappoint.

"You what?" he exploded. "Mary Grace, whoever is behind this are killers. They want to eliminate any loose ends and that includes you."

Trying to lighten the tension, she tilted her head. "Why, Ned, I didn't know you cared."

His jaw started working again and she almost wished his face were still covered in bushy hair. Her mountain man. She shook her head. No, not *her* mountain man. He would never be her mountain man. With that sobering thought, she apologized.

"Okay, I'm sorry I jumped the gun without discussing it with you first. We're in this together and I didn't act like a team player."

His shoulders finally relaxed, but when he glanced at her, she saw something that resembled guilt in his eyes, but he quickly recovered. She was an excellent observer and didn't try to talk herself out of what she knew she had seen.

"Uh-huh. You're giving me grief, but you've also done something. I take my apology back."

His lips bloomed into a full smile, but Mary Grace knew she'd probably never see that smile again if her PI came back with proof against Finn.

"You can't take back an apology."

Humor laced his words and her heart fluttered, but she ruthlessly buried the feeling.

"Can, too."

He actually laughed. "You sound like a three-year-old."

She laughed back and added, "Do not."

They both sat there for a minute and the camaraderie faded away.

"I recruited my brother to help before we touch down in Washington."

Now that piece of information got Mary Grace's attention. "And your brother's name?"

"Not important. What is important is that he has a lot of contacts and he tapped into the rumor mill. He spread the word that I'm dating a journalist who is very interested in what happened to me and Finn."

She gave him an incredulous look. "And you think I shouldn't have contacted Hensley? Your brother just painted a bull's-eye on both our backs."

But then her journalist's brain started churning out possibilities. "Actually, this might work into my plans. If your brother's information hits Washington pretty quick, maybe Hensley will get wind of the rumors and be more willing to meet with me."

"With us."

"Huh?" she said, jerked out of her musings.

"If he wants to meet, it'll have to be with both of us. You don't leave my side."

She almost smiled at his rough command, but before she had a chance to say anything, Ned told her to buckle up, and not long after that the plane's wheels ground against the asphalt. They were in Washington, Mary Grace's home turf.

FIFTEEN

They deboarded the plane and Ned strode toward a parked car waiting for them on the tarmac. Mary Grace started asking questions the minute he put the vehicle in Drive. Her job suited her well. He didn't doubt that everyone she interviewed eventually just gave her the answers she wanted to stop her from badgering them. But on the other hand, he was getting used to her constant chatter. The peaceful solitude he'd enjoyed on his mountain didn't seem quite so enticing any longer.

"Is this a private airport? I assume it's private and that's why you didn't have to go inside and do any paperwork. And who handles leaving the cars that have been waiting for us at the airports?"

She didn't wait for him to answer, but kept talking.

"I'd like to swing by my place first." She gave him the address.

He drove the car into a business parking lot, put the address into his phone, then pulled back onto the street. "We'll have to be careful. The people after us may have your place staked out."

"I thought about that, but it's worth the risk because Bobby may have been able to slip into my house and leave us some kind of information. Maybe Hensley will have responded to my email by the time we get there, and we can set up a meeting."

"I doubt Bobby would hang around Washington while he's hiding. He's probably all the way across the country by now."

She shrugged. "It's worth a shot and Bobby has a key."

Her eyes lit with determination and something else, something he saw reflected in his own mirror at times: the thrill and excitement of the hunt. His heart flipped and it brought a mix of emotions. The longer he was around Mary Grace, the more he didn't want her to get hurt, but all he could do was his best to protect her. He had to remind himself that as a journalist, she was likely exposed to danger. Maybe not the kind they were facing, but certainly disgruntled and angry people whose crimes she had exposed.

He turned right onto her street and scouted the area. No odd-looking vans or cars parked on the street. Then he noticed the place had an urban feel. It sat just outside DC, the type of place large cities were revitalizing, catering to young professionals. She pointed at two parking places, one of which had a used upscale car parked in it.

"That's my car. I took a cab to the airport when I flew to Jackson Hole, so I wouldn't have to deal with airport parking. Park next to mine. I'm allotted two spaces."

Ned pulled into the spot and cut the engine, searching the area for anything that looked out of place. They appeared to be in the clear. Maybe the people after them never dreamed they'd come to her place. It wasn't logical that they would return. Sitting in Mary Grace's lap, Tinker Bell whined. Mary Grace reached to open her car door, but Ned laid a hand on her arm.

"Wait."

She froze and jerked her head around. "What is it?"

Ned scanned the area one more time. The patio homes were built close together with a small strip of grass in between. There were twelve houses lining the street. He peered over his shoulder at the small playground across the road. He still didn't see anything out of the ordinary, but for some reason his gut told him something was off. It wasn't screaming a warning, but something was going on. It could be that they were just being watched from a distance.

Tinker Bell whined again and Mary Grace spoke with urgency. "She has to be let out and a double whine means it's serious."

"Okay, I'll come around to your door and you stay close while your dog does her business. Then we'll go inside."

Constantly scanning the area, Ned got out of the car and rounded the hood. He huddled her forward in front of him. As soon as they hit the grass, she put TB down and he almost heard the dog heave a sigh of relief. Krieger followed suit and relieved himself, as well.

Ned chuckled when he realized what he was doing. If his old comrades could only see him now. Traveling with a journalist and her rat dog was a unique experience, but one he was enjoying more with every passing moment.

He shielded Mary Grace as they moved toward the tiny front entrance and waited while she unlocked the door. He pulled her close to his side and stopped in the foyer after they entered. He closed and locked the door after his dog followed them in.

"Krieger, check it out."

It was one level and Krieger was back in minutes. He sat in front of Ned—the all-clear signal—and Ned released Mary Grace.

Knowing they were safe for the moment, he became curious about her personal living space. In the past, he found that you could gather a lot of information by studying a person's environment.

In the foyer stood a corner coat tree with a bench seat. He moved forward and prowled through the living/kitchen area. There were three bedrooms, two small and one master. The master had a private bath and one of the smaller bedrooms had been converted into an office. He estimated about fifteen hundred square feet. Everything smelled and looked new.

He grimaced at the huge Christmas tree and all the decorations peppered throughout the place, but became very interested in the framed pictures lining the mantel on the fake fireplace. After being at her grandmother's house, he'd have thought Mary Grace would be the type of woman who'd want a real messy fireplace.

She came and stood beside him. "I wanted a real fireplace, but they aren't allowed here."

Ned picked up a picture of a teenage girl wearing braces and standing on a bicycle. Beside her, a young boy was straddling a banana seat bike. They both wore wide grins.

She took the picture from his hand and stared at it. "This was right after my mother married Bobby's dad. I was so happy to have a sibling. I was thirteen and had been an only child for all those years, spending most of my time at Gram's."

Ned's heart hammered against his chest as he heard the sadness in her voice. He couldn't help himself, he placed a finger under her chin and lifted her head. Slowly, ever so slowly, telling himself he was all kinds of a fool—but not able to stop—he lowered his lips to hers and the warmth of the kiss began melting the frozen, cynical wall he'd built to protect himself.

He pulled away and gazed into her soft golden eyes, wanting to believe in her with every fiber of his being, but he reminded himself of the item she had found in the shack that she hadn't shared. He retreated instantly. As he stepped back, he didn't miss the hurt in her eyes, but she recovered quickly and took several steps away and cleared her throat.

"Yes, well, I'll look around and see if Bobby left any clues and check my email for a response from Hensley."

She disappeared into her small office. Ned took one step forward, but stopped himself. He shook off the kiss and tender feelings she evoked. Until she came clean, he couldn't trust her and he had to keep his mind clear. He had a job to do.

Hands trembling, Mary Grace slipped into the chair behind her desk and started booting up her computer. Leaning sideways, she peeked into the living area. Ned had his back turned to her and was once again studying the pictures on her mantel.

She stared blankly at the computer screen while it was booting up and thought about that kiss. It had been so warm and precious until he pulled away, mistrust flickering in his eyes. She slumped in her chair. He had every right not to trust her because she was with-holding information, even if it was for his own good. Maybe she should just tell him about Bobby's letter, but even if she did, it would probably make matters worse. Mistrust was better than accusations in her opinion.

She typed in her password, went straight to her email account and there sat an email from the private investigator she had hired. She stared at it for a moment, then closed her eyes and prayed not only that God would show her the truth, but that both she and Ned could handle the fallout in a worst-case scenario.

Taking a deep breath, she opened her eyes and clicked the email. She read it twice before closing her eyes once again. It was definitely a worst-case scenario and she had to tell Ned. Now, before things went any further. She briefly wondered why Bobby hadn't been able to find the information himself, but maybe the place where he was hiding didn't have internet service. She swallowed hard and quickly pushed aside the thought that maybe he wasn't alive and able to do the search himself.

Feeling like an old woman, she pushed herself out of her chair and walked into the living room. Ned turned at her approach and lifted a bushy questioning brow. She motioned toward the sofa.

"Let's have a seat."

He moved toward her and stopped so close she could feel his breath on her face. Gently placing both hands on her arms, he demanded softly, "Tell me."

Mary Grace gazed into those intelligent green eyes of his and wondered if this would be the last time they would be together. Would he leave after she told him what she'd discovered?

"I—I found something at the shack that I haven't shared."

To her surprise, Ned's lips curled at the corners and his expression softened. He led her to the sofa and pulled her down by his side. She felt the warmth emanating from his body, but she shivered in spite of it.

"I've been waiting for you to tell me the truth. I knew you found something at the shack, but I wanted you to tell me on your own, because you trusted me."

"You knew?" she whispered. "Ned, Bobby left me another letter for my eyes only in a place where no one would look. A secret hiding place we used when we were kids. It was behind a loose board in the wall of the shack."

She swallowed again, forcing the words past her lips, "I didn't tell you because I wanted to check out what he had to say before I shared. And after I read it, I didn't want you to get hurt."

His eyes narrowed, but she forced the words out. "Bobby named a second person that he highly suspects is connected to what happened to you and Finn."

Ned was a smart man, and she could almost see his brain churning out the possibilities.

"Go on." His words weren't quite as soft now and his eyes had narrowed.

With tears in her eyes, she lifted her chin and told him straight, with no embellishments. "Bobby suspects Finn of being involved in selling the state secrets you two were trying to uncover." Before he could explode, she talked fast. "On the plane, I emailed a private investigator I've used in the past. I trust him implicitly. He ran a deep search on Finn. Half a million dollars was placed in an offshore account in Finn's name two days before the failed mission. Another half a million was deposited into the same account two days after the mission."

Her heart in her throat, Mary Grace found that she couldn't breathe while she watched a drastic change come over Ned. He didn't make a sound, seemingly frozen into place until his intense green gaze landed directly on her.

"And you expect me to believe something your brother wrote in a letter to his sister? A brother probably trying to save his own skin? You expect me to believe that Finn, a man I grew up with and have known all my life, betrayed me? You think he planned an event that would place him in a wheelchair for the rest of his life?"

Mary Grace shivered. Ned didn't sound like the gruff, exasperated mountain man she'd come to know. The affable Scottish guy was long gone, too. She didn't recognize the man sitting beside her, staring at her with accusing eyes. He had kept this part of himself hidden from her: the intelligent warrior willing to die for what he believed in, and he didn't believe in Mary Grace and Bobby. He believed in Finn.

Mary Grace hardened her resolve, fell back on her professionalism and stared him in the eye. "I have proof. My PI found the deposits made in Finn's name."

Ned's lips curled into a cynical smile. "Let's see. What is it you made me promise about Bobby? That someone could have set him up and I should wait to make sure before I go after him? Don't you think the same thing could have been done to Finn?"

Mary Grace had to concede the point, but her reporter's gut was screaming that Finn had betrayed Ned.

She gave a stiff nod. "Fine, I agree. It's possible that

Finn could have been set up. We'll have to follow all the leads and see what shakes out."

She softened her voice. "Listen, Ned, I know it's hard to believe that Finn could do something like this—"

His words sliced into the air, effectively cutting her off. "Finn did not do this and I'll prove it."

Mary Grace peered into his beautiful eyes, eyes that had previously warmed her heart, but the only thing reflected back at her now was a green as hard and brittle as colored glass. He was lost to her, if they even had a chance to begin with. Even if they found Finn innocent, she doubted Ned would ever forgive her for putting him through this. But she knew, deep down, that for some unknown reason Finn had betrayed his best friend, and it was something Ned might never recover from. Ned had trust issues and this would place him out of her reach forever. He'd crawl back to his mountain and hibernate for years.

Gram had always taught her to keep moving forward, no matter what was going on in her life, and Mary Grace did just that. She'd had plenty of practice with her mother and stepfather. When she was a teenager, she sometimes wanted to crawl into a hole and stay there, but Gram always pulled out her Bible and reminded Mary Grace that God loved her, and stood beside her, no matter what.

She wrapped her mind around those old scriptures— they gave her strength—and straightened her shoulders.

"Do we stay together, or would you prefer we handle our investigations separately?"

He smiled, and it wasn't a team-player smile. Mary Grace almost laughed at the thought. Ned definitely wasn't a team player. She briefly wondered how he would fare at one of those team-building conferences that companies made their employees attend. He'd probably scare the daylights out of everyone there.

She stopped her semi-hysterical train of thought, knowing from the past it was a coping mechanism unique to her.

"Oh, we'll stay together. You aren't leaving my sight until we find your brother."

And wasn't that just nice? But she had to remind herself this was hard on Ned, too.

"Fine, but, Ned? I really do hope both Bobby and Finn are completely innocent in all of this. I'm sorry I had to tell you what I found out about Finn, but it had to be done."

Calling herself all kinds of silly, Mary Grace felt the waves of pain coming off him and she found herself still wanting to soothe the heartache he was experiencing due to the information she had unearthed.

But Gram had taught her to be practical, and no matter her feelings for Ned, she had to find Bobby, make sure he was alright, and then she would expose the person, or persons, responsible for what had happened to Ned and Finn, and if Finn was involved, well, God would have to take care of the rest.

SIXTEEN

Ned refused to believe that Finn was in league with traitors to the country and had betrayed him. Finn hadn't had the best family life growing up, but they had saved each another's lives on more than one occasion when they were in the army. Someone had to have set Finn up. The alternative was unthinkable.

He counted himself fortunate that he hadn't completely fallen for the woman sitting next to him. Or had he? No, he wouldn't even allow that possibility to enter his mind. He had to remember her main goal was to prove her brother innocent, and if she could point the finger elsewhere, it was to her benefit.

It felt like a giant fist was squeezing the blood from his heart, but he focused his mind on the mission ahead and compartmentalized all other emotions.

He ruthlessly ignored the sadness on Mary Grace's face. "Did you receive an email from Hensley?" He almost winced as he heard his own voice, so similar to his brother's clipped, terse tone.

She searched his face one more time before shrugging her shoulders, and that bothered him, that she could dismiss him so easily. "No, I haven't heard from him, but he may be tied up with official business. I say we grab some lunch. I'll send another email asking him to meet us somewhere away from prying eyes. There's a small park just outside the city that's fairly secluded."

He nodded his assent and watched as she shuffled toward her small office. He stayed seated and gazed at the pictures on the mantel once more. Just how far would Mary Grace go to save her brother? Restless, he rose and began pacing through the dainty town house. He could search online, see if he could track Bobby himself, but Mary Grace's brother was a computer wizard and knew enough to stay offline if he didn't want to be found. He could also run a deep check into Finn, but that would mean admitting he didn't trust his friend.

He stopped in the foyer and lifted his chin. A few seconds later, Krieger was by his side and the dog released a low growl. It was an alert, not a full-blown warning. Ned opened the front door and scanned the area. A few kids were on swings in the playground under the watchful eyes of their mothers. He remembered the odd feeling he had gotten when they arrived. It hadn't been a feeling of immediate danger, just that something was off.

He spied a man walking his dog down the street, but that was it. He closed the door. Maybe Krieger was reacting to Ned's own turbulent emotions. Dogs were very sensitive to their handlers. Mary Grace came up behind him. She was dressed to leave.

"I heard back from Hensley. He'll meet us at the park at six o'clock. I'd like to see his reaction in person. We'll pick up something to eat while we wait."

She acted like she wanted to add something, but her lips tightened. Ned found himself aching to smooth the worry lines from her forehead, but he only nodded and grabbed his coat from the rack in the corner.

TB was already tucked safely into the dog carrier and Krieger trotted out behind them. Mary Grace swirled around to face him. She had her car keys in her hand.

"After everything that's happened, maybe it would be best if we part company. If you'll give me your cell number, I'll keep you apprised of any information I uncover and I'd appreciate it if you would return the favor."

Caught off guard by the sudden change of plans, he stood there and just stared at her, his mind a whirlwind of emotions. The woman had turned his life inside out. He was torn between wanting to distance himself from her and aching to glue himself to her side forever.

Receiving no response, she gazed at him one last time, then pivoted on her heel toward her car. Frozen to the spot, he watched as she opened the car door and slipped inside. Away from him, that's all he could think about. Through the side window, he watched her pull TB from the carrier and place the dog on the passenger seat. She leaned forward to insert the key into the ignition and warning bells exploded in Ned's head. Mary Grace's car had been sitting there the whole time she'd been gone. Plenty of opportunity for someone to tamper with it. The feeling that something was off crystallized in his mind.

Both he and Krieger were already moving when she turned the key and the engine caught. Rounding the hood of the car, he ripped her door open, pulled her out of the car and made a flying leap into the air. He heard Krieger behind him and dearly hoped his dog would save the rat. Mary Grace would never get over losing her dog.

He might not trust her, and he was very angry with her, but he didn't want her to die.

About fifteen seconds after they hit the ground and cleared the car—Mary Grace protected beneath him—a small explosion blew through the air and light debris stung his back as it seared through his shirt and jacket.

Before he could catch his breath and assess the situation, a sharp elbow almost caved in his trachea as Mary Grace fought her way out from under him. Shifting his weight off her, she scrambled to her feet and frantically swiveled her head around.

"Tinker Bell! Where's my dog?" she shouted.

Ned got to his feet and breathed a sigh of relief when Krieger padded toward them with TB dangling from his mouth, hanging inside the ugly Christmas sweater. At least it was good for something.

Ned scanned the area for any lingering danger while Mary Grace gingerly removed her dog from Krieger's jaws and gently soothed TB's nerves. After making sure her dog was okay, she dropped to her knees and threw her arms around Krieger. She praised Ned's dog and told him he was a hero. It was the first time Ned had ever been jealous of his dog.

Disgusted with himself, he turned away from the tender scene and scanned the area once more, but didn't sense anyone lurking about. He was glad to see no one on the playground. They must have left while he and Mary Grace were inside the town house. He wasn't surprised to hear sirens in the distance. An explosion, even a small one, wasn't something this neighborhood would be familiar with and a neighbor had probably called the cops.

Mary Grace got to her feet and walked slowly toward

him, resolution written on her face. She stopped in front of him, her precious dog still trembling in her arms.

"You saved my life and Krieger saved Tinker Bell. I thank you for that." She took a deep breath and lifted a defiant chin. "I know it was wrong of me to withhold information from you, but I honestly did it so you wouldn't get hurt. If the PI I hired hadn't found anything on Finn, I never would have mentioned Bobby's letter to you." She took what appeared to be a defensive step back. But before she could say anything else, a city police cruiser pulled to the curb in front of her driveway.

Mary Grace watched the policeman walk briskly toward them, keeping a sharp, questioning eye on Krieger. Ned mumbled low so only she could hear before the cop got within hearing distance.

"Don't say anything, let me handle this."

She nodded her assent. The day was waning, and they had an important meeting to make in a few hours. If Ned and his connections could move this along, it was more than fine with her.

Ned moved toward the cop and held out a small piece of paper. Naturally curious, Mary Grace moved close enough to hear.

"If you'll call this number, everything will be taken care of."

Suspicion filled the cop's eyes until he glanced down at the paper. He stepped away, never turning his back to them and pulled out a phone. He spoke to someone for a few minutes, then ended the call and moved back toward them. He scrutinized Ned for a moment, nodded, handed the piece of paper back, got in his car and left.

Mary Grace was incredulous. She stared at Ned. "What just happened?"

He grinned at her, and just like that, they were back on even ground. He stared at her for a moment, as if he wanted to say something, then shook his head.

"I gave him the direct line to the CIA and a guy I know there who handles situations such as this. Let's get going." He went quiet for a moment. "This looks like a professional job. Just enough of a boom to get the job done, but not enough to attract major attention."

She followed Ned to the car that had been left at the airport for them and they loaded up. She rubbed the top of Tinker Bell's head and the white silky fur soothed Mary Grace. Dogs really were good therapy. Krieger jumped in after Ned opened the rear door and hung his head over the back of Mary Grace's seat.

She grinned, then sighed at the expression of adoration in the big dog's eyes as he stared at Tinker Bell. The animals reminded Mary Grace of her and Ned in reverse. She hoped she didn't wear that sappy expression when she gazed at Ned.

Ned folded his large body into the driver's seat and started the car. Putting forth great effort, she told him of a good local restaurant where they could pick up something fairly fast. Everything was somewhat back to normal. She stared out the window, thankful to be alive.

They'd eaten and arrived at the park an hour early. As Ned scoped out the area, Mary Grace waited in the car. She'd promised to keep all the doors locked and be ready to start the car and leave if anything suspicious happened.

Sitting behind the wheel, she glanced at Krieger in

the rearview mirror. "Like I'd leave him at the first sign of trouble."

Krieger rumbled back, obviously unhappy at being left behind to protect Mary Grace and Tinker Bell. Fifteen minutes later, Ned cleared the woods and Mary Grace scooted across the console so he could have the driver's seat. A whoosh of cold air flowed into the car with him.

"Everything's clear. The temperature's dropping."

"Well, it is December." She sighed longingly. "Christmas is almost here. I hope we resolve this soon. I'd like to spend Christmas with Gram—" she hesitated to finish her sentence, almost afraid to upset their unspoken, tacit agreement to work together "—and Bobby."

Broodingly, he stared out the windshield as a flake of snow drifted onto the glass. "One step at a time," was all he said.

Tentatively, trying to make conversation, but also very curious about this secretive man, she asked, "Do you usually spend Christmas with your family in Jackson Hole?"

Surprisingly, he answered, "The house in Jackson Hole is our home base in America. My family travels a lot, but we try to get everyone together in the same country for Christmas."

That didn't tell her much of anything, but it didn't surprise her. She briefly wondered if he would ever trust her enough to tell her about his family.

She couldn't help herself; she had to throw in another more personal question. "And do you still believe in the true reason for the season?"

His large hands gripped the steering wheel. "God allowed someone to betray me and Finn, and He allowed Finn to get injured." He paused and relaxed his fingers. "I come from a family of believers, but during my time in the army, I witnessed so-called religious figures in many countries commit atrocious crimes, all in the name of their religion."

Mart Grace nodded sagely. "Just what I thought."

He snapped his head around. "What?"

She twisted sideways in her seat and smiled at him. "It's okay, Ned, God understands you're angry right now, but He will bring everything to rights. In the end, even if it's not what we envisioned, it will be the right thing, the best thing for us." She paused, gathering her thoughts because this was so important, especially if they ended up proving Finn, his best friend, had betrayed him. "Ned, God will reveal the truth about everything, and we, as believers, have to accept it."

He smiled and it wasn't a nice smile. "So you're going to be able to accept it, just like that, if we prove your brother is partially responsible for what happened to my best friend?"

Mary Grace jerked her head back as if she'd just been slapped. Would she be able to accept it if Bobby ended up in jail? She didn't have time to ponder the question because they both sat up straight when a car pulled into the empty parking lot, the fluttering snow having sent the last of the park visitors home before their guest arrived.

Ned reached for his door handle. "Stay in the car while I make sure it's safe, then you can join us."

Mary Grace protested him going alone.

Exasperation written on his face, Ned said, "Would you, just for once, do what I say? I'm trying to protect you."

She leaned back in her seat with a huff. "Fine, but don't ask him anything until I get there. I want to gauge his reaction."

Finally, she noted a spark of humor in his eyes. "Don't worry. I know you're the expert talker. I'll give you full control after I make sure it's safe."

Mary Grace nodded her assent and he climbed from the car. They had parked in a corner of the lot under some bare tree limbs, but Hensley spotted Ned coming toward him as soon as he got out of his car. Not willing to take a chance on Ned's life, Mary Grace reached over the console and quietly opened the driver's door.

"Krieger, protect Ned."

If a dog could smile, Krieger was grinning as he flew over the seat and jumped out of the car. Mary Grace was impressed when the dog took to the woods and quietly circled around behind Chief of Staff Hensley.

She watched the man approach Ned and thought the meeting was going nicely—until Hensley pulled a handgun from inside his coat and pointed it straight at Ned's heart.

SEVENTEEN

Ned wasn't surprised when Hensley pulled a gun on him. Under the circumstances, he would have done the same thing in the other man's shoes and would have respected Hensley less if he hadn't taken the precaution, but that didn't mean he trusted the man. Not at all.

He raised his hands in the air, just enough to show the man he meant no harm, but he'd palmed a knife inside one fist in case things went downhill fast. One throw to the trachea and Hensley would be dead.

The president's chief of staff kept his eyes on Ned. The man was definitely out of his element.

But Ned never underestimated anyone.

Hensley spoke first. "Do I know you?"

He was studying Ned intently. But before he could respond, Ned was startled to see Krieger lope out of the woods and sneak up behind Hensley. His dog assumed attack position and stared at Ned, awaiting a command.

Ned wanted to close his eyes in frustration, knowing this was Mary Grace's doing, and he was proven right when she hopped out of their car and came striding across the parking lot. His heart in his throat, he wanted to strangle her and throw his body in front of her at the same time. The woman continuously elicited conflicting emotions in him, even now when he needed to defuse the tense situation in front of him.

From inside the dog carrier, TB gave a bark of greeting as Mary Grace hurried to his side. He was angry, but also impressed with the way she quickly defused the situation.

She kind of puffed her hand at Hensley. "Sir, please put the gun away. There's no need for that and you're scaring Tinker Bell to death."

With disbelieving eyes, both men stared at the happy fluffy white rat dog with its tiny head sticking out the top of the dog carrier snuggled against Mary Grace's chest.

She made a show of calming the already perfectly calm dog and Ned almost barked out a laugh. Even though he still wanted to strangle her, he admired her pizzazz.

She stared pointedly at Hensley until the chief of staff finally lowered his weapon to his side, but he didn't put the gun away. She gifted him with her big Georgian smile.

"Now, I've interviewed you in the past, and you know I'm a trusted journalist. I just need a few moments of your time."

Now that the high probability of danger was past, Hensley gave both of them a nervous look, then ran slim fingers through his thinning hair and cleared his throat.

"I want to know what this is all about."

Mary Grace held out both hands. "I really just have one important question." Ned marveled at the change that came over Mary Grace. Her jaw hardened and her eyes narrowed.

"Are you trying to kill me or my brother?"

Hensley's brows arched toward his hairline and he clumsily placed his gun back inside his jacket.

"What? Why on earth would I want to kill a White House press correspondent? I don't even know your brother. And what does this have to do with your email? You said you had information that might negatively impact my career. That's the only reason I came here."

Hensley took a deep breath, like he was settling in for a long-winded tirade, but Mary Grace cut him off at the knees. Still alert, Ned relaxed a tad and enjoyed watching Mary Grace do what she did best: talk. She placed her hand on TB's head and went for the soft touch.

"Chief of Staff Hensley, it really is for your benefit that I contacted you. You see, Ned is here to protect me, and someone has made several attempts on my life. During the course of my investigation, I came across information that led me to you. You have been targeted in a cover-up that goes to the top of the pecking order in Washington. If the information becomes public, you will be ruined whether you're involved or not. You know how it works."

She shook her head sadly and Ned bit back another grin.

"I have interviewed you, and my resources tell me you work hard and have never been involved in any kind of cover-up."

Indignant, Hensley lifted his chin. "I don't know where you received your information, but I'll do everything in my power to help you find the culprits. My background is clean, and I plan to keep it that way."

Hensley stared at Ned, an assessing look in his eyes. Ned knew the moment the man snapped the puzzle pieces together. The pieces connecting Mary Grace and a cover-up to a man named Ned. Hensley was high enough on the power grid in Washington to be aware of Ned's reputation. His eyes widened slightly, the only indication he gave at figuring out who Ned was, a man known only as Ned by a small, select few. A man who worked for the CIA, but whose identity was kept quiet. Ned didn't mind being partially revealed because he never intended to do undercover work again. He was leaving the CIA for good. After what had happened with Finn, and the betrayal they both experienced, he'd never trust anyone enough to put his or anyone else's life on the line again.

Ned didn't know if Mary Grace saw the indicator, but as sharp as she was, he'd have been surprised if she missed anything. He had his answer a second later.

With a winsome smile, she indicated with her hand. "I see you understand what's at stake. After speaking with you, my gut tells me you're a pawn in this nefarious conspiracy, maybe set up to take the fall for something you didn't do, but if you work with me, I hope to expose the person, or persons, responsible. We've had someone spread rumors and specific information in Washington. Information we hope will bring those responsible to the surface. There's the possibility you might receive a small amount of bad publicity, but I'll make sure you end up a hero in the press."

Hensley's face literally turned red with anger. "I don't know what's going on, and I wouldn't give credence to anything you're saying if it weren't for the man standing beside you, but I'll play along for the time being because I don't want my reputation torn to shreds."

Mary Grace smiled, but the tone of her words ensured he understood she meant business. "I said I'll make sure everything works out right for you."

Hensley's face went from red to white. " I'll do my part to help with anything you need. I'm a man of the people."

Mary Grace said briskly, "Good."

Ned was very impressed, and he realized if her brother were anything like his sister, it was no wonder the CIA had recruited him. Mary Grace was the epitome of intrigue.

Behind the men, Krieger stood at attention and pointed his nose toward a bare tree line. Ned didn't see anything, but he trusted his dog's instincts. "Krieger, check the perimeter."

Their visitor was visibly shaken when he realized a huge German shepherd had been sitting behind him the entire time.

"I want everyone to casually walk to their cars and leave quickly. My dog gave me an imminent danger signal."

They dispersed swiftly. Ned kept his eyes trained on the wooded area Krieger had pointed out while herding Mary Grace to the car. As he scanned the tree line, the setting sun glinted off the long barrel of a gun. He looked closer and saw an unusual lump about midway up the tree. A sharpshooter. Ned moved fast, just as the first bullet barely missed them and pinged off the car.

"Mary Grace, get in the car. Now!" he shouted as he whipped his pistol out and started running across the parking lot while firing toward the guy hidden in the tree. Hensley turned, saw what was happening and pulled out his gun. Ned prayed Hensley was innocent in all of this, because if the shooter was someone he'd brought with him, Ned and Mary Grace were in deep trouble.

Mary Grace dove into the driver's seat. Her hands shook as she turned the key in the ignition. It would be her fault if Ned got shot. She berated herself for always being so stubborn. She had set up this meeting and if someone got killed, she would carry the weight of that for the rest of her life.

The car roared to life and she hit the gas pedal right when Hensley lifted his gun. She'd have no qualms about running the man down if he dared to turn his weapon on Ned, but when she got closer to them, she realized Hensley was trying to help. Both men were shooting toward the trees.

She whooshed out a breath of relief as she slammed on the brakes, skidding to a halt right behind Ned. His gun still in his hand, and his eyes scouring the area, he opened the driver's car door.

"Scoot over."

She wanted to argue that she was perfectly capable of driving the car, but decided this wasn't the time to argue. She slid into the passenger seat and yelped when Krieger leaped through the open door and landed in the back seat. She breathed a sigh of relief when she saw Hensley running toward his car, then climbing in to safety.

Gun still in hand, Ned slid into the car, put it in Drive and drove with one hand, his eyes never leaving the surrounding area. He didn't slip the weapon into his jacket until they were well clear of the park.

Both cars had escaped without anyone getting hurt and Mary Grace closed her eyes.

"Thank You, dear Lord, for protecting us." She breathed the prayer out loud.

She lifted her lids and stared out the front window. That had been a close call. Too close. She laid a hand on Tinker Bell's head, as much to soothe herself as her dog and released a nervous chuckle.

"Well, I'd say Hensley is in the clear. Bobby's information must have been wrong."

Without saying a word, Ned lifted his brows and glanced at her before looking at the road again. She blew out a breath of frustration.

"I know what you're thinking."

He didn't say a word. He was going to make this hard on her, but she really didn't blame him.

"Fine, maybe Bobby was wrong about Finn, too, but we still need to follow up on that money in the offshore account in Finn's name."

The man-of-few-words only nodded, and it was maddening.

"Aren't you going to say something? Anything?"

He stayed quiet.

"Fine, I was wrong to put the two of us and Hensley at risk like that and I want to apologize. It's just that I'm so worried about Bobby and I really want to find whoever is after us. I have to follow every lead, but I could have handled this differently. Safer."

She stared out the window, expecting his condemnation, but was shocked when she sneaked a peek in his direction, unable to believe her eyes.

Mountain Man was grinning.

He shocked her when he finally spoke. "The meeting was the right thing to do."

Her first reaction was relief that Ned didn't think she'd messed up big time by placing them in danger, but then she slumped in her seat, thinking about what she planned to do. Her gut declared that Finn was involved, but it was also screaming another name, and if Mary Grace was right, things were about to get much more dangerous than she'd ever dreamed.

This time she refused to accuse anyone Ned trusted without proof. She prayed he wouldn't be angry when he learned what she was really preparing to set in motion, but what did it matter? It was very unlikely they'd ever have any kind of a relationship, anyway. There were too many things standing between them.

It was also the story of a lifetime. She glanced at Ned and wondered where they'd be after this was all over. Would he learn to trust her, or would he walk away forever when he found out she'd once again withheld information?

EIGHTEEN

Ned gripped the steering wheel harder as snowflakes swirled and darkness descended, relieved only by the streetlights as they crossed the bridge over the Potomac River.

"Where are we going? I know it's not safe to go to my town house."

He glanced in the rearview mirror, but didn't see anyone following them. "I have a small town house in Washington I keep available for whenever I'm in town. Excluding family, no one knows about it, so we can re-group there."

Curiosity laced her next question. "Do you spend much time in Washington?"

After the close call at the park, Mary Grace didn't seem upset. The woman was pretty remarkable, but Ned ignored the tiny spark in his heart robustly trying to grow into a flame and broached a subject Mary Grace wouldn't be happy to hear instead of answering.

"I have a proposition."

She slid him a sideways glance. "I don't like the sound of this."

He plowed forward, even though he knew it was

probably futile. "The further we get into this thing, the more dangerous it becomes, and I think you should stay behind, where it's safe."

She twisted sideways in her seat and exploded right on cue, the gold in her eyes sparking fire. "Oh, no, you don't. You might live like a Neanderthal on that mountain of yours, and you might think like one, but I've been taking care of myself for a long time and I refuse to hide in safety while you take all the risks. Taking risks is part of my job description and you need me to put my plan into action."

Mary Grace reminded him of a frontier woman, soft on the outside but tough at the core, able to endure just about anything thrown her way.

He grinned, knowing it would drive her crazy. "It was worth a try."

He wasn't surprised when she socked him in the arm and followed that with a fierce glare.

"Just what exactly is your plan? You were pretty vague with Hensley."

She plopped back in her seat and became quiet. Ned sensed her plotting. He was becoming so attuned to her, it was unsettling.

"I want to do some interviews that will hopefully prompt those responsible for this mess to make a move. We'll refine it when we get to the town house."

For some reason, Ned couldn't shake the feeling that she wasn't telling him everything, but he ignored it because he wanted to trust her as he hadn't trusted anyone in a long time.

He pulled into a middle-class neighborhood and pressed the automatic garage door opener he kept on his personal key chain as he guided the car into the driveway of a benign town house, built identical to the others surrounding it. That's why he'd bought the place. Nothing about it stood out and the neighbors kept to themselves.

The garage door closed behind them and automatic lights flicked on.

Mary Grace shifted in her seat. "Somehow, I just can't imagine Mountain Man living in a town house."

Her humor had his lips twitching and his mind shifted gears. He didn't want to think about someone trying to kill them, or about Finn being in a wheelchair for the rest of his life, or the gut feeling that she was plotting again. He'd hidden it, but the shooting at the park had shaken him to the core. He was comfortable with danger, but the thought of anything happening to Mary Grace, the possibility of a world without her in it, even if they weren't together, was unthinkable.

Even though he knew it was a mistake, because after this was over they'd go their separate ways, and he wasn't ready to admit that his feelings might be something…more for Mary Grace, he wanted to kiss her—right here, right now, as affirmation of their survival after the shooting. When she'd driven the car toward Hensley at the park with fierce determination blazing in her eyes, Ned's heart had almost jumped out of his chest. First in fear for her, and then because he realized she was risking her life to protect him.

Her eyes widened when he slowly reached across the seat and pulled TB from the dog carrier pouch. He placed the dog in the back seat with Krieger and twisted back around. Mary Grace didn't move a muscle until he lifted her chin with a finger.

He was very seldom surprised or caught off guard,

but he was startled when she jerked forward and wrapped her arms around his neck, pulling his head forward. When she placed her lips against his, Ned felt as if he had come home. The world was no longer filled with evil and betrayal, but…possibilities. His heart beat wildly as her kiss brought hope for the future. A future he never dared dream possible for a man like him, a man who'd seen too much of the depraved side of humanity.

Even in the middle of an impossible dream, Ned's subconscious instincts stayed focused and he immediately sensed another presence. In one swift move, he pulled away from Mary Grace, shoved her head down, whipped his pistol from inside his jacket and pointed it at the man standing beside his car window.

He immediately recognized the person and so did Mary Grace. She grabbed Ned's arm and forced the gun down.

The joy in her voice reflected a far different reaction than Ned's.

"Bobby!"

Mary Grace scrambled out of the car and ran around the hood toward Bobby. She threw her arms around him and squeezed tight. "Thank You, Lord! Thank You for protecting my brother."

She pulled back and studied him intently. He was tall and lanky, and although he was twenty-five years old, he still only managed to grow what resembled peach fuzz on his face. He had unkempt dark blond hair and he pushed his glasses up the bridge of his nose in a familiar, endearing way. Some might call him a nerd, but to Mary Grace he was one of the sweetest, most honest people she knew.

A blush worked its way up his neck and spread over his face when he reached behind him and tugged a woman forward. With a mixture of shock and confusion, Mary Grace said, "Fran?"

During their short reunion, Ned had slipped out of the car and was leaning against the driver's door. He gave his niece a hard stare.

"Yes, Fran, what are you doing with Mary Grace's brother?"

Before Fran had a chance to answer, Bobby stepped forward and squared off in front of Ned, who towered over him, reminding Mary Grace of the large, immovable mountain he lived on. Bobby surprised Mary Grace, first with his bravery, because Ned wasn't the type of person most people would directly challenge, and second by the accusation in her brother's voice.

"You were kissing my sister."

Ned growled back, "What are you doing with my niece?"

Mary Grace had always been the one to protect Bobby, not the other way around. She appreciated his standing up for her, but Ned could squish her brother like a bug if he chose to. Determined to get everyone settled down, she stepped between the men.

"Let's take this inside. I'll make some coffee and we can talk."

Bobby looked like he wanted to punch Ned and Ned looked like he wanted to wring answers out of Bobby's thin neck, which would easily snap under Ned's large hands.

. She was grateful when Fran stepped forward and grabbed Bobby's hand. She led him toward a door Mary Grace assumed opened into the town house.

Ned's eyes flared hot when he saw Bobby's and Fran's interlocked hands.

Mary Grace knew she had to defuse the volatile situation. They followed Bobby and Fran through the door Fran had opened after punching in a code. Ned must give his family access to his properties.

They entered through the kitchen and Mary Grace was disappointed to find nothing personal in the area. The inside of the town house was just as bland as the outside. The living room sat across a small hallway from the kitchen and it appeared as if two bedrooms and baths made up the rest of the small space.

Bobby and Fran sat on the sofa and Mary Grace winced when she noticed they were still holding hands. Not because she didn't like Fran, but because of Ned's reaction. It was obvious he was protective of his niece and Mary Grace had experienced his fierce protectiveness.

Ned took a seat in a cushy chair, leaned back and crossed his arms over his chest like a big grumpy bear. The two men glared at one another and Fran looked miserable.

"Let me make some coffee and then we'll talk," Mary Grace said.

Mr. Man-of-Few-Words laid down the law. "No coffee. We talk now, and it better be good."

Mary Grace knew when to gracefully give in. She took the only other chair in the room. Tinker Bell jumped in her lap, Krieger lay on the floor beside her and she started the ball rolling. Better coming from her than Ned.

She managed a wobbly smile. "Bobby, I'm so glad you're alright. I was worried."

Bobby tore his gaze away from Ned. "I didn't mean for any of this to happen. You know I would never intentionally put you in danger."

"Of course you wouldn't," she responded swiftly, knowing in her heart that his words were true. Bobby was naive and too trusting and at times people tended to abuse that sterling quality.

Bobby glanced at Fran, tightened his grip on her hand and sat up straighter. "I know you've had to pull me out of a few scrapes over the years, and I appreciate that, sis, but I'm a man now. I'm responsible for my own actions."

Mary Grace wanted to cheer and cry at the same time. Bobby had grown up and she had to accept that fact. It was no longer her job to look out for bullies and people who might hurt him.

Ned leaned forward in a threatening manner, placing his elbows on his thighs, and Mary Grace forced herself not to jump into the fray again. Bobby was right. He was twenty-five. Time to stand on his own. She suspected Fran had something to do with Bobby's newfound courage and she applauded the woman for bringing her brother out of his timid shell.

"I suggest you start at the beginning, and I advise you to leave nothing out because not only have you placed your sister in danger, somehow you have dragged my niece into this mess."

Ned's words hung in the room like shards of ice, but Mary Grace settled back in her chair. She sent up a quick prayer that this would end well, because judging by the way Fran and Bobby were gazing at each other, she just might be involved in Ned's life whether he wanted her there or not. She felt a momentary pang at the thought, but focused her attention on Bobby's explanation.

He gazed directly at Ned and Mary Grace's heart burst with pride.

"As I'm sure you know, I was recruited straight out of college by the CIA based on certain aptitude tests I took. They offered to pay off my school loans if I agreed to work for them for five years." He smiled at Fran before continuing. "I only have one more year left, and after that I'd like to create Christian video games based on Bible stories."

"I'm not interested in what you do in the future, but what you've done in the past. Your future will be determined by that," Ned interjected in a harsh voice.

Mary Grace gave her brother credit, instead of squirming in his seat, he faced Ned like a man.

"My job is to analyze information and occasionally assist with missions that require help with computerized security cameras and such. They never explain what, or where, the mission is, just what my small part of the job will be and when I should do it."

Ned gave him a hard look and Bobby's words came out faster.

"What no one is aware of is that I have another talent. I love puzzles and I can pretty much decipher any code. Everything I worked on had information they didn't want me to see in code." He shrugged. "I guess they assumed it was safe from prying eyes."

Ned nodded. "Go on."

Bobby took a deep breath and continued, "They put me on standby—which means I had to be at my desk, ready to move—to disable some security cameras in a certain art gallery. I got curious and searched for the file that fit the timeline of my assignment. I found it, and when I realized what I was looking at, I was shocked. Everyone I work with had heard of *Ned* but no one knew his true identity. I'd heard all kinds of stories about the man, but didn't believe half of them. It was impossible for one man to have done all that."

Ned leaned back in his chair in a relaxed position, but Mary Grace knew him well enough to know he was strung as taut as a bowstring. She watched both men, willing Bobby to move it along. Curiosity was eating her alive.

Bobby finally lifted his head and Mary Grace detected a touch of fear in his eyes. "I found out who Ned really is. Who you are."

Mary Grace drew in a sharp breath. Bobby knew everything about Ned!

He went on, "I noticed something else in the file, something odd that caught my eye."

"Aye? And what was that, Bobby?"

"Your escape exit from the location. There wasn't one."

Mary Grace jerked when Ned tore out of his chair and started pacing the floor. "That's because we were supposed to be dead."

Mary Grace swallowed hard and waited for Bobby to continue.

"That was my assessment. I didn't know what to do, or who to trust, so for a long time, I carefully poked around and finally located another file, one that had been approved and showed your escape route. I assume that's the one they sent you. At that point, I knew I didn't have much time before I was discovered looking in places I shouldn't, but I was able to find several emails sent between Hensley and Finn. It was made to appear that the two men were conversing about your current mission, but something didn't feel right. It's easy to send an email from someone else's server if you know what you're doing. I didn't have time to read them all. I stayed offline the whole time I was in hiding so no one could track me, so I never had a chance to dig deeper."

Bobby swallowed hard. "When the mission went down, I disabled all the cameras like I was supposed to, but left one live." He rubbed his right temple, as if reliving the scene, then looked up. "Not that it proved who was responsible, but I did see what happened. You were set up. I didn't record the event because I knew if I was right, my superiors would be able to track the recording on my computer. People who work for the CIA have been known to disappear.

"I don't know if Hensley and your friend, Finn, were set up to take the fall, or if they were actually involved. I got out of there as fast as I could. It was too dangerous to contact Mary Grace directly, so I had a friend of mine slip a note inside her tote bag. Before they were onto me at CIA headquarters, I spent some time tracking your past and came across a corporation named RBTL—the company that owns your mountain." Bobby grinned. "Sneaky name. Read Between The Lines is a computer acronym."

He turned serious once again. "At the same time, I got a list of your relatives, and that's how I knew about Fran. I was afraid they would go after Mary Grace because she's my sister and a reporter, and after reading your file, I knew Mary Grace would be safe with you. I went to the swamp shack in Georgia to leave two letters. One hidden for Mary Grace, the other in case you were with her. I knew you didn't trust me and wouldn't pay attention to the name I left you if you saw Finn on there. You worked together, and I figured you were probably friends, so I left that information for Mary Grace's eyes only, to do with as she felt best in case something happened to me. I knew if I went missing, she would eventually look there. Then I headed to Jackson Hole hoping to connect with both of you so that the letters at the swamp shack would never be needed."

A blush stole up his neck when he glanced at Fran. "I was hiking up the mountain, about to turn back around, because after thinking about it, I was afraid you might think I had something to do with the mission gone wrong, and that's when I heard a snowmobile. It turned out to be Fran."

"After we talked a little bit, I explained things to her, and at that point I needed some help. I had to trust someone. Fran agreed to hide me in a utility building behind the family home where she and her mother were staying. We both agreed for her to go to your cabin and see if Mary Grace was there, and maybe talk to you, see if she could find out if you blamed me for what happened. But when she came back and told me about the explosion, and that you two were okay, I decided to stay put until I could come up with a plan."

He gazed at Mary Grace earnestly and her heart tripped with love. "I knew you'd be safe with Ned." He turned back to Ned. "I didn't find out anything new and figured you'd head to Washington. That's when Fran told me you had a town house here. We were hoping you would end up here. Fran had access to the security code and we waited inside, then came out here when we heard the garage door open."

Bobby shot Ned a nervous look and Mary Grace intervened before Ned had a chance to strangle Bobby for placing his niece in danger.

"Ned and I have a plan." She explained what they were planning to do, then said, "It's time for me to set up some interviews and plant some seeds." Mary Grace prayed Ned would forgive her when her real plan was revealed. One particular interview would be used as a tool to reveal the person she was sure was in this thing up to their neck.

NINETEEN

That evening, after having a pizza delivered, Ned made sure Fran and Mary Grace were ensconced in the two bedrooms. He left Mary Grace working away on a laptop he kept at the town house, and after tossing a few blankets around, he and Bobby shared the living room floor. He took immense satisfaction in the fact that Bobby tossed and turned all night long—hopefully out of fear. Ned made it clear he didn't trust Bobby, with his life or with his niece. Mary Grace's brother was going to have to prove himself to Ned.

Early the next morning, Mary Grace had insisted Ned call CIA Director Madeline Cooper because she'd promised her she'd run any kind of future story by the director first, due to possible security issues. She insisted the director would be aware of her movements due to her interest in what was going on.

Leaving the dogs with Fran and Bobby, they'd met at an out-of-the-way café and Ned was surprised at Madeline's response to Mary Grace's information implicating Chief of Staff Hensley in the involvement of selling state secrets. She'd been pleased. Maybe a little too pleased? Ned felt his soon-to-be ex-boss had jumped the gun when they found out later she'd gone behind Mary Grace's back and called a press conference for that day, which was where they were now. Leaning against a wall at the back of the room, Ned watched Mary Grace in her element. She was in the front row and the reporters surrounding her began shouting questions when the CIA director took the stage. She majestically held up a hand until the reporters quieted. Uneasiness rippled down his spine when Madeline Cooper looked at the group before she ducked her chin and hid a small self-satisfied smile. He straightened from the wall, his gut screaming and his eyes locked on the woman.

He glanced at Mary Grace and his unease strengthened in force. He recognized the determined jut of her chin. Something big was about to happen. Something he wasn't going to like and wasn't privy to.

The small smile was replaced by a forlorn expression as Madeline Cooper lifted her head and started talking. "Some unfortunate information has come to my attention. It will, of course, be investigated thoroughly, but I feel the American people have a right to know what's going on." She gripped both sides of the podium and leaned slightly forward. She had the reporters in the palm of her hand, everyone except Mary Grace.

"For some time now, we've been aware that state secrets have been making their way into enemy hands. There was one mission in particular that went awry because someone knew we were coming. I won't get into the details of that mission, but one of our people was severely injured during the process." She paused, then added dramatically, "They were betrayed and now we have information that sheds light on that unfortunate circumstance." She took a deep breath, drawing it out, gaining more time in the spotlight.

"We will be opening an investigation into Chief of Staff Hensley."

The room exploded, but Ned kept his gaze zeroed in on Mary Grace. The truth hit him like a fist in the chest and he knew what was coming. She had set up Madeline Cooper, actually wanting this press conference to happen. Betrayal sliced through him like a serrated knife. He watched and waited for the proverbial ax to fall.

Madeline Cooper held up a hand and the room quieted. Mary Grace shouted out a question before anyone could stop her.

"Director Cooper, isn't it true you were in a position to know the circumstances of the mission you just spoke about? Couldn't you have been involved in the selling of state secrets and a failed mission that left one of our own disabled for life?"

The director's head snapped up and her bewildered expression quickly turned to granite. "Just what are you implying, Miss Ramsey?" she asked stiffly.

Pushing aside the pain of yet another betrayal, Ned prepared to swiftly remove Mary Grace from the premises if things went bad.

"I'm implying that I've studied this situation from all the angles and I think you should be investigated instead of Chief of Staff Hensley." Mary Grace took a deep breath and plowed forward, using the CIA director's own words against her. "It has come to my attention that there's an offshore account in your name that shows recent activity. Did you, or did you not, transfer half a million dollars to someone right before, and right after, the mission that went wrong?"

Ned wanted to howl. Mary Grace had once again withheld information from him, and at the same time he was stunned that a woman he'd worked with for several years had fooled him.

Shock, and a touch of fear, shone in Madeline Cooper's eyes, but she closed the press conference with a bright, false smile. "I don't know where Miss Ramsey acquired her information, but I suggest her employer, Future Broadcasting Company, review her journalistic practices."

She turned to leave the podium and Ned pushed his way through the maddening throng of shouting journalists. He grabbed Mary Grace by the arm and shielded her as he bulldozed them through the crowd and out of the room.

She twisted around, facing him the moment they were clear, true regret written on her face. "Ned, I'm sorry I didn't tell you about Madeline Cooper, but you were so upset over Finn when I told you about him, I was afraid you'd try to stop me. After we met with Hensley, I got suspicious because I felt like he was innocent. Last night, I contacted the PI I hired earlier and had him dig deeper. Madeline Cooper tried to make it appear as if Hensley paid out the money, but my PI finally traced it all the way back to Madeline. She did a good job of covering her tracks, but not good enough."

Reporters were filing out of the room and several veered toward Mary Grace. He took her by the arm and started moving. "Let's get out of here. I want to speak to Madeline in private. I know where she lives. I've visited her house on two occasions over the past few years. I'd rather go alone, but I know you'll have none of that and I don't have time to argue."

He shoved his emotions into a box, closed the lid and didn't say another word until they pulled up to a gate protecting the privacy of the owner of a large house sitting at the end of a curved driveway. With gratification, he punched numbers into the box attached to a pole several feet from the gate.

Madeline hadn't had time to change the code. He stopped at the front entrance of the house and got out of the car. He was so angry that he didn't even notice Mary Grace had followed him until she laid a hand on his back. He heard a small sniffle and then, "I'm so, so sorry, but I didn't have a choice. I had to do this."

He ignored the warmth from her hand and stabbed the doorbell. The door swung wide and there stood the director's bodyguard.

Ned's fists clinched and he snarled. "I'm here to see her."

The bodyguard, Henry, recognized him and slapped out a palm. "You know the drill."

Ned handed over his cell phone and weapon and motioned for Mary Grace to hand over her own phone. Once they were over the threshold, Henry ran a wand over their bodies and winked.

"Wouldn't want any recording devices in the house. She'll see you in the library."

Ned strode forward and Mary Grace scuttled behind him. The library doors were open and he stepped inside. Madeline sat behind her antique cherry desk and motioned toward the two chairs across from her.

Ned strode up to the desk, leaned over and gripped the edge of the wood. "Tell me Mary Grace is wrong. Tell me you're not responsible for Finn ending up in a wheelchair. Tell me you haven't betrayed your country."

She tsked. "Now, Ned, I'm not happy that you and your little friend here have upset my plans for Hensley, but you know I won't go down for this. I have too much power."

Ned would make sure she was convicted for what she'd done, but he reined in his temper because, more than anything, he wanted answers.

"At least tell me this. I was working for you. Why were you trying to kill me and Mary Grace, and why did you transfer money into an offshore account in Finn's name? Was he a backup fall guy in case Hensley didn't work out?"

A sly grin filled with hidden secrets tilted her lips. She leaned forward and whispered, "I highly suggest you talk to your friend before you start accusing anyone of attempted murder."

Ned reared back as if she'd punched him. What was she implying? That she'd harm Finn if Ned came after her?

He had to ask. "What do you mean?" His words came out sounding hoarse.

She waved a hand at Henry, whom Ned had known all along was standing just inside the doorway.

"Henry, please show our guests out."

Ned shoved away from the desk and grabbed his weapon along with his and Mary Grace's phones from Henry's hand before he strode down the hall and out of the house. He wanted to hit something because he was afraid Madeline Cooper was going to hold Finn's innocence as collateral for her career. There was a trail of money movement, but that could disappear. She had the connections to make it happen.

He and Mary Grace got in the car at the same time

and he tore out of there, slowing to a normal speed when they hit the street. He started to head back to the town house, but had himself together enough to spot the dark sedan coming up fast behind them. "Hold tight," he warned, just before he jerked the car down a residential side street, trying to rid them of their tail.

Mary Grace braced herself as the car took a sharp right. "Ned, what is it?" she asked tightly while trying to hang on. He took another hard left and her body swung in that direction.

"Looks like Madeline was one step ahead of us and had someone waiting until we left to tie up a loose end. The loose end being us. I should have paid better attention and we never should have gone there. It was a decision based solely on emotion and I know better." His voice sounded so cynical that Mary Grace didn't think anyone would ever be able to penetrate the wall of distrust that now surrounded him.

A bullet pinged the lower back of the car and Ned yelled, "Get down!"

Her heart hammering in her chest, she ducked and the car made several more sharp turns. She was about to sit up straight when the back of their car was rammed by the one chasing them. Her head hit the dash and stunned her for a second, but she rallied and looked sideways at Ned from her bent over position.

"Give me your gun," she said through gritted teeth. She'd had about enough of this whole mess and she was sick of getting shot at.

The look of surprise on his face was only momentary before he handed her his pistol. "You sure you know what you're doing?"

She glared at him before sitting up, opening her window and shooting at the car behind them. The first two bullets missed, but the third was a bull's-eye. She hit the right front tire and the vehicle swerved in the road until it finally hit a telephone pole.

She calmly handed the gun back to Ned and sat straight, staring out the window. She was tired of people trying to kill them, and if Ned wanted to crawl back to his mountain and hide, well, she'd deal with those emotions later. All she wanted right now was to hug Tinker Bell and have a few calm minutes to herself, but she did realize she needed to apologize, even if to deaf ears.

"Listen, I'm sorry about what happened. I know you trusted Madeline Cooper, but even if you never speak to me again, I had to handle things the way I did. If you had confronted her directly, which you would have, the truth would never have come out."

Having said that, Mary Grace also knew she wouldn't have changed the way she handled the situation. She was a seeker of truth, from a personal and professional standpoint. She prayed that Ned would understand, but his tight grip on the steering wheel indicated otherwise.

She was surprised when he finally spoke. "I'm fine with the way you handled the director, but I have one question."

"Yes?"

"Do you still think Finn betrayed me? That he was in league with Madeline Cooper?" He glanced at her bleakly. "Because if he is, that would mean my best friend has been trying to kill both of us." He gritted his teeth and his jaw worked itself back and forth. "For money."

Mary Grace wanted to tell him everything would be okay, but that wouldn't be the truth. As a child, she'd learned to face truth head-on, even if it hurt. Her mother and stepfather had forced her to learn that friends and family didn't always have your best interest at heart. She could literally feel his pain coming in waves, filling the car, and had no words to comfort him because deep inside she knew Finn had indeed betrayed his best friend, so she didn't say anything.

The car was quiet and they were soon back at the town house. Bobby and Fran were full of questions after seeing the press conference on television, but Mary Grace steered them away from Ned and into the kitchen. Ned disappeared into one of the bedrooms and closed the door.

She took a deep breath, pasted on a bright smile and faced her brother and Fran. "I think Ned needs some time alone. Why don't I make us some coffee?"

She scooped Tinker Bell into her arms when her precious baby came running into the kitchen full tilt, Krieger close on her heels. Burying her face in her dog's soft fur, Mary Grace felt the first tear fall for everything that could never be.

She felt a pair of thin arms wrap around her and Tinker Bell. Bobby gave her a good hug, then stepped back and pulled her toward a chair at the breakfast nook, gently pushing her into the seat.

"Come on, sis. You've looked out for me all my life. It's my turn to take care of you."

Mary Grace sniffed and lifted her head, staring at her brother with new eyes. "You grew up when I wasn't looking."

He glanced at Fran and blushed. "Yes, well, things change." He gave her a knowing, gentle smile. "You're in love with him, aren't you?"

Astounded, Mary Grace stared at the two of them as

Fran sat down. The question didn't exactly catch her off guard, but…somewhere along the way, had she fallen in love with the gruff mountain man? A man who at times isolated himself on that mountain of his away from the world. A man filled with pain at the betrayals he had experienced. She looked deep within herself, and realized that yes, she had fallen in love with Ned. But it was an impossible situation, especially after this latest betrayal he'd experienced at the hands of Madeline Cooper. Mary Grace didn't think Ned would ever fully trust anyone again, especially her because she'd withheld information from him yet again.

Bobby arched a brow and Mary Grace responded, "Maybe, but nothing will come of it."

Bobby reached for Fran's hand. "Remember what Gram always says, 'Have faith. God can do anything. Even open the heart of a stubborn man.'" He paused and leaned back in his chair, changing the subject. "Tell us what happened today."

Placing Tinker Bell in her lap, Mary Grace shared everything that had happened, including her withholding information from Ned and someone shooting at and ramming their car. They were shocked at the audacity of the director of the CIA.

At the end of her tale, Bobby wrapped her hand in both of his on top of the table. "Listen, sis, if Ned really loves you, he'll come around. If he's foolish enough to allow other people's choices to stand in the way of love, then he's the one who will be left out in the cold."

Mary Grace closed her eyes and prayed they'd all live long enough to find out if Ned really could learn to trust and love someone.

TWENTY

The next morning, Ned announced they were flying to Scotland, and when they arrived at the tarmac, Madeline Cooper's sly innuendos about Finn still rang in his head, making him more determined than ever to prove his best friend's innocence. His patience wore thin when Bobby and Fran accompanied them to the airport, only to insist on boarding the plane when they arrived. They promised to stay out of the way and babysit the dogs when he talked to Finn.

He finally gave in just so they could be on their way. Without inviting Mary Grace to join him, he climbed into the cockpit and revved the plane's big engine. He'd filed a flight plan the night before, so if anyone checked, primarily the CIA director, they would know where he was headed. He'd be ready for them this time.

He concentrated on getting them off the ground, and soon they were soaring through the sky. It was going to be a long flight.

He brooded for the first four hours and no one bothered him, but soon after that, Mary Grace poked her head through the door with a cup of coffee and a Danish in hand. He thanked her curtly and she ducked back out.

He promised himself that after he proved Finn's innocence, he would get on with his life, but it was hard to think of the future when someone was trying to kill them.

He spent the rest of the flight planning what he would say to Finn and worrying about everyone's safety. Confronting Madeline Cooper had given them some answers, but if she was the one trying to kill them, he'd awakened the sleeping giant. They had given her one more reason to get rid of them all, including Finn.

He checked his watch after he set the plane down. It was 20:00 hours eastern time, which meant by the time they drove to where he'd stashed Finn it would be about two in the morning in Scotland.

He debated whether to wait but wanted to get it over with. He also considered whether to call Finn and warn him they were coming but decided against it. He trusted Finn, but his gut told him to make it a surprise visit so he could gauge his friend's reaction. That would help prove Finn's innocence to Mary Grace.

He left the cockpit and herded everyone off the plane. He waved at the guy who had stepped out of the building of the small airport and caught Mary Grace's small smile at the fact that he didn't have to handle any paperwork. That was going to change soon because he would no longer be working for the CIA.

He tried to prevent Bobby and Fran from getting into the car with him and Mary Grace, but Bobby insisted he was part of this and had a right to be there. Ned agreed with him, but they had a heated discussion when Fran refused to be left behind. Even the dogs hopped into the car.

Everyone was quiet while Ned steered the vehicle

through the crystal clear night on small curvy country roads. The closer they got to the cottage where he'd stashed Finn, the more uneasy he became. He believed in his friend's innocence, but what if he were wrong? He was risking the life of everyone in the car.

He pulled to the side of the road a quarter of a mile from their destination and cut the engine. Mary Grace reached across the console and laid her hand on his.

"Ned, are you okay? We're in this together." She went quiet for a moment, then spoke in a soft voice. "For your sake, I pray Finn is innocent. I know how much his friendship means to you. But if he isn't, I pray God will give you the strength to overcome this."

A tumult of emotions clashed and roared inside him. He had always been a man of absolute control. His life had depended on it. He wanted to give something back to Mary Grace, but he was frozen inside. He found himself at a crossroads in life. If Finn were guilty, he didn't know if he'd ever be able to trust anyone again.

Slowly, he pulled his hand away and Mary Grace's warmth left him. He glanced into the back seat. "You two get out here." He pointed to the side of the road. "You can wait in that old shack."

They both opened their mouths to protest, but he placed a hand in the air. "This is not up for negotiation. Get out of the car. We'll pick you up on our way back."

They must have realized he meant business because they opened their doors and clamored out. Mary Grace rolled down her window and handed Tinker Bell to Fran. With a wobbly voice, she made Fran promise to take care of her beloved dog if something happened to her.

Ned wanted to howl in frustration. Nothing was going to happen to her because Finn was innocent. He just didn't want Fran and Bobby there to cloud the meeting. They'd pick them back up in an hour or so and everything would be fine.

Krieger had gotten out of the car and Ned cracked his window and gave a command. "Follow."

Mary Grace folded her arms over her stomach and stared out the passenger window at the thick forest and inky black night. "If you think Finn is innocent, why'd you leave them behind and order Krieger to follow on foot?"

Ned wasn't in the mood for chatter, but he answered curtly, "I didn't think it fair to Finn to involve anyone else in this discussion and it's force of habit with Krieger. He's always been my front man. He'll stay in the shadows until I tell him otherwise."

Ned knew Finn would be alerted by the security he himself had installed for his friend's safety. Finn would have a small warning that company was arriving, he just wouldn't know the identity of his visitors.

Ned's stomach churned the closer they got to the cottage, and all too soon, he pulled the vehicle into the short graveled driveway. Lights in the house were blinking on, and soon Mary Grace would know the truth, that Finn was innocent. Dressed in pajamas, Finn rolled his wheelchair onto the front porch, and in that moment, something that had been eluding Ned ever since the conversation he and Finn had had while Ned and Mary Grace were in Georgia crystallized in his mind, but it was too late. Too late for everything. Mary Grace had already slipped out of the car.

Exhaustion weighed heavily, but Mary Grace opened her car door when they arrived at Finn's cottage. She took a deep breath and said a quick prayer, because whatever happened would most likely determine the rest of her life. She had only known Ned a short time, but after talking to Bobby, she finally admitted to herself that Ned was the only man she'd ever love. The feelings she'd had for other guys she'd dated in the past didn't even come close to what she felt for Ned. She now realized it wasn't her dysfunctional childhood that had destroyed all her relationships. She just hadn't met the right man and her heart had known the difference.

She took a deep breath and studied the guy sitting in a wheelchair under the front porch light. He was light where Ned was dark. From a short distance, he appeared to be a good-looking man with blond hair and quite a good physique, considering he was confined to a wheelchair. He spotted Ned and waved them forward just as a large man stepped out of the house and stood at Finn's side.

Mary Grace kept moving but stopped when Ned met her at the front of the car. She saw him make a small movement with his right hand and surmised he knew where Krieger was and had just given him a command. That meant something wasn't right.

With a hand on her elbow, he moved them forward but spoke under his breath. "Be ready to move fast if I tell you to."

Questions burst forth in her mind, but she did as she was told and walked to the front porch with a smile pasted on her face. "You must be Finn. I'm Mary Grace and I've heard so much about you." Her words didn't come out as smooth as she'd hoped, and Ned appeared relaxed at her side, but she knew he was wound tight. Tension radiated off him in waves. She didn't know what was going on, but his grip tightened on her elbow when his gaze swung from the large man standing at Finn's side to his friend.

"Why, Finn?"

Mary Grace's heart broke at Ned's pain-filled, gruff words.

Finn gave Ned a crooked grin. "You always were too smart for your own good. What gave me away?"

The man standing beside Finn pulled out a handgun and pointed it at them. Ned dropped his hand from her elbow in a seemingly natural manner.

"You did. When I spoke to you on the phone, you knew Mary Grace's name. I hadn't told you her name." He glanced at the big man standing beside Finn under the bright porch light. "Violet eyes. I saw your henchman's unusual eye color when he tried to take down Mary Grace on my mountain. Did you have other hired men trying to kill us while your killer made his way back here? Were you behind all the attempts on our lives? Why, Finn? I thought we were friends."

Mary Grace readied herself to move when Finn's lips twisted into an ugly smile. "You have it all, Ned. You've always had it all." Eyes bright with jealousy and bitterness swung toward Mary Grace.

"Did you know Ned's a famous painter? He's known all over the world as the elusive *Ned* because the public has never met him. His family is rich, but he got even richer with his own paintings and he didn't even need the money. Did you know his family owns a huge castle here in Scotland?"

Finn glanced back at Ned. "I always tagged along during holidays—the charity case—and I promised myself one day I'd be as rich as your family."

Ned took a halting step forward and Mary Grace wanted to weep at the pain vibrating in his voice. "Finn, it doesn't have to be this way. We can work things out. I'll hire you the best attorney money can buy."

Finn shook his head and his lips twisted in a parody of a smile. "I really didn't want you dead, but I knew you'd never give up until you found out who had betrayed us. An admirable trait most of the time, but it was interfering with my plans. When Madeline Cooper and I realized Bobby had left one of the cameras running while our mission was being carried out, we knew we had to cover our tracks and dispose of anyone who might discover us. We figured Bobby would contact his sister, and if he actually knew anything he would share it with her, a well-known reporter. Oh, and we knew you were holed up on your mountain, we were just biding our time, hoping to make your death look like an accident, but then my man followed Mary Grace to your mountain and we had to try to get rid of both of you. I truly am sorry it has to end this way, but that's life. Oh, and one more thing before we say goodbye forever."

Mary Grace gasped when Finn pushed himself out of the wheelchair. Ned didn't move a muscle, just choked out one word. "Why?"

Finn's lips spread in a wide smile. "The bullet did graze my spine, but after I left the hospital and you moved me here, I hired a really good physical therapist. It was hard, but I regained my mobility." His lips twisted again. "The stupid guy who accidentally shot me is no longer with us." He shook his head in mock sorrow. "You just can't find good help these days."

"But why didn't you tell me you could walk?"

The grief and sadness in Ned's response made Mary

Grace want to throw her arms around him and let him know everything would be okay, but that wouldn't be right because she didn't know if anything would ever be okay for Ned after a betrayal that cut this deep.

"Why, Ned, you wouldn't believe how many people underestimate a man sitting in a wheelchair. You're a prime example."

Finn glanced over his shoulder at his henchman and nodded. "Make it quick."

Everything happened at once. Ned shouted a German command for his dog, pulled a handgun from the inside of his jacket and pushed Mary Grace to the side in one smooth movement.

She went down sideways and her shoulder hit the graveled driveway, but she ignored the pain and scrambled to her feet. In a flash she saw Krieger coming up behind the big man holding the gun, but she knew it would be too late if the guy fired. She automatically threw herself in front of Ned just as both men's guns went off. She watched the large man fall as a burning sensation ripped through her side before she crumbled to the ground. She heard the loud report of a second shot, and from her prone position on the ground, prayed as she watched Ned move around her and charge his best friend. They struggled over a gun in Finn's hand. Krieger stood guard over the fallen body of the first man, saliva dripping out of his mouth.

Black dots peppered her vision, but she fought to stay conscious. She prayed nothing would happen to either man, because if Ned had to kill Finn in order to stop him, he would never forgive himself.

Just as her vision wavered even more, Fran slipped an arm under her head. She and Bobby must have followed them on foot, and Mary Grace was thankful they did. Fran's voice quaked as she spoke to Mary Grace.

"You have to be okay, Mary Grace. My uncle loves you and he'll never leave his mountain if you die."

Mary Grace wanted to reassure her, but the black dots were becoming thicker. Her heart jerked in fear when she saw Bobby out of the corner of her eye jump onto the front porch to help Ned, but Fran breathed out in satisfaction.

"It's okay. They have both men subdued and they're tying them up."

A few moments later, Ned bounded off the porch and kneeled at Mary Grace's side. He replaced Fran's arm with his own and leaned close, his heart pounding in fear that she'd been shot. Golden eyes filled with sadness and an expression he hoped was love stared back at him. It was in that moment he knew that all the betrayals in the world didn't matter as long as Mary Grace always looked at him as she was now. His heart expanded and filled with love for this feisty, beautiful woman, All the negative emotions he'd been clinging to—distrust, anger and betrayal—simply disappeared.

His Scottish brogue filled with gruff emotion, he said, "Aye, me luv, 'tis my fault this happened to ye. Ye have to hang on, ye hear me. I luv ye and find I canna live without ye." He pressed a gentle kiss against her forehead. A tear fell from his chin and hit her cheek before he whispered, "Ye saved me life, Mary Grace. I trust ye and I find meself trusting our Lord. I pray ye will live through this so I can shower ye wi' love for the rest of me life. Please say ye will marry me?"

Mary Grace's pain filled eyes stayed on Ned and the

corners of her lips curved upward. "I love you back, Mountain Man, and yes, I'll marry you."

He bent down and gave her a warm kiss, then pulled back. "'Tis a happy man, I am, but if ye'd see fit to marry yerself to this mountain man this Christmas, I'd be the happiest fella on earth."

"I'll marry you, Mountain Man, if you'll rebuild that mountain cabin of yours." She gave him a shy grin. "I'd love to show our children where we first met."

A big whoop, something that sounded like a war cry from times past, filled the air and Ned kissed her again, right on the lips.

EPILOGUE

It was good that the bullet wound had just been a graze, because in her wildest imagination, Mary Grace never dreamed she'd be walking down the aisle of a five-hundred-year-old church on the grounds of an ancient castle on Christmas Day. Happiness surged through her as she stood at the entrance of the building, waiting for the "Wedding March" music to begin, and she said a silent prayer of thanks. The stone structure was bursting with people and the decorations were beyond beautiful. Simple but elegant small tree branches were attached to each pew with red bows and a huge Christmas tree stood behind the minister. The handmade ornaments on the tree looked as old as the church.

Her gaze found Gram Ramsey sitting proudly in the front row. Mary Grace's heart swelled at the thought of Ned flying her grandmother to Scotland and formally asking for Mary Grace's hand in marriage. He made a pledge to Gram that her home in Georgia would be in good hands for future generations. She chuckled, remembering Gram's response to *Eli*. "You'll do fine, my boy, just keep to the Word and everything will work out."

Bobby and Fran sat beside Gram, holding hands.

Mary Grace smiled, recalling the stir they'd caused by breaking tradition. Fran had insisted on sitting on the bride's side of the church with Bobby. That had brought quite a few raised eyebrows.

Her gaze swung to Laird Duncan, Ned's irascible grandfather sitting on the opposite aisle with Ned's gorgeous sister. Gram and Angus Duncan had enjoyed a few heated debates over the wedding, especially the short amount of time they had to plan it, but unless Mary Grace was mistaken, those two were keen on each other, as the laird's wife had died many years ago.

At last, she allowed her gaze to drift to the front of the church where Ned stood beside his older brother, both men standing tall and proud, dressed in historically befitting kilts. The clan's tartan colors were red and gray, and the church was filled with neighbors and friends wearing the same color. Early that morning, she had been presented with her own tartan sash, which she'd slipped over her white wedding gown.

The only kink in the day sat on the third pew, glaring at Ned's brother. The woman was an American librarian hired by Ewan to catalog the massive number of books in the old castle. Ned didn't trust the woman, said he sensed something off there, but Mary Grace ignored the moment of worry and turned her head to gaze at her future husband.

His smile rivaled the sun pouring through the church windows. He had come so far in such a short amount of time. He trusted her and had fully opened his heart to love. Finn's betrayal had hurt, but he finally realized he couldn't shoulder the burdens of the world—that was God's job. But it hadn't stopped Ned from trying to help Finn. He had indeed hired the best attorney money could buy. The rest was in God's hands.

The day before, Mary Grace had submitted her article. They'd found enough proof in Finn's cottage to force the CIA director to come under investigation, and Mary Grace alluded that Chief of Staff Hensley was instrumental in making this happen.

The music swelled in the small church and everyone stood. Her eyes trained on Ned, Mary Grace followed the path of pink rose petals and stopped at his side. She grinned and he smiled back. Before they turned to the minister, Ned surprised Mary Grace by whistling and looking back down the aisle. The whole church tittered when Krieger and Tinker Bell, both dressed in doggy tartans, padded down the aisle and sat beside their owners.

In a long Georgian drawl, Mary Grace brought more laughter to the congregation when she said, "You ready to get hitched, Mountain Man?"

"Aye, that I am."

* * * * *

Thick snow squalls blew down the Toronto shoreline
of Lake Ontario, turning the city's annual winter
wonderland into a haze of sparkling lights. The cold
hadn't done much to quell the tourists, though, Detective
Liam Bearsmith thought as he methodically trailed his
hooded target around the skating rink and through the
crowd. Hopefully, the combination of the darkness,
heavy flakes and general merriment would keep the
jacket-clad criminal he was after from even realizing he
was being followed.

The "Sparrow" was a hacker. Just a tiny fish in the
criminal pond, but a newly reborn and highly dangerous
cyberterrorist group had just placed a pretty hefty bounty
on the Sparrow's capture in the hopes it would lead them
to a master decipher key that could break any code. If
Liam didn't bring in the Sparrow now, terrorists could

turn that code breaker into a weapon and the Sparrow could be dead, or worse, by Christmas.

The lone figure hurried up a metal footbridge festooned in white lights. A gust of wind caught the hood of the Sparrow's jacket, tossing it back. Long dark hair flew loose around the Sparrow's slender shoulders.

Liam's world froze as déjà vu flooded his senses. His target was a woman.

What's more, Liam was sure he'd seen her somewhere before.

Liam's strategy had been to capture the Sparrow, question her and use the intel gleaned to locate the criminals he was chasing. His brain freezing at the mere sight of her hadn't exactly been part of the plan. The Sparrow reached up, grabbed her hood and yanked it back down again firmly, but not before Liam caught a glimpse of a delicate jaw that was determinedly set, and how thick flakes clung to her long lashes. For a moment Liam just stood there, his hand on the railing as his mind filled with the name and face of a young woman he'd known and loved a very long time ago.

Kelly Marshall.

Don't miss
Christmas Witness Conspiracy *by Maggie K. Black,*
available wherever Love Inspired Suspense books
and ebooks are sold.

LoveInspired.com

HARLEQUIN

Heartfelt or suspenseful, inspiring or passionate, Harlequin has your happily-ever-after.

With new books published
every month, you are sure to find the
satisfying escape you know you deserve.

Love Harlequin romance?

DISCOVER.

Be the first to find out about promotions, news and exclusive content!

f Facebook.com/HarlequinBooks

𝕏 Twitter.com/HarlequinBooks

◎ Instagram.com/HarlequinBooks

𝓟 Pinterest.com/HarlequinBooks

ReaderService.com

EXPLORE.

Sign up for the Harlequin e-newsletter and download a free book from any series at **TryHarlequin.com**

CONNECT.

Join our Harlequin community to share your thoughts and connect with other romance readers! **Facebook.com/groups/HarlequinConnection**

Get 4 FREE REWARDS!

We'll send you 2 FREE Books plus 2 FREE Mystery Gifts.

Love Inspired books feature uplifting stories where faith helps guide you through life's challenges and discover the promise of a new beginning.

FREE Value Over **$20**